...rogue
always gets
what he wants....

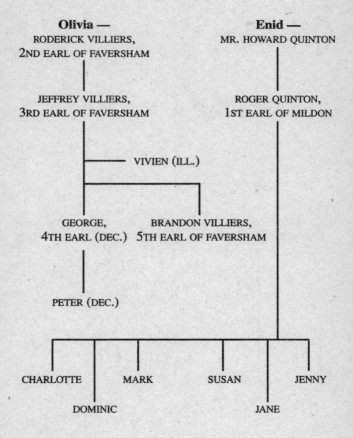

Olivia —
RODERICK VILLIERS,
2ND EARL OF FAVERSHAM

Enid —
MR. HOWARD QUINTON

JEFFREY VILLIERS,
3RD EARL OF FAVERSHAM

ROGER QUINTON,
1ST EARL OF MILDON

VIVIEN (ILL.)

GEORGE,
4TH EARL (DEC.)

BRANDON VILLIERS,
5TH EARL OF FAVERSHAM

PETER (DEC.)

CHARLOTTE

MARK

SUSAN

JENNY

DOMINIC

JANE

Prologue

It began as any typical evening in the city.

Brand Villiers, fifth Earl of Faversham, lounged in a private parlor at an exclusive brothel, a beautiful doxy on his lap, an excellent set of cards in his hand, and a glass of fine Bordeaux wine at his side. Many a man would have envied his circumstances. Yet Brand felt a restless boredom, a discontent that he was loath to acknowledge. "Damned perfect life," he muttered.

Scowling, Sir John Gabler looked up from his cards. "What's that?" With his freckled face and rumpled fair hair, Gabler looked too young to be smoking the cheroot clamped between his teeth. His cravat was tied inexpertly as if he hadn't yet mastered the intricate knots.

"There's nothing better than having an armful of pretty woman," Brand said, stroking Jewel's silk-covered back. Smiling, she lowered her eyelids to half-mast, her dark eyes smoldering with seductive promise. She was a new girl, and he looked forward to sampling her services. Maybe then he could rid himself of this vague sense of ennui.

"She isn't yours yet. We haven't concluded our wager." Gabler exchanged two of his cards for new ones from the deck. The moment he saw them, his pale blue eyes flickered. With an air of gloating triumph, he slapped down a trio of aces. "Try to top that, old boy."

Brand lifted an eyebrow. "Quite impressive."

"Jewel, come here. You'll have me tonight." Gabler crooked his finger at her.

But Brand kept one hand tucked firmly around her slender waist. With his other hand, he spread out four kings on the green baize tabletop.

Gabler's eyes widened. He slumped in his chair like a sulky boy. "Blast you, Faversham! I should have known not to be suckered into a game with you. You've the devil's own luck."

Brand acknowledged the truth in that. Over the years, he'd won more games than he'd lost. From an early age, he'd developed a knack for cards and dice, the keen ability to read an opponent's facial expressions, to calculate the odds, to heed his instincts. He knew when to take a risk and when to fold. But it was more than a quick mind that favored his chances. He also had been blessed—or perhaps cursed, some might say—with consistently good fortune in gambling. There were even those who whispered he'd sold his soul to the devil himself.

Brand saw no need to correct the supposition. He'd learned long ago that people would believe what they willed.

"Run along and find yourself another bed partner," he told Gabler. "This beauty is all mine." Jewel nestled against him so that he could feel every luscious curve of her heaven-made form. Beneath the table, her hand sought the placket of his breeches. "And kindly shut the door on your way out."

Gabler muttered an imprecation, shoved back his chair, and stomped across the plush blue carpet. As he departed the chamber, another man pushed his way inside.

A froth of graying curls bordered the newcomer's beaky features. His greatcoat flapping like the wings of a crow, he flew toward the table. "Faversham! Thank God I found you!"

"Trowbridge," Brand said testily. "In case you haven't noticed, I'm engaged at the moment."

With nary a glance at Jewel, Viscount Trowbridge rattled on. "I must speak to you. Alone. It's a matter of life or death."

"A broken fingernail is a matter of life or death to you." But even Trowbridge usually adhered to the rule that protected a gentleman's right to privacy. Resigned to hearing him out, Brand lifted Jewel aside.

"Make haste, darling." Her lips full and pouty, she blew him a kiss. "I'll be waiting for you."

That soft, sultry voice roused anticipation in him, and he didn't appreciate the interruption. The moment he and the viscount stepped into the opulent corridor, Brand snapped, "What is it? If this is another of your harebrained schemes—"

"It isn't. I swear it." Trowbridge fumbled in his pocket and drew forth a crumpled piece of paper. His hand trembling, he pushed it at Brand. "Read this. It came in the evening post."

Brand unfolded the sheet and moved closer to the oil lamp that flickered on a table. Two words were neatly penned on the plain white stationery: *You're next.*

Brand returned his attention to the distraught man. "What the deuce is this? A prank?"

"Nay," Trowbridge said in a quavery voice. " 'Tis the phantom."

"The phantom."

As if expecting a specter to glide out of one of the private chambers, the viscount glanced up and down the deserted passageway. "The phantom of the league. Haven't you heard?"

"I've heard that Mellingham died in a duel he should never have fought. That Wallace got so drunk he fell down a flight of stairs and broke his neck. And Aldrich suffered a heart seizure the way we'd all like to go— with a whore's legs wrapped around his waist."

Trowbridge gave a violent shake of his head, making his curls bounce. The grayness of fear tinged his angular features. "Someone is trying to murder me—to murder all of us. One by one. Every last man who belonged to the Lucifer League."

Brand felt a cold prickling of unease. Discounting the sensation, he stuffed the note back into Trowbridge's hand. "You're exaggerating."

"Someone's out to kill me, I say!" Wild-eyed, the viscount seized Brand's lapels. "You must help me find out who, I beg you!"

Brand regarded him with cool scorn. "It's a jest, nothing more. Someone is having a good laugh at your expense."

"If you don't give a damn for me, then do it for yourself. You could be next—after me."

"Go have a few drinks and forget about it. That's what I intend to do."

Pivoting on his heel, Brand returned to the private

parlor. He stood for a moment by the door, fingering the scar at the side of his mouth and wondering at his callousness. Over the years, cynicism had crept upon him, like the steady rise of water, centimeter by centimeter, until he felt he was drowning, gasping for a breath of clean air. Beneath the surface lurked shadows that he didn't care to examine. Shadows that had grown darker since the deaths of his brother and nephew a decade ago.

Shadows that shrouded his guilt . . .

Fool. He wasn't one to get carried away by maudlin sentiments. A long time ago, he had adopted a casual indifference to such conventional nonsense. He had learned that wickedness made life far more interesting, and that he himself belonged firmly on the dark side.

Jewel slid her soft arms around him. "Lie with me, m'lord. You've made me wait long enough."

Brand carried her across the chamber and pressed her down onto a chaise. The warmth of her body kept the shadows at bay. Lost in eroticism, he forgot the outside world until the next morning when he heard the chilling news.

Lord Trowbridge was dead.

Chapter 1
THE DEVIL'S DUE

London, one month later

"I'm here to see my grandmother," Lady Charlotte Quinton told the butler as she entered the mansion on a draft of wintry air. She set down Fancy's basket in the foyer, then stooped to release the leather catch.

A bushy brown dog hopped out, skidded on the marble floor, and leapt straight into Charlotte's arms, nearly bowling her over. She fought for balance on feet numbed by the cold. Her muscles were stiff from sitting in the coach for the past two days, confined with her chatterbox maid, Nan.

But personal comforts were of little consequence when Grandmama had been injured. Charlotte would endure anything for the sake of her beloved grandmother— even enter the lair of her sworn enemy.

Brand Villiers, the infamous Earl of Faversham.

Charlotte's stomach clenched. Never had she expected to find herself here, standing in the foyer of his London house.

Sixteen years ago, when she was just a girl, Brand had broken her heart. He had given Charlotte her first kiss—only to scorn her romantic dreams of love. She had fled from his mocking laughter, stumbled into a hearth fire, and suffered burns over her right arm. The combination of physical and emotional scars had left her bitter and angry.

Eleven years ago, when the time came for her to make her debut at age eighteen, she had been too self-conscious to face London society. While other ladies married and started families of their own, Charlotte had remained at her parents' house in Devon.

Five years ago, selfish and immature, she had set her sights on Brand's best friend, Michael Kenyon. She had tried to end Michael's budding romance with Brand's half sister, Vivien. She had stolen a necklace and made Vivien look like a thief.

Brand, unfortunately, had been the one to uncover Charlotte's plot.

She still cringed at the memory of her folly—and the lash of Brand's rebuke. As punishment, she had been banished by her family to the north country of Yorkshire, a banishment that she now realized she'd sorely needed. No one knew better than Charlotte just how much growing up she'd done in the past five years. Or just how much she wanted to make amends.

Amends, that is, with everyone except Brand.

Two days ago, she had received an urgent message that her grandmother had been injured in a carriage accident and was convalescing in, of all places, Brand's London house. Charlotte had had no choice but to journey to the home of the man she viewed as the devil himself.

Clutching her dog Fancy against her merino cloak, Charlotte regarded the butler, whose jowly, ancient face bore a look of befuddlement. "I'm Lady Charlotte Quinton," she explained. "My grandmother is Lady Enid Quinton. She's staying here while she recovers from the accident."

Dragging his rheumy gaze from the dog, the butler raised a fastidious white eyebrow. "Of course, m'lady. I wasn't informed of your impending arrival."

"There was no point in sending a message since I left York straightaway. Have my parents arrived? Or any of my brothers and sisters?"

"Nay, you've been her ladyship's only visitor."

Charlotte frowned. Her family had always been caught up in their own squabbling, but they all loved Grandmama and Charlotte had expected them to make the journey from Devon. Why hadn't they come? "If you'd be so good as to take me straight to Lady Enid."

"I'm afraid that's impossible."

"Impossible? Why?" Dread honed Charlotte's voice, as sharp and cold as the blustery evening. The hastily penned summons from Lady Stokeford had revealed precious little information, only that Grandmama and her two dearest friends had been injured in a carriage crash. Now, all the worry and fear of the past forty-eight hours overwhelmed Charlotte.

Was Grandmama . . . dead?

Horror must have shown on her face, for the stooped old butler said quickly, "There's naught to fear. 'Tis only that the physician is presently with the ladies."

A measure of relief eased the knot in her breast. "How fares my grandmother? How badly was she hurt?"

"Your questions are best directed at the doctor," he intoned. "Might I take your wrap?"

As he approached, holding out his white-gloved

hands, Fancy growled in the circle of Charlotte's arms. "It's all right, darling, he won't hurt you," she murmured, stroking the dog's fluffy head. To the butler, she said, "I'll keep my cloak, thank you. May I ask your name?"

"North, m'lady."

"I will speak to the doctor, North. Take me to him at once."

"I'm sorry, but the earl has given orders—"

"Lord Faversham is here?" Her insides clenched again, this time with dismay. It had been too much to hope that Brand would be gone to a gaming hell with his dissolute cronies. This was his house, after all. She knew he despised her after her behavior five years ago. And the feeling was mutual.

But that was the least of her worries.

"His lordship just returned from visiting friends out of town," North said. "If m'lady would care to be shown to a chamber—"

"No," Charlotte said firmly. "While my maid settles my luggage, I'll see Grandmama. You may tell the earl that I insisted."

North hesitated, then made a creaky bow. A tonsure of gray hair cupped his balding pate. "As m'lady wishes."

He led the way up the broad marble steps, and the lamp in his hand cast a wavering light over the simple elegance of the décor. Charlotte was hard-pressed not to gawk at the fine paintings and exquisite furnishings. Because of the longtime friendship between their grandmothers, she had known Brand for her entire life. However, although she'd often visited his country estate in Devon, she hadn't traveled to London for her debut and had never before seen his town house.

It was a deplorable twist of fate that Grandmama and her two friends had suffered the coach accident on their way into the city. Charlotte could only hope that she wouldn't encounter Brand until the morrow.

Her footsteps blended with the butler's shuffling gait. As they reached the top of the stairs and headed down a murky passageway, Fancy quivered, her bright black eyes peering from the ball of brownish fur.

Perhaps she sensed her mistress's unease, Charlotte thought, stroking the animal. Fancy had grown plumper in the fortnight since Charlotte had rescued her from a gang of ruffians in York. With loving care and a steady diet, the thin, woebegone creature had filled out. A daily brushing had lent a sheen to her ratty coat, and the bald patch on her back leg was growing new fuzz. Now if only Grandmama could learn to love Fancy . . .

North stopped outside an ornate door framed in gilt moldings. "Permit me to announce you, m'lady."

Charlotte gave a distracted nod. As the butler vanished into the chamber, she set Fancy on the floor and then paced the long corridor, the dog shadowing her. Slipping off her cloak, Charlotte tossed it onto a spindly chair. No mirror hung on the blue-striped wallpaper, so she patted her untidy chestnut hair and hoped for the best. She was hungry, weary, and teetering on the ragged edge of patience. But she couldn't rest until she had assured herself of her grandmother's improved health.

What was taking North so long? Were Grandmama's injuries worse than the man had reported?

Charlotte reached for the door handle just as the gilded panel swung open again. The butler's aging form reappeared, but he merely nodded to her and trudged down the passageway. Starting into the chamber, she came to an enforced halt.

She stood face to face with Brand Villiers.

Tall and lean, he blocked the doorway. His ice-gray eyes held the worldly amusement that had always both intrigued and annoyed her. He was clad almost entirely in black with only a gray waistcoat to temper his devilish image.

Five years hadn't changed those saturnine features with the small scar that lifted one corner of his mouth in an eternal smirk. Nor had the passage of time altered his wicked handsomeness—or the telltale warmth that suffused her body. Except for a few threads of silver in the dark brown hair at his temples, he looked exactly as he had on the day he had caught her in the throes of malicious mischief.

Her heart skittered inside her breast. Sweet heavens, he could still awaken a tangle of intense feelings in her. Humiliation for the way he so callously treated her after their kiss—her first kiss. Shame for the wrong she'd done to her friend Vivien—Brand's half sister. Resentment than he had so relished the chance to chastise Charlotte. And an involuntary tug of something else, something soft and aching. Despite all the history and rancor between them, she still remembered how it felt to have his hard male body pressed to hers.

"Look what an ill wind blew in," he said.

Charlotte forced a polite smile. Not for the world would she let him guess her reaction to him. "I see you're as charming as ever," she said coolly. "If you'll excuse me, I'd like to visit my grandmother."

He remained in place, lounging against the door

frame. "The doctor is finishing his examination. There's time for us to have a little chat."

"My only interest is Grandmama. How is she?"

"Both of our grandmothers are well enough, all things considered. So you can curb that impatience of yours and speak with me."

"I've nothing to say to you."

"Then I'll do the talking. Perhaps you've heard that Vivien and Michael have been happily married for five years now."

Charlotte felt herself blush and hated that betrayal of her emotions. So he wouldn't let the matter drop. Although she had made a horrible mistake in trying to win Michael for herself, she didn't need to hear so again from Brand. "Of course. I'm happy for them."

He cocked a disbelieving eyebrow. "They've added two children to their family."

"Then I wish them well," she said with more sincerity than he would ever believe of her. "If that's all you have to say . . ."

"It's only the beginning."

His indolent gaze sauntered from her bedraggled garb down to the tips of her muddied half-boots. For a heartbeat, she regretted not taking the time to freshen up in her chamber. She should have been girded in her best gown instead of this drab, wrinkled brown designed to withstand the dirt and splatters of traveling. She should have faced him with her hair brushed and tidied into an elegant chignon. Not because she cared to impress him, but because she needed armor against his scorn.

"Kindly move aside," she said.

"All in good time." He gazed down at Fancy, who peeked out from behind Charlotte's skirts. "I see you've found at least one creature that will tolerate your company. If indeed that hairball is a dog."

He reached down as if to pet Fancy.

A growl vibrated from Fancy's throat, and although it wasn't in Charlotte's nature to retreat, she stepped back, the dog keeping close to her. "Don't touch her. She's frightened of men."

"Like her mistress?"

"I've no fear of you. Only disgust."

Brand chuckled. "Good old Char. I always did enjoy your frankness."

"I'm not here to give you pleasure."

Again, his gaze slid over her form. "A pity. You don't know what you're missing."

"I regard it as a blessing, not a pity."

Charlotte brushed past him, and when he didn't move aside, their arms touched. She caught her breath at the shiver that sped over her skin. It was impossible that she could still suffer such a reaction to him. Yet her blood flowed faster and her heart beat out of control. In defiance of common sense, she noticed every detail about him: his spicy scent, his masculine form, his brooding mouth. Awareness coursed downward to her bosom and lower, settling in her nether regions with a familiar, irksome ache.

Blast him. He was a worthless reprobate. Thank heavens she had the sense to prefer a man like Mr. Harold Rountree. Charlotte latched on to that thought. Mr. Rountree had more scruples in his neatly trimmed fingernails than Brand Villiers had in his entire wicked body.

The dog trotting at her heels, Charlotte hastened through a small antechamber with an arrangement of chairs, an alabaster bust on a pedestal, a flickering oil lamp. Peeling off her kid gloves, she made a conscious effort to tamp down her anxiety. It wouldn't do to appear worried. She must greet Grandmama with an encouraging smile.

Provided, of course, that Grandmama was conscious.

An old, lanky gentleman carrying a leather satchel came through the doorway of the bedchamber. She extended her hand to him. "I'm Charlotte Quinton, Lady Enid's granddaughter. Are you the physician?"

"Dr. Spencer, at your service." As he made a quaint, courtly bow, he stopped short, his gaze fixed on her hand.

She resisted the old habit of hiding her scars behind her back. People often stared at the ugly network of whitened flesh that extended up her right arm. At least her long sleeve covered the worst of it. "Burns," she said, preferring bluntness to pretense.

Blinking, he returned his gaze to her face. "Er . . . I see. Her ladyship is resting comfortably. You'll be pleased to hear she's much improved today."

"How badly was she injured?"

" 'Twas a clean fracture, and the bone should mend quite nicely."

"Fracture?"

"She's suffered a broken arm, my lady. There's a bottle of laudanum on the bedside table. Two drops every four hours should relieve her pain and help her sleep."

"I'll be sure she takes it." Somewhat heartened by his prognosis, Charlotte went past him and through the open doorway.

Inside the spacious, high-ceilinged chamber, several candelabra cast golden haloes of light, while shadows gathered in the corners. A fire burned on a hearth of pale marble, tended by a housemaid, who curtsied to Charlotte and then retreated into an adjacent chamber. Across the room stood three ornate beds with identical hangings of deep maroon velvet tied back by gold tasseled ropes.

Charlotte paused at the sight. How like the Rosebuds to arrange to be together in one chamber. The three old ladies had been fast friends for more than half a century. In their first season, as celebrated debutantes, they had been dubbed the Rosebuds for their youth and beauty. They often spoke fondly of their glory days, though Charlotte suspected there was more to their stories than they let on.

But now she could think only of how happy she was to see them again. And how grateful that they had survived that awful crash of their coach.

On the left, dainty Lady Stokeford reclined against a mound of feather pillows. Strong-willed in spite of her fragile appearance, she was grandmother to the three Kenyon brothers, whom Charlotte had known while growing up. A dapper, white-haired gentleman sat in a chair beside her.

Lady Faversham occupied the center bed, her iron-gray hair and gaunt features stark against the white linens. Her head was turned as she spoke to Lady Stokeford. Pinch-mouthed and grim, she was Brand's grandmother.

Turning to the right, Charlotte felt her heart fill her throat as she spied her own dear grandmother. Stout and matronly, Lady Enid Quinton lay asleep. Even on her sickbed, she wore a turban over her graying ginger hair, this one of yellow silk. Her broken arm in its sling rested on the white counterpane.

It was not the reunion Charlotte had envisioned on many a lonely night, with the wind wuthering around the eaves of her isolated cottage on the outskirts of York. She had imagined herself returning in the peak of summer to Quinton's Lodge in Devon, with roses blossoming and Grandmama welcoming her with open arms, along with Mama and Papa and her younger brothers and sisters. After five long years of exile from her family, Charlotte felt her heart overflow with love for her grandmother.

She hurried across the thick carpet and halted beside the bed. Dimly, she heard Lady Faversham and Lady Stokeford call a greeting, but Charlotte could think only of her grandmother.

With a shock, she noticed how old and feeble Lady Enid looked. The lines of age that were etched over those plump features had grown deeper. Her skin appeared ashen in the candlelight. Charlotte's vision blurred with tears as she touched her grandmother's wrinkled brow.

Those stubby, ginger lashes fluttered. A set of familiar brown eyes blinked thrice, then warmed with wonder. "Charlotte?" she said in a quavering voice. "Have you come home, then? Or am I dreaming?"

A sob strangled Charlotte's throat as she embraced the old woman, taking care not to jostle the injured arm. She breathed in the familiar scent of caramel and vanilla. Gladness suffused her as she kissed the soft, seamed comfort of her grandmother's cheek.

"I'm here, Grandmama. Not home, but here in London with you." Her voice caught on a tremor of joy and remorse. Lady Enid's love had always been unconditional, yet Charlotte had risked it all in one stupid, wicked act of folly . . .

With her good arm, Grandmama returned Charlotte's hug. Languid fingers stroked her hair. "There, there, my sweet girl. You mustn't weep. 'Tis only a broken bone. Why, I'll be up and about in no time."

"Quite the contrary," Brand stated.

Startled, Charlotte turned to see that he had followed her into the chamber. He stood in a pool of shadow near the foot of his grandmother's bed. He went on. "Even for the young, a broken bone takes six weeks to mend properly. At your age—"

"Pish posh," interjected Lady Stokeford from the far bed. "There is no need to remind us of our decrepit state."

"Indeed so," Lady Faversham grumbled from the middle bed. "I've half a mind to get up and show you how well I can get about." Clad in a plain, modest night-gown up to her chin, she stretched out a hand for the ivory-topped cane that rested against the bedside table.

Brand moved the cane out of his grandmother's reach. "You'll remain in bed where you belong. You wouldn't have fractured your ribs if you'd had the sense to stay home with your knitting instead of haring off into a blizzard."

"Knitting!" Lady Faversham said with a snort. "If ever you spy me in a rocking chair with knitting needles, you may as well order my coffin."

"We did what we had to do," Lady Stokeford added. "*I* may have been fortunate enough merely to have a few bumps and bruises in that unfortunate accident, but I would risk my life again for such a cause."

"As would I," Lady Enid concurred. "Snowstorm or not."

Bewildered, Charlotte asked, "What cause? Why *did* you travel all the way from Devon to London during a blizzard?"

"That's precisely what I'd like to know, too." Brand's gaze flicked to her, then returned to the three old ladies. "They've yet to explain themselves."

Lady Stokeford glanced at her friends. " 'Twas my fault, I fear—"

"Enough, Lucy," said the old gentleman beside her. Belying his stern tone, he gallantly kissed the back of her blue-veined hand. "I won't have you blaming yourself."

Lady Stokeford cast him a miffed look. "I'll do as I please. Oh, I'm sorry, I haven't yet introduced you to Charlotte."

She did the honors, but Charlotte had already guessed his identity. He was Nathaniel Babcock, Lady Stokeford's devoted suitor these past few years. His blue eyes twinkling, Nathaniel stood up and bent from the waist in a deep, old-fashioned bow.

"Nathaniel's right, Lucy, you mustn't be so hard on yourself." Lady Faversham took a shallow breath, her palm resting on her injured rib cage. "You only did what any loving grandmother would do."

"We were coming to London to stop Samuel's wedding," Lady Enid told Charlotte. "But just outside the city, our coach slid off the road and went into a ditch. It's lucky we were only a few miles from here."

"Samuel?" Charlotte questioned. "Do you mean Mr. Firth?" He was Lady Stokeford's bastard-born grandson whom Charlotte had never met. A wealthy, self-made businessman, Firth apparently held a grudge against the Stokeford family. Lady Stokeford had only learned of his existence the previous year, and he'd rejected her attempts to make him a part of the family.

"Yes," Lady Stokeford confirmed in a subdued tone. "I knew naught of Samuel's intent to marry until I received a message from him four days ago."

"The wedding was scheduled for the following day," Lady Faversham added grimly. "So we had no choice but to set out immediately. Alas, we arrived too late. And in no condition to stop anything."

"Would that I'd been with you three," Nathaniel Babcock said. "You must have ordered the coachman to set too fast a pace."

"But why did you wish to stop the wedding?" Charlotte asked the Rosebuds.

"Because they're meddling, as usual," Brand put in. "Firth is a grown man. He has the right to marry whomever he pleases."

"Not when his bride is merely fifteen years old," Lady Faversham snapped. "She is Lady Cassandra, daughter of the Duke of Chiltern. The villain gave her to Firth to repay a gaming debt."

"A shy, country-bred girl is no match for a man of the world," Lady Enid added.

"Rather, a man *angry* at the world," Lady Stokeford said. Her voice broke as she lapsed into a fit of coughing. "Oh, this dreadful London air. I vow, my lungs can't tolerate it."

Nathaniel Babcock fetched her a glass of water, and the elderly woman gratefully took a sip. "If that new tonic from the doctor doesn't work," he said, "you're heading straight back to Devon."

"You won't be here to order me about," Lady Stokeford said loftily. "You're leaving tomorrow for Lancashire, remember?" To Brand and Charlotte, she added, "Poor Cassandra has fled to her father's estate. Since we Rosebuds can't get about, Nathaniel has agreed to be our emissary. He'll see if an annulment can be arranged."

Charlotte sank down on the edge of the bed. Unlike Brand, she couldn't blame them for interfering. Their concern for Lady Cassandra's welfare was more than justified. Although the Rosebuds could be exasperating at times, manipulating family members at will, they always meant well.

"It's damned lucky the three of you are still alive," Brand said. His hands clasped behind his back, he paced the blue and gold carpet with quick, agitated steps. "You've the brains of a peahen, venturing out into such a storm."

"Don't curse," Lady Faversham said. "And don't criticize your elders."

He returned his grandmother's glare. "I'll criticize as I please. I saw the coach in the stables. The entire side was caved in."

"Dear heavens," Charlotte whispered, reaching out to grasp her grandmother's plump hand. "Then it was truly a miracle that you survived." On any other occasion, she would have admired the Rosebuds for their courage. She herself aspired to be like them, feisty and energetic into old age. Yet now, she had a keen awareness of Grandmama's frailty. "I intend to stay until you're back on your feet."

"I was hoping you would," Grandmama said fondly, squeezing Charlotte's fingers. "You mustn't tell your brothers and sisters, dear, but you've always been my favorite grandchild. Do you know you smiled at me for the first time on the very day of your birth?"

Her throat taut with tenderness, Charlotte smiled now. Indeed, her grandmother had told that tale many times over the years. But she rather suspected it was being the first grandchild that gave her a special place in Grandmama's heart.

How she'd missed all of her family—her two younger brothers and three sisters, and her dear parents, who had always been loving although somewhat stolid and dull. Papa was a retired naval officer who had been created Earl of Mildon more than a decade ago for his bravery in battle. He had since settled into the placid life of a country gentleman, content to stay within the confines of his estate. But Charlotte had yearned only for escape. Growing up, she had disliked her hectic life as eldest of six children. She had been expected to tutor her younger siblings and mediate their frequent disputes. Banishment to Yorkshire had given her the chance to live alone for the first time in her life.

It had also given her the opportunity to think and reflect. In taking a close look at herself, Charlotte had been appalled to recognize the self-pity and bitterness that had twisted her thoughts for too long. She had vowed to change for the better, to make amends for past mistakes by devoting herself to charity work.

And she had discovered just how much she could pine for the familiar tumult of family life.

"Where are Mama and Papa?" she asked now. "Surely you sent word to them, too."

Lady Enid made a desultory wave of her hand. "Oh, I bade them stay home in Devon. You know how they prefer the country. Besides, I knew *you* would be the perfect nurse to me."

Charlotte was glad she'd been the one summoned. Much as she wanted to visit with her family again, they could be rather boisterous, and Grandmama needed her rest.

Briskly, she turned to the bedside table to fetch the brown bottle of laudanum. A small yelp issued from the floor. She'd bumped Fancy.

Charlotte picked up the dog. "I'm sorry, darling," she crooned. "I'd completely forgotten you were there."

"Little wonder," Brand said. "The beast looks more like a dustmop than a dog."

He stood watching her intently, his shoulder propped against the bedpost. Ignoring the fickle warmth inside herself, Charlotte placed the shaggy canine on the counterpane. "Grandmama, meet Fancy."

"An ambitious name, as well," Brand muttered.

"What a dear, sweet creature," Lady Enid said, smiling as she petted the dog. "She's rather scrawny, though. And there's a bald patch on her leg, poor thing."

"She was living on the streets when I found her. Do you like her?"

"If you love Fancy, then I do, too."

Fancy sniffed Grandmama's hand, turned around three times, and plopped down against her side.

"Look at that," Charlotte said in delight. "She trusts you already. I was thinking that perhaps you'd like to keep her. After I leave, of course."

"Keep her?" Grandmama's eyes filled with loving concern. "Oh my stars, I couldn't take her from *you*, dear."

"She's my gift to you. But you needn't decide right this minute."

"How considerate," Brand said to Charlotte. "Your grandmother breaks her arm, and you give her a dog to take on walks."

Charlotte shot him a glare. He really was the most irksome man she'd ever known. Bending down to the dog's level, she said distinctly, "Slippers, Fancy. Fetch the slippers."

Two ears perked up from the nest of fur. Fancy hopped off the bed and poked her nose under the bedside table and a nearby chair, then snuffled her way along the carpet.

"It's a wonder she can see through all that fluff," Brand said.

Pursing her lips against a retort, Charlotte crossed her fingers inside the folds of her skirt and hoped that Fancy remembered her training.

The dog made a circuit of the chamber, then vanished into the adjacent dressing room, emerging a moment later with two pink slippers in her mouth. She trotted back to the bed and dropped the footwear near Charlotte, gazing up and wagging her tail.

"Good dog!" Proudly, Charlotte scooped up the animal and hugged her. Fancy licked Charlotte's chin and wriggled with happiness.

The Rosebuds clucked and exclaimed. Nathaniel Babcock chuckled.

"Such a clever creature," Lady Stokeford said admiringly. "What else can she do?"

"That's all as yet," Charlotte said. "I've only been teaching her for a week or two. But she's very bright and learns fast. She'll be a great help to Grandmama when I leave here."

"Well, *I* think she's splendid," Lady Enid declared. "But I do hope you're not planning your departure already."

"Of course not. We'll have a nice, long visit. It'll take weeks to properly train Fancy."

"Perfect," Brand said. "Lady Enid should be fending for herself by then."

Charlotte clenched her teeth as she placed Fancy back on the bed. "Grandmama will need a guardian angel. If she were to fall, she might be unable to reach the bell-cord. I'll train Fancy to run and fetch a servant."

Brand's gaze remained skeptical, burning into Charlotte, making her annoyingly aware of him as a man. "Better yet," he drawled, "teach her some medical skills. Think of the money you'll save on doctors."

Charlotte sent him a withering look. "Run along. I'm sure there's a sewer somewhere that would suit you."

"Perhaps Brandon would show you the sights tomorrow," Lady Stokeford piped up. "You've never been to London before."

"I rather doubt I'd enjoy *his* sort of entertainment," Charlotte said. Firmly turning her mind to her plan, she stepped toward her grandmother. "However, I wouldn't be averse to joining society while I'm here."

A clamor of excited delight burst from the Rosebuds.

"We'll procure invitations to the best parties," Lady Faversham said.

"Oh, what fun," Lady Enid said, her eyes alight in her rounded face. "I do wish we could go, too."

"Perhaps I could persuade Lady Jersey to sponsor

you," Lady Stokeford added. "You must be introduced to all the eligible gentlemen."

"I'll be sure to warn them," Brand said in an undertone. "They'll need to know what a shrew you are."

Like the devil incarnate, he lounged against the bedpost. His curled lip and quirked eyebrow expressed doubt that any man could ever want her.

Meeting his keen stare, she felt another lurch of longing. It had always been this way. Even when he insulted her, he made her heart beat faster. Not even her hardwon maturity had banished her foolish attraction to Brand.

Charlotte turned her back on him and addressed the Rosebuds. "I'm pleased to say, I've already met a fine gentleman in York a few months ago. We attend the same church there. He's visiting London at present and—"

"Who is he?" Brand asked. "I'll send him my condolences."

"I'm telling my grandmother, not you." Determinedly, Charlotte focused her attention on Grandmama's warm brown eyes. "His name is Mr. Harold Rountree, and he's running for election to the House of Commons."

"Rountree?" Brand repeated.

Charlotte ignored him. "Mr. Rountree and I have come to know one another quite well. You might say we have a certain . . . understanding."

The Rosebuds gasped in unison. "Oh, my stars!" Lady Enid said, lifting her head to stare goggle-eyed at Charlotte. "Are you betrothed?"

Chapter 2
A SECRET ADMIRER

"You had no right to pull me out of there," Charlotte said the moment Brand hauled her into the corridor, the dustmop trotting at her heels. "I was in the middle of an important conversation with my grandmother."

Preoccupied with his dark thoughts, Brand steered her down the corridor. "You and I have a certain matter to discuss."

"I've no interest in anything *you* have to say."

"You'll be interested to hear what I know about your *beloved*." He imbued the word with grim sarcasm. Ever since Trowbridge's death over a month ago, Brand had conducted a quiet investigation that had yielded no answers. He had searched for a reason why someone would kill four members of the disbanded Lucifer League. He had sought out and interviewed several former members.

Including Harold Rountree.

Was it mere happenstance that Rountree was now courting Charlotte? Brand found himself suspicious of such a coincidence.

"Mr. Rountree is respectable, hard-working, and sober—everything you're not," Charlotte stated. "He's also a highly regarded barrister in York. I can't imagine how you could know him—unless he represented you in a criminal case."

At any other time, Brand would have chuckled. He'd almost missed parrying insults with her these past five years. Of all the women he knew, Charlotte alone could match him jibe for jibe.

There was something different about her, and he tried to put his finger on exactly what it was. Banishment from her family and friends had given her an aura of maturity that transcended her waspish nature. Tendrils of dark, chestnut hair had escaped her untidy bun. A patch of mud stained the hem of her gown. She didn't seem to fuss much over her appearance anymore. Nor did she wear gloves to hide her scarred arm.

For a moment he fantasized about undoing the buttons down her back, stripping off her bodice, learning all the secrets of her lush body. He imagined her moaning and sighing and begging him to take her to bed.

She was more likely to knee him in the ballocks.

Damn, he must be desperate. It had been a month since his brief liaison with Jewel. Prolonged celibacy could be the only reason he was lusting after a tart-tongued spinster.

And letting himself be distracted.

"Rountree isn't the paragon you think he is," Brand said.

Charlotte's green eyes flared with indignation. "Bother your insinuations. Speak plainly or I'll leave."

"As you wish. I met Harold Rountree several years ago. He was once a member of the Lucifer League."

Reaching the head of the stairs, Charlotte came to an abrupt halt and stared at him. "The . . . *what*?"

"The Lucifer League was a hellfire club that disbanded four years ago. Rountree was an active member."

She gave him one of those disdainful looks that would have withered a lesser man. "Hellfire clubs are common enough. What sins was he committing? Drinking and card playing?"

He considered telling her. But she'd be scandalized by the truth. There had been whores, orgies, opium, the sort of debauchery that a well-bred lady had no business knowing about. Brand had been only an occasional participant; he was too particular about sharing his women. "More than that," he said, letting Charlotte think what she willed. "If you'd like, I can describe the activities in explicit detail."

"No, thank you. I've no interest in all your sordid affairs." Heightened color in her cheeks, she started down the wide marble stairs. "And you're mistaken about Mr. Rountree. It must be someone else you're remembering."

"No I'm not," Brand said, following her. He lagged a few paces behind so that he could enjoy the view. Damn, she had a fine figure, with a slim waist and womanly hips that made him think about wild, unrestrained bedsport. How he'd like to pluck the pins from her bun and let all that thick chestnut hair tumble to her waist . . .

"I was there at the last meeting."

"I don't doubt *that*. But the part about Mr. Rountree can't be true. You had too much to drink and mistook another man for him."

"Believe what you please. Only consider yourself warned." Brand hoped that for once she'd heed his emphatic tone. The last thing he wanted was to reveal his suspicions of foul play.

She glided down the stairs as if they were discussing

nothing more important than the weather. "I'll ask Mr. Rountree myself when next we meet."

"He'll deny it."

"Then I'll take his word against yours," Charlotte said over her shoulder. "If that's all you have to say, good night."

An uncustomary anxiety gnawed at Brand. Was she so dazzled by Rountree's sterling façade? He couldn't let her confront the man. The little fool might endanger herself—and ruin Brand's investigation.

Reaching the bottom of the stairs, he stepped in front of her and put out his hand to block her path. She collided with him. For an instant, her lush bosom pressed into his arm. Her eyes widened to big green pools, and she flinched, her cheeks flushed and her posture stiff.

He found himself staring at her parted lips and wanting to kiss her. Again. This time, she was no longer an immature girl. She was a woman in need of a man's seductive touch.

"Excuse me," she said icily. "You're standing in my way."

He dragged his mind back to their conversation. "We need to talk."

She glowered, all indignant maiden. "I've heard quite enough from you for one night."

"Too bad. I'm not finished." Damn, why couldn't she just cooperate for once? "Tell me, how long has Rountree been in London?"

"Over a month. And lest you think he's been inattentive to me, he's written every day."

"Of course. He wants your dowry and your aristocratic name." Or was it something more? Something to do with Charlotte's connection to *him*? The possibility chilled Brand. Perhaps there was nothing to the matter, yet he had to be certain. Like all the other men in the Lucifer League, Rountree was a suspect. He had to be presumed dangerous until proven otherwise.

"You know nothing of his intentions," she snapped. "He happens to be extremely considerate and kind. We care for each other, not that you'd understand that."

Her rigid bearing made Brand realize he'd insulted her. He cursed under his breath. Things weren't going the way he'd wanted. Prickly or not, Charlotte was a woman, and women required tender handling. It always made them much more amenable to persuasion.

"I'm advising you to be cautious, that's all. Steer clear of Rountree. There are plenty of other men in society who would be happy to court a beautiful woman like you."

Her eyes widened slightly, soft and leaf-green in the dim light of the entrance hall. For a moment, he could have sworn she was attracted to him. That she wanted him to pull her into his arms and kiss her. The heat of anticipation gripped his body. But when she spoke, her voice dripped scorn. "Why are you trying to flatter me? Your compliments mean even less to me than your other lies."

"I've never lied to you, Char. You know that. So heed me now and don't mention this matter to Rountree."

"You've offered nothing but hearsay. It's only fair that I get his side of the story."

Brand clenched his jaw. Damn, she was stubborn—stubborn enough to get herself killed. Like it or not, he had to make her aware of the danger. "If you must know," he said in an undertone, "there's a possibility that Rountree could be guilty of murder."

She stared in blank incredulity. *"Murder?* That is the most ridiculous, idiotic, outrageous—"

"Keep your voice down. Anyone could be listening. We'll continue this conversation in private."

He led her across the entrance hall, his footsteps ringing on the pale, speckled marble. The lighter tap of Charlotte's half-boots sounded beside him. A familiar quarrelsome expression pinched her lips, but at least she had the sense to bide her tongue.

At the rear of the hall, he entered a deserted parlor and shut the door behind them. The tall casement clock in the corner ticked away the seconds with precise monotony, and the night-darkened windows reflected the fire that hissed on the hearth. Tastefully decorated in muted greens, this was his grandmother's favorite room, the place where she'd often called him for a scolding whenever they were in town.

The thought of her, lying injured upstairs, shook him deeply. Had the mishap with the coach been an accident—or not?

The question nagged at Brand. The Rosebuds had been present at the country estate where the breakup of the Lucifer League occurred four years ago. At the time, with their usual flair for meddling, they had come across the members of the league. Now, Brand couldn't shake an uneasy feeling about their single encounter with the hellfire club. What if the murderer was out to kill every person who could identify the members of the league? The notion seemed far-fetched, but he intended to investigate it first thing in the morning.

Charlotte flounced to a chair by the fire, letting the dog sprawl like a fuzzy rug across her lap. Craving a drink, Brand went to a rosewood cabinet and uncorked a bottle of wine.

Crystal clinked as he filled a goblet. He took a taste and found it a tolerable burgundy, so he brought another glass to Charlotte. "Here, you'll need this."

She waved him away. "I'm waiting for your explanation. And it had better be good."

He set her glass on a nearby table and savored a sip of his wine. "I'll get straight to the point, then. Over the past few months, several members of the league have died under unusual circumstances."

"Unusual in what way?" she said with blatant skepticism.

He propped his elbow on the mantelpiece. "Lord Mellingham took part in a duel, but his gun misfired and killed him. Simon Wallace had too much to drink and fell down a flight of stairs. Sir Raymond Aldrich suffered an apoplectic seizure, and he was younger than I am."

"If one leads a dissolute life, one will come to an untimely end."

Once again, Brand felt a flare of dark humor at her straitlaced manner. But this was no time for banter. "That's not all. Lord Trowbridge came to see me a few weeks ago. He'd received an unsigned note that read, 'You're next.' "

"A hoax."

"I didn't believe it, either. But when he was attacked and killed by ruffians only a few hours later, I could no longer dismiss it as coincidence. Someone really is trying to murder the members of the league."

Charlotte stared at him for a long, measuring moment. Then she stated flatly, "Mr. Rountree is not a murderer."

Brand knew he had to tread carefully. "That may very

well be true. All I'm asking is that you don't quiz him about the league right now. At least not until I can look into the matter."

"You? It would be best to hire a Bow Street Runner."

"A commoner has no connection to society. I'm far better qualified to investigate these men. I attend the same parties, belong to the same clubs."

"Mr. Rountree hails from York. He doesn't share your social circle. That proves he isn't guilty."

"Nevertheless, he once belonged to the league. Every member must be treated with equal suspicion."

"Including yourself?"

Annoyed, Brand tossed back the rest of his wine and set down the glass. "Don't be cheeky. Why would I tell you all this if I were the culprit?"

"To implicate an upstanding citizen."

"Is he truly so honorable? Harold Rountree has a solid motive for murder. He would lose the election if rumors circulated about his not-so-sterling past."

Charlotte sat very still. From her stricken expression, it was clear that she was wrestling with the ugly specter of doubt. Brand willed her to believe him, to not let their animosity sway her judgment. Abruptly, she set Fancy on the floor and sprang to her feet. "That is a ludicrous charge, and I won't listen to you any longer."

"You'd better listen. You'd be a damned fool to tangle with a possible murderer." Brand couldn't resist adding, "But then, you've always been a fool for certain men. Myself included."

Her wide eyes fastened on him. She had to be remembering that incident long ago when she'd thrown herself at him, begging him for a kiss. In no uncertain terms, he'd crushed her romantic dreams. She'd despised him ever since.

Damned shame, that. Charlotte was no longer a young girl. She was a woman with unfulfilled needs. It would be an unparalleled challenge to awaken the passion buried inside the spinster.

He was aware of how alone they were. The whisper of the fire, the closed door, the darkened windows, created an aura of utter seclusion. His imagination served up a feast of her strong limbs wrapped around him in ecstasy.

"Conceited dolt," she snapped. "I can't imagine anyone else in the world whom I detest more than you."

"Is that so?" Goaded, he came closer, crowding her against the chair. Another woman would have resumed her seat, but not Charlotte. Defiant and willful, she held his gaze. He stood so close his legs brushed her skirts. In that moment, he could have sworn she *did* still desire him. He sensed it in the warmth radiating from her, in the slight widening of her eyes, in the tensing of her body.

And what a body she had—fiercely feminine with rounded breasts and curving hips. She would not be easily conquered.

Bending closer, he inhaled her clean, no-nonsense aroma. "You don't detest me, Char," he murmured. "I proved that to you once, a long time ago. Remember?"

She held her ground. "I was young and stupid. But thankfully, I've learned from my mistakes. A pity I can't say the same for you."

"Sin can be quite enjoyable. You should try it." He caressed her shoulders, trailed his fingers up to her throat, where her skin was warm and velvety. "I wonder if you still kiss like an eager, naïve girl."

Her gaze softened, but only for an instant. Her hands flew up to thrust him away. At the same instant, something sharp attacked his ankle.

Brand jumped back. "Bloody hell!"

"Isn't your reaction a bit extreme?" Charlotte mocked. "I hardly touched you."

He bent down to examine his throbbing ankle. "She bit me. The little furball sank her teeth into me."

Fancy had retreated to the safety of Charlotte's skirts. In a menacing stance, the dog watched him. A growl issued from somewhere inside all that hair.

Sinking to her knees, Charlotte cuddled the cur to her bosom. Her scarred hand stroked that ridiculous mop of a head. "Are you all right, darling? Did the big bully kick you?"

"I hesitate to interrupt such a touching scene," Brand said with heavy sarcasm. "However, *I'm* the injured party."

Charlotte glanced up. They made quite a pair, Fancy in that hostile stance and Charlotte with prim lips and reproachful eyes. "She didn't really hurt you, did she? Are you bleeding?"

He lifted his trouser leg and examined his black stocking. "Apparently not. But it throbs like the devil."

"I suppose you expect an apology."

"Oh, have you taught her to speak, too?"

"Very amusing. Fancy only nips when she feels threatened. Or when someone threatens *me*."

Brand straightened, putting his weight on his wounded leg. The pain had subsided already, not that he'd tell Charlotte so. "Marvelous. You're giving your grandmother a vicious animal."

"It's only men Fancy dislikes. She has excellent instincts as to those who cannot be trusted."

"Then it's time she learned to trust the master of this house."

Brand scooped up the dog, tucking her into the crook of his arm. Fancy yipped and squirmed. But she was all hair and little substance, and he easily controlled her.

A look of horror on her fine-boned features, Charlotte advanced on him. "Put her down this instant!"

"All in due course." Keeping a firm hold on the scruff of the dog's neck, he encouraged Fancy to sniff his hand. When she snapped at him again, he rubbed her perky little ears and scrawny neck. "Steady, girl. There's no cause for alarm. I only want to be friends."

Charlotte hovered at his elbow. "You're frightening her. Give her to me at once."

"Not until she realizes I'm no threat." Under his determined petting, Fancy gradually ceased struggling. Ever so slowly, her tail began to wag. After a few moments, she even licked his hand. "There now, that wasn't so bad. All you needed was a little disciplining."

Charlotte made a scornful sound. "*You,* advocating discipline? The man who wouldn't know a moral from a molehill?"

Grinning unrepentently, he handed Fancy to her. "No more biting," he warned the dog, "or you'll be banished to the stables."

Tail swishing, Fancy ducked her head submissively. He allowed himself a certain satisfaction at having won over Charlotte's man-hating pet.

"Don't worry, darling, I won't let him put you out of

the house." With the protectiveness of a mother, Charlotte clutched an armful of dustmop. As she cooed, the dog nuzzled her. A flat pink tongue emerged from the fur to lave Charlotte's slender throat and delicate chin in slobbery, canine kisses.

Damn, now he was envious of a dog, Brand thought in disgust. To give himself something to do, he went to the sideboard and poured himself another glass of wine. "Nevertheless, she'll abide by the rules. Just as my dog always did."

Charlotte gave him a curious glance. "You no longer have Hector?"

"He died three years ago." Brand kept his voice impassive. Aware of an emptiness inside himself, he drank the wine. It was odd how much he still missed the dog's companionship. At times, he half expected to see the big mastiff padding down a corridor or rising from his pallet by the hearth.

"I'm sorry," Charlotte murmured.

Before she could pry into his unmanly sentiments, he changed the subject. "So you think you can teach that scraggly beast a few parlor tricks."

"They're more than tricks. I've trained five animals so far, each for someone in need, the infirm and the elderly."

"You've never cared about anyone but yourself. What brought about this flood of benevolence?"

She eyed him sulkily as if debating whether or not to take umbrage at his rudeness. "A few years ago, I met an elderly woman in Yorkshire who suffered from the gout. When I saw her terrier fetch a ball of yarn that had rolled away, I had the idea that dogs could be taught to do a number of simple tasks."

"Light the fire, pour the tea, make the bed?" he said for the sole pleasure of riling Charlotte.

For once, she didn't rise to his bait. She lifted her dainty chin with that prideful defiance. "You'd be surprised at the number of helpful things a dog can learn to do—open and close the draperies, find an article of clothing, carry a message to a neighbor. Dogs can be especially useful to the blind."

"Oh?"

"There was a man I used to see on my trips into York, a young man whose eyes had clouded prematurely. He would sit on his front stoop, afraid to venture into the busy streets." She petted Fancy, her scarred hand moving in long, sweeping strokes. "I'd found a half-grown collie pup left in a sack alongside the road. Samson, I named him. For months, I walked Samson along certain routes and taught him to obey commands until he could lead Mr. Snyder to church and to market without a single misstep."

"Amazing," Brand muttered.

"Isn't it? I think so, too." She clearly didn't see that he was taken aback more by her zeal than the innate abilities of dogs. Her green eyes sparkled and her face glowed. It was a look that disarmed him, made him see her as a woman of passion. A woman who had never tasted sensual pleasure.

Brand put a halt to the fantasy with the memory of her spiteful nature. Five years ago, Charlotte had plotted to end his half sister's budding romance with Lady Stokeford's grandson, Michael Kenyon. Charlotte had stolen a costly necklace and hidden it beneath Vivien's pillow so that Vivien would be accused as a thief. If not for Brand's quick intervention, his half sister would have been sent to prison.

No newfound charity could make Brand forgive that.

"Why so philanthropic?" he asked. "Are you making up for past sins?"

Charlotte blinked, and he could see the moment she remembered. Her shoulders firmed, the light left her gaze, and cool disdain ruled again. "I don't have to explain myself to you."

"Quite, I understand you well enough. For an intelligent woman, you're damnably thick-skulled. Especially about Harold Rountree."

"I'm an excellent judge of character," she said, looking him up and down. "At the risk of repeating myself, Mr. Rountree isn't a murderer."

"You can't afford to take that chance."

"What I do is none of your concern."

"It is so long as you live in my house." Not to mention, his grandmother would strangle him if anything happened to the granddaughter of one of her dearest friends.

"Spare me your masculine blustering," Charlotte said. "It's better spent on a more gullible woman." Her head held high like a damned princess, she walked out of the parlor, leaving him to brood alone.

The moment she entered the guest bedroom, Charlotte sank onto a yellow hassock and pressed her fists to her eyes. At last she could give in to the shock and pain that she'd hidden from Brand. Had Mr. Rountree belonged to such a vile group? Was he capable of committing cold-blooded murder?

It was outrageous, fantastical, impossible. Mr. Rountree had never given her the slightest cause to think him a reckless profligate, let alone a killer.

He was a mild-mannered, thoughtful gentleman. Whenever he came to call, he always brought her a bouquet of wildflowers or a packet of her favorite sugared almonds. When he went out of town, he faithfully wrote to her. If he had any fault at all, it was that sometimes his honorable character made her feel inadequate.

Or perhaps the fault lay in her.

Deep down, she didn't feel deserving of such a decent man. She had betrayed Vivien in the most horrid way possible. Looking back from the distance of time, Charlotte scarcely recognized herself in that malicious act. Her only consolation was that she hadn't meant for Vivien to be imprisoned, only to be sent *away.* So that Charlotte could claim Michael for herself. Michael had always been kind to her, and in return, she had been thoughtlessly cruel to the woman he loved.

Mr. Rountree didn't know that sordid story. Charlotte had never been able to bring herself to admit her crime to him.

Remorse threatened to swamp her, but she reminded herself that she had atoned for the sins of her past. Banished to York, she had lived quietly and productively, devoting herself to charity work. Now she desired only stability and respect, the chance to marry a good man and raise a family.

She *had* to believe in Mr. Rountree. She wouldn't let Brand ruin her plan for her life. He'd always been that way, laughing at her romantic dreams or making some derogatory remark.

Something warm and wet lapped her elbow. Fancy

stood with her paws propped on the ottoman, head cocked to the side, ears barely visible in the thick strands of fur.

Charlotte lifted the dog into her lap and pressed her cheek to the thick coat, taking comfort from its warmth. "I hate him, Fancy. I'm glad you bit him. He deserved it."

But it was the doubt she hated. The doubt that Brand had planted in her, the doubt that nagged at her peace of mind.

A lilting Yorkshire voice broke the silence. "Is it the master thee hates?"

Charlotte lifted her head to see her maid standing in the doorway to the dressing room. A plump, fresh-scrubbed sixteen-year-old, Nan exuded an aura of abundance, from her much-freckled face to the carroty hair beneath her white mobcap. Her generous bosom strained at the seams of her bodice, negating the modest cut of the fabric.

Charlotte sat up straight. "I'm sorry, I didn't know you were here."

"Talkin' about the devil earl, aren't tha?"

"Aren't *you*," Charlotte corrected automatically. "And that's no way to refer to the master of the house." *As much as he deserves it.*

"Master of the underworld, more like," Nan said, her brown eyes bright with interest. "Have tha—*you*—seen him, then?"

"Yes." There was no need to elaborate; Nan was already too curious for her own good. "Who's been spreading gossip about Lord Faversham?"

Without invitation, Nan drew up a stool and seated herself near Charlotte. " 'Tis the talk of the household, m'lady. They say downstairs that he's bedded every lady in London. He doesn't chase the serving maids, though, more's the pity. I'd like t' let him dip his wick—"

"Nan! That's quite enough." The heat of a blush suffused Charlotte from head to toe. She didn't know whether to be vexed with her maid or angry at Brand for his infamous reputation. "You're not to listen to such loose talk."

"Why not?" Nan asked in her frank manner. " 'Tis the truth, and thee likes me t' be honest."

"I don't want you to lie or steal. But it isn't seemly to gossip, whether the topic is true or not." When Nan opened her mouth to argue, Charlotte held up a forestalling hand. The girl had had a rough, unschooled upbringing, and it was imperative that she learn restraint. "Besides, if you listen too avidly, the other servants will expect you to talk about yourself in return. And you know how important it is to conceal your past."

"Aye, miss, but—"

"Keep to yourself, behave modestly, and you'll earn a good name. Otherwise, I won't be able to keep you as my lady's maid." Charlotte placed Fancy on the floor. "Come, you may help me out of these traveling clothes."

Readily distracted, Nan followed her into the dressing room, its yellow-draped window and dainty French chairs more sumptuous than Charlotte's cottage back in Yorkshire. "Will we stay in London for a long time?" the girl asked. "Will his lordship have parties for dukes an' duchesses?"

"We'll stay until my grandmother's arm heals," Charlotte said, wondering how she could tolerate Brand's company for weeks on end. "As for the parties, I really don't know who is in his circle of acquaintances."

"Such an adventure this is." Unfastening the back of Charlotte's gown with nimble fingers, Nan heaved an exultant breath. "So many fine houses we saw from the coach. An' Lord Faversham's is the grandest of them all."

Charlotte unbuttoned her cuffs. "Dwelling on material wealth isn't good for your character."

"But 'tis exciting t' see. On my day off, I mean t' find those streets paved with gold. Dick swore on his mam's grave that 'tis true."

"Dick is telling tales," Charlotte said, slipping out of her gown and petticoats. "And you know you're not to mention his name."

"But . . ." Reflected in the dressing-table mirror, Nan's face settled into sulk. "I do miss him betimes. He's a fine figure of a man."

Dick was a liar, a thief, and a criminal. It horrified Charlotte to think of Nan falling under his spell again. "There's more to a man than his physique. He must be trustworthy, morally strong, and faithful. Never forget that."

Charlotte felt like a hypocrite for speaking so sternly. Even after all these years, she still felt an errant attraction to Brand Villiers, who was the antithesis of the ideal man.

Dressing for bed, she diverted Nan with instructions on her schedule for the upcoming days. But Charlotte couldn't divert the memory of Brand. His aura of danger, of carnal delights, stirred a secret thrill in her. She had hoped—feared—that he would kiss her. Again.

There are plenty of men who would court a beautiful woman like you.

Silly chit, that's what she was. Only swooning girls

heeded the compliments of a rogue. A mature woman chose a reputable gentleman like Mr. Harold Rountree.

Closing her eyes, she pictured Harold's affable features, not breathtakingly handsome, but pleasant and solid, his brown hair always well-groomed. He made her feel safe and secure, with her feet planted on firm ground. Even his courtship had been slow and steady and respectful.

He couldn't be a murderer. *He couldn't be.*

Yet doubt whispered its insidious message. Somehow, she had to find out the truth.

Chapter 3
THE MISSING FOOTMAN

" 'Twas me own fault 'er ladyship was 'urt," the coachman told Brand.

The late morning light illuminated the small, tidy chamber above the stables. A burly fellow in his middle years, Butterfield sat up in the narrow bed. A bandage circled his head, concealing all but a patch of his coarse, salt-and-pepper hair. Shame-faced, Butterfield kept looking away from Brand's eyes. "I know ye won't be keepin' me, but I beg leave t' stay until I can walk without me 'ead spinnin' like a top."

Determined to get some answers, Brand drew up a rough wooden stool and sat down. "I didn't come here to dismiss you. I want to know exactly what happened."

"I fear I'll be no 'elp, m'lord. 'Tis all a blank in me mind. One minute I was guidin' the 'orses through the snow, an' the next, everythin' went black."

"Surely you recall something," Brand prodded. "Tell me the last thing you remember before the accident. Did the wheels hit a rut? Or a patch of ice?"

"Might 'ave, I suppose. 'Twas snowin', and I urged 'er ladyship t' stop, but she insisted we press on."

Brand nodded. His grandmother could be quite formidable. "Go on."

"I kept the team to a slow pace. I wasn't goin' to risk the ladies' lives no matter what they said. There was a fair amount o' drifts, ye see." Rubbing his grizzled jaw, Butterfield stared into the distance.

"What is it?"

"I just remembered somethin'. Bein' as it were cold, we sat together atop the coach, me an' Tupper."

Brand frowned. "I don't recall my grandmother employing a footman by that name."

" 'E were new, only a week on the job. 'E come from service to the Duke o' Bedford. An' 'e did 'is job well enough."

"It was only the two of you, then?"

"Aye. Right afore we left, 'Obbs came down wid the trots, an' so did Newcastle. Fit as fiddles one minute, runnin' fer the chamber pot the next. The ladies was in a 'urry, so we left short'anded."

A coincidence? Or a conspiracy aided by the mysterious Tupper? "Tell me what else you recall. Particularly right before the crash."

Butterfield scratched beneath his bandage. "Lemme think now. As we was nearin' the outskirts o' London, Tupper looked back and saw one o' the straps 'ad gone loose on the luggage. 'E said 'twas flappin' in the wind. So 'e climbed back t' fix it."

"And then?"

"Then . . . I know naught else." The coachman spread his meaty hands wide. "Perhaps, as ye say, we hit a rut or a patch o' ice."

"It seems to me you'd remember more—at least until the moment you lost control of the coach."

Butterfield looked abashed and miserable. "I'm sorry, m'lord. I recollect only Tupper climbin' t' the back, then a flash o' pain . . ."

Brand went tense. "He struck you?"

"I . . . I can't rightly say fer certain. But nothin' was stolen. The ladies still 'ad their jewels. So why would 'e?"

Why, indeed?

Brand stood up from the stool. "I'll have a word with him."

"Beggin' yer pardon, but 'tis impossible. Tupper took off the day o' the crash."

"What the devil—Where did he go?"

"Don't know, m'lord. 'E weren't nowhere t' be found." The coachman shook his head. "The bloody bugger ran away an' left the ladies t' fend fer themselves. I was out cold, y'see, an' 'tis lucky a farmer came by an' went fer 'elp."

Ugly suspicion clutched at Brand. "Lucky, indeed," he said grimly. "Describe Tupper."

" 'E's tall and thin wid buck teeth. Blue eyes and darkish hair. A pockmark on his cheek. Right about 'ere." The coachman poked a stubby finger to the side of his mouth.

"Where is his family from?"

Butterfield shook his head. "The fellow kept t' 'imself, 'e did. But wait—'e said 'e 'ad an auntie what owns a fish stall in Billingsgate Market. Beggin' yer pardon, m'lord, but 'tis all I know."

His thoughts racing down a dark path, Brand placed his hand on the man's shoulder. "My thanks. You've been more help than you can imagine."

Charlotte was walking Fancy in the winter-dead garden when Brand emerged from the stables, leading a coal-black gelding.

The crushed-shell pathway crunched beneath her half-boots, and a bitterly cold breeze stirred the ribbons of her bonnet. She squinted against the bright sunlight. Most of the snow had melted, but small patches lingered in the shadows and beneath the bushes. Here and there, a flash of green showed where snowdrops had pushed tender shoots out of the soil.

When Charlotte spied Brand in his dark blue coat and black breeches with gleaming knee boots, her heart performed a cartwheel. The mere sight of him made her feel fluttery inside. He wore no hat, and the wind ruffled his deep brown hair. Intent on adjusting the girth of the saddle, he didn't appear to notice her.

She ought to remain silent. She ought not wonder at the seriousness of his expression. She should stay right here and resist the pull of his wicked magnetism.

Fancy decided the matter. Tail wagging, the dog strained at the leash and drew Charlotte to the clipped hedge that separated the garden from the stableyard. Keeping a tight hold on the dog, she said, "Hullo. You're looking rather grim-faced this morning."

Glancing up, Brand lifted an eyebrow. "Charlotte. What a pleasure to see you in my garden."

His sarcastic tone belied the polite phrase. His gaze swept over her dismissingly, and she was irked at the melting warmth he inspired in her. Nevertheless, she would be pleasant. "I confess, I'm surprised to see you up and about before noon. Are you off to the shops?"

"I'll leave the shopping to the ladies."

"I thought you should know I sent a letter to Mr. Rountree with the early post, informing him of my arrival."

He shot her a glare. "You're determined to be a damned fool, then."

"I can watch out for myself."

A twist of his lips indicated his skepticism. "You're not to meet with him alone."

"Naturally. It wouldn't be suitable." She couldn't resist adding, "But of course you're accustomed to a different sort of *lady*."

His gaze flicked to her bosom, lingered a moment, then returned to her face. "Yes, women who have more sense."

He swung into the saddle. Nodding to her, he rode through a back gate that a groom held open for him.

Her breasts tingled from that look. Disliking the response, Charlotte turned around toward the house. How was it that he could stir such a jumble of emotions in her? Mortification, longing, anger.

And curiosity.

His haste intrigued her. Where was he going? She had thought indolent rakes lolled about all day until it was time to go out carousing in the evenings.

She resumed her stroll through the garden. While Fancy sniffed every bush along the concentric pathways, Charlotte looked up at the house. The distinguished, Italianate façade had tall windows interspersed with columns that marched along the honey-hued stone. She hadn't known his mansion on Grosvenor Square was so terribly impressive, for she'd never before had occasion to visit here.

At eighteen, she'd forgone a season in London, too self-conscious about her scarred arm to risk appearing in society. She felt stronger now, less intimidated. Maturity had given her the wisdom to realize that those who whispered or criticized weren't deserving of her acquaintance.

Now, she also had a purpose.

When she had sent out her note to Mr. Rountree with the early morning post, she'd noticed the neat stack of letters the Rosebuds had penned to the principal hostesses of the *ton*. Once the invitations started arriving, Charlotte hoped Mr. Rountree could be persuaded to attend as her escort. She was anxious to further their acquaintance and win his affections. If—*when*—he proposed, she would happily settle down to marriage and family.

Unless he was a murderer.

No, she couldn't believe that. She would *never* believe it.

Yet she caught herself staring at the gate where Brand had exited the yard. Was he off to question one of the reprobates from that hellfire club? Would he put himself in danger? She cared only because his death would cause pain to his grandmother.

"Never mind him," she said aloud. "He isn't worth a second thought."

Looking up, Fancy cocked her head and wagged her bushy tail.

Charlotte coaxed the dog back inside and headed down the long passageway to the front of the house. Canine nails clicked on the marble floor, blending with the tap of her own footsteps. Statues filled niches along the elegantly papered walls. Now that she could see the place in the daylight, she found herself admiring the stylish appointments. Brand must have hired someone to refurbish the house quite recently, for she could still smell the faint odors of paint and wallpaper paste. Letting herself be nosy, she peeked into room after room, each one more spacious and lovely than the last—a music room, sitting room, library, and drawing room.

"Ah, there you are, m'lady."

In the entrance hall, Charlotte spun around to see the butler approaching from yet another corridor. "North. Were you looking for me?"

Fancy growled, and North gave the animal a pained, disapproving glance. "You've a visitor," he intoned. "A Mr. Rountree."

Charlotte's heart leapt. Dared she hope that Mr. Rountree's swift response to her letter indicated the strength of his interest in her?

On the heel of that thought came a more sobering one. His presence meant she would have the chance to confront him sooner than she'd expected.

Removing her heavy cloak and bonnet, she strove for calm. "Where is he? And would you please ask him to wait a few minutes longer?" She needed to dash up to her bedchamber, to arrange her hair and don a finer frock than this simple blue gown.

"After you, m'lady." North waved a white-gloved hand at the staircase.

Was the old man senile? "You're to take my message to Mr. Rountree," she reminded him.

"Mr. Rountree awaits you upstairs," he said as if that were the most natural event in the world.

"I beg your pardon?"

"He is visiting the, er, Rosebuds. When I went to their chamber in search of you, the ladies asked me to show the gentleman up."

"Oh, my. Never mind, I'll go there straightaway."

Fancy trotting alongside her, Charlotte headed for the stairs, restraining the impulse to race up the steps like a ten-year-old hooligan. What were the Rosebuds saying to Mr. Rountree? What if they asked too many personal questions and frightened him off? Thank goodness they didn't know Brand's wild tale of murder, else they would be interrogating poor Mr. Rountree like Runners from Bow Street Station.

It *was* a wild tale. It had to be. So why did a knot of tension pull taut in her breast? Although Nathaniel Babcock had departed a short time ago for Lancashire, there could be no danger in the Rosebuds' being alone with Mr. Rountree.

Forgoing a stop in her chamber, she hastily patted her hair and then opened the door to their bedchamber. The congenial tone of Mr. Rountree's voice reassured her. It was his friendly, meeting-constituents manner.

She found the Rosebuds out of bed and ensconced in the sitting area, Lady Enid on the chaise longue, flanked by Lady Stokeford and Lady Faversham on chairs. For three elderly women who had survived a coach crash only a few days earlier, they looked remarkably chipper in silk dressing gowns, their hair elegantly styled. A chorus of *good morning*s issued from the old ladies.

In front of them, on a straight-backed chair, sat Harold Rountree. Unremarkable in stature, he had pleasant features saved from the ordinary by thick-lashed brown eyes. His unadorned blue coat and buff breeches were quietly fashionable.

He sprang to his feet, and a sincere smile warmed his face. "Ah, Lady Charlotte. What a pleasure it is to discover that you've come to London."

"I'm surprised that you'd respond so quickly to my note."

"I couldn't stay away." Walking forward, he took hold of her gloved hands. "Permit me to say I've missed you, my lady. These past few weeks have been rather dull without you."

She basked in the glow of his regard. The warm clasp of his fingers made her doubts seem unmerited. Seeing him in the flesh, being the object of his admiration, reassured her of his integrity. Mr. Rountree couldn't possibly be a killer. He couldn't have belonged to that dreadful hellfire club.

But what if she was wrong?

A low growl gave Charlotte only half a second's warning. "Fancy—!"

Mr. Rountree released a startled oath and staggered backward, his arms wheeling. In the next instant, he thumped down onto the carpet.

Out of the corner of her eye, Charlotte saw Fancy streak away. Horrified, she snapped, "Bad dog!"

Hanging her head, Fancy scuttled under Lady Stokeford's chair and peeked out. The Rosebuds made exclamations that Charlotte barely heeded.

Looking stunned, Mr. Rountree sat on the floor, and she rushed to kneel at his side. "I'm terribly sorry! Fancy dislikes most men. I ought to have left her in my room."

Rubbing his ankle, Mr. Rountree managed a half-hearted laugh. "It's quite all right. There's no harm done. Er, I didn't know you had acquired another dog."

"I rescued her from a throng of ruffians on the day you left York. Did she break the skin?"

Without thinking, she started to lift his trouser hem

and examine his leg, but he scooted away, his cheeks flushed. " 'Tis nothing. A mere trifle."

"Allow me to cleanse the wound. It's the least I can do. If you'll excuse me, I'll fetch some bandages—"

"Nonsense. I couldn't permit you to fuss over me." Looking somewhat nonplussed, he got to his feet and tidied his coat. "I'll run along and let my valet take care of it."

"You're leaving so soon?" she said in dismay. "But we haven't had a chance to visit."

"I've no wish to tire the Rosebuds. They've been exceedingly generous with their time."

The Rosebuds exchanged a glance in that secretive way of theirs. "You mustn't keep him, Charlotte," Lady Faversham said with a terse nod.

"There will be many opportunities to see your beau at parties," Grandmama added.

"We've made arrangements for you to attend the Pomeroys' musicale on Thursday," Lady Stokeford put in. "You'll need to spend the afternoon tending to your wardrobe."

Mr. Rountree bowed over Charlotte's hand. "I shall look forward to our next meeting, fair lady."

Charlotte was torn between staying to ask their opinion of her beau and seizing the chance for a moment alone with Mr. Rountree. Duty won out. "I'll walk you downstairs," she said.

"*Must* we tell her?" Lady Enid Quinton asked shortly after her granddaughter and Harold Rountree had vanished out the door.

Olivia, Lady Faversham, sat rigidly upright despite

the pain she must be feeling from her fractured ribs. "It's our duty to set her straight."

"He's a wretch of the worst ilk." Lucy, Lady Stokeford, brought her dainty fist down onto the arm of her chair. "Imagine, passing himself off as a decent gentleman when he was a member of that dreadful hellfire club."

At the last meeting of the Lucifer League, the Rosebuds had been searching for a valuable statue stolen by one of the club's members. The Rosebuds had spied Harold Rountree in the throng of men, although today was the first time they'd been formally introduced to him. "Perhaps we shouldn't say anything just yet," Enid ventured. "It would be cruel to break my granddaughter's heart. She's paid for her sins, and she deserves to be happy."

Lucy cast a sympathetic look at Enid. "If Mr. Rountree is hiding his sordid past, it would be far more cruel to let her go on believing he would make a suitable husband."

"Perhaps he's reformed," Enid said hopefully. "He did seem a likable gentleman. If they love one another, I wouldn't wish to separate them."

"Love, bah," Olivia said, her hands curled clawlike around the ivory knob of her cane. "You mark my words, he's after her rich dowry. And *our* connections in society."

Her mind in a muddle, Enid cradled her aching arm. "How will we find out his true character? We can't play the sleuth when we're confined to the bedchamber."

"It's quite simple," Lucy said. "We must ask Brandon what he knows."

"Ah," Olivia said morosely, "that incorrigible grandson of mine. There was a time when I thought he and Charlotte . . ." Her voice trailed off into a sigh, and she turned her gaze out the window at the barren winter landscape.

Enid's heart went out to her. Olivia didn't complain much, but her hope of seeing Brandon happily wed seemed farther away than ever. He was thirty-seven years old and showed no sign of settling down to raise a family.

Her throat thick, Enid said, "Remember how we once plotted ways to get them together under one roof? Here they are at last, but their lives are set on such very divergent courses."

"I wonder," Lucy said slowly. A halo of white hair surrounding her delicate face, she looked pensive. "Did either of you notice how aware they were of one another yesterday evening?"

"They quarreled," Enid said glumly. "They always quarrel."

Olivia moved her hands restlessly on the rounded top of the cane. "I doubt those two could ever agree on anything. If one of them were to say the sun rises in the east, the other would dispute it."

"Yes," Lucy said. "Yet I can't help but think . . ."

Recognizing the shrewd contemplation on Lucy's face, Enid felt a flicker of interest. "Think what? Do tell us."

"That we Rosebuds never give up." Lucy motioned to them. "Come, dear friends, let us put our heads together and devise a plan."

Lest the dog take a notion to bite again, Charlotte firmly held Fancy in the crook of her arm. She had already apologized half a dozen times to Mr. Rountree on their way down to the foyer.

A footman handed Mr. Rountree his overcoat and hat, then resumed his post by the door. Harold Rountree made a distinguished figure in his double-breasted coat, the sleek-fitting trousers, and brown leather pumps. The fact that he was a pillar of the community had drawn Charlotte to him.

For years, she had tried to atone for the sins of her past. She had kept herself busy with charitable works— until she had celebrated her twenty-ninth birthday with only a stray dog and a serving maid to keep her company. She had faced the prospect of spending the remainder of her life alone, without having someone to share in day-to-day events, someone to sit with by the fire in the evenings, someone to hold her close at night.

Someone to father her children.

She'd had her fill of notoriety. Now, Charlotte desired only the sort of quiet, conventional life that her parents enjoyed in the rolling countryside of Devon. She wanted a brood of children running up and down the stairs and giving her sticky jam kisses. Harold Rountree had all the makings of a devoted husband and doting father. So what if he didn't excite wicked longings in her as Brand did? She wanted a union based on trust, not lust. Mr. Rountree was reliable, decent, honorable.

Or was he?

"I need a moment of your time," Charlotte said abruptly.

He turned to smile at her. "Certainly. Perhaps I could return on the morrow—"

"Now. Please."

"If it's so important, of course I'll stay."

His graciousness only made her fret all the more. As he approached, Fancy growled and he made a wide detour around them, heading into the adjoining library. Charlotte couldn't help but remember how decisively Brand had tamed her dog.

Brand was a forceful, overbearing rascal. In time, with more gentleness and subtlety, Mr. Rountree would befriend Fancy, too.

He waited politely while she seated herself on a blue-striped settee. Removing his hat, he took the opposite chair. "If you fear my reaction to your presence here," he said, "please be assured that I've resigned myself to the situation."

Settling Fancy in her lap, Charlotte looked up in confusion. "Resigned yourself? You *don't* want me here in London?"

"You misunderstand me. I meant *here* in Lord Faversham's house." His lips compressed. "The fellow's a notorious rake—not that I would expect a fine lady like yourself to know about his affairs, his gambling, his . . . women."

Oddly enough, Charlotte bristled. Though she shared Mr. Rountree's low opinion, Brand was like family and she didn't care to hear an outsider criticize him. During her youth, Brand had taught her to ride a horse astride, slipped her extra sweets at teatime, even helped her rescue an old monkey from a traveling fair a long time ago.

He had given Charlotte her first kiss. A long time ago . . .

She reined in her wayward thoughts. Better she should concentrate on her purpose. On the awful doubts Brand had sowed in her mind.

Harold Rountree would lose the election if rumors circulated about his not-so-sterling past.

Charlotte forced herself to speak. "If what I've heard is true, you aren't one to cast stones."

He blinked. "Pardon? Have I offended you in some way?"

"Rumor has it that you once belonged to a hellfire club known as the Lucifer League."

His gaze fled hers. He glanced around the library as if seeking escape from her accusation. She waited in tense silence, aware of the spicy scent of leather-bound books on the oak shelves. The watery daylight cast a dull shine on the globe by the window. A long-dead Faversham countess in an old-fashioned ruff smiled benignly from the oil portrait on the mantelpiece. Had that lady ever felt so overwrought? Had she ever faced the possibility that the man of her choice might have feet of clay?

"Blast Faversham," Mr. Rountree mumbled. "For all his other faults, I never thought him a tattler."

Her heart took a dive. "It's true, then."

"Alas, to my great regret." He looked at her again, mortification in his expression. "Will you permit me to explain?"

"I'm listening."

He cleared his throat. "Several years ago, an aquaintance persuaded me to attend a party—a house party hosted by one of the league's members. Do understand, it wasn't my usual sort of entertainment. I meant only to observe, not to participate . . ." Blowing out a breath, he dropped his hat on a nearby table. "Oh, blast. I shan't make excuses for my lapse of judgment. It was wrong, and I've regretted it ever since. I hope you can forgive me."

If he had blustered or made denials, it would have been easier for Charlotte to give vent to her anger. She felt betrayed, for she had believed in his integrity, and resentful, for he had proven himself to be less than ideal.

Hypocrite, she scolded herself. Who was she to condemn Mr. Rountree? The secrets in her own past were every bit as reprehensible, perhaps even worse. She ought to confess right now, then they could forgive and forget, perhaps even share an abashed laugh over their youthful errors.

But her mind turned to the murders, and she swallowed hard. "Have you seen any of these men since then?"

"Absolutely not. I promise you, I never associate with scoundrels."

"Who else belonged to this league?"

"Men of ill repute, that's who. They call themselves gentlemen, but they aren't fit for a lady's company." He glowered. "Including Faversham."

"Tell me their names, please."

Mr. Rountree shook his head firmly. "Such rogues are of no concern to you."

"But I'll need to know which men to avoid here in London," Charlotte improvised. Something kept her from confiding Brand's suspicions of a murder plot. If by some horrid stretch of the imagination, Mr. Rountree was killing the former members of the Lucifer League, one by one . . .

The fine hairs prickled at the back of her neck. It was absurd to feel so edgy. She was perfectly safe here in the library, half a dozen servants within earshot of a scream. Besides, Mr. Rountree was *harmless.*

Studying his candid brown eyes, she ached to believe that.

"You needn't fear for your virtue," he said. "I'll be your protector when you enter society. No rogue would dare to bother you in my presence."

He looked so serious that Charlotte didn't know what to say. She desperately needed to be alone, to think things through. "Thank you, but I doubt that will be necessary."

As if she hadn't spoken, he went on. "Of course, there's the matter of procuring the invitations to the best parties. Perchance I might prevail upon the Rosebuds to use their influence—"

"No."

"No?" He sprang up and walked forward. From Charlotte's lap, Fancy growled a warning, but Mr. Rountree seemed oblivious. Falling to one knee, he fixed his intense gaze on Charlotte. "You're angry," he said, his voice full of regret and an unusual fervency. "What can I do to earn your forgiveness? If you give me half a chance, I vow I'll spend the rest of our lives proving myself worthy of you."

The impassioned speech took her aback. "Really, Mr. Rountree, you needn't grovel—"

"Yes, I must. You see, my lady, I can't bear to lose your respect. Especially now, when I can wait no longer to express my most ardent affection for you." Reaching out, he took her hand and clasped it to his chest. "Will you do me the great honor of becoming my wife?"

Charlotte sat speechless, her emotions in a muddle. This was the moment for which she had been yearning, the proposal that had been her fondest aspiration. But his deception had changed all that. And she faced the dismaying realization that until the murderer was caught, she could never fully trust Mr. Rountree.

Before she could formulate a reply, disaster struck. Again.

Fancy lunged at him, teeth snapping.

Mr. Rountree reared backward—too late. Gasping, Charlotte yanked Fancy away. A loud ripping sound rent the air.

A ragged piece of fine blue cloth dangled from the dog's mouth. And a large hole marred Mr. Rountree's sleeve.

Chapter 4
SOMETHING FISHY

In the predawn darkness, when Brand departed his club, only a few dedicated gamblers remained around the candlelit tables.

The swift clip-clopping of his mount's hooves echoed through the deserted city streets. The wind cut like an icy blade through his greatcoat, but the heat of urgency kept him from freezing. Gradually, the elegant town houses of Mayfair gave way to rundown shacks and cramped hovels. An occasional dark shape slunk through the shadows, though whether human or beast, Brand couldn't tell. He kept a sharp eye out for footpads, but on this bitterly cold night it seemed that even the most desperate of thieves had taken shelter.

As he neared the Thames, the frosty breeze carried a seaweedy odor. The glow of torchlights and the distant buzz of voices heralded Billingsgate Market. He had come here the previous afternoon, but the place had been nearly empty and a crossings sweeper had told him to return in the early hours, when the fishing boats brought in their catches.

Now, he flipped a silver coin to a hungry-looking youth who huddled in a doorway, and bade him watch the gelding. Then Brand joined the mob of fishmongers wheeling their handbarrows into the crowded square.

The stench was overpowering. Baskets and barrels held oysters, herrings, shrimp, sole, cod, and a hundred other varieties of seafood. One end of the market featured whelks piled by the sackful, the edible meat curling like corkscrews out of muddy yellow shells.

The shouts of hucksters bombarded him from every direction. "Fine mussels, a shillin' the lot!" "Live eels, only ten left!" "Fresh bloaters! Who'll have these fat beauties?"

While the rest of London slept, the streetsellers shoved and jostled. They poked at the goods on display, picking up this fish and that one, then throwing it back down.

As he made his way through the throng, Brand kept alert for a man fitting Ralph Tupper's description. There were costers in greasy caps, their faces gaunt in the torchlight. To his right, several men quarreled loudly over the price of a basket of lobsters. Ahead, a tall porter staggered under the weight of a massive oyster sack, the back of his canvas coat wet from the drippings.

It was impossible to be discreet. Stares met Brand from every direction, some suspicious, others merely curious about the presence of a gentleman in their midst. Ignoring them, he reached the perimeter of the square and began his inquiries.

He stopped at a table where a skinny merchant hawked strings of turbots, the white bellies of the fish shining like mother-of-pearl in the light cast by a sputtering pitch torch. The man pocketed a few coins from a customer and bared his blackened teeth at Brand. "Freshest fish ye'll find. Swimmin' an 'our ago. Five shillin's fer the lot."

"I'm looking for a man named Tupper. He has an aunt who works a stall here."

"Never 'eard o' the bloke."

"Perhaps you know him by another name. He's tall and thin. Blue eyes and buck teeth. And a pockmark beside his mouth."

"Sorry, guv'nor." Losing interest in a conversation that brought him no profit, the man shouted, "Get yer fresh turbots! They're goin' fast!"

Brand moved methodically from booth to booth, asking the same questions and receiving the same response, a shake of the head, a disinterested cold shoulder. He paid particular attention to the older women on the chance that one of them might be Tupper's aunt. At least they were more willing to talk to him, and more than once he had to parry a wink and an invitation to a nearby room.

The sky began to lighten. He went through the opening at the end of the market and found himself at the wharves, where he could see the tangled riggings of the fishing boats and the red worsted caps of the sailors who sat huddled on deck, smoking their long pipes and watching the crowd. Sellers milled here, too, busy with their transactions. Bursts of laughter rang out as they called good-natured insults to one another.

Brand gave out Tupper's description so many times he could recite it by rote. He faced the fact that his slim chance had dwindled to almost nothing. Until he questioned a stoop-shouldered coster who jerked his thumb toward a stall at the end of the row.

"Seen 'im down there, I did. Tried to cozen me into buyin' yesterday's cod. Toff like ye'd be easy pickin's fer that one."

"I appreciate the warning."

Taut with expectation, Brand approached the stand where barrels of fish stared with sightless eyes. A heap of reddish-brown shrimp lay in a pool of slime, and live eels wriggled in a basket lined with wilted cabbage leaves to keep them from escaping.

Behind a rickety table, a huge woman stood haggling with a customer. Tufts of wiry gray-black hair stuck out of her voluminous cap. The limp tails of several fish dangled from the pocket of her soiled apron.

She concluded her sale and turned, smirking, to Brand. "Wot ye like, sir? A fine codfish? Or may'ap a tumble in yonder alley?"

He controlled a grimace. "I'm looking for a man named Tupper. He was a footman for Lady Faversham."

She blinked. Her massive head moved slightly, as if she had checked the impulse to glance behind her. A door stood open to the shadowed interior of a warehouse where a torchlight glowed somewhere out of sight.

"Wot's 'e done?" the woman asked warily.

"He left without his wages. This belongs to him." Brand plucked a guinea from his pocket and held it up.

Her eyes gleamed with avarice. " 'E's me nephew. I'll give it t' 'im."

She made a grab for the gold coin, but Brand closed his fingers around it. "I'll deliver it myself. Just tell me where I might find him."

The woman licked her chapped lips. "Well, now. 'E might've gone off already—"

"Bloody baskets is too 'eavy, Auntie." A grumpy young man toting a basket of fish emerged from the warehouse. The gray light of dawn showed his slightly protruding front teeth and the blemish beside his mouth.

A hard knot twisted in Brand. "Ralph *Tupper*, I presume."

Tupper scowled. Staying behind his aunt, he clutched the basket like a shield. "Wot's it to ye?"

"You were lately employed by my grandmother. You left your post rather abruptly."

Tupper flashed a cocky sneer. "Didn't suit me no more."

"Didn't suit ye?" his aunt mocked, cuffing him on the ear. "Ye lied t' me about yer wages, ye worthless cur. Ye said ye only earned a shillin', an' 'is lordship brung ye a guinea."

Tupper ducked the blow. "I told ye the truth. I swear it."

"The fact of the matter is," Brand said, "I've a few questions for you, Tupper. You'll earn the guinea by giving me the right answers."

"Ain't got time fer no questions."

"You do, indeed." Brand took a menacing step forward. "On the day my grandmother's coach crashed, you were riding beside Butterfield, were you not? What exactly happened?"

" 'Twas snowin' an' we went into a ditch. Ain't nuthin' more t' say."

"Butterfield told me that you'd climbed back to fix a strap on the luggage. The last thing he recalls is feeling a sharp pain at the back of his head. Perhaps you can explain *that*."

Tupper shifted from one foot to the other. "The old mucker was drinkin', that's wot. Don't want ye t' know 'e was sotted."

Brand restrained his rage. "Then why did you vanish? Why didn't you stay to give aid to the ladies?"

"I fell t' the ground. Must've hit me head, too, an' wandered off in a daze. Don't recall aught else."

Brand believed that about as much as he believed in the freshness of the fish on display. "Then permit me to revive your memory," he said. "The crash was no accident. You took the post at Faversham House for the express purpose of harming my grandmother. When the opportunity presented itself, you struck Butterfield over the head and caused the coach to overturn."

"Nay! 'Tis a lie."

Brand drew back his greatcoat to reveal the brace of pistols tucked into his waistband. "Someone hired you to do the craven deed. It'll go easier for you if you give me the man's name."

Tupper's gaze widened on the guns. Heaving the basket at Brand, he darted into the darkened warehouse.

Brand dodged the rain of fish and lunged after him.

Tupper's aunt moved with surprising speed, throwing her substantial form into the doorway. "Leave 'im be," she screeched. " 'E ain't done nothin'."

Brand was sorely tempted to ignore his grandmother's teachings and give the woman a hard shove. Instead, he tossed the guinea onto the filth-strewn floor. While she squatted down to scrabble for the coin, he leapt over her and entered the building.

Tupper had snuffed the torch, and the blackness was impenetrable. The reek of rotting fish hung like a pall in the frigid air. Drawing one of his pistols, Brand stopped to listen. Only the muffled cries of the fishsellers filtered in from outside.

The footman could be hiding anywhere amid the piles of boxes. Then, as his eyes adjusted to the dark, Brand spied a faint square of light across the room. Had Tupper escaped out that doorway?

Wending through the clutter, Brand kept watch for any sign of the man. The rustle of movement came from a short distance to his left.

He spun toward the noise, the pistol ready. "Show yourself. I'll pay you well for the information I want."

The stillness mocked him. Had he heard a rat? Or a rodent of the human variety?

His senses alert, he advanced deeper into the darkness. He had only a split second of warning before a tower of crates toppled into his path. He jumped back, and the loud clatter rang in his ears. At the same instant, a black figure sped toward the rear exit.

Brand gave chase, thrusting boxes out of the way. Tupper reached the door first and ran outside.

Trailing by several yards, Brand emerged into a narrow alley cluttered with refuse. One end led to a side street. At the other end, Tupper raced toward the busy square. Brand sighted down the barrel of the pistol, then lowered it with a curse of frustration. He didn't dare risk a shot, not with so many people milling around.

Stuffing the weapon back into his waistband, he sprinted after his quarry and spied the tall footman slithering like an eel through the sea of fishsellers.

Fueled by rage, Brand shoved costermen and merchants aside, ignoring their oaths and shouts. All the while, he kept his gaze trained on Tupper's dark, bobbing head. He steadily gained on him until, at the far edge of the square, he caught a handful of Tupper's sleeve.

The footman's frightened gaze flashed over his shoulder. Jerking himself out of Brand's grasp, he crashed into a stall. Baskets and barrels went flying like ninepins.

People screamed and shouted. Lobsters scuttled for freedom. A cat pounced on a fat fish. The beefy merchant hurled a string of blue curses at the two men.

Brand swung at Tupper's face. The satisfying blow reverberated up his arm. His nose dripping blood, the footman yelped and ducked for cover beneath a table. Brand hauled him out by the scruff of his neck and landed another strike to his jaw. But Tupper rammed his head into Brand's midsection, momentarily knocking the wind out of him.

The villain scrambled across a carpet of cod. Sucking in a painful breath, Brand went after him. His boots slid in something slimy and he went down hard, landing on his side in the brine from an overturned barrel.

Avid-eyed onlookers formed a solid wall around him. The ruddy-faced shopkeeper shook his fist and sputtered dire threats.

Brand rolled to his feet. He pushed his way through the mass of spectators, but he was too late.

In those few seconds, Tupper had vanished into the seething crowd.

"His lordship has not yet arrived home," North said in answer to Charlotte's query outside the breakfast chamber.

Brand's absence took Charlotte aback. She had wanted to speak to him about the coach accident. "Did he say where he was going so early?"

The ancient butler regarded her with a somewhat abashed expression. "Begging your pardon, m'lady. I have not spoken with the master since yesterday."

"Yesterday? Are you saying . . . he stayed out all night?"

"It would seem so."

As he toddled away, mournfully shaking his head, Charlotte compressed her lips. Brand was up to his old tricks. Not even with the Rosebuds in residence would he temper his wicked ways.

At this very moment, he was no doubt lying in the arms of one of his hussies. They might be doing all manner of unchaste deeds. The very thought made her hot . . . with anger.

"Blast him," Charlotte said under her breath.

Marching upstairs, she donned her pelisse and jammed a bonnet onto her head. When Fancy whined eagerly, she put the dog on the leash and went downstairs again.

All the while, a discomfiting mix of emotions burned in Charlotte, the foremost of which was curiosity. She had only a sketchy notion of what took place in the bedchamber, enough to wonder what Brand did to make so many women eager for his company. He was handsome, she allowed, and he did possess a certain sinful charm. In her youth, she had seen the ladies flocking around him, simpering and flirting, vying for his attention. At the time, in the first blush of innocence, she had been one of them.

She knew better now.

Their obsequious fawning was an affront to womankind. Had they no pride, no self-respect? *She* would never be so foolish as to relinquish her virtue to a scoundrel.

Mr. Harold Rountree made a far superior companion—if she could prove his integrity, that is. The doubts that Brand had planted in her throbbed like a sore tooth. Consequently, she'd had to parry Mr. Rountree's long-awaited proposal. She had put him off with a promise to give him an answer in a fortnight. He'd required a bit of soothing, especially after Fancy had taken a bite out of his best coat.

"Men," she muttered. "They're entirely too much bother."

As if in agreement, Fancy wagged her tail and led the way to the back door. Emerging onto the verandah, Charlotte saw a gardener garbed in a thick coat and slouch hat, trundling a barrow of refuse toward the back gate. The otherwise deserted pathways looked forlorn in the fitful daylight.

She gave Fancy a few moments to tend to her business in the bushes, then headed toward the stables. The door opened on well-oiled hinges. Blinking to adjust her eyes to the dimness, Charlotte inhaled the familiar odors of hay and horses. A groom hastened out of the tack room at the end of the long corridor.

Fancy growled, and the bandy-legged man prudently halted a few feet away. He doffed his cap and held it to his chest. "M'lady. We weren't told ye wished the carriage made ready."

"I'm not going out for a drive," she said. "I'd like to see Lady Faversham's coach."

If the groom was surprised by her request, he gave no indication of it. He motioned to her to follow him past the stalls of horses and to the rear of the building.

Brand kept his stables to exacting standards, Charlotte thought, observing the freshly painted white trim and neatly swept floors. Unlike the mews behind smaller town houses, this place had room for ten horses and a variety of carriages. Windows let in ample daylight.

The groom waved his gnarled hand at the vehicle parked inside the closed double doors. "There she be, m'lady."

"Thank you, that will be all."

As he departed, Charlotte could only stare in disbelief at the mangled coach. The back wheels were splintered and the axle was bent. The entire right side was crumpled like a giant wad of black paper, and the window bore a star-shaped crack. Thank heavens the Rosebuds hadn't been cut by shattered glass.

Charlotte leaned her gloved hand against the coach to steady herself. The accident came alive for her: Grandmama's terror at the sudden jolt . . . the wild tilt as the vehicle rolled over . . . the occupants tumbling on top of one another, their belongings tossed to and fro. It was a miracle the Rosebuds hadn't suffered heart failure in addition to their other injuries. Their shock and pain must have been dreadful. How long had they lain there, waiting for help to arrive?

What of the coachman? And the footmen? Surely they too had been injured. If their fate had been worse, Grandmama would have said so.

Charlotte gazed up at the coachman's box. One side of the wide bench had been damaged, and stuffing spilled out of the torn black leather. She could just see the smashed door to a compartment beneath the seat. On impulse, she tested the footrest and hoisted herself up so that her chin was on level with the floor of the box.

Something shiny glinted inside the compartment. Reaching inside, she pulled out a pewter flask. She uncorked it and sniffed the contents. Her eyes watered from the unmistakable aroma of spirits.

An ugly suspicion took root in Charlotte's mind. Were the Rosebuds wrong in attributing the crash to the snowy weather? What if the coachman had been drunk?

Frowning, she wondered if Brand had considered that possibility. But, of course, he was too busy with his sordid nighttime activities to spare a thought for the accident. At the earliest opportunity, she would speak to him. Such a servant must be disciplined—or better yet, dismissed.

As if sensing her agitation, Fancy whined. Charlotte clambered down and stroked the animal. "It's all right, darling. You can be sure I'll protect Grandmama. I intend to find out exactly what happened."

Clutching the flask, she drew Fancy back out into the chilly air. And in a repeat of the previous morning, she spied Brand in the stableyard.

He had just dismounted from his black gelding. Oddly enough, several cats milled around him. Fancy yapped and jerked on the leash, straining to give chase to the cats.

Or perhaps to nip Brand again. Charlotte refused to believe that he had tamed Fancy so easily.

She picked up the wriggling dog. "Do behave yourself, darling."

As the bandy-legged groom led the horse into the stables, another scrawny cat emerged from the shrubbery and joined the others. This one was brazen enough to rub its head against Brand's knee-high boot and meow piteously.

Unkempt as any rake after a wild night, Brand stepped around his feline harem. His hair was mussed, his cravat missing. Mud and other unidentifiable substances stained his greatcoat and breeches. With his unshaven cheeks and the scar beside his mouth, he looked every inch a man . . . a dangerous man.

His gaze met hers. He grimaced as if none too pleased to see her.

Nevertheless, an involuntary thrill weakened Charlotte's knees and wreaked havoc with her heartbeat. She dismissed the reaction and walked briskly toward him. Upon drawing closer, she realized what had attracted the cats.

A malodorous, fishy stench emanated from him.

Turning her head away, she waved her hand to banish the odor. "Phew! When I accused you of rolling in the gutter, I meant it merely as a figure of speech."

"Spare me your quaint observations." His gaze swept past her as if he had more important things on his mind. Without another word, he strode toward the house.

Charlotte set Fancy down on the ground; the dog lunged at the cats and made them scatter. That task accomplished, she trotted after Brand, pulling Charlotte along by the lead. They reached the verandah as he was opening the back door. Fancy halted at his feet and gazed up at him in faithful adoration, tail wagging hopefully.

He paid no heed to the animal. With a distracted scowl, he held the door for Charlotte.

She stepped into the back hall. "I expected you to come home smelling of ladies' perfume, not stinking of fish. Where have you been?"

"Billingsgate."

"The fish market," she said in mock surprise. "You've sunk rather low in your search for women."

Shutting the door, he gave her a pointed stare. "I could have sunk lower."

"Your foul humor exceeds even your foul smell." Tightening her fingers around the flask in her hand, she added, "If you can manage to be civil for a few minutes, I must speak to you. On a matter of grave importance."

His frown deepened. "Has my grandmother taken a turn for the worse?"

"No, the Rosebuds were still asleep when last I checked—"

"Then your little crisis can wait." Stripping off his leather gloves, he started down the passageway.

She went after him, and their footsteps mingled with the clicking of Fancy's claws on the marble floor. "It's about the accident," Charlotte said. "The coach accident."

Abruptly, he swung around to face her. "What of it?"

This time, to her surprise, Charlotte held his attention. His keen gray eyes were fixed on her, searching her face. A little nonplussed by his sudden interest, she said, "I've been thinking about what happened—and wondering if we've leapt to the wrong conclusion."

"What the devil do you mean?"

"There was a snowstorm, of course, and the roads were icy. However, there may have been extenuating circumstances that caused the crash."

"Such as?"

His air of grim intensity fed her suspicion that she'd guessed correctly. She held out the flask. "This. The journey from Devon was long and cold, and it's quite likely the coachman drank spirits to keep himself warm."

Brand took the flask, uncorked it, and sniffed the contents. Then he tilted his head back and took a long swallow. Moisture glistened on his lips, quirked in that eternal smirk. He dropped the flask onto a nearby chair.

"Gin," he pronounced. "Vile stuff, too. I prefer wine myself."

"Your preferences are irrelevant," she snapped. "It's the coachman's drinking habits that concern me. He must have tippled too much."

"Tippled."

"Aren't you listening? I'm saying it's quite likely he was inebriated. That's why the coach veered off the road and went into a ditch."

"No one was *tippling*. I've already spoken with Butterfield. So you may put the matter out of your mind." Turning away, Brand resumed walking toward the foyer.

"So Butterfield denied it," Charlotte said indignantly, keeping pace with him and trying not to breathe in his odor. "Will you simply take the man at his word?"

"Yes."

"There must have been a footman or two with him who might bear witness to his imbibing. Have you thought of that?"

"Don't pester me, Char. I'm too damned tired." In the front hall, Brand removed his smelly coat and threw it over the mahogany newel post. He ran his fingers through his hair, enhancing his wickedly dangerous image. "Run along now. And take the furball with you."

Charlotte pulled on the leash to stop Fancy from jumping up and down in an effort to catch Brand's attention. "This is too important to be ignored. If the coachman is a drunkard, he must be dismissed. Next time, he could kill your grandmother—and mine." The thought made her throat tighten.

"You're being melodramatic—"

"I'm being sensible. And if you refuse to look into the matter, then I shall do so myself."

Brand opened his mouth as if to speak, but the butler's stoop-shouldered figure shuffled into the foyer. His fastidious nose wrinkling, North picked up Brand's coat between his white-gloved forefinger and thumb. "Will you require breakfast in your chamber, m'lord?"

"Yes, at once."

"Very good." The butler paused, then added morosely, "I'll order hot water for a bath, too." Shaking his head and muttering to himself, he walked away.

Brand bent down to grab Fancy and tucked her in the crook of his arm. "Your mistress is still a meddlesome brat," he told the dog. "She never gives up. I don't know how you tolerate her."

His long fingers scratched behind the dog's furry ears, much to Fancy's delight and Charlotte's ire. "I intend to protect my grandmother," she stated stiffly. "With or without your help."

Brand unfastened the lead from Fancy's collar and tossed it to Charlotte. "You leave me no choice, then," he said. "There *is* more to the incident than meets the eye. Follow me and I'll tell you about it." With that, he started up the grand staircase.

Charlotte hastened after him. "Do you mean there really was negligence involved?"

Over his shoulder, he said, "No more questions until we're alone."

She huffed out a breath. "Where are we going?"

"To a place we can talk away from listening ears." As they reached the top of the wide marble stairs, he looked at her, his insolent gaze roaming downward to her bosom, then returning to her face. "My bedchamber."

Chapter 5

THE SUMMONS

Charlotte faltered on the top step. "We can speak just as well elsewhere," she countered. "In the library or the drawing room."

"I'm filthy. I want to wash up." A trace of diabolical humor crooked his lips. "It won't be the first time we've been alone in my bedchamber."

His smirk resurrected the memory of that mortifying encounter at Faversham House some sixteen years ago. He had come home to Devon for the Christmas holidays, a dashing buck of twenty-one, the stuff of girlish dreams. Charlotte had been instantly smitten. With all the fervency of budding womanhood, she had trailed after him like a lovesick puppy, determined to catch his notice. But he had viewed her with absent-minded indifference.

Until in desperation she'd followed him into his bedchamber and begged him for a kiss. She could still recall her giddy joy at his compliance, and her anguish upon realizing he'd only wanted to humiliate her . . .

"What are you doing?" she asked, still dazed from her first real kiss. It had been deep and melting, and if she hadn't been sitting in his lap, her legs surely would have collapsed. Then, to her shock, he had reached be-

neath her skirt, his caressing fingers boldly moving up her stockinged calf.

"I'm giving you what you want, Char. What you've been begging for these past few weeks."

She squirmed, afraid of the intensity of longing inside her, yet even more afraid of appearing young and gauche. "Stop it! I never begged you to put your hand under my gown."

"You've asked for it with every sway of your hips, with every come-hither smile. And this is what happens when you tease a man." His hand roved higher, to stroke the tender back of her knee . . .

A bolt of pleasure made her panic. Charlotte boxed his ears and scrambled to her feet. He lounged in the chair, amused and superior, his eyes full of secrets she couldn't begin to decipher.

"Run away, little girl," he'd said. "And let this be a lesson to you."

Charlotte snapped back to the present to see him walking down the corridor. She hastened to catch up. "After one appalling experience in your bedchamber, why would I agree to another one?"

Idly, he stroked Fancy until the dog almost purred. But his attention was fully on Charlotte. "Perhaps I shouldn't have brought up that day," he said musingly. "It can't be a very pleasant memory."

"I should think you'd enjoy gloating over how you took advantage of a gullible girl."

"I was referring to what happened afterward."

Her burns. Odd that she had separated the two incidents, when the they were connected irrevocably. Rather than retreat to her chamber to lick her wounds, she had gone straight to Brand's best friend, Michael Kenyon. In an effort to soothe her battered heart, she had flirted with Michael, snatching his book away and backing too close to the hearth.

She had stumbled into the fire. An inferno had engulfed one side of her gown, going straight up her thin sleeve.

Time had given the disaster a fragmented, nightmarish quality. The whoosh of flame. The searing heat. The echo of her agonized screams.

Michael's quick action had saved her life. He had thrown her to the floor, wrapped her in a rug, and extinguished the blaze. Too late. Her arm had been hideously burned. She could only be thankful that the thickness of her petticoats had prevented further injury.

In the long weeks of painful convalescence, Michael had visited often. He had brought her flowers and read books to her. She knew he had meant only to be kind, but nonetheless, she had transferred all her youthful affection to him.

There had been only hatred left for Brand.

"It happened ages ago," Charlotte said stiffly. "It's best forgotten."

"Perhaps." Brand glanced at her arm. "Yet you carry the reminder."

Charlotte resisted the old impulse to move her hand behind her back, even though she was dressed for the wintry weather in a pelisse and gloves. If only he knew that the aftermath had been worse than the accident itself. She had worn long sleeves even on the hottest days of summer, a self-conscious adolescent acutely aware of every pitying look and horrified whisper. She had turned into a bitter young woman who lashed out at the world.

But no more. *No more.*

She gave him a steely stare. "If people can't accept me as I am, then I've no use for them."

"I quite agree."

Why was he commiserating with her? She found herself saying, "You left for London without visiting my sickroom."

He raised an eyebrow. "Did you really want to see me again?"

"Only for the chance to throw the chamber pot at you."

"A pity I denied you the pleasure of doing so."

Oddly enough, his wry smile loosened the knot of tension inside her. It made her remember happier times, when they had been part of an extended family, linked by the Rosebuds. There had been holidays spent together, rehearsing mock theatricals and going on picnics. They had been as close as cousins, Brand, the Kenyon brothers, and Charlotte's family.

Then the illusion of camaraderie vanished as Charlotte rounded the corner and spied her maid.

Nan toted a bundle of laundry that reached her chin. She appeared to be quarreling with a thin-faced man in a plain brown suit who blocked an open doorway.

Giffles, Brand's valet.

Dismayed, Charlotte slowed her steps. So much for slipping in and out of Brand's bedchamber without anyone noticing.

"Good morning, my lord, my lady," Giffles stated calmly, as if accustomed to seeing his master in disarray, stinking of fish, and escorting a woman to his chambers.

A low warning rumble came from Fancy. Holding the dog securely, Brand frowned at the girl. "What's going on here? Who the devil are you?"

"This is my maid, Nan," Charlotte said quickly. "I can't imagine what she's doing in this wing of the house."

As Nan sketched a curtsy, made awkward by her burden, she stared at Brand with frank interest on her freckled face. "Beggin' thy pardon, m'lord. Lost my way, I did."

"She entered your chamber," Giffles said on a note of disapproval. "As if she had the right to wander wherever she pleases."

She cast him a resentful look. " 'Twas a mistake. I told thee so."

"Mistakes will not be tolerated," Giffles intoned. "This is the home of the Earl of Faversham, not a shepherd's hut in the wilds of Yorkshire."

"Huh. I hail from the city. So don't be callin' *me* a bumpkin—"

"Nan," Charlotte said. "That's enough."

The maidservant fell silent, a rebellious glint in her brown eyes.

The two men exchanged a glance, and Charlotte had the impression that an unspoken message passed between them.

"I'll escort you down to the laundry," Giffles told Nan. "That way, you won't go *astray* again."

As he started down the corridor, the maid minced after him, imitating his nose-in-the-air manner. She looked so ridiculous with the bulky canvas sack that Charlotte had to cough to cover an hysterical laugh.

"That went well," she said, upon following Brand into a spacious bedchamber decorated in blue and gold. "Now everyone on the staff will know I was here. And by nightfall, everyone in the neighborhood, too."

"My valet doesn't gossip. Better you should worry about your maidservant."

"Nan will hold her tongue," Charlotte said.

Brand cocked a dubious eyebrow. As he shrugged out of his coat, Charlotte spied the brace of pistols stuck in his waistband.

All thought of scandal fled her mind. "Good heavens! Have you been dueling?"

"Not since last autumn—when I winged that young fool Lambert for accusing me of cheating at cards." He put Fancy on the floor, then went to a mahogany rolltop desk and placed the pistols inside a leather case.

Watching him, she fit the facts together in an inescapable conclusion. The pistols, the fishy stench, his air of grim preoccupation. "So that's why you were at Billingsgate Market," she said slowly. "It was something to do with the Lucifer League."

"Your cleverness astounds me." He vanished into his dressing room, Fancy trotting at his heels.

Too upset to take offense at his sarcasm, Charlotte peeled off her kid gloves and dropped them on a table. Her scars ached from the cold, and she absently massaged them. All the while, she wrestled with a worrisome fear. Until this moment, the danger hadn't seemed real to her. She had been too caught up in her own problems with Mr. Rountree to wonder much about Brand's investigation. But the sight of those weapons sent an icy shudder of awareness through her.

Brand had put his life at risk. Not only by hunting the murderer, but also by the simple, deadly fact that he too had belonged to the league.

He could be next.

The sounds of him washing up came from the dressing room. The urge to rush in there seized Charlotte. She wanted to command him to leave the matter to the proper authorities. She wanted to put her arms around him, to feel the reassuring beat of his heart against her bosom. She wanted to beg him to stay out of danger.

She took a step toward the dressing room, then stopped. What utter nonsense. Brand Villiers meant about as much to her as the postman or vicar. He was merely an old acquaintance, tied to her by the friendship between their grandmothers. And by a shared past.

Taking measured breaths, Charlotte sought to calm the turmoil inside herself. Brand had been a thorn in her side for most of her twenty-nine years, and she knew his every fault and foible. His wicked nature ran contrary to everything she wanted out of life—respectability, normality, marriage. Because they were so different, he wasn't someone who truly mattered to her.

But she didn't want him to *die*.

Unable to remain still, she paced around his bedchamber. The furnishings suited him—masculine in the lack of frills and furbelows. Dark blue draperies hung from the tall windows that formed two sides of the room, and a trace of spice in the air underlay that fishy odor. Charlotte studiously avoided looking at the four-poster bed that dominated the chamber. Instead, she headed to the gray marble fireplace, where a few books rested on a round mahogany table beside a blue armchair, well used from the look of the cushions.

A battered, tubelike artifact on the mantelpiece caught her attention. Picking it up, she smiled in surprise. His spyglass. A long time ago, he and the Kenyon brothers had been fond of playing pirates in the woods. Why had

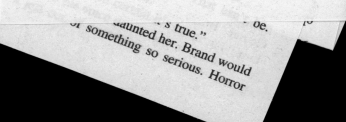

Brand kept it all these years? Was he more sentimental than she'd thought?

He probably spied on the neighbors.

Charlotte raised the instrument to her eye. The circle of wavy glass magnified a silver snuff box on a table across the chamber. Making a circuit of the room, she paused on the bed with its blue coverlet and bank of feather pillows . . . the bed where he entertained his lovers.

Her thoughts veered down a forbidden path. What would it be like to lie there with Brand? To let him touch her? To let him put his hand all the way up her skirts?

Flushed, Charlotte replaced the spyglass on the mantel. It was shocking how readily she could imagine herself with Brand. She had never entertained such lascivious thoughts about Mr. Rountree. Perhaps temptation took on an unforeseen luster in the bedchamber of a notorious rogue.

But she was a sensible woman . . . occupied a chamber on the . . . known this part . . . here onl . . .

idly scratched her belly. But there was som . . .
rolled onto her back, her tail swishing. With his toes, he
He leaned against the bedpost. At his feet, Fancy
prompted, "I'm waiting."
black stubble on his cheeks. In a more subdued tone, she
did look exhausted, with shadows beneath his eyes and
Charlotte perched on the edge of the seat. He truly
with you."
"I've been up all night, and I'm too weary to quarrel
"Sit," he said, pointing at the chair by the hearth.

. . . does one fellow drunkard protect
. . . mand, then you
gaz

George. Brand had bloodied the . . . lying in the dirt. Now, that same fierce det . . . tion burned in her. By heaven, she would pr . . .
grandmother.

"Give me the names of the men who belonged to the Lucifer League," she said. "When I go into society, I'll help you investigate them."

"You'll do nothing of the sort," he said sharply. "I told you the truth only so you'd cease blaming Butterfield."

Unable to sit still, Charlotte rose from the chair. "You should have told me anyway. My grandmother suffered a broken arm because of this villain. I intend to see that he pays."

Brand strode to her. "This is no childish adventure, Char. The man is extremely dangerous. He's already murdered at least four men."

Charlotte held his icy glare. "He nearly killed three sweet old ladies, too. I won't hide while he goes after the Rosebuds again."

"He can't get near them. They're safe here."

"Tupper invaded your country house," she pointed out. "Perhaps the murderer already has another minion in place here, as well."

"No one new has been hired in the past year." His features set in stone, Brand prowled to the fireplace. "Nevertheless, I'll assign someone to guard the doors, day and night."

"Someone reliable, I hope. Men can be bought."

"So can women. How well can you trust your serving maid?"

Pinned by his stare, Charlotte fought the urge to squirm. If ever he found out about Nan's criminal past . . . "As well as you trust your valet."

"Giffles has served me for nearly twenty years. Nan can't be more than sixteen. She's a saucy wench whose head is easily turned."

"You needn't worry about Nan," Charlotte said with more confidence than conviction. "She's very grateful to be a lady's maid. She wouldn't do anything to jeopardize that."

Or at least Charlotte hoped not.

The sound of commotion snapped her attention to the door. A solemn-faced Giffles entered the bedchamber at the head of a procession of maidservants who carried cans of steaming water into the dressing room.

The valet bowed to Brand. "Lady Faversham wishes to see you, my lord."

"I'll go, too," Charlotte said. "I want to check on my grandmother."

"Ahem." Giffles looked rather discomfited. "Begging your pardon, but Lady Faversham requested a private audience with his lordship."

As the valet discreetly faded into the dressing room, Brand gave her the gloves that she'd tossed onto a table. "Go on with you now," he said. "And don't tell anyone what we talked about here. Especially not the Rosebuds. I won't have them worried."

Charlotte bristled at being dismissed like an unwanted servant, first by the valet and now by Brand. She resented even more the implication that she couldn't be trusted.

It made what she had to admit more difficult. She hesitated, then said, "There's something you should know. Something about Mr. Rountree."

"Yes?"

"Shortly after you left yesterday, he came to call on me. The Rosebuds invited him upstairs to their chamber."

"The devil you say!" Brand swore viciously under his breath and took a step toward her. "Are you mad? He could have shot them or slipped poison into their tea."

"Mr. Rountree isn't like that," Charlotte said, though a sliver of doubt throbbed in her. What if he *did* turn out to be the mysterious killer? The Rosebuds would have been in grave danger.

Brand aimed a black look at her. "If you want to play the fool and trust Rountree," he said, "I can't stop you. But don't do it in my house."

"I had no choice in the matter. He was already with the Rosebuds when I came in from the garden."

"Then I hope to God you hurried him straight out of there."

"He did depart rather quickly," she admitted. "Fancy bit him."

Brand hunkered down to rub the dog's belly. "Excellent work, furball. You've more sense than your mistress."

Annoyed, Charlotte kept mum about Mr. Rountree's marriage proposal. It would only give Brand more ammunition to harangue her. "What, did you expect *me* to bite him?"

"Not in front of anyone else, I would hope."

She resented his secretive smirk. As if he were telling a jest she didn't understand. "At the risk of repeating myself," she said, "I didn't know the Rosebuds were a target. *You* didn't bother to warn me."

Brand arched an eyebrow. "Then I'll make myself perfectly clear. Harold Rountree is barred from this house. If he so much as places his big toe on my front doorstep, I'll put a bullet through his heart."

• • •

"Will you be wanting a shave, my lord?" Giffles asked as he entered the dressing chamber and went to a cabinet to retrieve the necessary equipment.

It was a perfunctory question, and Brand grunted an assent. Having just emerged from the copper tub, he wore a crimson robe tied at the waist. Steam from the water fogged the mirror. Using a linen towel to rub his hair dry, he worked at scouring Charlotte from his mind.

The trouble was, she beviled him like the aftereffects of imbibing too much wine. He couldn't forget the shapely thrust of her breasts beneath that form-fitting pelisse. The no-nonsense way she'd looked him straight in the eyes. The pert sway of her backside as she'd marched out of his room.

He liked his women soft and sensual, well versed in the art of pleasing a man, the antithesis of Lady Charlotte Quinton. Yet from the moment she had entered his chamber, he'd thought far too much about getting her into bed. He wanted to transform all that righteous indignation into passion.

For him.

Disgusted, he threw down the towel and it caught on the foot of the brass tub, one edge plopping into the still-steaming water. He should have taken a cold bath instead of a hot one. Only a harebrained dunce would desire the woman who had nearly succeeded in sending an innocent woman to prison.

The snick-snick of metal broke into his thoughts. As Giffles sharpened the razor on the strop, his rigid posture conveyed disapproval.

Welcoming the chance to vent his ill temper, Brand

growled, "Go on, speak your mind. I shouldn't have brought Charlotte here."

"She *is* a lady," Giffles said. "And a guest of the Rosebuds. It would be most unwise to seduce her."

"Don't fret. The lady wears iron underdrawers."

"And you do like a challenge, my lord."

Brand felt the nudge of deviltry. "Remember Lady Marchbane? The biggest cock-teaser in London. The biggest tits, too."

Adding a trickle of water to the shaving soap, Giffles wore a long-suffering look. "It is a woman's virtue that matters, not the size of her . . . bosom."

Charlotte had a fine bosom. Keeping that thought to himself, he said, "Virtue makes a damned dull bed partner."

The valet took a hot damp towel from the hearth and wrapped it too tightly around Brand's face to soften the whiskers. "Virtue is its own reward."

Brand pushed the cloth aside. "Don't be pious. I saw the way you looked at Nan."

A slight flush colored those bland features. "I beg to differ, my lord. There was nothing untoward in my regard."

"You were eyeing the wench. Ogling her *bosom*."

"I was making note that her bodice was entirely too tight."

"A pity I can't ask the housekeeper to order new gowns for her. You'll have to continue to enjoy the view."

Giffles stirred the shaving soap so intently that foam spilled over the sides of the china cup. The uncustomary sloppiness proved his agitation. "The girl is far too free-spoken. She needs to learn discipline and discretion. On the way down to the laundry, she had the effrontery to call me . . ."

"Go on. Tell me."

"A stick-in-the-mud."

Brand chuckled. "Bloody good judge of character." Then he sobered. "Can she be trusted?"

"I wouldn't know, my lord." Giffles lifted an inquiring brow. "Why do you ask?"

In unvarnished detail, Brand related the threat to the Rosebuds, including the fact that the killer had planted Ralph Tupper in his grandmother's household.

"I knew that no good would come of your association with the Lucifer League," Giffles said with a dour shake of his head. "However, I shall do what I can to assist you. Perhaps I could speak to the valets of the former members."

"I had something else in mind, too," Brand said. "Nan is the only new servant in this house. I want you to keep an eye on her."

Giffles looked as if he'd bitten into an apple and found half a worm. "But my duties to you—"

"I can fend for myself." Despite the grave circumstances, Brand rather enjoyed the valet's dismay. He took the shaving brush from Giffles and lathered his own face. "Henceforth, you're to watch Nan very closely. Become her shadow. Find out everything you can about her."

Chapter 6

THE LOCKED DRAWER

Charlotte crouched down to let Fancy sniff the small metal object in the palm of her hand. "Key," she said, repeating the word several times. Then she placed it on a chair across the library.

"Key, Fancy. Fetch the key."

Fancy cocked her head questioningly, her black eyes barely visible through the veil of dense, brownish fur. Turning, the dog trotted straight to the chair. Planting her front paws on the leather cushion, she sniffed the key and carefully picked it up in her teeth. She brought it back to Charlotte and dropped it at her feet.

Charlotte cuddled her in a hug. "Good dog. You're so much easier to train than the master."

Wriggling with pleasure, Fancy licked Charlotte's chin.

Thinking of Brand, Charlotte frowned up at the ceiling, wondering why the Rosebuds had asked to see him. She could only surmise that they had recognized Harold Rountree and intended to ask Brand's opinion about revealing the truth to Charlotte.

But had they also realized the accident was the result of foul play? Surely not. For them to reach such a conclusion, they would have to know about the murders, and that was something Brand would never tell them. For once, Charlotte agreed with him. Their grandmothers would only try to meddle and might even end up getting themselves killed.

Tamping down her anxiety, she scanned the library, which also served as Brand's study. His absence gave her the chance to accomplish her real purpose here.

She went to the doorway and furtively glanced up and down the corridor. The entrance hall was deserted except for a footman carrying a silver tray of letters up the stairs. He didn't appear to notice her.

So much the better.

Charlotte eased the door shut and hastened to the mahogany desk. Having informed the butler that she was training Fancy and needed to be left alone, she counted on having an adequate interval of privacy.

As she sat down in the big leather chair, the faint scent of beeswax perfumed the air. A few scratches marred the expansive surface of the desk, proof that it was well used. Here, Brand would sit and sign papers. Even a profligate had to tend to estate business from time to time.

When Charlotte grasped the handles of the top drawer, Fancy whined. The dog sat beside the chair, ears cocked. Inexplicably, those watchful eyes made Charlotte feel a pang of guilt.

"I'm snooping for a good cause," she murmured, rationalizing it more to herself than to the dog. "I can't allow Grandmama to be harmed again, can I? This is the only way for me to find out the identities of the other members of the Lucifer League. Your friend Brand won't tell me anything."

Did that tail wag a little faster? Surely Fancy didn't

recognize his name already . . . or perhaps she did. The fickle animal viewed him as something of a doggie deity.

At a gentle tug, the drawer slid open on well-oiled runners. Inside lay a typical hodgepodge of items: feather quills, a pen knife, scissors, bottle of black ink, and a small key unlike the ornate one to her bedchamber which she'd used to train Fancy. Charlotte rummaged in the back of the drawer, plucked out a small, leather-bound ledger, and flipped the pages.

The two columns of tidy sums appeared to be in Brand's penmanship. Each number had a date beside it, a name, and a place, most often a gentleman's club. In the longer column, the numbers were much larger and the bottom balance totaled nearly a hundred thousand pounds. With a sickening jolt, Charlotte realized she was gazing down at a list of his winnings at the gaming tables.

She couldn't begin to fathom what induced a man to risk large sums of money on the flick of the dice or a shuffle of the cards. How many hapless fools had he beggared? She didn't want to know.

Then Charlotte realized she'd struck gold. Using pen and inkwell, she copied down the names of the men on a sheet of stationery imprinted with the Faversham crest. There was no guarantee that any of them had belonged to the league, but at least the list gave her somewhere to start.

She clapped the book shut and slipped it back into the drawer. Methodically, she searched through the other drawers, one by one, discovering mostly files of legal documents unrelated to her quest.

The bottom drawer on the right was locked. That alone intrigued Charlotte. Remembering the key inside the top drawer, she retrieved it, inserted it into the keyhole, and the bottom drawer opened easily.

"That wasn't a very clever hiding place, was it?" she said to Fancy. "Why bother locking up if the key is so close at hand?"

Fancy tilted her head inquiringly.

The drawer was half empty, containing only a few papers and a small leather sack of guineas, the gold glinting dully in the morning light. Charlotte picked up the one other object, a miniature painting in an oval gilt frame. To her great surprise, she found herself looking at the image of a girl, perhaps eight years of age, with curly copper hair and a bright-eyed smile. Judging by the style of her gown, the likeness was a fairly recent one.

Charlotte sat frozen, staring down at the miniature clutched in her hand. Why would Brand keep this picture locked up? Who was the girl? His love child? A hot rush of emotion scalded Charlotte, jealousy that he had fathered a child and anger that he would hide her away like a nasty secret.

Yet something faintly familiar about those dainty features nagged at Charlotte. All of a sudden, recognition bathed her in foolish relief. This was Amy, Michael Kenyon's daughter from his first marriage, and Lady Stokeford's great-granddaughter. Charlotte had met the little girl five years ago.

Was Brand her godfather?

Charlotte couldn't remember, for she hadn't attended the baptism due to a nasty cold. But it was the only explanation. Growing up, Brand and Michael had been best friends—although they'd had a falling-out some years ago over a matter neither man had been willing to discuss. That must be why Brand didn't display the likeness in a place of prominence on his desk. Because he still despised Amy's father.

It didn't matter. Brand's personal life had no bearing on her present purpose.

Replacing the miniature exactly where it had been, Charlotte bent down to peer into the depths of the drawer. A sheet of folded paper caught her attention. It was a cheap handbill, the ink smudged and garishly bold.

> *Repent, for the End is Near! Heed the message of doom in the Sacred Scriptures! The Most Reverend Sir John Parkinson, Church of the True Believers, 25 February, 8 o'clock in the Evening.*

Charlotte frowned. It was the sort of advertisement one might pick up on the street and then toss into a rubbish bin. Yet Brand had taken the trouble to place it in a locked drawer.

An inescapable conclusion wormed into her mind. Maybe Sir John Parkinson had a connection to the Lucifer League . . .

Impossible. A minister who lectured on religious topics wouldn't have belonged to a hellfire club. But she wasn't naïve enough to believe that a man's outer appearance always revealed his true character. Look at Mr. Rountree.

A dull throb of pain assailed her, but she ignored it, examining the handbill again and memorizing the address.

25 February.

Tomorrow night.

Tomorrow night, the Rosebuds had arranged for her to attend a musicale at the home of Lord and Lady Pomeroy. If she devised a ruse and slipped away early, she might just catch the end of the lecture.

As Brand strode into their chamber, the Rosebuds sat on identical chaises, their backs to the bank of windows. A medicinal scent hung in the air. From their serious expressions, they had Something Important on their minds.

Perhaps they'd heard he'd stayed out all night. Or perhaps this had to do with their visitor the previous day.

He'd lay heavy odds on both possibilities.

"Grandmother." He leaned down to kiss the parchment of her cheek. She looked the same as always, peevish and sharp-eyed. Yet affection stirred in the wasteland of his heart. "I see you're finally well enough to leave your bed."

"I broke a few ribs, not my legs," Lady Faversham said, as peppery as ever. "I won't be confined like an invalid."

"But we aren't ready for dancing at parties," Lady Enid said, resting her bandaged arm on a pillow.

"Nor will we be for some time to come," Lady Stokeford added.

In a familiar conspiratorial manner, the three old ladies traded a glance. Brand braced himself. Whatever they were plotting, he was at the center of it.

He lowered himself to a crimson hassock. "All right. Out with it. And kindly be quick. I'm weary and want my bed."

"Indeed," Grandmama said, her lips forming a prune of disapproval. "I understand you were out all night. And you returned home an hour ago, stinking of fish."

He ticked off number one. "My life is my own. Go on now, you must have another reason for summoning me."

"A very important reason," Lady Enid trilled. "We're hoping you can help us with dear Charlotte."

Instantly wary, he repeated, "Charlotte?"

"It isn't so much *her* as her choice of a suitor," Lady Stokeford clarified, her delicately seamed face showing worry. "We met him yesterday when he came to call on her."

His grandmother gave a crisp nod. "To be perfectly blunt, Mr. Harold Rountree is a cad."

Brand ticked off number two. "Ah. And you have proof of this?"

The Rosebuds exchanged another cryptic look. "He belonged to that dreadful hellfire club," Lady Enid said.

"We saw him when we were looking for that stolen statue four years ago," Lady Stokeford stated.

"You should know," Grandmama said to Brand. "You were there, too."

Her stern look of censure still had the power to make him feel abashed, even though he was thirty-seven years of age and an unprincipled profligate. But he kept his gaze steady. "It seems to me you ought to be having this conversation with Charlotte. Tell *her* about him."

"We're loath to break her heart," Lady Enid said. "She's paid for her mistake, and it's time to end her banishment. She deserves some happiness in her life."

"She won't find it in a marriage to that man," Lady Stokeford added.

His grandmother gave him a significant look. "That's where you come into the picture, Brandon."

For one mad moment, he was struck by the horrifying thought that they wanted *him* to marry Charlotte. Everything in him recoiled—except for the tall man down in his breeches, who had a lusty mind of his own.

Brand sprang to his feet. "Blast it, Grandmama. I'm not in the market for a wife. And even if I were, Charlotte would be at the bottom of the list of prospects."

Lady Faversham cracked a tolerant smile. "Calm down, my boy. I wasn't suggesting *you* wed her. Although in truth, I'd enjoy a great-grandchild or two before I die. Not to mention, an heir for the title."

His gut twisted. If she'd swung at him with her damned cane, she couldn't have struck him more solidly. *His fault.* It was his fault the heir had died. His fault that both his brother and nephew were dead. He'd killed them as surely as if he'd put a gun to their heads.

But Grandmama didn't know that Brand blamed himself. No one would ever know.

He pushed the thought from his mind. "Then what *are* you suggesting?"

"We were hoping *you* would tell Charlotte about Mr. Rountree," Lady Enid said. "Warn her that he isn't the man he pretends to be. She always set great store by your words when you two were children."

"Perhaps when she was five years old."

His grandmother glared. "It's a small favor to ask."

She was right, and if that was all the Rosebuds expected of him . . . "Consider it done." He felt the relief of a fish let off the hook. Little did they realize, Charlotte already knew about Rountree. "If that's all, I'll take my leave."

"Now that you mention it, there *is* something else," Lady Stokeford said, her blue eyes keen on him. "The

Pomeroys are giving a musicale tomorrow evening. Charlotte will be attending."

"So will you," Grandmama said in her brook-no-nonsense voice.

The hook caught him again. "Sorry, but that's impossible," he said. "I've already made plans." Tomorrow evening he intended to keep Sir John Parkinson under close scrutiny. Over the past few weeks, Brand had been going down a list he'd made of those who had known the murder victims. Parkinson's transformation from rake to cleric made him a prime suspect. It was vital to observe the man in his surroundings, to judge if perhaps he'd gone over the edge into madness.

"Won't you change your plans and do this one act of kindness for us?" Lady Stokeford coaxed. "We're indisposed, and the poor girl won't know anyone in society."

"She needs someone to introduce her to all the right people," Lady Enid said. "You're just the man to do it."

"I'm the last man," he countered. "If she's seen with me, her reputation will be ruined."

"Nonsense," Lady Stokeford said placidly. "Everyone knows you two grew up together. You're like brother and sister."

He almost choked. His interest in Charlotte was anything but brotherly. "People will assume the worst. Especially of a scoundrel."

"Then for once in your life, do something worthwhile," his grandmother snapped. "Help us find a husband for Charlotte."

Chapter 7

SPARK AND TINDER

"I shan't tolerate anything less than perfection at my wedding," Lady Belinda said, her sharp-nosed face showing the arrogance of the very rich and very aristocratic. "As the daughter of a marquess, I must set the standard for excellence. All the arrangements will be made to my complete satisfaction, from the hymns to the wedding breakfast. We're having caviar imported all the way from Russia, you know."

"That sounds wonderful," Charlotte said, though she had no earthly idea what caviar was. Nor did she care to ask. As Lady Belinda continued to expound on her nuptials, Charlotte listened with only half an ear.

A few steps away, Brand stood chatting with their host and Belinda's father, the Marquess of Pomeroy, a thin-faced man with a receding chin. Brand looked heart-stoppingly handsome in his dark blue coat and silver waistcoat, the candlelight gleaming on his rich brown hair and illuminating the stark masculine angles of his face.

Then he turned his head toward her. A faint smirk touched his mouth. Dear God, she was doing it again, staring at him. Aware of heat in her cheeks, she looked away, feigning an interest in her surroundings. It was not entirely pretense, for she felt a whirl of giddy excitement.

The crystal chandeliers cast a golden glow over the rich furnishings of the drawing room. Dressed in evening finery, the guests laughed and conversed in dulcet tones. On a platform at one end of the long chamber, the small orchestra tested their instruments, harp and violin and pianoforte.

How she had missed the glitter and excitement of such affairs! Although she had shunned a formal season in London, too self-conscious at age eighteen to face the pitying whispers, Charlotte had attended a number of fancy balls at Stokeford Manor and Faversham House in Devon.

Tonight, the Rosebuds had taken charge of her transformation. They had summoned the best modiste and spent hours debating the merits of silks and sarcenets. Charlotte had been ready to order the first bolt of cloth presented to her. But the Rosebuds had overriden her choice of a simple gray muslin and paid an extra fee to have the gown ready on short notice, and she had to admit they had done well.

The sea-green velvet of her gown complemented her eyes and enhanced the chestnut highlights of her hair. Although she had no qualms about baring her scars, she had donned the long gloves required of a lady. There had been a few pointed stares from some of the older guests, enough to make her suspect they recalled the gossip about her burns.

Let them. She was only sorry that the evening would end early. If her hunch was correct, Brand would soon make an excuse to slip out.

"Ah, there he is," Lady Belinda said, making doe eyes

at someone in the crowd. "My beloved Colonel Tom."

A debonair, blond-haired man wearing a blue cavalry uniform emerged from the throng of guests. At his side hung a sword in a gleaming scabbard. Heads turned and ladies whispered in admiration, but he paid no attention to them. In a flamboyantly gallant gesture, he took Lady Belinda's hand and kissed the back. "Dearest, I've been looking for you everywhere."

Lady Belinda giggled. "I've been right here all along, my silly sweetcakes. 'Twas *you* who vanished from the receiving line."

"I went to fetch a glass of your favorite bubbly." He handed her a flute of champagne, then turned a smile on Charlotte. There was something rather reptilian in his bold blue gaze that made her uneasy. "I see you have a companion."

Simpering at her fiancé, Lady Belinda made the introductions. He was Colonel Tom Ransom, a name Charlotte recognized from Brand's gambling ledger. Her interest sparked, she studied Ransom closely. They were an oddly mismatched couple, Ransom so strikingly handsome and Lady Belinda plain to the point of homeliness. As the colonel bent down to kiss Charlotte's hand, Brand stepped to her side.

Her contrary heart skipped a beat, and she felt the rise of that wretched desire. It had always been like this; whenever he was near, her body reacted to him with insufferable longing.

Perhaps because of her acute awareness of him, she noticed the slight narrowing of his eyes and sensed the watchfulness in him.

He didn't like the man.

"Tom Ransom," Brand said, extending his hand. "I understand congratulations are in order."

"Faversham," Ransom said tersely. As they shook hands, he cast a sidelong glance at his fiancée, then looked back at Brand and shook his head slightly.

On several occasions, Charlotte reflected, Ransom had lost large sums to Brand. It was obvious the colonel didn't want Lady Belinda to know about their past association.

Lady Belinda's demeanor had turned frosty. She regarded Brand as if he were a dung beetle. "Lord Faversham. I wasn't aware your name was on the guest list."

"A last-minute addition," Brand said glibly. "My grandmother sent a note."

"Did she?" Lady Belinda's voice conveyed both skepticism and censure, and she slid her arm through her fiancé's as if to protect him from evil influences. "Sugar cake, you never mentioned that you knew Lord Faversham."

"We attended Eton together. It was a long time ago." His bland smile minimizing the acquaintance, the colonel patted her hand, which rested on his arm. "Well, dearest, perhaps we should mingle. All of your guests will want a chance to converse with the beautiful bride-to-be."

His compliment worked wonders. Lady Belinda melted into a simpering idiot again. "My dear colonel, you're always the perfect gentleman. A blessing you're not like"—she flashed a snooty glance at Brand—"like that despicable Lord Byron."

Her insult to Brand couldn't have been clearer, Charlotte fumed. Shocked at the power of her resentment, she said quickly, "What do you mean about Lord Byron?"

Lady Belinda's nostrils flared. "Why, everyone knows how shabbily he treated his bride, the Lady Annabelle. Just last month, he threatened her with his pistol, and she was forced to flee for fear of her life. Now the poor girl has petitioned the court for a formal separation. Oh, the shame of it all!"

In spite of her distaste for gossip, Charlotte was appalled by the story. "He writes such romantic verse, I never dreamed he could mistreat his own wife."

Lady Belinda leaned closer. "You've been too long in the country," she said, sotto voce. "Let me warn you, some men are merely charming on the surface. But they are scoundrels, through and through."

Charlotte couldn't agree more. And clearly the woman had no notion at all that her beloved colonel was a gamester.

"Sweetest, you mustn't spoil this lovely evening with such unsavory matters," Ransom said. "Come, I'll take you for a turn around the room."

As they strolled away, Lady Belinda leaning on his arm and simpering at him, Charlotte asked Brand the question that had been nagging at her. "Was he a member of the Lucifer League?"

Brand steered her in the opposite direction. "Byron? No. He runs in a more literary circle."

His touch on her arm made her skin tingle. "Don't pretend to misunderstand me," she said. "I'm referring to Ransom. It was obvious he wanted to hide his disreputable past."

"Naturally. The poor devil can't risk losing such a rich plum."

"Do you mean poor—literally?" she whispered, so that no one around them could overhear. "Did he lose all his money at the gaming tables?"

"Who told you he was a gambler?"

Charlotte parried his sharp stare. The midst of a party was not the time to reveal that she had compiled a list of suspects from his private ledger. "It's a reasonable assumption. After all, he associates with you."

"Associated," he corrected. "I don't make wagers with those who cannot pay their debts. Ransom's vowels could paper the ballroom at Buckingham Palace."

"And Lady Belinda doesn't know."

"He's always been extremely discreet about his vices. It's logical to conclude he isn't motivated by her beauty or charm."

Charlotte couldn't let his sarcasm slide by without a challenge. "Not every man is like you. It's entirely possible that Colonel Ransom loves and respects her. That he's determined to change his wicked ways and share his life with the woman of his heart."

Brand's mouth settled into that all-too-familiar smirk. "Why do I suspect you're speaking of yourself and Harold Rountree?"

His keen stare made her squirm. Charlotte wondered if she really *had* spoken so heatedly because of a hidden wish to convince herself of Mr. Rountree's reformation. "That's ridiculous."

"People don't change, Char," Brand murmured for her ears alone. "Once a scoundrel, always a scoundrel."

She gave him a meaningful look. "Exactly."

"I've never presented myself as anything else. But Rountree has."

"Mr. Rountree is a respectable barrister. He's a far better man than you—"

"Well said," spoke a hearty voice from behind them. "Though it doesn't take long to find a fellow better than this reprobate."

Charlotte turned—and lowered her gaze to a man who stood no taller than her chin. Stout and swarthy, he had rather coarse features that reminded Charlotte of a troll. His black-currant eyes stared straight at her bosom for a moment before he aimed a grin at Brand. "Faversham, old chap. Never thought to see you at so tame a gathering."

"Nor I, you. Where's your wife?"

"Right over there, chatting up our host." He inclined his head toward a willowy brunette in a form-fitting bronze gown, who must have stood a full head taller than her husband. "Lydia's a beauty, ain't she? But no more lovely than your companion." His leering gaze returned to Charlotte, making her skin crawl. "Do make the introductions."

"I think not," Brand said.

When he tugged on her arm, Charlotte resisted. If this stranger had been a part of Brand's degenerate past, she wanted to know his identity. Ignoring convention, she put out her hand. "I'm Lady Charlotte Quinton."

"Lord Clifford Vaughn, at your service."

Vaughn. Just as she'd hoped, his name was on her list.

As Vaughn lifted her gloved hand to his lips, he gave a theatrical gasp. She thought for a startled moment that he'd glimpsed her scars. But he merely produced a hairpin, holding it up for her inspection. "This must have fallen from your coiffure, my lady. If you'll permit me to replace it . . ."

Brand snatched the hairpin and handed it to Charlotte. "Never mind his juvenile tricks. He tries that one with all the ladies."

"I think it was quite clever," Charlotte said. To Vaughn, she added, "You must have plucked it out when you came up behind us."

Affording her a broad wink, he said, "I'll be happy to tell you all my secrets. Perhaps you'll come and watch the race tomorrow afternoon at Hyde Park. The FHC will determine the best driver."

"FHC?"

"Four-in-Hand Club," Brand told her. "Unfortunately, you'll be otherwise engaged."

"No I won't, and I'd like to attend."

"I withhold my permission. I'm sure your grandmother would concur."

"What's this, you're her chaperon?" Vaughn loosed a rumble of laughter. "Now there's the fox guarding the henhouse. My lady, watch that he doesn't try to pluck off your feathers and share your nest."

"I wouldn't wish to," Brand said. "She already henpecks me enough."

He exerted firm pressure on her arm, and short of causing a scene, Charlotte had to accompany him past the chattering throngs of guests. Their hips brushed as they walked, further adding to the agitation inside Charlotte. "I'm perfectly capable of arranging my own schedule," she said heatedly. "And I don't henpeck."

"You do, and this time you're poking your nose into a hornet's nest," he said for her ears alone. "Stay away from Vaughn."

"Why? Are you afraid I might question him about the Lucifer League?"

Brand narrowed his eyes at her. "To hell with the league. He's a notorious womanizer."

She glanced back over her shoulder, but could no longer see Vaughn through the press of people. "That little troll?"

"Women find his assets charming, or so he likes to brag. Before you know it, he'll coax you into a dark room and have his hand up your skirt."

"I thought that tactic was *your* specialty."

Brand's moody gaze wandered over her bosom and dipped lower, as if he were imagining her unclothed. "Any time you'd like a demonstration, I'll be happy to comply."

A wicked fantasy flowed through her mind. His lips on hers, kissing her madly. His scent of spice and leather, enveloping her senses. His hands moving over her body, caressing places no man had ever touched . . .

Charlotte snapped back to reality as he found chairs for them in the last row. He sat down and studied the crowd, a trace of impatience defining his high cheekbones and taut mouth. He leaned forward, his elbows on his knees, his fingers tapping a restless tune.

He must be planning his departure. Little did he know, she intended to follow him. "Don't you like music?" she asked innocently.

"Only when I have a glass of wine in one hand and a deck of cards in the other."

Charlotte hid her amusement. "Sit up properly," she chided. "The performance hasn't even started, and you're behaving like a child."

Looking more disgruntled than ever, he straightened

his back. "I despise these affairs. I'm only here at the request of the Rosebuds."

"A charming compliment. Thank you." Yet foolishly, madly, she'd hoped he was here because of her. Because he had forgiven her. Because he wanted to kiss her again.

You're a beautiful woman . . .

His face softened a little. No, it was only a deepening of that perpetual smirk. "We've never minced words, you and I," he said. "And I know you don't want to be here with me, either."

"Yes, I'd rather be with Mr. Rountree," she said just to taunt him. "He knows how to please a woman."

To her irritation, Brand chuckled darkly. "You should hope he does. By the way, where is Casanova tonight?"

"I wouldn't know. Being from York, he isn't acquainted with Lord and Lady Pomeroy."

"A social outcast. The fellow's quite a prize. Even the Rosebuds don't like him."

"They hardly know him," she said through her teeth. Weary of defending Mr. Rountree, Charlotte turned the topic back on Brand. "I wonder that the Rosebuds would allow you to escort me tonight, given your bad reputation. They must be going soft in their old age."

He gave her an enigmatic stare. "Can't you guess? It's one of their games."

"What do you mean?"

"I mean they're deliberately pushing us together. Hoping we'll go mad for each other. That I'll fall on bended knee and propose like some moon-eyed calf."

Flummoxed, Charlotte stared at him. Her heart beat fast and furious. On the dread hope that she'd misunderstood, she stated, "They want *us* to *marry*?"

"Actually, they asked me to help you find a husband. But I know their modus operandi. They love to meddle."

She drew a deep, calming breath. At least now she knew the real reason why the Rosebuds had summoned Brand to their chamber. It wasn't just to ask him to accompany her into society, as they had told her. How could they even think Brand Villiers had the ability to love her—or any woman—more than he loved his wicked ways?

"They've picked a hopeless cause," she said with feeling. "We could never fall in love. We're far too different."

His insolent eyes regarded her. "For once, we're in agreement."

"We don't share the same standards, and we certainly aren't pursuing the same course in life."

"We're like oil and water."

"Spark and tinder." And how he could make her burn. The notion of being his wife caused an ache that she didn't care to consider.

"They believe you've turned into a crusading do-gooder," Brand said, one corner of his mouth lifting to show his disbelief in her transformation. "Now they're hoping you'll reform me, too."

"A more futile effort I can't imagine."

He nodded. "I'm glad we understand each other. I won't be made into a family man who stays home every evening and dandles children on his knee."

"I wouldn't dream of it." That was stretching the truth, but he couldn't know it. He *wouldn't* know it. Hardening her undisciplined heart, Charlotte gave him a saucy look. "I recognize an impossible task when I see one. You're the last man in England I'd ever consent to marry."

It was easier to escape than he'd anticipated.

Standing outside the Pomeroys' house, Brand glanced up and down the street in Mayfair. Coaches and carriages lined the curbstone, the horses breathing plumes of smoke into the frosty night air. Here and there, small groups of coachmen gathered around the fires they'd lit in cast-off iron containers. Most of the footmen were inside the house, helping to serve the guests in exchange for a few coins.

Brand spied his coach halfway down the row to the right. He set off at a brisk pace, his hands in the pockets of his greatcoat. He should have ample time to reach his destination, accomplish his purpose, and return by the end of the evening to fetch Charlotte. She probably wouldn't even notice how long he was gone.

The strains of music drifted from the drawing room. He could see the violinist outlined in the candlelit window, his arm manipulating the bow across the strings. Thank the devil, Charlotte was engrossed by the concert. As soon as the first piece had begun, he'd told her he was going to drum up a card game with a few other malcontents. She had merely given him a sharp look and a dismissing wave.

It was almost as if she'd *expected* him to leave.

Charlotte couldn't possibly know where he was heading, so that meant she thought him an inveterate rogue who had to sneak out of parties in order to feed his obsession with gambling. That was the image he fostered, the role in which he felt comfortable. It was no one else's business how he squandered his time or his money.

Yet the fact that she'd believed his excuse so readily rankled him.

He motioned to his driver. The burly man sprang up from the circle of servants warming themselves around a small blaze.

"M'lord?" Turley said. "Where does ye wish t' go?"

No surprise showed on that ruddy face. After some fifteen years, Turley was accustomed to Brand's caprices. He didn't even inquire as to Charlotte's whereabouts.

Brand gave him the address, then climbed into the coach. The well-appointed interior was shadowed and cold, befitting his mood. Rocking slightly, the coach started down the street, leaving behind the Pomeroys' house and the lights of the party.

And Charlotte.

Brand drummed his fingers on the padded leather seat. The slow, cumbersome pace of the vehicle irritated him. Had he not been coerced into escorting Charlotte, he would have driven the curricle tonight, despite the wintry weather. In truth, he wouldn't have attended the tedious affair at all.

He turned his mind to the murders. But thoughts of Charlotte kept trespassing on his concentration. The Cupid's bow of her lips when she was annoyed. The faint, flowery scent of her skin. The enticing glimpse of her breasts pressed against her low décolletage.

Ever since she'd descended the stairs at his house earlier in the evening, sleek and slim in a form-fitting gown, he had existed in a deplorable state of semi-arousal. Cold air and distance hadn't cured him of lust.

Lust for Charlotte, who had spent the past five years in exile for almost ruining his half sister's life.

Hell.

He needed release, that was all. When he returned to the party, he would scout around for a willing woman. He'd seen several tonight who had given him that unmistakable, come-hither look. He would arrange a rendezvous, drop Charlotte at home, then go back out to meet his chosen partner. A long bout of fornication would satisfy the restless hunger in him.

The coach rumbled to a halt. With a start, Brand realized he'd reached his destination on the seedy outskirts of Covent Garden. He climbed out, bade Turley wait, and walked toward a ramshackle brick building.

The wind flapped the edges of a handbill that had been nailed to the door. In the gutter lay a bunch of violets, a trampled herald to the approach of springtime. The muffled shout of laughter came from a tavern down the narrow lane.

Opening the door, Brand entered a small, rubbish-strewn foyer. Something scuttled through the darkness, probably a rat. The faint glow of light and a booming voice led him through another set of doors and into the cramped confines of a theater.

Or at least it had been a theater at one time. A half-circle of balconies faced a modest stage lit by torches in wall sconces. On the columns near Brand, the gilt paint had peeled, revealing the raw wood beneath. A skinny man clad in pristine white robes stood onstage at a podium, quoting eloquent passages from the Bible.

The congregation consisted of a scattering of people perched on hard benches on the main floor. Here and there, a few careworn women huddled inside their cloaks. A number of men wore the plain garb of laborers as if they had stopped in on their way home from work. One, a gangly fellow in a workman's cap, scribbled notes in a small book. Some of the listeners were vagrants, judging by their ragged clothing, who had come inside to escape the bitter bite of the wind.

Or perhaps hoping to hear a message of salvation.

"The Scriptures warn that the time of tribulation is nigh," boomed the preacher. "Evil lurks among us, temptation runs rampant. God shall strike down and punish those who have disobeyed his commandments. He will send earthquakes and plagues upon the land. The oceans will boil and the skies will rain fire. Death will come knocking on the doors of all sinners, bringing a fate so ghastly it cannot be imagined by those of pure mind."

Taking a seat in the shadows of the back wall, Brand studied the speaker. Sometime in the past four years, Sir John Parkinson had abandoned his foppish attire for the robes of a minister. His thick brown curls, once his vanity, now spilled untidily down to his shoulders. In the torchlight, his eyes glowed like hot coals, and the rafters rang with the thunder of his voice.

Brand doubted anyone in the audience knew that their holy evangelist had once been an enthusiastic member of the Lucifer League.

"The Lord has vowed to guard His faithful," Parkinson raved on, his sleeves flapping as he waved his arms. "He will transport His followers to Heaven on winged chariots guided by angels. You have a chance to join that exalted multitude in the Church of the True Believers. Repent now and be saved, or dwell forever in the burning flames of hellfire. Amen!"

"Amen!" echoed the scraggly throng.

His lecture was winding to a close, and Brand thanked God for that blessing. A pair of young women dressed in angelic white passed the collection baskets. Watching the progress of the handmaidens, he allowed a cynical grin. Trust Parkinson to entice two nubile disciples into his fold. It made one wonder how else they served him.

Out of the corner of his eye, Brand spied a latecomer entering the theater. The woman—for that slim, shadowed form could only be female—paused as if to survey the audience. He couldn't discern her features in the gloom. But something about her riveted him.

A lady, he thought, his gaze drilling into her. That perfect posture and fine cut of clothing could only belong to a lady. But why the hell would a lady venture alone into this rough part of town?

She took a few steps forward. The torchlight from the stage cast a weak illumination upon her face.

Brand bit out a disbelieving curse. Several people in the back rows turned around to glare at him, including the weedy man with the pencil and notebook.

She swiveled toward him, as well. Exuding a meddlesome determination, she headed straight toward him, primly lifting her fancy velvet skirt to avoid the refuse on the floor.

Brand surged to his feet. His mind raged, but his mouth barely worked. "Charlotte?"

Chapter 8
BRAND'S MISTRESS

As the faithful shuffled out of the theater and into the cold night, Charlotte reminded herself to exercise patience. She must stay calm, composed, resolute. Of course, Brand was angry. Men always were when a mere woman dared to encroach on their plans.

"Keep your voice down," she whispered. "Undue attention will only hinder our investigation."

"You are *not* my partner," he snapped, though in a lowered tone. "I don't know what in bloody hell induced you to come here, but you're going straight out to the coach to wait for me."

Calm, composed, resolute. "I intend to find the man who threatened my grandmother. Anyway, two heads are better than one."

"Not when one of the heads belongs to a woman." Brand raked his fingers through his hair in a classic male gesture of extreme frustration. "Damn it, Char. How the devil did you manage to follow me, anyway?"

"I hired a hackney."

"Don't be obtuse. It was one of the other coachmen, wasn't it? He overheard me giving out the address."

Charlotte made a noncommittal sound. She deemed it prudent not to chastise him for using profanity—or to admit that she'd found the handbill in a locked drawer of his desk. She glanced at the stage, where a thin man robed in white took the collection baskets from his two angelic assistants. The faint clink of coins sounded through the emptied theater. Her voice a mere breath of sound, she asked, "Reverend Parkinson was a member of the Lucifer League, wasn't he?"

Brand glowered at her. "No. I'm here for a card game."

"Oh? Let's go question your gambling partner before he leaves, then." Charlotte headed toward the gloomy aisle along the outer perimeter of the theater.

Brand stalked at her heels. As she reached the curving wall, he took firm hold of her arm. Their hips bumped, and his warm breath made her neck tingle. "If you wish to endanger yourself, then so be it," he muttered. "But I'll do the questioning. If you say one word—just one— I'll drag you out of here and show you who's master."

His grim expression convinced Charlotte that he meant what he said. A deep-seated quiver disturbed her, a sensation comprised in equal parts of apprehension and anticipation. She had the shocking impulse to put herself at his mercy, to taunt him until he mastered her with a kiss.

Or at least to let him *try*.

His gaze dipped to her parted lips. As if he had read her carnal thoughts and found them lacking, he released her. He made his way down the aisle, leaving her to follow this time.

Calm, composed, resolute.

Charlotte concentrated on regaining her equilibrium. She mustn't be distracted from her purpose. A woman was far better at interpreting the nuances of conversation than a man. She must listen closely, learn what she could. Grandmama's life could depend upon it.

As they quietly mounted the steps alongside the stage, Brand pointed at the dusty crimson curtain. "Stay," he muttered. It was the same stern tone he used with Fancy, and it made Charlotte bristle.

Calm, composed, resolute.

She forced herself to take up a stance in the shelter of the curtain, where she could see and hear the proceedings.

Brand walked to the middle of the stage. His footsteps resounded on the floorboards. "Parkinson. Don't go yet."

The Reverend Sir John Parkinson whirled around. Despite his white surplice and the Bible tucked in his arm, he didn't resemble any minister Charlotte had ever known. Those hawklike features and shoulder-length curls belonged in the portrait of a cavalier from the immoral court of the second King Charles.

Parkinson squinted as if he needed spectacles. In a snappish tone unlike the booming delivery of his sermon, he asked, "Who's there?"

"The Devil himself."

An undignified titter came from the pair of robed angels who flanked Parkinson. They too looked less than virtuous on closer inspection. Keeping close to the curtain, Charlotte judged them to be younger than herself, though both had the weary features and hollow eyes of women who had lived on the streets.

"Faversham?" Parkinson asked in obvious astonishment. He stood stock still for an instant, then strode forward to vigorously shake Brand's hand. "God be praised, it truly *is* you. What an unexpected gift from heaven. You've come to be saved!"

The irony of that struck Charlotte. Had the circumstances not been so dire, she might have been amused by the preacher's misguided notion.

"I'm afraid that isn't—" Brand said.

"God has answered my prayers. He has sent a miracle to support my ministry." Parkinson motioned excitedly to his minions. "Angels, hasten to rejoice with me. This is indeed a glorious day, a mighty blow in our war against the Evil One. Brand Villiers, the wicked Earl of Faversham, has come to repent his sins."

The two women scurried forward, eyeing Brand with less than holy interest.

"I'm not here for salvation," Brand stated in a clipped voice. "I want to ask you some questions. About your association with the Lucifer League."

Parkinson recoiled. He glanced furtively at his gawking lackeys and cleared his throat. "*Former* association. That was a long time ago. Like the prodigal son, I've atoned for my sins. The Father in heaven has sanctified my soul and cleansed me with the waters of forgiveness. Amen!"

"Amen!" echoed the angels.

"Be that as it may," Brand said tersely, "I'm wondering if you still keep company with any of the members."

"Absolutely not. How could you even suggest such a sin? I've devoted my life to spreading the word of God. Er, do excuse me for a moment." He hustled the angels out a door at the rear of the stage. Then he swooped back, his manner edgy. "My followers know only the rudiments of my imperfect past. I wouldn't want to arouse confusion in their pretty heads, you know."

What a hypocrite, Charlotte thought. Not only was he

keeping secrets, he had the gall to imply that women were stupid. A retort sat poised on the tip of her tongue, only to languish unspoken when Brand turned to frown at her. How did he know she'd been tempted to speak out?

"Is someone else there?" Parkinson asked, peering past Brand as if straining to see her in the gloom of the curtain. "Who's that? A woman?"

"It's only my mistress," Brand said. "But never mind her. She's too daft to heed anything we say."

Mistress? Daft? Charlotte pulled in an angry breath, then thought better of blistering him with a reproach. Now was *not* the right time.

"Your strumpets aren't welcome here," Parkinson said, shifting uneasily from one foot to the other. "Nor are you, Faversham, unless you've come to repent."

"Then answer my questions, and I'll be on my way. When exactly did you turn against the league?"

"Why, four years ago, at that last meeting, my blind eyes were opened to the evils of iniquity. From that moment onward, I followed the light of hope and redemption." He held out his robed arm to Brand. "You too must accept the true path. Give up your gambling and womanizing before it's too late."

Brand raised an eyebrow. "Do you believe that God should punish the members of the league?"

"Why, 'tis inevitable, of course! If a man wallows in a cesspit of sin, then he must someday endure the fires of eternal damnation."

Ice descended Charlotte's spine. Was she looking into the face of a murderer? Did those zealous brown eyes and lush curls hide a mind capable of plotting death?

"I wonder if you've heard the news, then," Brand said to Parkinson.

"News?"

"Mellingham died in a duel in December. A fortnight later, Wallace fell down a flight of stairs and broke his neck. Then in January, Aldrich suffered a heart seizure in his mistress's bed. A few weeks ago, Trowbridge was waylaid by a gang of ruffians and killed."

Parkinson's jaw dropped. He clutched his Bible to his chest, his knuckles gone white. "Dear God. Wallace and I attended Eton together. And Trowbridge . . . we used to have dinner at White's every Friday evening. I never knew Mellingham or Aldrich very well, but to hear they're gone . . . it can only be God's judgment."

"Or man's," Brand said, the ring of irony in his voice. "I understand you paid a call on Wallace last autumn."

"Yes. I . . . I'd hoped to rescue him from a life of debauchery. But he tossed me out of his house and told me never to return." Tears glinting in his eyes, Parkinson sank down onto a stool. He bowed his head and ran his fingers through his hair, further mussing the curly waterfall. "Now nothing can save him, poor soul."

Charlotte felt a fleeting glimmer of sympathy. If Parkinson was innocent, he had suffered a grievous loss. And if he was guilty? Then he had to possess the cunning of a madman in order to feign such anguish.

She could see Brand's profile, stark and uncompromising in the torchlight, as he gazed down at Parkinson. "How appropriate," he jeered, "that we're standing on a stage. That's a brilliant piece of acting."

Parkinson's head jerked up. "Acting? What in heaven's name are you saying?"

"That you knew each one of these men. You knew

their habits and their weaknesses. And now you're on a mission to murder every last member of the league."

"Murder?" Parkinson squeaked, his face aghast. "Are you saying . . . that someone *murdered* Wallace? And the others?"

"Bravo. You portray astonishment as well as you do grief."

The minister jumped to his feet, his robes flapping. He shook his fist at Brand's face. "How dare you make such an accusation! To me, a man of God!"

"Outrage is in your repertoire, too, I see."

"Blast you to hell, man. If there was foul play involved in Wallace's death, I want to know every detail."

"Give me your Bible," Brand said abruptly.

Parkinson eyed him suspiciously, then handed it over. "What's this all about? If you mean to steal the book, you may have it with my blessing. If ever a man needed to read the Holy Scriptures, it's you. And make certain you pay strict attention to Revelation."

"Thanks for the advice, but this is all I wanted." Brand withdrew several sheets of paper from inside the pages.

"Hold on now, that's my sermon," Parkinson objected, lunging for the document. "It took me hours to draft."

Brand folded the papers and tucked them into an inner pocket of his coat. "I'll keep it for the present. I want to compare the penmanship to a note Trowbridge received right before his death."

"Note?"

"You know. The one that said, 'You're next.' "

"If you're implying that *I*—"

"That's precisely what I mean." With a tight, humorless smile, Brand returned the Bible. "By the way, you'd do well to review Deuteronomy and the Ten Commandments, especially the fifth. 'Thou shalt not kill.' "

Parkinson clamped his arms around the book. "I've heard quite enough of your monstrous implications. Leave here at once. And take that whore of Babylon with you."

"Her?" Brand said casually, nodding his head at Charlotte. "She isn't from Babylon, she's from York."

Charlotte released an angry huff. Stepping out from the shelter of the curtain, she advanced on the two men. "To clear the air, Reverend, I am *not* his strumpet. I'm a lady, and I've come with some questions of my own. Did Tom Ransom or Clifford Vaughn belong to the league?"

Parkinson looked staggered by her question. "Yes, but . . . good God, have they been murdered, too?"

"No, they're very much alive," Brand said, seizing Charlotte by the arm and half dragging her to the steps at the edge of the stage. Into her ear, he growled, "Which is more than I can say for *your* prospects."

"You told me she was your bit o' muslin," Parkinson said in an aggrieved tone. "And she doesn't seem daft to me."

"She's a blabbermouth shrew," Brand said, "and no one you'd care to know. She's leaving town tomorrow, going far abroad to join her family in China or India or somewhere. Thankfully, we'll never see her again."

As they headed up the main aisle, he aimed a warning glare at Charlotte. She glared back, even though she knew his outrageous lie was meant to protect her identity from a possible killer.

Over her shoulder, she saw Parkinson onstage, his

feet planted in a wide stance. The shadows cast by the torchlight gave him the aspect of an avenging angel.

"Remember my message, Faversham," he called out in ringing oratory. "Until passing over into the next life, no one is beyond hope, not even you. Relinquish your vices—or suffer the fate of the damned."

Chapter 9

ENCOUNTER IN THE KITCHEN

Brand maintained his grip on Charlotte's arm until he had her safely ensconced inside the coach. Ignoring convention, he sat beside her, prepared to take evasive action if she tried to slip out the other door.

But as the coach set off in a swaying rhythm, she merely arranged her skirts, keeping a circumspect few inches separate from him. In a tone as frosty as the night, she said, "Kindly move to your own side."

"No. Henceforth, you'll consider me your warden."

"You aren't my guardian, my husband, or my blood relative. And definitely not my lover. You've no jurisdiction whatsoever over me."

He restrained the urge to shake some sense into her stubborn head. Or perhaps kiss her into submissiveness. For once, he'd like to hear her sighing in ecstasy rather than lashing him with her sharp words. "I'll bind and gag you if necessary," he said. "You should never have left that party in the first place. Tongues will flap when you and I both turn up missing."

"I told Lady Pomeroy that I had a headache and you were taking me home."

A cynical laugh burst from him. "And you think she believed you? Dammit, Char. You're a babe in swaddling clothes when it comes to society. And even worse at handling yourself around potential murderers."

"Don't curse. And I can take care of myself."

"Right, that's why you said, 'Hello, I'm Lady Charlotte in case you'd like to track me down and murder me in my bed.' " The thought made his blood run cold. He was still shaken by the sight of her, stepping out into the light of the stage, more courageous than any woman he knew.

No. More the damn fool.

"I didn't say my name," Charlotte said. "Besides, you can only blame yourself. Since you wouldn't tell me the truth about Vaughn and Ransom, I was forced to find out for myself."

She was blaming *him*? "You took an exceptionally stupid risk," he said through clenched teeth. "If Parkinson is the killer, he could go after you, too."

"He presents no threat to me," she said. "Thanks to you, he thinks I'm a whore . . . from York."

Her snippy tone stirred a dark humor in him, taking the edge off his anger. "Does that offend you, Char? To pose as my mistress?"

"Need you ask? You knew it would irritate me. That's why you said it."

"It was the most logical explanation for your being there with me."

She gazed steadily at him through the darkness. He could smell her indefinable essence, a scent that stirred his blood. The gentle rocking of the coach made him fantasize about taking her right here, lifting her skirts and riding her until he'd tamed her brazen spirit.

"Logic has nothing to do with it, Brand. You're actually quite predictable."

He sat bolt upright. He had been accused of many sins in his life, but never of being a dullard. "The hell I am."

"It's true. Why else can I usually guess what you'll say and do?"

"You can't. I don't follow society's rules. I live life my own way."

"Yes, and that in itself makes you predictable. For instance, tonight I was *expecting* you to sneak out of the musicale. It's exactly the sort of behavior that fails to surprise me."

He glowered at her indistinct form. He, who prided himself on being free and footloose, avoiding convention like the plague, was as set in his ways as an old man with a pipe and rocking chair?

Not bloody likely.

"We were speaking of *your* behavior," he said tightly. "You put yourself in extreme danger tonight—"

"I'm not finished," she broke in. "I've always wondered why you felt the need to defy a civilized code of manners. You must have been taught the proper rules. George was always the perfect gentleman. It doesn't make sense that you'd turn out completely opposite to your own brother."

Brand went cold inside. Why the hell had she brought that up? The past was over with and done. So what if his older brother had garnered the academic honors while Brand was sent down from Eton for being caught with a serving maid in his chambers? So what if George had followed the straight-and-narrow path, while Brand walked on the wild road?

For as long as he could remember, he'd always been the bad seed. While George earned praise for his impeccable behavior, Brand was thrashed for sneaking out of church or banished to bed without supper for not minding the governess. It was his flawed nature, his father had proclaimed in a fury. Brand could never measure up to his elder brother. And since George was the best at everything, Brand had set out to become the worst.

In the end, his wickedness had killed George and George's son.

Denying a flash of pain, Brand shoved that parcel of guilt into the cellar of memory. But he could never really forget. The darkness always lurked at the edge of his consciousness.

Needing a distraction, he focused his attention on Charlotte. "I'll tell you what's predictable," he said savagely. "The way you keep changing the subject away from *your* foolish behavior."

"All right, then. We may as well discuss the investigation." Rummaging in her reticule, Charlotte pulled out a small square of paper and unfolded it, then angled it toward the meager light from passing windows. "Tom Ransom and Clifford Vaughn are on my list, as are all four of the murdered men. Parkinson is not, presumably because he no longer gambles. That leaves at least eight gentlemen unaccounted for, including James Weatherby, Uriah Lane—"

"What the devil are you talking about?" Brand snatched the paper from her. Disbelieving, he could see just enough in the gloom to scan the roster of his gaming acquaintances. "Where did you get this list?"

"I compiled it myself. From your betting book."

Her words were a knife in his gut. "Jesus. You went through my desk?"

"I had little recourse. You wouldn't tell me anything. And I meant it when I said I'd do anything to protect my grandmother." Charlotte paused, then added in a somewhat placating tone, "I'm sorry it had to come to this."

Unwilling to let her see his panic, he fought to control his breathing. God! No wonder she'd known exactly where to find him tonight. She hadn't had to ask a coachman. She'd read that handbill. The one he'd kept locked in the bottom drawer of his desk.

What else had she seen in that drawer?

The question dried in his mouth. He didn't dare ask, didn't dare draw her attention to the miniature of Amy. Charlotte would want to know why he kept a likeness of Michael's daughter locked away. She'd poke and pry and bedevil him for answers. If ever she learned what it meant to him . . .

But that was one secret she would never unearth. No one but he and Michael and Vivien knew the truth about Amy's paternity.

No one else ever would.

"Damn you, Char." Needing an outlet for his seething emotions, he tore the list into bits, opened the window, and hurled the scraps onto the cobbled street, where the icy wind whipped them away into the darkness. It was a juvenile action that did little to relieve the knot that strangled him.

Her hands folded in her lap, Charlotte sat watching him. "I expected you'd do that," she said. "But no matter. I've already memorized the names."

"Then you brought it out just to taunt me, is that it?"

She shook her head. "Of course not," she said in that cool, irksome tone. "I wanted you to realize how very serious I am about this investigation. I'll do what I must, even at the risk of making you angry."

Angry? He was furious, livid, enraged. He wanted to drive his fist through the wall of the coach. No, he wanted her to stop talking, and there was only one sure way to accomplish that.

He pushed his face close to hers, enough to glimpse the widening of her eyes in the darkness and her deceitful, delicate features. "You've succeeded. And here's my predictable response."

Trapping her against the seat, he fit his body to hers in a primitive statement of dominance. He heard her swift intake of breath in the moment before he found her mouth. So he'd surprised her, after all. But he couldn't gloat; he could only revel in the pleasure of kissing Charlotte.

She was everything he remembered and far more, a woman in need of mastering. He took advantage of her shocked submissiveness by deepening his relentless assault on her lips. Despite her tart nature, she was sweet and soft with the mysteries of femininity. And warm. So warm he could fool himself into believing she enjoyed his kiss. Her fingers pressed into his shoulders as if to hold him close. He could feel the rapid rise and fall of her breasts, the slim womanly form beneath the layers of clothing.

Then *she* surprised *him*. Wreathing her arms around his neck, Charlotte kissed him back, albeit somewhat tentatively. Her response was unschooled, far too unsophisticated and far too virginal, yet a powerful heat flared in him. And somehow the kiss altered from punishment of her into torture for him. He could think only of being naked, between her legs, tutoring her in the art of passion.

Cursing the bulky winter garb that separated them, he fumbled with her pelisse and cupped her breasts, caressing the silky mounds above the low-cut bodice. But the cloth barrier only fed his frustration. In some dim part of his brain, Brand knew he was behaving like a lout, a predictable lout, and that it would take skill and finesse to seduce her beyond a kiss.

Yet the feel and taste of her made him insane. He couldn't control the desperate pulsing of his blood, couldn't stop himself from tugging at her skirts, working his hand beneath the twisted petticoats, over silk stockings and garters and slender thighs. He couldn't keep his needy fingertips from brushing tight curls, from dipping into moist, velvety, feminine heat. Charlotte's heat, Charlotte's honey—

A blow struck his hand away. Brand found himself shoved backward. At the same moment, the coach turned a corner and he almost fell off the seat.

He caught the brocaded handrest, and a rush of cold air from the open window blew sanity into him. Through the darkness he could see Charlotte calmly straightening her skirts.

Charlotte. What the hell had he been thinking?

He hadn't been thinking, that was the problem.

Although he knew he owed her an apology, her poise provoked him. "Dammit, Char. You shouldn't have done that."

"Nor should you," she said. "A word of advice. Next time, you should ask the lady's permission."

Her voice was low and steady, with no hint of the turmoil he felt. His breathing raged out of control; his heart thundered in his chest. Even his hands were shaking. *Shaking.*

When was the last time a woman had affected him like this? He couldn't remember, couldn't piece together two thoughts.

But he forced himself to be cool. "You were kissing me back. You *gave* me permission."

She uttered a husky laugh. "It would be foolish of me to dispute that, wouldn't it? However, the enjoyment was only momentary."

"Like hell." Brand craved the truth from her. He wanted her to acknowledge that she'd felt as overwhelmed as he did. She had been hot and damp between her legs, and he would hear her admit it out loud. "You can't deny the carnal attraction between us, Char. It's always been there. You felt it, too, just now."

"If you wish me to be perfectly honest . . ."

Charlotte paused, and he studied her through the darkness, trying to read the expression on her shadowed face. Maidenly reserve had caused her to push him away. She was a twenty-nine-year-old virgin, for God's sake. Ballock brain that he was, he'd gone too fast for her.

Now was when she'd divulge that as much as she desired him, she could never engage in a love affair. And he'd beg forgiveness, woo her with pretty words, bide his time and . . .

Seduce her. If it earned him a place in hell, he'd possess Charlotte, spoil her for all other men, make her his mistress.

"Yes," he prodded, "I want you to be honest. I want complete candor from you."

"All right, then." She touched his arm, not like a lover, but in the apologetic manner of a friend sharing an unpleasant confidence. "Quite frankly, Brand, I'm surprised that you have such a reputation with the ladies. Your powers of seduction are vastly exaggerated."

His jaw dropped. He tried to assimilate her words, but only one stood out. *Exaggerated?*

The coach came to a halt, and she glanced out the window. Then she delivered the coup de grâce to his lust, by saying in a breezy tone, "Ah, we're home and just in time. I'm rather weary, aren't you? I was afraid I might embarrass myself with a yawn."

The moment Nan crept into the gloomy kitchen from the garden, she knew she was in bad trouble.

The banked fire gave off only enough illumination to see the bricks of the hearth and the empty rocking chair where ofttimes Cook had her afternoon nap. Shadows concealed the rows of copper pots and the massive stove with its array of modern ovens. The cupboards were big black shapes in the darkness.

But one light shone from across the kitchen. One person stood in the doorway to the servants' staircase. One man whose glower could make her romantic haze shrivel like a dead leaf.

That stick-in-the-mud Giffles.

The candlestick in the valet's hand cast a harsh glow over his severe features. He wore a gray dressing gown cinched at the waist over his nightclothes. Any hope she'd had of ducking down beneath the tables died a quick death.

He was glaring straight at her. "Miss Killigrew. What were you doing outdoors after midnight?"

"I . . . had t' visit the privy." Nan kept her chin up.

She had learned long ago the fine art of telling false-hoods. The principal rule was to meet the accuser's gaze without flinching.

"There are indoor conveniences provided for that pur-pose."

Did his cheeks take on a ruddy hue? The notion of having embarrassed Giffles gave Nan a heady sense of confidence. For all his blustering, he was a harmless old fussbudget.

She wended her way past the long wooden tables and stopped in front of him. "I prefer the privy t' a chamber pot," she said in an innocent tone. "When a girl is havin' her monthly courses—"

"Spare me the details."

"But sir, I only wish t' know what t' do. Shall I ask thy permission next time?"

"Don't be impertinent. There won't be a next time."

He *was* blushing, she'd swear to it. "Beggin' thy par-don, sir, but when the need arises—"

"You're not to go outside after dark, not for any rea-son," Giffles cut in. "Do I make myself perfectly clear?"

Dismay sliced into Nan, taking the fun out of pester-ing him. She *had* to slip out of the house. Dick had come all the way to London just to visit her. She had another tryst planned in two days' time and if she didn't appear, if she didn't accomplish what he'd asked her to do, he might take up with another girl, mayhap that red-haired floozy he was admiring in the pub . . .

"Well?" Giffles prodded.

Feigning meekness, she said, "Aye, sir."

The valet still looked suspicious. Abruptly, he said, "Did you encounter anyone outside?"

Her stomach lurched. There was no way he could

have seen Dick, for they'd parted in the mews behind the brick wall. Quickly she schooled her face into a virtuous smile. "La, sir. And who would a simple maid from York be meetin' out in the earl's garden on a frosty night like this—"

Giffles caught her by the arm, and the flippant words lodged in her throat. His fingers had a frightening strength. His face took on a sinister anger in the candlelight. Just like that, he changed from a somber old puritan to a cold, hard stranger.

"Tell me the truth," he snapped. "Were you meeting someone out there?"

Nan's legs wobbled. Her heart raced so swiftly she feared she might swoon. How horribly she'd misjudged him. But she forced her chin high. "N-nay. I swear it."

Giffles gave her a look of contemptuous disbelief. "By God, you'd better not be lying. If I find out you are, I'll beat you to within an inch of your deceitful life."

He released her, raised his hand. His solid, masculine hand.

Nan didn't think, didn't question. She reacted out of blind instinct, sinking to the stone floor and hunching herself into a ball at his feet, bracing herself for the blow.

It never came. Her heart boomed, her teeth chattered. Though she held herself rigidly, convulsive shudders gripped her. She crouched with her arms clutching her knees and her face tucked into the protection of her skirt. The starched smell of the cloth gagged her.

His feet moved. Elegant bare feet shod in leather slippers. She could just see them from the corner of her eyes.

Jesus, Mary, and Joseph. If he kicked her, she might end up badly hurt. A broken rib or a bruised back she could hide, but any visible wounds would cost her this post, her one chance at a decent life . . .

"Don't," Nan whispered, hating herself for pleading, hating the tears that threatened to spill. "Please don't hit me."

He uttered a low-pitched sound in his throat. She flinched violently at the touch of his hands on her shoulders. But he merely drew her up and enfolded her in his embrace, tucking her face against the silk lapel of his dressing gown.

"Hush, lass. I won't harm you. I only meant to frighten you."

A noisy sob escaped her clenched teeth, yet still she didn't weep, didn't trust him. Uncontrollable shivers racked her, and his warmth seeped into her cold, cold body. His arms were muscular yet gentle, the way she had imagined a father's arms ought to be. Long ago, when she'd been too young and stupid to know the worthlessness of such dreams.

He pressed a neat, folded handkerchief into her fingers, and that one small kindness undammed the flood of tears. While she bawled, he muttered soothing sounds and patted her back. Gradually, the fury abated and she noticed things about him.

The broad firmness of his chest. The scrubbed odor of soap. The pressure of a telltale enlargement at his loins.

Giffles. This was *Giffles*.

A faint horror invaded her. She had sobbed all over him, turned his handkerchief into a crumpled ruin. He would want something in return—didn't all men?

She groped for his hand and shaped it around her breast.

For a moment, he held her cupped in his warm, strong fingers. And in spite of everything, she felt a thrilling pulse low in her belly. Mayhap the valet wasn't so stuffy, after all. It wouldn't be so bad to bed him . . .

Then he stepped back, dropping his hands to his sides.

His face cold and contemptuous, he said, "Go on upstairs. Return to your chamber at once."

Nan stared uncertainly at him, finding no hint of interest in those hostile features. She'd been wrong again. Giffles didn't want her.

The stupid urge to cry came over her again. She fled through the doorway, half stumbling up the winding, wooden steps.

Whatever had made her think that a toplofty man like him could ever desire a common thief?

Chapter 10
COLLISION COURSE

Charlotte sat next to Brand as he drove the curricle through Grosvenor Gate and into the winter-barren expanse of Hyde Park. After the noise of the street, the only sound was the clip-clopping of the matched pair of black horses. The day had been unseasonably warm, melting away all but a few patches of snow in the shadows of the trees. Now, the sun sat low on the horizon and the brisk breeze chilled her. Fancy nestled in her lap, her fuzzy head and inquisitive eyes peeking out from beneath the rug.

Today, Brand had paid more attention to the dog than to her.

Ever since she had left him in the coach the previous night, thoroughly put in his place, he had treated her with cool detachment. At breakfast, it had been "Pass the salt cellar, please" spoken from behind the newspaper. Seeing her in the corridor, he had given a formal nod and nothing more. She had intended to hire a hackney for this trip, but when she had emerged from the house, Brand had been driving his carriage up to the curbstone.

That had surprised her. After the way she'd mangled his manly pride, she had expected him to forbid her again to go to the meeting of the Four-in-Hand Club. But he had silently given her a hand up, tossed a lap rug to her and Fancy, and snapped the reins. All of her attempts at conversation had received clipped, single-word answers.

Now he gazed straight ahead as if she didn't exist. She, on the other hand, was entirely too aware of him. Sliding a glance his way, Charlotte marveled at the rugged beauty of his face, the high slash of cheekbones, and the scar at the corner of his mouth that enhanced his rakish allure. A greatcoat of fine gray wool outlined his broad shoulders. With careless confidence, he directed the horses along the dirt road.

He probably no longer cared if she walked into danger. The thought dispirited her somehow. Brand hadn't forgiven her, which was exactly as she had intended. It was illogical to wish for a return of their witty banter. She had no regrets about insulting him.

Your powers of seduction are vastly exaggerated.

Blast him, he'd deserved the set-down. It was long past time someone knocked Brand off that arrogant pedestal of his. He thought he could seduce any woman he wanted, whenever the whim struck him, with no consideration for the consequences.

Didn't he know that she too had her pride? She wasn't one of his doxies, willing to have her skirts tossed up so he might fondle her at will.

Merciful heaven, the way he had touched her. The stroke of his finger at her most intimate place. The melting sensation elicited by his caress. The mad desire to part her legs . . .

In that marvelous, frightening moment, Charlotte had recognized the true extent of her weakness for him. The mighty wall of her morals had nearly crumbled. If she hadn't had the presence of mind to thrust him away, she would have surrendered to an irredeemable scoundrel.

The thought induced an inward earthquake. Brand had absolutely no interest in marriage or family, the conventional life to which she aspired. He was dedicated to the dark road of dissipation. She couldn't fool herself with the false hope that he might change. She knew him too well for that.

Which was why, after priding herself on her honesty these past five years, she had lied to him. To protect herself, she had struck a blow at his male conceit.

Your powers of seduction are vastly exaggerated.

It had taken all her willpower to utter that falsehood. She'd had to be convincing, to ensure that Brand would never again touch her . . .

"There," he said.

The sound of his voice startled Charlotte. For an instant, she feared that he had read her mind. That he could tell how breathless and flushed she felt just by looking at his handsome profile. He glanced at her, his eyes like chips of iron, cold and impersonal. Then she noticed that he was pointing his whip at a cluster of carriages under the bare trees a short distance ahead.

She feigned an interest in her surroundings. From this vantage point in the depths of the park, they might have been out in the country. No houses or shops marred the pristine view. The late rays of sunlight glinted off the peaceful waters of the Serpentine. In a thicket alongside the river, a deer grazed in the shadows.

Brand drew the horses to a halt at the edge of the gathering. Men called out greetings to Brand; ladies ogled him and murmured to one another.

Or perhaps they were wondering about *her*. In the past, he had probably brought his doxies to such events.

Disdaining his assistance, Charlotte climbed down from the high perch with Fancy securely tucked in the crook of her arm. While Brand saw to the horses, she crouched down to fasten the leather lead to the dog's collar. Fancy sniffed the barren ground, tail wagging, her furry little body quivering with excitement.

Lord Clifford Vaughn trotted out of the throng of people. A brown greatcoat flapping around his short, stocky form, he hastened toward Charlotte. Fancy growled, ducking behind Charlotte's skirt, but Vaughn had eyes only for Charlotte.

"Well, well," he said, rubbing his leather-gloved hands together like a gleeful troll. "So you talked the rum cove into bringing you, after all. Didn't I warn you he wasn't much of a guardian?"

"Chaperon," she corrected.

Vaughn flashed her a crafty grin. "I'll warrant, he did quite a lot of chaperoning last evening. I heard the two of you left early and didn't return to Faversham's house for hours."

Charlotte stiffened, her cheeks flaming despite the cold weather. Where had he gained his information? Had she and Brand been followed to the lecture? Or was Vaughn merely fishing for a nugget of gossip? "I was taken ill," she said coolly. "Better you should inquire after my health than suggest anything improper."

He waggled his thick eyebrows. "Playing the coquette, are you? I've a fondness for games—"

"Never doubt the word of a lady," Brand said, strolling up to them. His scarred mouth was hooked into a sinister half-smile. He clamped his hand onto the shorter man's shoulder so hard that Vaughn staggered a little. "I should be very disappointed to learn you're spreading false rumors."

Vaughn gave a nervous, hearty laugh. "Me? Gossip about my old chum? What rot."

"I'm glad we understand each other." Just like that, Brand dropped his hand and became the blasé reprobate again. He idly surveyed the gentlemen gathered around their carriages and arguing the merits of their horses, the ladies chatting in small clusters. "I see Barrymore has his new bays. Who else is racing today?"

Charlotte wondered if she'd imagined that hint of menace in Brand. Though grateful that he'd come to her defense, it would be foolish to read too much into it. She knew from observing her younger siblings that boys often used physical threats to get their own way. And like her, Brand wouldn't want anyone to guess the real reason they'd been out late.

Especially not one of the murder suspects.

Vaughn eagerly embraced the change in topic. "There's Lane, Sefton, and Harrowby. Besides me, of course." He flicked his finger at the large, charcoal-gray wheel of Brand's curricle, then sauntered forward to examine the sleek ebony horses. His cravat was so elaborate he had to bend at the waist in order to check one of the hooves. "What say you give these blacks a go, Faversham? There's four hundred at stake already. And to sweeten the pot, I'll wager another fifty guineas my chestnuts can outpace these nags."

"Done," Brand said.

"I'll be at the starting line in a jeffy, then. 'Twill be a pleasure to collect your gold." Greed on his swarthy features, Vaughn scurried toward a lavishly outfitted red-and-yellow carriage.

Brand went to his team to check the rigging, and Fancy bounded after him. But Charlotte didn't need the tug of the leash to make her follow. Keeping her voice low so that no one could overhear, she said, "You aren't really going to race against *five* carriages, are you?"

He adjusted the girth on one horse. "I should think it's quite predictable behavior for a miscreant."

"Don't be juvenile. This race sounds far too dangerous."

He gave her that keen look, the one that made her heart beat faster, the one she couldn't interpret despite her half-witted boast to the contrary. Was he still angry with her, or was he merely sulking? "I never refuse a challenge," he said, his voice musing as if over some hidden meaning. "Even we profligates have our code of honor."

"Honor," she scoffed. "Would you jump off a cliff if your friends dared you to do so?"

"If there was water beneath, I absolutely would. That's why you and I are so different. I live for adventure and you live for . . . monotony."

Taken aback, she said, "My life is *not* monotonous. Just because I can't . . ." *Can't give myself to a rake who sets my soul on fire.*

"Can't stop being a shrew," Brand finished for her. In a single, lithe bound, he mounted the high perch. "Do me a favor and keep a grip on the furball, will you? It would spoil everyone's fun to see her trampled."

"Someone's going to be trampled, that's certain."

"It shan't be me. You should know by now that I play to win."

For the first time that day, he flashed her that familiar cocky grin. She felt its effect arrow straight to her depths, nurturing a warm throb of desire. Then he drove away, leaving Charlotte to stew in silence.

She was irritated with herself for worrying about him. And ashamed of the persistent ache of yearning. How could she have allowed herself to become embroiled in such a stupid quarrel, anyway? She wasn't supposed to let him affect her anymore.

I live for adventure and you live for monotony.

She watched surreptitiously as he guided the curricle to a place in the thick of the carriages. Hopping down, he spoke to the other drivers, shaking hands and clapping backs in the manner of men. His tall, lean form moved with a feral grace that appealed to her woman's heart. Foolish or not, she yearned for him in a way that went beyond the physical.

Perhaps to Brand, her chosen life *was* monotonous. But she would sooner embrace occasional boredom than care about someone who risked his life in duels and carriage races and other idiotic acts.

Determined to put him out of her mind, she took Fancy on a walk around the perimeter of the gathering. Here and there, a few green spikes poked up from the underbrush, along with a cluster of unfurling violets. The air was cool and crisp and scented with an earthy odor that brought a nostalgic reminder of the moors.

She missed her cozy little house on the outskirts of York. She wanted to return to her normal life—even if it was monotonous at times. But there was her grandmother's safety to ensure first.

The men who weren't participating in the race gathered in a group, making wagers and exchanging opinions on the odds. Guiding Fancy away from them, she kept close to the ladies in their stylish hats and form-fitting pelisses. Near the refreshment table, women sipped tea from china cups and nibbled cakes. Several ladies whom she'd met the previous evening smiled a greeting or afforded her a polite nod. Others eyed her speculatively, but that was to be expected. She had, after all, arrived in the company of Brand Villiers.

At the front of the crowd stood a shapely brunette in a smart feathered bonnet and crimson pelisse, the color enhancing her vivid red lips and dark brown eyes. She peered through a lorgnette to watch the men at the end of the path, who were taking their sweet time about beginning the race.

Charlotte's interest sharpened. Clifford Vaughn's wife might provide a clue about the mystery.

Charlotte strolled to her side. "Good afternoon. I hope you don't mind if I join you."

Lady Lydia lowered the gold lorgnette. Her sharp gaze dipped to Charlotte's arm, then back up to her face. "Ah, Charlotte Quinton. My husband told me that Faversham had forbidden you to attend this meeting."

"My powers of persuasion prevailed." Wondering if the woman knew anything about the murders, Charlotte said quickly, "Are you alone? Perhaps we might watch the race together."

Lydia sniffed. "Well, you'd certainly be better conversation than my present companion." From behind her, she drew forward a fair-haired girl of perhaps eighteen, with downcast eyes and a shy demeanor. "This is Miss Darby, my husband's cousin. Margaret, say hullo to Lady Charlotte."

Miss Darby bobbed a curtsy. Her lips moved, but if

she spoke a greeting, Charlotte couldn't hear it.

"Speak up, girl," Lydia said, but gave Miss Darby no chance to do so. "She grew up on a dairy farm in Sussex. You very likely didn't see her at the party last night because she was hiding in a corner as usual."

The rude introduction stirred Charlotte's protective instincts. She put out her hand and said gently, "It's a pleasure to meet you, Miss Darby. I've lived most of my life in the country, too. Perhaps sometime we might share stories."

As they shook hands, Miss Darby darted her a glance, giving Charlotte a glimpse of big blue eyes and a strained smile framed by the drab brown hood of her cloak.

"Don't expect her to answer. I'll wager a guinea you can't get her to string five words together." Lydia snapped her gloved fingers at the girl. "I'd like to have a private chat with Lady Charlotte. Take her dog for a walk, will you? And don't venture too far afield."

Miss Darby obediently reached for the leather lead, but Charlotte didn't want to be a party to coercion. "Fancy can be a handful sometimes. Especially when there are men in the crowd."

In a soft voice barely above a whisper, Miss Darby said, "Please, m'lady. I don't mind."

She gave a little tug on the leash, but that was all the encouragement Fancy needed. Tail wagging, the dog showed an instinctive trust and an eagerness to go walking, so Charlotte set aside her misgivings.

As the girl and dog headed toward a thicket of elms, Charlotte couldn't resist saying, "She uttered exactly five words. You owe me a guinea."

Lydia frowned, then loosed a trill of laughter. She

patted her reticule of fringed gold silk. "I don't seem to have brought any coins. I'll have to settle up when next we meet."

"Consider the debt canceled. I don't really wish to profit off Miss Darby's shyness."

Lydia rolled her eyes. "Such timidity," she said in a tone of disgust. "It's been a trial keeping the chit occupied these past few months. I'm to find her a husband, can you believe it? If I'm not there to carry the conversation, she drives off her suitors with her silence."

Charlotte clenched her teeth. She mustn't make an enemy of this woman who might provide a clue to the killer's identity. "Not everyone can be as amiable as you," she said with forced admiration. "You and your husband must have many friends."

"Naturally, we're invited to the best parties." Lydia eyed her craftily. "Forgive me for speaking plainly, but I'm surprised that *you* had the audacity to attend the Pomeroys' soiree."

Charlotte froze. Had Lydia heard about Charlotte's banishment to York? Impossible, for only close family members knew the truth. Warily she said, "Pardon?"

"Why, I'm referring to your scars, of course. Everyone's heard how you were burned as a young girl." Raising the lorgnette, Lydia sent another pointed stare at Charlotte's arm as if to see through the long sleeve and kid glove. "How dreadful to be so disfigured. Were I you, I don't believe I'd be so brash as to show myself in polite society."

Charlotte just managed to stop herself from hiding her hand behind her back. As an adolescent, she had been acutely aware of being different . . . ugly beside other girls with their milky-smooth skin. Lydia's remark reminded her of those painful feelings of inadequacy, and the deliberate cruelty angered Charlotte.

She managed a coldly polite smile. "I'm not afraid of the *ton*. There are many who accept me as I am. As for those who would judge me by my scars, they're shallow, mean-spirited bigots."

Lydia didn't appear fazed by the rebuke. If anything, her fine features wore a faintly calculating sneer. "How very straightforward of you. But then, Faversham has always liked immodesty in a woman."

Once again, she had nonplussed Charlotte. Did she think Charlotte was Brand's *mistress*?

Charlotte's dander rose. But she reminded herself that her purpose was to probe for information. "Since we're being frank," she said, "perhaps you'll satisfy *my* curiosity. Do you always attend the same parties as your husband? Or does he have his own set of friends?"

Lydia waved her elegantly gloved hand. "We each go our own way. It's quite a convenient arrangement, if you understand me."

Charlotte frowned. Did that mean Lydia hadn't been present at any meetings of the league four years ago? Did she even know about her husband's past association with the hellfire club? "If I may ask, how long have you two been married?"

"Over a decade." Lydia's beautiful features took on a smug, assessing look. "Long enough to afford each other certain . . . privileges."

"Privileges?"

"Don't pretend innocence, Lady Charlotte. After all, you keep company with Faversham."

Charlotte flushed. Her gaze went to Brand's strikingly handsome figure among the men. From their gestures, they appeared to be debating the length of the course. "I believe you've misconstrued my friendship with him."

"Friendship." Lydia drawled the word as if it had a secret significance. "Let me say, I admire your discretion. Perhaps you'd care to become *friends* with my husband, hmm?"

"I *would* like to become better acquainted with both of you," Charlotte said uneasily. There was something avid in the woman's manner, an undertone she mistrusted. "Of course, if I'm being too forward—"

"Enough of this coyness," Lydia said. She tapped Charlotte on the arm with the lorgnette. "If you must know, Clifford was rather intrigued by your scars. If you'd like a liaison with him, I'll be more than happy to arrange it."

"A liaison—" Charlotte choked out.

"Have I shocked you, then? Faversham must be your first. I daresay in time, you'll hunger for more variety."

"I can't imagine any such thing."

A greedy envy tainted Lydia's beautiful face. "I've heard he's a marvelous lover. I shall have to ask Clifford to slip a suggestion in Faversham's ear. My husband and I often assist each other in these matters, you know." As if they'd just been discussing the weather, Lydia raised the lorgnette and peered at the group of men.

She procured partners for her husband. And in turn Vaughn gave her to other men. Was that the way marriages in the *ton* were conducted?

Swallowing her disgust, Charlotte turned numbly toward the field where the carriages were now lined up. How had the conversation gotten so out of hand? She had learned nothing—except for the fact that Brand's acquaintances were even more corrupt than she'd ever imagined.

She spied Brand, now seated in his sleek gray curricle on the outer edge of the contenders. Did he partake in such lewd pursuits? Did he seduce the wives of his acquaintances? Dear God, she didn't want to know.

"Look, the race is about to begin," Lydia said, "and it's about time. We've been standing out here in the cold forever."

Though Charlotte's stomach churned, she strove for lightness. "Why is it that men always feel the need to hold contests?"

"So we ladies can vie for the winner, of course." Lydia sent Charlotte a challenging stare. "Let it be known, I intend to reward the champion. If it's Faversham, you'll have to give him to me for the night."

A furious rush of emotion swept through Charlotte. If this woman dared to make an advance toward Brand, Charlotte would put a swift end to it.

Before she could examine her intense possessiveness, the crack of a gunshot split the air.

At the signal, the carriages set off, wheels rattling and brasswork flashing. Clods of dirt flew from thundering hooves. An aura of conviviality reigned among the spectators. The men shouted to their favorites while the ladies called out merry encouragements.

In the center of the tight mass, two carriages bumped wheels. As the vehicles slowed and fell behind the others, gasps and groans came from the onlookers.

Although tempted to close her eyes, Charlotte watched with throat-stopping fascination. The scene had a certain savage beauty that made her heart pound and her senses soar. Brand edged ahead of the others, including Vaughn's gaudy curricle. Dimly aware that she was exhorting him to win, rather than praying for his safety, she pressed her gloved hands to her mouth.

A movement flashed at the corner of her eye. Something streaked across the field, a small black feline, then a dog in hot pursuit.

Fancy?

With a cry of horror, Charlotte plunged after them. Too late.

The cat darted out in front of the racing carriages, the dog right behind. To avoid hitting the animals, Brand made a sharp turn straight into the path of his competitors.

Her heart in her throat, Charlotte saw Fancy and her prey escape into the underbrush by the river.

At the same moment, the carriages collided.

Chapter 11

AMY'S GIFT

Charlotte reached the site ahead of the other people.

To her vast relief, she saw that Brand was safe. Having veered to a halt in a nearby copse of oak trees, he struggled to calm his rearing horses. Another vehicle had gone into the mud on the banks of the river, and the driver was attempting to turn the team of horses. Miraculously, only one carriage had overturned.

The red-and-yellow curricle lay on its side, the wheel still rotating. Several grooms ran to untangle the frightened horses from the traces.

Charlotte spied Lord Clifford Vaughn sprawled face-up in a low boxwood hedge.

Aghast, she hastened to his side. His eyes were shut, his arms and legs lying akimbo. Bloody scratches marred his swarthy features. She could see no other visible wounds, but he might have suffered internal injuries.

He might be dead.

An eerie thought flashed in her mind. *Another member of the Lucifer League . . .*

"Lord Clifford," she said sharply. "Are you all right?"

He lay utterly still. There was no rise and fall of his stocky chest.

As she picked up his limp wrist, the sound of running

feet came from behind her, along with the keening cries of several ladies and the shouts of gentlemen.

Lady Lydia rushed up, her face white and pinched. Seeing her husband's supine form, she let out a piercing shriek. A gentleman nearby caught her as she wobbled on her feet. "Dear God, Cliffie! Is he dead?"

Charlotte was afraid to answer. When her trembling fingers couldn't locate a pulsebeat in his wrist, she pulled at his cravat, a stiff waterfall of starched, knotted linen.

She bent her face closer to him and lightly tapped him on the cheek. "Lord Clifford," she said again, urgently. "Please wake up."

Just like that, his eyes popped open. He grinned broadly. "Boo!"

As Charlotte jumped back, Vaughn burst into cackles of laughter.

Lydia marched closer and whacked him with her reticule. "Bloody prankster. I should have known a mere fall couldn't kill you."

Vaughn rolled off the bush and landed on his rump. "Aw, Lyddie. 'Twas only a bit of a jest. You know I can't resist an opportunity when it arises."

"Don't be a boor. Stand up now and apologize to Lady Charlotte for giving her such a fright."

He got obediently to his feet, brushing the twigs and dried leaves off his coat. Cocking a leg, he made a courtly bow to Charlotte. "Do forgive me, my lady. Though 'tis gratifying to know you care enough to come rushing to my rescue."

Her shock depleted, Charlotte didn't know whether to be angry or exasperated. "I'd have done the same for a beggar on the street."

"Oh ho. I'm humbled by your proper set-down. What

penance must I perform to earn my way back into your good graces?"

"You were never *in* my good graces."

The crowd tittered with laughter. Charlotte knew they had no inkling how sincerely she meant the insult. Nor did Vaughn or his wife, either, judging by their avid smiles. They looked like two spiders, waiting to lure her into their web.

Repulsed, she turned to see Miss Margaret Darby hovering by the overturned carriage. Her dainty features showed alarm and her blue eyes brimmed with tears. "I'm sorry," she whispered. "The leash slipped from my fingers . . ."

"Fool," Lydia pronounced, going to her. "You could have killed my husband. And look what you've done to the carriage. That's gratitude for taking you into our home."

Miss Darby cowered, though something flashed in her blue eyes before she bent her head. Resentment? Charlotte couldn't fault her for that.

She stepped quickly between the two women. "If you're going to blame anyone, blame me. I should have warned her that Fancy likes to chase cats."

"All dogs chase cats, and she should have known so. Come along, Margaret. We'll have to ride home with the servants." Lydia marched away with Miss Darby scurrying behind her.

With the show over, the circle of people began to disperse, the men going to check out the damage to the carriages and the ladies excitedly discussing the accident.

Charlotte had no wish to associate with any of them.

She started toward the river in the direction she'd last seen Fancy.

Brand loped toward her, the dog tucked in the crook of his arm. His hair was mussed, and dirt smeared his cheek. But he had never looked so wonderful.

Dear God, he could have died. The man she loved could have been crushed beneath the carriage wheels or trampled by horses.

The man she loved.

Struck by the thought, Charlotte stopped near a clump of gorse. Her gaze drank in his lean, fit form as he approached with long-legged strides. A flurry of tenderness tightened her breast. Yes, she loved Brand Villiers. She loved everything about him, the way he walked and laughed, his moody silences and his witty ripostes. He made her feel alive, keenly aware of the sensual needs of her body. Perhaps she had loved him all her life.

Even as the soft certainty engulfed her heart, she despaired of it. Loving Brand could only bring her pain. He would never return her affections. Not in the tender, steadfast way she yearned to be loved.

The way Harold Rountree professed to love her.

The last rays of sunlight illuminated the scowl on Brand's chiseled features. How she ached to throw her arms around him and rejoice in his narrow escape. Instead, she took the dog from him. She held Fancy close, heedless of the muddy paws. "Naughty girl," she chided. "I was so afraid I'd lost you." It was Brand she'd been afraid of losing, but she couldn't say so. She didn't dare reveal her foolish, newfound love.

Fancy licked Charlotte's chin in a raspy kiss.

Brand watched, his lips thinned. "I told you to keep a firm hold on her."

"Fancy wasn't with me." Gathering her composure, Charlotte related what had happened, that Miss Darby had taken the dog for a walk. She glanced over her shoulder, but Vaughn's wife and cousin were nowhere to be seen. "Poor Miss Darby. I fear Lydia will use this as an excuse to ill-treat her."

"If the girl has half a brain, she'll find herself a husband and get out of that house."

"Then you must know how perverted they are." Troubled, Charlotte told him about the conversation with Lydia, leaving out the nasty remarks about her scars—and Lydia's desire for Brand. "She actually offered to arrange a liaison for me. With her *husband*."

Not a muscle moved in Brand's face. His expression was harsh in the shadows of dusk. "Did you agree to it?"

Hurt and angry, Charlotte stiffened. "No, you jackanapes! How can you even suggest I'd partake in something so revolting?"

"You said you'd do anything to solve the case. You could wheedle all sorts of information out of him in the bedchamber."

If there weren't people nearby, she'd have boxed his ears. "You're being deliberately obtuse. You're overlooking my point."

"Then why don't you enlighten me?"

"I'm saying that Vaughn and his wife are capable of anything, perhaps even murder. But I don't understand *why* they'd kill those men."

Brand reached out to rub Fancy's head. "Debt," he said succinctly.

Charlotte's gaze flicked to Vaughn, who was examining his expensive carriage along with several other men. "Are you saying they're in desperate straits?"

"Vaughn owed a good deal of money to the men who died. In excess of thirty thousand pounds."

The news staggered Charlotte. It certainly gave Vaughn an ugly motive to kill. "Good heavens. Who else do they owe? Could those men be next?"

"I'm looking into the matter."

"You must have some ideas. Tell me."

"Another time. Let's get out of here." He grimaced at her. "Unless *you* want to be next."

As he started toward his carriage, Charlotte kept pace with him, frustrated by his abrupt reticence. "Is it Weatherby or Lane? I'd like to meet the other suspects."

"You'd have to develop a taste for the low life. And the Rosebuds might have an opinion on that."

"They don't have to know. Besides, I came here, didn't I?"

"It's different when you're at a party in a house with a lot of bedchambers and dark corners. Not to mention, with those who think nothing of taking advantage of a naïve spinster."

If the Vaughns were any indication, she couldn't dispute him. She *was* unsophisticated, at least to a degree. And foolish, too, for wishing Brand would lure her into a darkened bedchamber. For wanting to let him teach her all about passion . . .

"I'm becoming less naïve by the moment," she said dryly. "Thanks to you and your friends."

"Yet you refuse to recognize the danger. This game you're playing may well turn deadly."

Trepidation filled her, but she couldn't quail now. "My grandmother's life is at stake, Brand. I can't take any less risk than you. I'll do whatever it takes to catch the murderer."

His ice-gray eyes took on a hooded, speculative look. "So be it, then. I'll show you exactly how sordid my world is. There's only one difficulty."

"What? If you're thinking the Rosebuds will find out—"

"They're the least of your worries." Upon reaching the carriage, he touched her cheek in an unexpected caress that thrilled her—at least until he spoiled the effect with his next words. "In order to be convincing," he went on, "you'll have to pose as my mistress."

A short time later, Brand forgot all about the investigation and his satisfaction over how easily Charlotte had been lured into his trap. The moment they returned home, North had been waiting in the foyer. The old butler delivered one announcement, then toddled off, blissfully unaware of having turned the master's equilibrium topsy-turvy.

Michael and Vivien had arrived from Devon to visit the dowager Lady Stokeford. They were upstairs in the Rosebuds' chamber.

They had brought Amy.

The news was a fist to Brand's gut. He wanted to race up the steps at once. Not since the Christmas holidays two months ago had he seen his little girl.

No, not his. Only Michael had the right to call himself her father. Brand had come to that agonizing realization long ago—for Amy's sake. No one knew the truth except for Michael, Vivien, and himself. Not even the

Rosebuds had any inkling that Brand had sired Michael's eldest daughter by his first wife.

Not even Charlotte knew . . .

Agitation hurried his heartbeat. Keeping his face indifferent, he said abruptly, "You'll want to change out of your muddy clothes. You can join us for tea later."

"It's only my pelisse that's dirty. I'll go up straightaway." Smoothing her lustrous chestnut hair with a gloved hand, she headed toward the staircase. "I'll just need a moment to leave Fancy with Nan."

Brand wanted Charlotte gone, out of the picture, at least until he could get his raw emotions back under control. He caught up to her in two long strides and blocked her path. "Stay in your chamber," he ordered. "It's not a good idea for you to join us."

"Why not?"

"What, have you forgotten your cruelty already? I very much doubt that Vivien will want to see you."

Charlotte lowered her gaze. But not before he saw distress widen those green eyes, divulging a naked pain at his blunt words. He felt like hell for reminding her of that. From time to time, he'd glimpsed the fragility beneath her strength of will, a fragility that touched him deeply. Then he was angry with himself—and with her. She had no right to look so damned vulnerable after the way she'd almost sent his half sister Vivien to prison for a crime she hadn't committed.

"This is the first time you've seen Vivien since then, isn't it?" he prodded. "The first time since you stole that necklace and set her up as a thief."

Charlotte lifted her chin and met his gaze. She still had that wounded-doe look. "Yes. I know it can't make up for what I did, but I'd like the chance to apologize."

"Do it another time. You shouldn't plague them with your presence."

"I won't make a scene, I promise you that."

"Another point. Michael is married now. He and Vivien have three children. I won't have you going after him, breaking up their family."

It was an underhanded strike, and he regretted it the moment the words left his mouth. He knew Charlotte wouldn't stoop so low. At least, he was reasonably certain she wouldn't. Sometime in the past five years, she had shed her bitterness and acquired a new maturity. Maybe living on her own had forced her to grow up and change her spitefulness.

She stood facing him, her posture rigid and her face a pale oval. This time, her gaze didn't falter. "I behaved badly five years ago. Now I have to face the consequences. Without hiding in my chamber."

Turning her back on him, she ascended the staircase, her spine straight with a damnable show of dignity. For once, he found himself admiring more than the womanly sway of her hips. She could have taken the easy way out, avoided Vivien and Michael altogether. Instead, Charlotte seemed determined to make amends.

Damned stubborn, that described her. She was also too clever, too observant, too meddlesome. Had she seen that miniature in his drawer?

As Brand mounted the steps, two at a time, a cold sweat prickled his skin. God help him if she guessed the truth about Amy.

Upon entering the chamber with Brand, Charlotte paused by the door, unsure of her welcome. Darkness had fallen, and the light from several oil lamps illuminated the small family gathering.

The Rosebuds were arrayed on chaises, their ancient faces bright with happiness. Michael lounged beside the dowager Lady Stokeford, while dark-haired Vivien sat cross-legged on the floor at his feet, her stockinged toes peeking out from her blue skirt. Their eldest daughter, Amy, was nestled in the crook of her great-grandmother's arm, relating a story about Nibbles, her pet rabbit.

They made a picture-perfect family.

Charlotte couldn't move, couldn't bring herself to step forward. Brand was right; she didn't belong in this cozy group. She had forfeited that privilege five years ago. Her presence could only open old wounds that were better left healed.

Then she noticed that Brand had stopped, too. He stood beside her in the shadows, his face stern, his gaze fixed with a concentrated stare on the happy assembly. As if he too felt like an outsider.

Charlotte remembered that he and Michael had had a falling-out years ago. They were no longer the close friends of their youth, releasing frogs in church or building rafts to sail across the lake. She didn't know what they'd quarreled about, only that the incident had occurred around the time of Michael's first marriage. Apparently they hadn't ever mended the rift.

Charlotte felt an unexpected affinity with him. Brand had ghosts in his past, too. Somehow, knowing that made her feel less alone.

Grandmama was the first to notice them. A smile broadened her plump face beneath the cheerful yellow turban. She rested her broken arm in its sling on a pillow in her lap. "Why, look who's here."

Spying them in the doorway, Amy jumped up. "Uncle Brandon, you're home! What took you so long? I haven't seen you in *forever*!"

The girl came running toward him, her copper curls flying and her hazel eyes sparkling. The deep russet of her gown enhanced her beaming smile. He bent down and enfolded her in a hug, twirling her around and presenting his back to the Rosebuds and Amy's parents. But Charlotte saw his face.

For the barest moment, a flash of tender feeling softened the steel-gray of his eyes, and Charlotte felt an odd jolt of certainty. He loved this little girl. Truly loved her.

How startling, for he never spoke of Amy. But there was that miniature in his desk . . .

With a return of his casual manner, Brand teased, "Who are you? What happened to little Amy?"

The girl put her hands on her hips and gave him an indignant glare. "*I'm* Amy. Don't you remember me?"

"Ah, so I do." He looked her up and down. "But you've grown. Last time we met, you only reached my elbow."

"Did not. Anyhow, I'm nine and a half and that makes me almost a lady. Mama says I'll be as tall as her someday."

His mouth crooked in an indulgent smile, he ruffled the girl's hair. "Indeed you shall. And just as pretty, too, I'll wager. You'll leave a string of broken hearts from one end of England to the other."

Amy beamed. "I brought you a present," she said, digging in the pocket of her white pinafore. "Look, I drew it myself."

Brand unfolded the scrap of paper. "Your rabbit. And a very clever rendition. I'll have it framed and put on my desk."

If he was so fond of her, why didn't he keep the painting of Amy on display? Charlotte forgot that distracted question as Michael came forward with Vivien.

Vivien gave Brand a warm hug and kissed him on the cheek. They were brother and sister, having the same father, although Vivien had been born out of wedlock. The men gravely shook hands.

His smile reserved, Michael placed his hand on Amy's shoulder. "It *has* been quite a while, Brand. You should come to Devon more often."

"London suits me," Brand said with a careless shrug. "Not enough action for me in the country."

"There is when one has a small army of children tearing all over the house. Thank God we left the two younger ones fast asleep at my town house." But Michael's complaint was cheerful, his gaze soft as he shared a smile with his wife. Then he looked at Charlotte, and all hint of warmth in him faded. He afforded her a sober nod. "Charlotte."

That was all. Just her name, uttered in a tone of veiled reproach.

She wished fervently that the floor would open up and swallow her.

Everyone stared at her. The Rosebuds appeared worried, while Amy looked merely perplexed as if she sensed the undercurrents and was unsure of Charlotte's identity.

Tall and handsome with a hint of silver at his temples, Michael stood with his arm protectively around his wife.

The last time the three of them had met, Charlotte had still fancied herself in love with him. But he'd had eyes only for Vivien, and in a fever of bitter jealousy, Charlotte had devised a plan to discredit her rival. She had stolen a jeweled necklace and hidden it beneath Vivien's pillow, intending that Vivien be branded a thief and sent back to the gypsies who had raised her.

The ploy had worked. Too well. Instead of being banished, though, Vivien had been held for the magistrate.

Seeing Michael and Vivien now, Charlotte felt paralyzed with the renewed horror of her past actions. How they must hate her, both of them. She had nearly ruined their chance at happiness, nearly sent an innocent woman to prison. And now Charlotte had capered blithely back into their lives, as if a simple apology might earn their forgiveness.

Vivien broke the awkward silence. Her mouth curved into a polite smile. "Charlotte, it's a pleasure to see you again."

That expressive brown gaze held a gracious welcome that only made Charlotte feel more miserable. She didn't deserve to have the olive branch extended to her. She'd been thinking of herself, of lightening the burden of her guilt, when she owed Vivien and Michael the courtesy of never having to encounter her again.

Her eyes burned with tears she refused to let fall. "I'm sorry," she murmured. "I—I shouldn't be here."

Even as she turned to go, Vivien glided forward and linked arms with her. "Don't be silly. Come in and visit with us. We were just telling the Rosebuds all the family news."

Charlotte found herself being towed into the chamber,

settled on a hassock, and made a part of the group. Vivien brought her a cup of tea from the tray, and Charlotte wrapped her cold hands around the heated porcelain.

But she couldn't swallow a drop. Feeling like an interloper, she could only sit in numb silence and listen to the swirl of conversation.

"If we'd known how serious the accident was," Michael was saying, "we'd have come sooner. But Grandmama made light of it in her letter." He sent a speaking glare at the dowager Lady Stokeford, who looked as fragile as a fairy with pale skin, wise blue eyes, and a spun-silk cap of white hair.

"Fiddle-faddle," the old woman said airily. "I didn't wish to worry you unduly. Besides, we've had Charlotte and Brandon to keep us company."

"Nevertheless, you shouldn't have set out in the middle of a snowstorm," Michael said. "It's a wonder the three of you weren't killed."

He didn't know, Charlotte thought distractedly. Would Brand tell him in private about the murder attempt on the Rosebuds?

Amy threw her arms around the dowager Lady Stokeford. "Papa is right, Grammy. You mustn't ever, *ever* do that again."

Fond laughter rippled from the Rosebuds. Even the crusty Lady Faversham cracked a rare smile.

"There, there, darling," Lady Stokeford said, stroking Amy's smooth cheek. "All's well that ends well. Now go have a look at that book I gave you."

Amy pursed her lips as if to protest, then curled up in the window seat and began to turn the pages by the light of a candelabrum.

"Alas, our mission didn't end well," Lady Faversham

said in a lowered tone, her wrinkled face once again dour beneath her severely styled gray hair. "We were too late to stop the wedding."

Michael paced in front of the Rosebuds. "Has there been any word from Firth?"

Lady Stokeford's smile drooped, and she shook her head. "I'm afraid not. Samuel has gone off to the West Indies."

"And what of Cassandra?" Vivien asked, worry darkening her eyes. "Are you sure he left her behind?"

"We've sent Nathaniel to Lancashire to make inquiries," Lady Enid said in a quavering voice. "The poor girl's gone back to her father, the Duke of Chiltern."

Lady Faversham jammed the tip of her cane into the carpet. "As soon as we can travel, we intend to have a word with Chiltern ourselves. It appears he gave away his own daughter to Samuel as repayment for a gambling debt."

"I'm more concerned about Cassandra," the dowager said. "She's only fifteen and far too young to be abandoned by that ill-natured husband of hers."

"Perhaps he'll come back soon," Lady Enid ventured. "I cannot believe even Samuel could treat his bride so shabbily."

"I can," Lady Stokeford said, her voice full of pain. "I fear 'tis my fault for not keeping a closer eye on him. I knew how bitter he was about the circumstances of his birth."

"He's a bastard," Michael growled, "and there's no need to sugarcoat that fact. With Lady Cassandra's co-operation, I may be able to arrange an annulment."

"She'll still be ruined," Lady Faversham said, her lips

pinched with disapproval. "I wish we could remedy *that*."

"What does *ruined* mean?" Amy piped up. With her fair features and copper curls, she looked nothing like her dark-haired stepmother. But she had Vivien's mannerisms and sat cross-legged on the window seat with her shoes off.

"Amy," her father snapped. "You shouldn't be eavesdropping. Go on downstairs now and read in the library."

"But I want to stay with my grammy. *She* always answers my questions."

Lady Stokeford smiled indulgently. "Dearest, *ruined* just means a girl isn't happy anymore. Perhaps you should go and see if Cook has any more cakes. You may have your very own tray in the library."

Amy peered with suspicion at her great-grandmother, and then her father. "You're all going to talk about grown-up matters, aren't you? I'm old enough to listen."

"Don't be pert," Michael said sternly. "And unless you wish to be turned over my knee and paddled, you'll go now."

"Yes, Papa." With the air of a tragic heroine, Amy rose from the window seat and inched toward the door. "It isn't fair that I'm sent away every time there's something interesting to be heard. Is it, Mama?"

"You know the rules, little dove," Vivien said gently.

But Amy wasn't through. She turned her big-eyed look on Brand. "Uncle Brandon, won't *you* let me stay?"

Brand's gaze flicked to Michael, and Charlotte sensed something between them, as if they were rival dogs fighting over the same bone. The impression vanished in an instant when Brand turned a lazy smile on Amy.

"It's a pity to miss out on all the fun, isn't it?" he

said. "But perhaps you'd like to play with Lady Charlotte's dog."

Amy brightened. "A dog? Where?"

"Fancy is in my chamber," Charlotte said, finding her voice. "You can ask the footman to direct you there. If you like, you can help my maid give her a bath."

"Oh, yes!" The girl started toward the door, then stopped to bob a curtsy. "Thank you, my lady," she said in a very mannerly voice. "I do think I remember you now. A long time ago, Uncle Brandon was shouting at you about a missing necklace."

On that earth-shattering statement, she skipped out the door.

Amy had overheard that quarrel?

Mortification suffused Charlotte as she recalled the terrible moment of discovery. Having guessed the truth, Brand had confronted her and demanded a confession. The fury and loathing on his face would live forever in her memory. Now, her only consolation was that Amy had been four years old at the time and wouldn't know the significance of the event.

But everyone else knew.

Charlotte could see it in their faces, in the tightening of Michael's expression, the unhappiness in Vivien's eyes, the censure of Brand's stare. Even the Rosebuds looked troubled.

She had thrown away their respect long ago, destroyed it with her own stupid hands. How could she have ever hoped to make amends?

Charlotte put down her untouched tea and rose stiffly, willing strength into her legs. Tears prickled in her eyes again, but she held them back, determined not to make it seem as if she were making a bid for sympathy.

"I apologize for my daughter," Michael said in a clipped tone. "She didn't mean to be rude."

"She wasn't—not in the least." Charlotte forced herself to meet his gaze. At one time, she'd been willing to sacrifice everything, even her integrity, to win him. He had saved her from that fire when she was thirteen, and look how she had repaid him.

Twisting her fingers together, she glanced from him to his wife. "I—I have to tell you . . . how ashamed I am of what I did five years ago. It was wicked and cruel. You befriended me, and in return, I betrayed you."

Lady Enid made a small sound of distress, but Charlotte could only gaze at Vivien, standing by her husband, a wary expression on her exotic features.

"Yes, I know you have regrets," Vivien murmured. "You told me so in your letter."

"I also wanted to say it directly." Charlotte bit her trembling lip. "I know it can't ever make up for what I did, but . . . I'm sorry. Truly sorry."

Vivien's expressive brown eyes warmed. "You needn't think of it any longer, then. As her ladyship said, 'All's well that ends well.' "

Did Vivien mean it? Would she forgive and forget, just like that? Charlotte couldn't imagine it, yet she felt a flicker of hope.

"I don't happen to agree," Brand cut in. "I'm sure Michael doesn't, either."

Michael did have a skeptical air, as if he were about to concur. But Vivien placed her fingers over his lips.

"Ah, but my husband isn't entirely blameless in the matter," she said, giving him the evil eye. "He was prepared to send me to the gallows."

"An exaggeration," Michael protested. "I let you escape."

"Bah. I outwitted you, that's what. And then you came after me, confessing that the mighty Marquess of Stokeford had been wrong."

She smiled and he smiled back, and in the midst of her remorse, Charlotte felt the sharp ache of yearning. If only a man would smile at her with such love in his eyes.

Her gaze found Brand, but he was frowning at Vivien and Michael. "You're entirely too forgiving," he told his half sister.

"Here now," Lady Enid said stoutly. "Charlotte truly has atoned for her sins."

"She's devoted herself to doing good deeds," Lady Stokeford added.

"Unlike some people we know." Lady Faversham sent her grandson a quelling look.

Brand cocked an eyebrow and said nothing more. Yet from his hard expression, Charlotte knew bleakly that she would never have his forgiveness.

It shouldn't hurt, she told herself. His opinion shouldn't have the power to crush her heart. After all, he was no saint. He drank and gambled and seduced countless women. But had he ever done anything so reprehensible as betray a dear friend?

She doubted it. Although Brand was an incurable rake, he also adhered in some matters to the rigid code of behavior drilled into him as a child.

Dear God, he must never know what she had discovered just this day. That she loved him with a fervency that could not be denied. If only she could return to York, go far, far away from him, perhaps then she might forget. Instead, she must remain here in London, by his side.

To track down a murderer, she must pose as Brand's mistress.

Chapter 12
CAUGHT IN THE ACT

" 'Old Vicar Funk / Went to the trunk / To get his poor daughter a dress. / When he got there / The trunk it was bare / And so was his daughter, I guess.' "

Lord Clifford Vaughn lowered the sheet of foolscap and joined his audience in bawdy laughter. With his coarse features and short stature, he looked like a mirthful troll all dressed up in gentleman's finery.

Sitting beside Brand, Charlotte quelled her uneasiness and smiled. Never in her sheltered life had she heard such an array of ribald verses. Some were silly, others outrageous, but all were unfit for a lady's ears.

Other than Lydia, she was the only lady present at the party. The other women appeared to be fashionable impures, and their behavior with the men proved they had about as much moral fiber as the Persian rug.

The motley group of aristocrats had gathered in Vaughn's drawing room, an exotically decorated chamber that resembled an Arabian tent. Gold-striped fabric loosely draped the walls and ceiling. Clusters of candles created pools of light, while leaving other areas of the room in shadowy darkness, where a few couples had retreated. From their occasional giggles, it was embarrassingly clear they were engaged in lewd activities.

Charlotte concentrated on her mission here. According to Brand, Vaughn and his wife were deeply in debt. From the luxury of the place, it wasn't difficult to believe they lived beyond their means.

Footmen circulated with wine and other spirits. One drunkard lay snoring in the corner. Across the room, a bearlike gentleman openly fondled the bosom of his female companion. Scandalized, Charlotte averted her gaze. He was Uriah Lane, one of the men on her list.

The sweetish odor of smoke hung in the air. Several gentlemen languidly puffed on long pipes attached to a brass contraption on the floor. "What is that thing?" she whispered to Brand, who sat beside her, one knee crooked up in a casual pose.

"Hookah. Containing opium made from the finest Turkish poppies." He picked up a pipe, drew on the end, and blew out an idle ring of smoke. "Care to try it?"

Revolted, Charlotte shook her head. "No, thank you."

His mouth deepened into a smirk, drawing her attention to the half-moon scar, the one he'd gotten in a long-ago duel. How she longed to kiss him there, to confess her imprudent love for him. "You seem tense," he said in a husky undertone. "It might help you relax."

"I don't need to relax," she said as Vaughn read another verse to loud hoots from the throng. "Nor do you."

"I'm perfectly alert." But Brand wasn't observing the dissipated guests. He wasn't listening and watching for clues. Instead, his gaze wandered over her bosom.

Beneath the pale blue silk of her gown, her skin tingled and her breasts tightened. A scandalous heat spread through her depths. Just looking at him, sitting so close, made her giddy. She craved his touch in the most shocking places . . .

Was this what love did to a woman? Made her forget all else but the object of her affections? "Put that silly thing down," she hissed in his ear. "We're supposed to be solving a mystery."

Brand took one last puff before setting the implement aside. Then he brushed his fingertips over her cheek. "Don't get your petticoats in a twist," he said, his voice a breath of sound. "It's all part of the ruse."

Pleasure curled in her belly, a feeling she resisted. That small caress had the stamp of ownership. It was meant to show anyone watching that she was his mistress.

His lover.

Charlotte cudgeled her shameful longings. Determined to preserve a semblance of self-respect, she drew back slightly. "Don't overdo it, Brand."

Chuckling, he subjected her to a lazy, unnerving stare. Ever since that kiss in his coach, she'd caught him studying her that way far too often. He hadn't objected to the time she'd spent with Vivien, slowly rebuilding their friendship. Did he finally believe her apology was sincere?

She didn't know, and she wouldn't ask.

To distract him—and herself—she whispered, "I wonder where Miss Darby is."

"Keeping to her chamber, if she has any sense."

Charlotte hoped so. She worried that the Vaughns might try to taint the innocent girl. But perhaps even they knew the boundaries of bad behavior.

"Stop murmuring, you two lovebirds," Vaughn called out. "I don't believe either of you are listening to my naughty verses."

Charlotte summoned a quick smile. "I'm sorry," she

said. "Am I to understand that you composed the rhymes yourself?"

Preening, Vaughn pointed his finger at her. "He-he. I'm a poet and you didn't know it."

"Your talents are quite di*vers*ified," Brand said.

"Di*vers*ified. Ha! Did you hear that, Lyddie? Faversham must want me to read another. Mayhap I'll dedicate the next one to his beauteous lady."

His. Charlotte kept the pleasant smile on her face, though her insides churned. She should be happy; the plan was working. Everyone assumed she was Brand's lover—because not even Brand Villiers would dare bring a decent lady to such a risqué gathering.

Lydia stirred on the couch beside her husband, a glass of wine in her hand. She aimed a look of barely veiled displeasure at Charlotte. Then her expression turned lascivious as she gazed hungrily at Brand.

Without thinking, Charlotte edged closer to him. The mere thought of that woman enticing him stirred a powerful resentment in her.

Thankfully, he didn't appear to notice the undercurrents between the two women. Of course, it had lasted only a moment.

One instant, Lydia was narrowing her eyes at them; the next, her expression lightened as she looked up at her husband. "Another ditty, dearest? Not everyone wants to hear your silly rhymes. You'll put Lady Charlotte to the blush."

"Ah, but this ditty is witty, indeed." Vaughn cleared his throat. " 'There was an old rake from Kildady / Who wanted to tup a young lady. / He unbuttoned his pants / And gave her a glance / And she hollered for her nursemaid-y.' "

Charlotte managed an uneasy laugh along with the other guests. Clifford Vaughn certainly had a gift for vulgarity. She oughtn't be surprised by his writing abilities; it only proved there was more to him than met the eye. Thankfully, his leering attention left her as an elegant blond man strolled into the chamber. Colonel Tom Ransom.

Vaughn scurried forward and clapped him on the back. "Ho there, Ransom. You've missed my poetry reading."

"I was held up by Belinda. The damned doggess made me attend the opera with her." His handsome face disgruntled, Ransom sprawled onto a cushion and took a draw from the hookah.

Charlotte tensed to hear him refer to his fiancée in so unsavory a manner. She met Brand's gaze, and he arched an eyebrow as if to say, *See? Ransom is marrying Lady Belinda for her rich dowry.*

One of the other smokers looked up, a thin lanky man with bleary eyes. He appeared so affected by the opium that he could barely keep his head from wobbling.

James Weatherby, Charlotte thought with distaste. His name was on her list.

"I've—I've an idea," Weatherby slurred. "P'raps Vaughn could—could write a poem for Belinda. He could read it at—at your weddin'."

"A capital notion," Vaughn said, rubbing his palms. "Let me see now. 'There was a rich bride who was cursed / By a poor colonel with an eye for her purse—'"

"Shut up, both of you," Ransom said, glaring balefully. "That's a damned stupid idea. And if either of you dares to foul my marriage plans, you'll meet me at dawn."

Weatherby shrank against the cushions. "Only jest—jesting."

"Well, keep your jest–jests to yourself. I've no need for them."

The angry exchange sent a shock wave through Charlotte. Was Ransom so desperate for money that he would kill anyone who might reveal his sordid past to his bride?

At the same moment that thought struck, she spied a flick of skirts in the corridor, a glimpse of someone hovering just beyond the doorway.

"I'll be right back," she murmured to Brand.

Though he frowned at her, she rose to her feet, glanced around to make sure no one else was watching, and slipped out of the chamber.

The passageway was refreshingly chilly after the hazy warmth of the drawing room. The smoke had made her a little dizzy. Blinking, she peered down the dim corridor.

A dainty shape moved in the gloom. A woman.

Charlotte hastened toward her. "Miss Darby," she said in a loud whisper. "Is that you?"

The figure spun around. The familiar pale oval of a face gleamed before she lowered her head and waited like a ghost in the shadows.

"It *is* you," Charlotte said on reaching the girl. "I was hoping we'd meet."

Miss Darby cast a furtive look toward the drawing room, where the convivial sounds of laughter echoed. Her voice almost inaudible, she said, "My lady. I—I'm not supposed to be watching."

"I understand, and please be assured I won't tell anyone. Is there somewhere we might talk in private?"

Miss Darby wrung her fingers. "I shouldn't . . ."

"Please, Miss Darby. I've something important to tell you." *And I hope you can tell me something important in return.*

"Perhaps . . . in here."

Silent as a wraith, she glided through a darkened doorway halfway down the corridor.

Charlotte followed and found herself in a sitting room illuminated by a single stream of silvery moonlight. Most of the room lay in deep shadow. When Miss Darby hovered uncertainly in the middle of the rug, Charlotte took the lead and motioned for her to sit beside her on a chaise.

Deciding to be blunt, she clasped her hands in her lap. "I've been worried about you, Miss Darby."

The girl gave a start of surprise. But she said nothing, and her expression was hidden in the dimness.

"I hope you'll forgive me for speaking candidly," Charlotte went on. "Your cousin and his wife have quite a number of unsavory friends. Have any of them bothered you in any way?"

"Bothered?"

The girl was a complete innocent. Or was she? She had been listening at the door . . .

The Vaughns must have ordered Miss Darby to remain in her chamber. Charlotte pictured her sitting alone, a timid girl wondering about the secret revels going on downstairs.

Curiosity was something Charlotte understood. Too well.

Choosing her words carefully, she went on. "Sometimes a man will touch a woman in an improper manner.

If ever that happens to you, I trust you'll send word to me. I'll help you find a safer place in which to live."

Another muted discharge of hilarity drifted down the corridor. Miss Darby was silent. She reminded Charlotte of a bashful little puppy cowering in a corner.

"I only want us to be friends," Charlotte said, gently touching the girl's arm. "If you'd prefer that I don't meddle, I won't."

Miss Darby flinched. "N-no. It's just that . . ."

"Yes?"

"It's just that . . . you're not like *them*."

The shyly spoken comment held an implicit question, one that Charlotte didn't really want to answer. But she couldn't prevaricate, not if she hoped to gain Miss Darby's trust. "You're wondering why I'm present at this party, aren't you?"

Miss Darby nodded slowly. "It's not my place to ask . . ."

"Nonsense, it's perfectly natural for you to express your doubts. You see, Lord Faversham is an old friend of mine. We grew up together in Devon. And now . . . now we keep company together." Because even that indirect statement sounded sordid, Charlotte couldn't stop herself from adding with throaty candor, "I must confess, there's never been anyone else for me. All other men pale in comparison. Perhaps you'll understand that someday."

"Ah." Miss Darby's voice was a breath of sound. "I believe I *do* understand."

Her earnest manner took Charlotte aback. Did the girl have a beau, a particular gentleman she admired from afar? Pray God he was someone decent. A gallant knight who could rescue her from this lion's den.

Another possibility jolted Charlotte. Or was he someone whom Miss Darby had met here in this house, a man whose evil she didn't grasp? Perhaps a former member of the Lucifer League?

The urgent question was poised on the tip of Charlotte's tongue when the shadowed figure of a man stepped into the sitting room.

Brand.

His voice rang out like a shot. "Excuse me."

Miss Darby gasped and jumped to her feet. "Oh, my. I *must* go." Without another word, she darted from the room.

Irked, Charlotte marched straight to Brand. "You have exceedingly poor timing," she said in a sibilant tone. "I was in the midst of asking Miss Darby some very important questions."

"It sounded more as if she were questioning *you*."

"Pardon? How do you know what—"

" 'Keep company,' " he muttered. "What the hell kind of euphemism is that?"

The realization swept over Charlotte. She blindly struck out and her fist connected with his chest. "Scoundrel! You were standing out there eavesdropping."

"So add another black mark to my catalog of sins." Flattening his palm to the small of her back, he gave her a push to the doorway. He glanced up and down the passageway, then murmured, "It's clear. Come along."

The pressure of his hand stirred that deep ache of longing. What else had he heard? She stepped away from him and folded her arms. "Come where?"

His grin flashed in the darkness. "Around me would be good. In lieu of that, however, I'll have to make do."

He caught her wrist and drew her around a corner and up a flight of stairs.

Charlotte felt a twinge of alarm. She picked up her skirt to keep from tripping. "You're not making any sense," she said. "I'm going back before we're missed."

"Spoilsport. We'll never have a better chance than this."

"A chance for what?" Her heart lurched into an unsteady rhythm. She stopped on the landing, halfway to the second floor. "Brand Villiers, if you think I'm *stupid* enough to let you lure me into one of the bedchambers—"

He chuckled darkly. "More to the point, I'm not stupid enough to think you're easily lured. But we are going to a bedchamber. Vaughn's."

When he continued up the steps, Charlotte sprang after him. "To search for clues?"

"Don't sound so bloody eager. If we're caught, there'll be hell to pay."

Their entire conversation had been conducted in whispers, but Charlotte found herself looking back down into the gloom of the stairwell. "We might run into Miss Darby."

"I saw her go off in the other direction. Her room is at the front of the house." He took Charlotte's hand in an impersonal grip and guided her down a corridor lit sporadically by candles in sconces. "The Vaughns' suite of rooms are back this way, over the gardens."

How did he know all that? Charlotte didn't bother keeping the resentment from her voice. "Do you always know the location of ladies' bedchambers?"

His gait took on a cocky strut. "I'm a man and by definition that makes me logical. And logic tells me the poor relation would be put in a room looking out over the noisy street."

"You're a man and that means you're too arrogant to consider everything that could go wrong. Someone else will come looking for us. Someone from the party."

"Not straightaway. That's the beauty of it. They'll assume we're off having a bit of fun."

A flush burned in Charlotte's cheeks, and she was glad for the shield of darkness. "I want you to know this is extremely awkward. I never thought we'd carry the ruse so far."

"Did you think you could just tell people we were 'keeping company' and keep our affair nice and quiet?"

"We *aren't* having an affair." But oh, how intriguing that sounded. "Besides, I couldn't bring myself to be so blunt."

"It's no trouble for me," he said. " 'Lady Charlotte Quinton is my mistress.' The statement has a fine ring of irony to it."

"It has *no* ring to it. No exchange of vows, no wedding, no honor."

This time, his laugh had a razor edge. "But that's our subterfuge, darling. You wanted this scheme, and if you can't live with it, then you're free to go home."

Darling. Her heart leapt at the endearment, though he was only taunting her, of course. "I'm not leaving. But the Rosebuds are bound to find out. Unless we're more discreet."

He plucked a candle from one of the sconces. "Discretion is my middle name."

"Your middle name is *rogue*. And they'll force you to marry me."

By the wavering light of the candle, his features hardened into a dangerous look and his eyes were shards of ice. "No one forces me to do anything, Charlotte. I'm not marrying anyone. Do I make myself clear?"

A curious sensation sank into her. It was anger, *not* disappointment. "You needn't be so emphatic. I don't want to marry you, either."

"We're in agreement, then." He quietly tested the knob and opened the door. "Although I was beginning to wonder after what you said downstairs to Miss Darby."

Charlotte froze. "What I said?"

" 'There's never been anyone else for me. All other men pale in comparison.' "

To hear her words tossed back in her face, uttered in that mocking tone, was a blow to her heart. Not that she would let Brand see her reaction. Aware of his sharp gaze, she snatched the candle from his hand. "You should be thankful that I sounded so convincing. It's the ruse, you know."

Charlotte brushed past him and went into the darkened bedchamber. By the small circle of light cast by the taper, she saw a tall chest of drawers, the typical scattering of chairs and tables, and a big, canopied bed. The décor was surprisingly tame. She would have thought the Vaughns' taste for vulgarity would extend to the bedchamber. "What exactly is it we're looking for?"

"Evidence," Brand said, heading past her. "Something to link the Vaughns to the murders."

"A collection of bloody knives?"

He cast her a blighting look, brought over another candle, and lit it from hers. "A signed confession would be helpful, too. In lieu of that, any sample of their handwriting will do. And anything that might hint at the identity of their next victim." He moved silently across the room and searched the bedside table.

Her stomach knotted. What if Brand himself was next?

He glanced over his shoulder and snapped, "Go on. This should come easy to you after rifling through my desk."

Grateful that he'd mistaken her hesitation, Charlotte didn't take issue with his snide remark. She walked to the table at the other side of the bed. While poking through the top drawer, she stole glances at Brand. He looked utterly delicious in a charcoal-gray coat that stretched across his broad shoulders and black breeches that delineated his long legs. She ached to brush back the lock of dark brown hair on his brow. His strong profile and efficient movements exuded a competence that defied his rakish image.

Was it only self-interest that spurred him to unmask the killer? Or was there a decent man inside him, a man who would risk his own life to save others?

She shouldn't wonder, shouldn't care. All that mattered was protecting Grandmama.

Charlotte returned her attention to the drawer. "Lydia certainly uses a lot of salves and ointments." Curious, she peeled off her kid gloves, picked up a blue jar, and wrenched it open, sniffing the musky aroma of the oil. "I wonder why she keeps them here instead of on her vanity table?"

Brand's mouth had an enigmatic twist. His gaze seemed to hold secrets as he studied her. "Don't wonder, just be quick. We haven't all night."

A pity we don't.

All too aware of the wide expanse of the bed, Charlotte closed the top drawer and opened the bottom. Her eyes widened, her stomach lurched, and her knees gave way. "Dear heavens."

"What is it?"

"I think . . . you had better come look at this."

Brand reached her side in under two seconds. He had a small book in his hand and he tossed it on the table. Crouching down beside her, he held his candle high to view the interior of the drawer.

Astonishingly, he laughed. "Ah. It's just the usual collection of whips and chains."

"How can you be so blasé? There are *weapons* in here. Shackles to bind some poor, unwitting victim."

"Rather, a very willing victim." Brand examined a riding crop. "I'm sure Cliffie and Lyddie have lots of fun with these toys."

"Toys?"

"Yes. There are those who enjoy using such implements in bedsport."

Charlotte looked from him to the collection. The sight took on a whole new meaning. A perverse, furtively fascinating meaning. Weakly, she said, "You're jesting."

He ran the shaft of the whip lightly down her cheek. "Believe the expert. You've quite a lot to learn about sensual games."

His knowing smile should have offended her. But her feverish mind was too absorbed in questions to take more than passing notice. Did Brand actually tie up his women? What did he do to them, then? Or did he let his lover bind *him*? Did he give her the freedom to touch his body at will, to have him completely at her mercy?

Dear sweet heaven. Why was she even wondering?

With effort, Charlotte pushed the drawer shut and found her voice. "Well, I think it's disgusting."

"You can't be sure until you've tried it," he said in a stirring tone that somehow made her skin tingle.

"If the Vaughns engage in such lewdness, then I *am* sure."

Brand looked amused by her vehemence. "Methinks the lady doth protest too much."

"No, you think everyone is like *you*."

"More's the pity. Everyone should be like me." Apparently he possessed at least some wisdom, for he changed the subject. He picked up the small book from the bedside table. "I found something, too. More of Vaughn's poems."

"If you plan on reading them aloud, please do it when I'm not around."

He riffled through the pages. "Actually, I was more interested in his sloppy penmanship."

Charlotte tilted the book so that she could view a page. "Look at all those blots. And his letters are like hen scratchings."

"Precisely. It's safe to say his handwriting doesn't match the note I saw."

"Then perhaps Lydia wrote the note—"

"Shh." Brand's manner snapped to alertness. He tilted his head in a listening pose.

"What is it?"

"Voices. Someone's out there."

Jolted, she strained her ears. From the corridor drifted the softness of a woman's voice, then the deeper tone of a man answering her.

"Oh, no," Charlotte moaned. "We'll be caught."

"But not at spying." Springing to his feet, Brand set

Chapter 13
THE MAN DOWNSTAIRS

Charlotte's feet were bolted in place. She could hear the laughter of the couple out in the corridor, yet she couldn't bring herself to lie down beside Brand. "You're mad if you think I'm going to climb into bed with *you*."

"This is no time for maidenly quibbles. They could walk in at any moment."

Still, she stalled. "Are the linens fresh?"

"Dammit, Char. They smell like a frigging summer breeze. Now, *move*."

She swallowed her misgivings and lowered herself to the mattress, keeping a decent six inches away from Brand.

Instantly, he scooted closer and pulled the sheets up to their necks, locking her in his embrace.

Charlotte stiffened, overwhelmed by the heat of his body and the feel of his muscular chest against her bosom. The solid weight of his leg lay over hers. A deep pulse of awareness affected her, but she resisted the urge to snuggle against him, to lay her head in the cradle of his shoulder.

She could endure this intimacy for a few minutes. Nothing would happen. They were fully clothed, after all.

In fact, she was safer here in bed than she'd been in his coach. He wouldn't dare try anything wicked, not when someone could come into the chamber at any moment.

Then she gasped as Brand nuzzled her cheek. His raspy skin and warm lips sent ripples of sensation through her. Out of self-preservation, she angled her face away. "Kindly keep your distance."

His gruff chuckle made her imagine all the things they could do in the darkness. Amusement filled his gaze along with something else, something hot and dark. "You'd like that, wouldn't you?" he said. "But how believable will it be if someone finds us lying at opposite sides of the bed?"

The truth of that made her tremble and from more than his closeness. They could be in grave danger if she refused to play her part. *He* would be in danger, for Brand had been a member of the Lucifer League.

"Blast this ruse," she said with feeling.

He grinned. By the feeble light of the candle, she could see every long, dark lash framing his eyes. Beautiful eyes, smoky gray, mysterious. And that scarred mouth that she wanted the freedom to kiss. *Brand*. Lying with him like this had long been the substance of her secret dreams.

The reality was so much better.

"It wasn't my idea to bring you to the Vaughns' party," he reminded her. "I'd have rather left you home. However, now that we're here . . ." His fingers trailed up and down her back, and a silken note entered his voice. "You do realize we're going to have to make this look realistic."

She *was* realizing it. Far too feverishly.

"Not until whoever it is walks into the room," Charlotte said, hoping she didn't sound breathless. "*If* they walk in at all."

"We'd better be prepared. They're still out in the corridor. I can hear them."

She could hear only the rapid beating of her heart, smell only his spicy masculine scent, feel only the welcome weight of his body. The bedcovers held them in a cozy cocoon. His mouth was so close, she felt the warm exhalations of his breath. If she tilted her head toward him just a bit, her lips would brush his ... To distract herself, she asked, "Who do you suppose it is?"

"Probably someone from the party. They mustn't guess that we came up here to spy."

His gaze was directed at her mouth. Dear God, he was thinking about kissing her. But with any luck, he was also remembering how she'd wounded his masculine pride.

Your powers of seduction are vastly exaggerated.

If ever he guessed what a lie that had been, she would be lost. Already, a dazed anticipation threatened to rob her of sanity. She quickly murmured, "Perhaps it's only a maid and a valet having a chat before they go about their duties."

"Then they'll be coming in to light the fire and turn down the bed." With bone-melting strokes, Brand massaged her shoulders. His husky tone deepening, he murmured, "You're really far too tense for a lover, Charlotte. I believe it's time I did something about that."

He brought his hands up to cradle her cheeks. And then he kissed her. A sweet kiss unlike the angry one in the coach. A gentle kiss that melted her resistance like hot wax. His fingertips stroked her face, traced the whorls of her ear, played with the fine hairs at the nape of her neck. Utterly entranced, she was only half aware of the small, needy sounds coming from her throat.

Any hope she'd had of hiding her longing for him vanished into a blur of sensation and pleasure. A deep, drowning pleasure that went on and on.

Brand. This was Brand who kissed her so tenderly, as if she were precious to him. As if she were a desirable woman instead of a spinster who had never known the fullness of love. When he held her like this, it was easy to pretend that he truly cared for her. To pretend they were husband and wife, and she was free to express her love for him.

Lifting her arms, she threaded her fingers into his hair, the dense silk of it stimulating her skin. She kissed him back, parting her lips at a nudge of his tongue. Long delicious moments passed, yet still he kept the kiss soft and restrained, light butterfly sips that wreaked havoc with her restraint. Or at least what was left of it.

Moaning, she opened her mouth wider, wordlessly begging him to delve deeper. He obliged, but only to a degree, not enough to satisfy her. She wanted more . . . more heat, more pressure, more of *him*. His arms surrounded her, yet she ached to be closer, ached so much that she lifted her hips and arched her breasts. Craving contact with his muscled body, she moved sinuously in the need to alleviate the growing frustration inside herself.

He eased his head back slightly, all the while licking, nibbling, tasting as if he couldn't get enough of her lips. "Lie still," he muttered. "You're inciting the tall man downstairs."

Befuddled, she opened her eyes to his strained expression. "Who?"

"This man." Before she could fathom his meaning, he took her hand and moved it under the covers, all the way down to cup the front of his breeches.

Charlotte froze, every fiber of her attention focused on what lay beneath her fingers. Something long and hard and thick. Something so blatantly masculine, she felt a bone-deep rush of desire.

And awareness.

She snatched back her hand, wrenched herself away from him. "*Don't* . . . that's completely . . . why did you *do* that?"

In a casual move, he leaned on his elbow and regarded her. "You needed to know how your squirming affects me. And what did you mean, 'completely'?"

Completely amazing. Completely enticing. "Completely beyond the bounds of our ruse, that's what."

The rugged angles of his face settled into a characteristic smirk. "Things were getting out of control," he said. "I had to put a stop to it before I ravished you."

"You might have said so in words."

"Unfortunately, you were beyond hearing." His gray eyes slumberous, he deepened that hateful smile. "I must say, you performed your role quite convincingly. Anyone would think you feel a true passion for me."

He looked too pleased with himself, too arrogant and superior. Charlotte choked on the perception that filled her beleaguered mind. In a shattering realization, she made the connection between her insult in the coach and his declaration before the carriage race.

Your powers of seduction are vastly exaggerated.

I never refuse a challenge. Even we profligates have our code of honor.

He had viewed her affront as a dare. He had set out to prove himself irresistible to her. And she had played right into his hands.

She ought to be angry at him for leading her on, angry at herself for being so idiotic. But her raw emotions lurked too close to the surface. At least she'd had the presence of mind not to blurt out her love for him. Then he truly would have been gloating. With a glance at the closed door, she untangled herself from the sheets and stood up, shaking out her skirts with unsteady hands.

Brand hadn't moved from the bed. He must be waiting for her to deny her desire for him. So that he'd have another chance to demonstrate his power over her. She wouldn't give him the satisfaction.

Conscious of his watching eyes, she copied his untroubled manner, walking to a darkened mirror in the pretense of tidying her hair. She could see the pinprick of candlelight on the bedside table behind her. "It's safe to get up now," she said over her shoulder. "I can't hear any voices out in the passageway."

"They've been gone for at least ten minutes," Brand said.

She whirled around to see him roll out of bed, all cool, callous rogue. "Ten *minutes*!"

All that time he'd been kissing her, holding her tenderly as if she mattered to him. And she had been kissing him back with all the unreserved love in her heart and soul.

"The door was locked, anyway," he went on, adding insult to injury. "I'd turned the key when we came in."

Brand had known that no one would disturb them. Or at least that they'd have ample warning of entry by a key rattling in the outside lock.

If he was the greatest lover in England, she had to be the stupidest clodpate.

Flushed with humiliation, she wheeled back toward the mirror. With her hair untidy, her shadowed image looked like a woman who had enjoyed a tumble with her lover. She drew the loose strands into a tight knot and jammed in the pins. "I suppose those were your friends out there, too. Did you tell them I was reluctant and needed a push into bed? Perhaps you even wagered on your success at seduction."

Charlotte meant to sound sarcastic, but her voice caught on the last few words. Tears burned her eyes and throat. She swallowed hard.

Don't weep. Please, God, don't let me weep.

Brand came closer. In the mirror she could see his shadowy form standing just behind her. "That isn't true," he said. "No one else knew about this. We came up here to look for evidence."

"Evidence of what? My gullibility?"

Brand didn't respond right away. He was probably calculating his next ravishment of her.

True to form, he put on a charming look of remorse, reached for her hand, and brought it to his lips. He kissed the scarred palm that still remembered the feel of him. "You're angry. Forgive me?"

Her foolish heart softened. But she found the strength to pull back her hand and regard him with cool disdain. "There's nothing to forgive, Brand. I insulted you, and in return you tricked me. We're even now."

. . .

His plan to coax a reaction out of Charlotte had worked.
All too well.

Brand cast a moody glance at her, seated beside him
in the open carriage. Her fine-boned face was composed
in the faint glow of the two brass lamps that lit their
way through the cold, darkened streets. The hollow clip-
clop of hooves filled the silence. She'd spoken scarcely
two words to him since that scene in the bedchamber,
and he had deemed it wise to leave her be. Irate women
needed a chance to sulk before they became amenable
again.

But Charlotte wasn't like most women. She had never
been amenable—except for an hour ago. In bed.

Jesus save him. The swiftness of her response had
been staggering. He had meant only to ignite the slow
burn of passion, to prove that he could put a crack in
that almighty restraint of hers. Instead he'd lit the fuse
to gunpowder.

The memory of her wildness consumed him. The
purrs of pleasure in her throat. The stroking of her fingers in his hair. The feel of her slim body undulating
beneath him. She probably hadn't even realized what
she'd been seeking. She was that naïve.

How he would like to educate her.

Numskull. For all her cleverness and wit, Charlotte
was a virgin, a respectable lady. She knew next to nothing about the pleasures of bedsport. But he could no
longer fool himself into thinking her a dried-up prude.

It had taken precious little to break down her de-
fenses. One diligently gentle kiss and all that ice had
melted. She had been so lost in passion he could have

lifted her skirts and entered paradise before she'd summoned any resistance. The temptation had been so strong, he'd had to end the encounter fast, lightning fast. By shocking her back to her senses.

The tall man had been less than pleased to be denied any more than that one brief touch of her hand. He was still refusing to lie down and die.

Brand's mind was every bit as obstinate. *Charlotte*. Prickly, irksome Charlotte wanted him with surprising ferocity. Tenderness was the key that had unlocked her lust. Armed with that dangerous knowledge, he could seduce her whenever he pleased.

He could make her his mistress.

There's never been anyone else for me. All other men pale in comparison. He would never forget standing out in the corridor, listening to her softly spoken words and feeling an ache inside himself that had little to do with lust. He'd had mistresses who had voiced ardent praise of him, a few who had declared their undying love though it was clear they'd only loved themselves. But no woman had ever spoken of him with such vibrancy of emotion.

Of course, Charlotte had been lying, embellishing for the sake of their ruse. Yet that hadn't stopped his craving to believe her. He'd wanted to hold her close, to hear her whisper endearments in his ear.

Damn, damn, *damn*.

Brand gripped the reins and focused on navigating the narrow streets. Only a half-wit would trust Charlotte, and he was privy to all her faults. It had been a mistake to take her to that party, sheer idiocy to entice her upstairs. Although he'd bought the Vaughns' silence by reminding them of the gaming debts they owed to him, he had to admit that Charlotte was right about the risk of her posing as his mistress. There'd be hell to pay if the Rose-buds found out.

The price would be even higher if he indulged his base urges and deflowered Charlotte. He'd destroy what little regard his grandmother still felt for him. Wasn't it enough that he'd caused the deaths of George and his son? Did he have to sow the seeds of more pain?

He inhaled a cleansing breath of frosty air, not that it helped to ease the tightness in his chest. If he ruined Charlotte, Grandmama would cut him out of her life al-together. She was all the family he had left.

No, not all.

There was Amy. If he made himself a pariah in his own family, he'd lose contact with Amy, too.

"What did you and Michael quarrel about?"

With uncanny accuracy, Charlotte's voice stabbed him. He jerked his head toward her, trying to discern her expression in the darkness. Nothing but simple in-terest showed on her indistinct features. She couldn't possibly know anything about the secrets of his past.

But why the hell had she brought that up now?

His palms felt like ice inside his gloves. "Devil if I remember. It was a long time ago."

"Was it a woman?"

He shrugged. "Might have been."

"Who was she?"

"No one important." Only Grace. Michael's first wife. A golden-haired temptress who had twisted Brand inside out and upside down. Their first and only amour had been the night before the wedding, and Grace hadn't been a virgin. Even then, he'd been moronic enough to believe her professions of love, not realizing her fairy-tale beauty had hidden a narcissistic woman who'd enjoyed playing two friends against each other. Looking back, Brand was appalled at his own blindness.

But he had no room for regrets.

Out of that brief liaison had come Amy. Sweet, innocent Amy whom he could never acknowledge as his own. That bitter fact wrenched his chest like nothing else. He would never hear Amy call him Papa, never kiss her good night, never walk her down the aisle on her wedding day.

Those privileges belonged to Michael. And Michael had made it clear in no uncertain terms that he would never relinquish those rights.

"This woman had to have been someone important to both of you," Charlotte said musingly. "You two are still barely civil."

"What, do you expect Michael and me to build tree houses together again? Face it, Char. We grew up. We pursue different lives. Don't make so much of it."

His sharp tone silenced her, and he hoped to God he'd allayed her interest in the matter. Charlotte was bright and perceptive, and she might put two and two together.

Especially since she'd seen that miniature in his drawer.

Bloody hell. She'd never mentioned it. She probably hadn't even noticed that he kept a likeness of Amy. He should bury this unnerving fear once and for all.

As he turned the pair of horses onto the side street that bordered his house, he noticed a furtive figure in the shadows. Someone stood at the entry to the mews. A man.

Brand's attention sharpened. There was something about that slouching, beanpole form that triggered a faint memory.

Then the man reached up to adjust his workman's cap, and Brand remembered. It was a man he'd noticed in the congregation at Parkinson's lecture.

And Brand didn't believe in coincidence.

He thrust the reins into Charlotte's gloved hands. "Hold the horses. I'll be right back."

"Where—"

Ignoring her startled question, he vaulted down from the high perch and took off running toward the stranger.

The man saw him and ducked deeper into the blackness of the alley. With all the cunning of a murderer, he faded from sight.

Brand paused to let his eyes adjust to the dense shadows. This mews served a number of wealthy homes with stables at the back of each property. Here and there, the barren branches of trees extended from the gardens. The intruder could be hiding anywhere, behind a rubbish bin, inside a garden gate, under a cart in one of the stableyards.

Or he could have jumped a fence and fled to the main street.

Brand hoped not. He was in the mood to throttle someone.

His senses alert, he entered the mews. He braced himself for a fight but no one jumped out at him. The odors of refuse and manure lent pungency to the cold air. Where had the devil gone?

Maybe he'd cut through a yard and doubled back. At this very moment, he could be creeping up on Charlotte.

Jolted by the thought, Brand threw a glance over his shoulder. He could see only the horses, not the carriage and not Charlotte. Then, out of the corner of his eye, he spied a slight movement in the shadows beneath a nearby tree.

The towering dark shape of a man.

Brand surged toward him, caught a fistful of rough coat, and thrust that struggling form up against the brick wall of the stables. He circled the scrawny neck with his fingers, pressing hard.

"Who the hell are you?" Brand snapped. "Why are you here?"

"Be happy to answer, m'lord," he choked out. "*If* you remove your hands from my throat."

That voice. Not aristocratic, but not common, either. An educated man.

And he knew Brand's identity. That *m'lord* hadn't been a placating compliment.

Brand patted him down and relieved him of a brace of pistols. Then he hauled the interloper by the scruff of his coat toward the light of the carriage lamps. From the high seat, Charlotte gave him a wide-eyed stare, but for once she had the sense to stay put.

The feeble glow revealed a gaunt, clean-shaven face with shrewd blue eyes and a hook nose. A dark workman's cap perched on a fringe of sparse brown hair. Brand was tall, but this man topped him by a good three inches.

"Speak up," Brand said harshly. "I'm waiting to hear why you were lurking behind my house."

"I'm here on official business. I'm Hannibal Jones, employed by the magistrate at Bow Street Court."

A Runner?

Taken unawares, Brand eased his hold and stepped back, making note of the officer's plain clothing. He had been certain this man was connected to the murders. "What proof have you of your identity?"

"My truncheon. If you'll allow me." With careful movements, Jones drew out the short club of polished hardwood from an inner pocket. A small brass crown gleamed on the top of the truncheon. All the Bow Street Runners carried the weapon as a badge of office.

Jones eyed Brand grimly. "I'm investigating the suspicious deaths of several noblemen," he went on. "And it's my duty to inform you, my lord, that you are under suspicion of committing murder."

Chapter 14
FAMILY SECRETS

While the younger children napped and Amy visited upstairs with the Rosebuds, Charlotte invited Vivien to take tea in the morning room. A coal fire hissed on the hearth, sending welcome waves of warmth into the cool air.

Vivien plopped into a chair, kicked off her slippers, and tucked her stocking feet beneath her. "My, it feels good to sit down for a moment," she said with the trace of an exotic accent. "The children do keep me busy."

But she looked utterly happy, and Charlotte wished she herself could be so content. And the least of her worries was that Bow Street Runner.

Hannibal Jones had only been doing his duty, checking out all the possible suspects. Somehow he had found out about the Lucifer League, arrived at the same conclusion as Brand, and had been conducting a stealthy inquest of the members. Jones had no proof whatsoever to connect Brand to the murders. Nor would he uncover any. In fact, Charlotte considered it a relief to know that a trained officer of the law was pursuing the case.

Brand hadn't shared her optimism. He and Jones had taken an instant dislike to one another. Consequently, ever since the previous night, Brand had been in a foul humor. He had gone out, muttering something about a visit to the boxing gymnasium.

Charlotte had seized this opportunity to speak to Vivien in private.

While they waited for the tea tray, they chatted amiably about the children, four-year-old William whose precociousness landed him into many scrapes, and two-year-old Lucy, who was as sweetly maneuvering as her namesake great-grandmother.

Once the footman had gone, and Charlotte had poured them both steaming cups, she cast about for a way to broach the tricky topic. She had never been more keenly aware of the slight awkwardness that lingered between them. There was a reserve in Vivien that hadn't been present five years ago, when she had come to Stokeford Abbey as a free-spirited gypsy and befriended Charlotte.

Charlotte went to close the door, then came slowly back to her chair. "Vivien, there's something I need to ask you."

Those dark velvet eyes regarded her. "I suspected you might have something particular on your mind. Has it to do with wherever you and Brand went last evening?"

Charlotte fought a blush. "The Rosebuds asked him to escort me to the Seftons' ball." That was misleading, but not an untruth. She and Brand had simply gone to visit the Vaughns instead. Her reputation hung on the hope that no one had noted their absence in the huge crush of guests. Before Vivien could ask for a report of the ball, Charlotte went on quickly. "But my question has to do with Michael and Brand."

"Ah. You're wondering about the chill between them."

"Yes. It doesn't make sense. Brand won't tell me

much, just that they quarreled over a woman a long time ago. But Michael is happily married to you now, so why would they still be at odds?"

Vivien gave her a strangely intense look, then turned her gaze downward, stirring her tea with a silver spoon. After a moment, she looked up again. "May I ask, what are your feelings for Brand?"

Taken aback, Charlotte fumbled, "I . . ."

"Please, I need to know the truth. It's very important."

Charlotte wanted to guard her secret inside her heart. Yet when she looked into Vivien's eyes, she knew instinctively that nothing less than complete candor would win Vivien's trust. She drew a deep breath and released it slowly. "I love him," she murmured. It was strangely liberating to speak those words aloud. "I can't explain why or how or when it came about, but I do love him. Even if he can never love me."

Vivien smiled gently, without surprise. As she sipped her tea, she wore a considering look as if pondering some secret. "Has Brand ever told you how he received his scar?"

"In a duel. Why do you ask?"

"Michael and Brand fought that duel. With swords."

Charlotte's teacup rattled as she set it into the saucer. Her mind flashed back to when Brand had first appeared with that scar some nine years ago after having shunned family gatherings for over a year. His long absence in itself had been peculiar; despite his other faults, Brand had always come home to Devon several times a year for holidays. But he had turned into a cynical stranger. At the time, Charlotte had attributed the change to grief for his elder brother, George, who had died the previous year.

She had never connected it to the animosity between Brand and Michael—or to that scar.

"Dear heavens," Charlotte whispered. "But I don't understand. Who was this woman they fought over? Wasn't Michael married at the time?"

"Yes," Vivien said very softly.

Charlotte was stricken by a realization so appalling, she almost couldn't put it into words. "Are you suggesting . . . they fought over . . . Grace? That Brand *seduced* Michael's *wife*?"

Vivien bit her lip and nodded. "I fear so. You see, they both had met Grace at the same time, and they both courted her. She was an extraordinarily beautiful woman, the toast of the *ton*."

"I know. I attended the wedding." Charlotte recalled being bitterly envious of Michael's lovely, flawless bride with her golden hair and smooth, perfect skin. She herself had sat at the rear of the chapel at Stokeford Abbey, her scars hidden by long sleeve and glove. Heartsore, she had wished fervently that she could have been Grace, pledging her life to handsome Michael.

"Grace professed to favor Brand," Vivien went on. "But at the time, he was merely a second son, with little hope of attaining the title. So instead she betrothed herself to Michael."

Charlotte knew the sort, women who craved lineage more than love. "That didn't give Brand the right to ravish her."

"It's my understanding that the ravishing was mutual. They had already begun the affair before the wedding. Michael didn't realize it at first, for Grace explained the loss of her virginity with the tale of a brief fling with a cavalry officer who'd subsequently been killed in battle."

"She sounds like Brand's sort of woman." Charlotte couldn't keep the sarcasm from her voice. "What happened then?"

"A short time after the wedding, Brand's brother George and George's son fell ill and died. Brand became Earl of Faversham."

"And he also became more acceptable to Grace," Charlotte guessed.

"It would seem so. On the night she died, Grace was running off to meet Brand. He was waiting for her at the coast, and they were intending to flee to the Continent. But there was a terrible rainstorm, a bridge had washed out, and Grace's coach went into the water."

"She drowned," Charlotte said numbly.

Vivien nodded. "Thank heavens she'd left Amy behind in London. Michael saw to it that no one ever found out his wife had abandoned her family."

Charlotte closed her eyes, imagining the horror of that accident, its tragic result unlike the crash that had involved the Rosebuds. Dear God! Grace had been so wild for Brand that she'd forsaken her husband and daughter. How could any woman leave her child?

Yet if she'd taken the baby, Amy might have been killed, too. Amy, who had been less than a year old at the time. Amy, who thankfully wouldn't even remember the heartless mother who had given life to her.

At least Michael had been there to love and cherish her . . .

And Brand, who kept a miniature of Amy in a locked drawer. Brand, who had revealed a flash of strong emotion when he had embraced the girl.

Charlotte's eyes snapped open. Her heart lurching erratically, she stared at Vivien. "My stars. Amy . . . ?"

Vivien's gaze wavered a moment. She looked troubled and hesitant. Then slowly she nodded. "Yes. Brand is her natural father."

Gripping the arms of her chair as an anchor, Charlotte sank into a welter of emotions. Shock, for she had never imagined such a momentous secret. Anger, for Brand had condemned her when he too had committed the sin of betrayal. Compassion, for she couldn't forget that look of tormented love in his eyes when he'd held Amy.

"Are you certain?" she asked Vivien. "Absolutely certain?"

"Brand has a birthmark. So does Amy, and so do I. It's right here." Smiling faintly, Vivien touched her hip. "It's a family trait."

Something occurred to Charlotte. "Then you're her aunt as well as her stepmother."

"I am, indeed." Vivien set down her teacup and leaned forward. "Charlotte, listen to me. You must never breathe a word of this to anyone. Only Brand and Michael and I know. And now you."

"The Rosebuds . . . ?"

Vivien shook her head. "Not even them, I'm afraid. It's Michael's wish, and I concur. The fewer who know, the better. If ever word of the scandal slipped out, society would whisper. Amy's reputation would be tainted."

"Blast those petty standards." Anger shot to the forefront of Charlotte's emotions. "Brand is to blame. He seduced the wife of his best friend. Let society censure *him,* rather than shun an innocent young girl."

But even as she spoke, Charlotte knew the futility of that wish. Society teemed with shallow, narrow-minded people who judged others by their pedigree. People like Grace.

"It's more than Amy's reputation," Vivien said fervently. "Michael has raised Amy as his own daughter. He loves her dearly, and he can't bear to let her regard anyone else as her papa."

"I understand."

"I hope so." Vivien rose from the chair, then dropped to her knees before Charlotte, gripping tightly to Charlotte's hand. "Please, for Michael's sake and for Amy's, give me your vow that you'll mention this to no one."

A lump filled Charlotte's throat. She felt humbled by the enormity of the gift Vivien had given her, to reveal such a secret after Charlotte had betrayed her so horribly in the past. Mere words of absolution couldn't have made Charlotte feel such gratitude in her heart.

"Of course you have my vow." Her voice broke, and she caught her friend into a fierce, heartfelt hug. "Oh, Vivien, thank you. Thank you for trusting me."

Vivien drew back and smiled, tears glossing her eyes, too. Yet she still looked a bit troubled. "I don't know if it's wise for you to tell Brand that you know."

"I won't let on that I heard it from you. I'll let him think I deduced it myself. You see, I found a miniature of Amy in his desk."

"I had that painting commissioned for him," Vivien confessed. "Michael stormed and shouted, but I finally convinced him it was only right." She squeezed Vivien's hand again. "However, I'm not worried about Brand being angry with me. I'm more concerned that he'll be angry with *you*. He's a very private man, my brother."

Charlotte knew that more than anyone. She also knew

Brand was a trickster, a charmer, and a rogue. But he loved Amy.

Dear God, he loved the daughter he could never acknowledge.

Brand rapped sharply on the ancient wood door. As he waited for a response, he paced the small porch of the town house on the outskirts of the Strand. The roof was sagging, precariously held up by two crumbling pillars. The windows looked grimy in the late afternoon light. He hadn't known James Weatherby lived in such a dump.

Had lived, Brand corrected grimly. This morning, Weatherby had been found dead.

Brand had been dressing after a bout of fisticuffs at the gymnasium when he'd heard the news. Uriah Lane had burst in, his well-fed face almost gleeful at being the first to broadcast the tidings. Lane had known nothing else, not even the manner of Weatherby's death. Only that his remains had been transported to the undertaker.

Another member of the Lucifer League had died. And Brand had to determine if Weatherby had been murdered like the others.

Dammit, why did no one answer the door?

Again, he pounded his fist on the wooden panel. A cold wind gusted, whipping at his unbuttoned coat and hurling a sheet of newspaper against the iron fence that surrounded the small front yard. A plump housewife in mobcap and cloak trudged down the cobbled street.

The door opened at last. A beetle-browed man with a ruddy face blocked the entryway. His rotund belly strained at the buttons of his drab waistcoat, and a splotch of egg yolk stained the collar of his shirt.

With glowering brown eyes, he regarded Brand. "If ye're another one o' them flippin' constables, ye can come back later. I'm 'aving me tea right now."

The door started to swing shut, but Brand put his hand out and kept it open a crack. "I'm Lord Faversham. A friend of Weatherby's. Are you the landlord here?"

"Aye. Shanley's the name, but—"

Brand didn't give Shanley a chance to finish. He thrust the door back all the way and walked into a small, dimly lit foyer. Dingy flowered paper covered the walls. Other than a chair and a table, the room was bare, the checkered marble floor scuffed and dirty. The place must have been a decent house until it had fallen into disrepair.

"See 'ere now, m'lord," Shanley protested. "If ye've come to collect a debt, the fellow's dead. An' two days afore the rent's due at that. Bugger already owed me for three months."

"How much?"

" 'Alf a guinea. An' cheap rent at that."

Brand found a pair of gold coins in his pocket and tossed them to the landlord, who caught them nimbly. "This should take care of it. Keep the rest for your trouble."

Those thick brows lifted. Grinning, Shanley displayed a set of pointy teeth, the front one bearing a gold cap. "Well, well. That's right good o' ye, m'lord."

"Show me to Weatherby's chamber. And tell me what happened."

His mood more expansive now, Shanley didn't question Brand's reasons. He motioned him to a curving flight of stairs, scurrying to lead the way up. "Ain't much to tell. Maid went to clean 'is chamber this mornin'. Found the poor bloke lyin' in bed, stiff as a board."

"Had he been stabbed or strangled?"

Shanley glanced back, indignation on his face. "I run a good establishment, lock on the front door an' back, windows secured. Ain't no one 'ere gets murdered in 'is own bed."

"So there was no sign of forced entry?"

The landlord shook his head. "Nay. Like that Runner said, 'tis an unfortunate matter that a man o' the quality could fall so low."

Hannibal Jones had been here. Restraining a rush of contempt, Brand asked, "What do you mean, unfortunate? How did Weatherby die?"

They reached the top of the stairs, and Shanley stopped, his face grave. "The gennleman snuffed 'is own life. Slit his wrists wid a razor, 'e did."

Good God. Was it possible this was a random horror that had nothing to do with the Lucifer League? That Weatherby's addiction to opium had pushed him into an abyss of despair? He had seemed despondent at the Vaughns' party. He'd said little, except for that one suggestion about the rhymes which Tom Ransom had summarily rejected.

Yet instinct told Brand this death was no coincidence. A murder could easily be made to look like suicide. In a drugged stupor, Weatherby wouldn't have put up much of a fight.

"What time did he return home last evening?" Brand asked.

Shanley scratched his balding pate. " 'Twas after midnight."

"Was he alone?"

"Aye. Allus was, that one."

"Did he have any visitors later?"

"Nay—unless 'twas someone 'e let in after I locked up."

So much for the safe household. "What of his valet?"

"Didn't 'ave one. Made do by 'isself."

"Did any of the other tenants hear anything?"

"Nay again. Them constables been badgerin' 'em 'alf the day, the rotters. They'll give this 'ouse a bad name wid all this talk o' murder an' mayhem." Dolefully shaking his head, the landlord threw open a door at the end of the corridor. "Ain't no murder wot 'appened 'ere. 'Twas a turrible mess, though, took the maid nigh on an hour to clean up."

Brand stepped inside the dim-lit room. The linens had been stripped from the bed, but the reddish-brown stain on the mattress remained as a memorial to violent death. Underlying the stink of vinegar and blood, the sweetish odor of opium smoke tainted the air. "Was anything stolen?"

"Dunno." Shanley winked unexpectedly. "If ye're of a mind to collect yer debt, I won't say nothin'."

Brand let the landlord assume his purpose was mercenary. From the casual way Shanley sauntered out, Brand suspected the man had already poked through the belongings for any valuables. Not that Weatherby had ever had more than two shillings to rub together.

His entire quarterly allowance had gone up in smoke. These past few years, he'd existed in a perpetual fog of dreams and delusion. The paraphernalia of his obsession resided on the bedside table, the brass hookah, the charcoal burner.

Damn *fool*.

Aware of a tightness in his throat, Brand swallowed. A third son, Weatherby had gone through his inheritance in short order. If memory served, he'd had two brothers, prosperous landowners in Hampshire who had cut off contact years ago. Would anyone even mourn his death?

Concentrate. Find a clue.

Brand surveyed the chamber with its meager collection of goods, the personal effects of a bachelor. A pair of black leather boots sat by the door. A brass-bound trunk lay open to a clutter of shirts and cravats and breeches. Papers scattered a plain wood desk.

He walked slowly around the room. A killer had trod this faded rug sometime during the night. Someone who'd gained entry without forcing a lock. Perhaps through a downstairs window? Or had Weatherby let in his own murderer? Was it someone he knew?

Going to the washstand, Brand picked up the razor and examined it. A small crust of shaving soap clung to the sharp edge. There was no sign of blood. If he'd had the slightest doubt, this confirmed the death was no suicide. Even if the maid had wiped the razor clean and replaced it on the stand, that bit of soap would have been gone.

So the killer had brought his own razor. Had Hannibal Jones taken that one away as evidence?

Brand resumed his survey of the chamber. There was no handy button lying on the floor, fallen from the intruder's coat. No ticket stub from the opera left by Ransom. No Bible passage left by Parkinson. No ribald verse by Vaughn.

That only left the note. Had Weatherby received the same warning as Trowbridge?

Brand leafed through the papers on the desk, but found only dun notices. The maid had been here, so the dustbin was empty. Spying a garment hanging from the back of a chair, he picked it up. Weatherby had worn this blue coat to the Vaughns' party the previous night.

Brand found an inside pocket. Empty. He was searching the other side of the coat when the scrape of a footstep trespassed on his attention.

The lamppost figure of Hannibal Jones towered in the doorway. Like a shroud on a corpse, a greatcoat swathed his cadaverous form. "Good afternoon, my lord. Looking for this?"

He held up a piece of notebook paper. Even from across the room, Brand could read the two neatly penned words: "You're next."

He strode forward. "Let me see that."

Jones tucked the note in his pocket. "With all due respect, my lord, this is documentation of a crime and property of the law."

Restraining his temper, Brand said tightly, "I only want to examine the penmanship."

"Or perhaps to destroy the evidence of your own treachery."

"Dammit, that isn't my handwriting. I'll be happy to provide you with a sample."

"I already have compared it to the betting book at your club. There are . . . similarities."

"Like hell. I hadn't any reason to murder Weatherby. We were friends." Or at least they had been before Weatherby's addiction had gotten the better of him.

"He'd lost a sizable sum to you at the gaming table several months ago. A waiter from your club verified that Weatherby signed an IOU. Did he ever repay you?"

"I forgave the debt," Brand said tightly. "You're grasping at straws."

Jones's mouth twisted in a caricature of a smile. "In my profession, I've learned that money can ofttimes move a man to kill. Where were you returning from last evening?"

Brand clenched his jaw. Though he hated being forced to explain himself, he knew the man could unearth the truth by other means. It would only look worse if Brand lied. "I attended a party at Clifford Vaughn's home."

"Another former member of this hellfire club."

"Who told you our names?"

"Never mind that. About last evening. I'm wondering why Lady Charlotte Quinton accompanied you." The slight sneer on his gaunt face indicated that he considered her a whore.

Brand seized a fistful of the man's coat. Not a wise way to acquit himself of a crime, he knew, yet his rage defied the leash of common sense. "Leave the lady out of this," he said through his teeth. "Or by God, I'll make sure you end up with your ass in the street and your head on a pike."

Chapter 15

FANCY'S FOLLY

Watching for Brand, Charlotte walked Fancy in the park across the street from the house.

The day was blustery and overcast with a chill wind that skirmished with her skirts and penetrated her pelisse. From time to time, an icy raindrop struck her face. But she kept to the graveled path where she could view the cobbled road in both directions. Brand's smart gray curricle was nowhere in sight.

Charlotte curled her cold, gloved fingers around the leash. Hoping to catch him alone before he went inside, she had been tramping the grounds out here for nearly an hour, and even Fancy was beginning to tire of barking at squirrels, sniffing bushes, and growling at the occasional male passerby.

Only the heat of Charlotte's feverish thoughts kept her warm.

She hadn't yet decided whether or not to talk to Brand about Vivien's revelations. She wanted to wrest the truth from him as to why he'd betrayed his best friend and had an affair with Michael's first wife. But her anger was tempered by the memory of that look on his face when he'd embraced Amy. Soft. Loving. Tormented.

Dear God, Brand had a *daughter*. Beautiful Amy with

her hazel eyes and impertinent manner. Now that Charlotte had had the chance to accustom herself to the idea, she could note a slight similarity of countenance. The girl had exactly the same carefree grin that Brand had had while growing up.

Did he regret never claiming Amy? Did he ever wish she'd call him Papa or come to him for comfort when she'd skinned her elbow? Did he ache at the thought of all he'd missed in her upbringing?

Charlotte felt a lump in her throat. No, Brand didn't want the responsibilities of a family. On more than one occasion, he had made that emphatic point, most recently at the Vaughns' party.

I'm not marrying anyone. Do I make myself clear?

Her heart felt so low she wanted to weep. Was he simply an incurable rogue who would never settle down? Or had he loved Grace so desperately that no other woman could ever take her place?

Now that the pieces of the puzzle were all in place, Charlotte realized that the change in him from insouciant rake to cynical misogynist had coincided with Grace's death. Grace, the woman he'd been intending to run away with to the Continent.

Fancy growled. But Charlotte heard it only on the periphery of her awareness. So when a male voice spoke, she jumped.

"Good afternoon, my lady."

Her hand on the bodice of her pelisse, she whirled around. Harold Rountree stood in front of her, a beaver hat topping his smiling features and a fine wool coat delineating his fit form. He swept off the hat and held out a bunch of violets and jonquils.

Charlotte took the bouquet and absently sniffed the

lovely aroma. "Thank you, but . . . good heavens. Where did you come from?"

"Faversham's house," he said, replacing his hat. "The maid said you'd gone for a walk, so I looked for you here."

"I didn't notice you at the front door."

"I went to the tradesmen's entrance." Mr. Rountree didn't look pleased to be forced to such measures. "Because of Faversham's ultimatum."

Her mind had been so focused on Vivien's revelations, it took a moment to recall what Brand had said. *If he so much as places his big toe on my front doorstep, I'll put a bullet through his heart.*

In a note to Mr. Rountree, Charlotte had related the gist of those words. With an apologetic smile, she said, "I'm sorry. Perhaps you'd care to accompany me on my walk."

Mr. Rountree frowned at Fancy, baring her teeth behind the curtain of Charlotte's skirts. "I'd like that."

"Don't worry about Fancy," Charlotte said, tucking the bouquet in the crook of her arm. "She won't bother you so long as you keep your distance. Now, tell me how your campaign is progressing."

As they strolled, he maintained a circumspect space between them. "I've made only moderate strides in aligning political support," he said. "It's a delicate matter, convincing people to support one's platform, especially when one has few connections among the nobility. But enough of that dreary talk. I came here to discuss a more personal matter. To find out if you've considered my proposal."

His proposal. His *marriage* proposal.

Guilt lurched inside her, for she'd lain awake into the

wee hours remembering another man's kiss. A man who would never, ever make her an honorable offer. A man who would never fulfill her dreams of marriage and family.

But Mr. Rountree wanted to give her all that. If only she could forget her hopeless longing for Brand.

"I'm afraid I haven't yet come to a decision," she hedged. "I thought we'd agreed on a fortnight."

"I couldn't stay away," he said with unusual fervency. "Pray forgive me for pressing you, my lady, but I can think of naught else but you. I would be proud to call you my wife."

The candor in his brown eyes called to her aching heart. Yet she mustn't trust him until the murderer was found. "Nevertheless, I'd like to think more on the matter. I'll give you my answer next week."

"It's that dreadful league." Clearly displeased, he jammed his hands into the pockets of his coat. "I do wish there was a way to assure you I've changed."

Charlotte seized the chance to question him, to see how he reacted to certain names. "Speaking of the league, did you hear the news about Sir John Parkinson?"

Mr. Rountree stopped and stared at her. "Parkinson? How do you know that knave? I hope to goodness Faversham hasn't been introducing you to all of his dissolute friends."

"I've met a few here and there, and it would help tremendously if you'd share your opinion of them. As for Parkinson, he professes to have shunned his evil ways. The news is that he's now a minister at the Church of the True Believers."

"Eh? Now there's a miracle, indeed."

Mr. Rountree couldn't have feigned that look of amazement. As they resumed walking, Charlotte tried him on another name. "I've also made the acquaintance of Lord Clifford Vaughn."

"Vaughn!" Mr. Rountree's disgusted look returned. "If that scoundrel offers to read any poetry to you, tell him to desist at once."

"Oh?" she said innocently. "Why is that?"

"Because it's not the sort of verse a lady should hear."

She was tempted to tease him further, but that might stir his suspicions as to where she'd been the previous night. "All right, I'll take careful note of your advice. I also met a Colonel Tom Ransom, lately of His Majesty's cavalry. He seemed a genial fellow."

"Bah. Another reprobate who hides his predilections from virtuous young ladies like yourself."

"But he must be an honorable man. He's betrothed to Lady Belinda, Lord Pomeroy's daughter."

"Pray God she realizes her error before it's too late." Mr. Rountree glanced right and left as if eavesdroppers lurked in the barren bushes. "You don't wish to associate with such a scoundrel. He's done acts that would put even Faversham to the blush."

"Truly? I thought Brand was the worst of all reprobates."

Mr. Rountree lowered his eyebrows. "Please don't ask me to elaborate on these matters. The topic is unfit for your ears."

Though intrigued by his secretiveness, Charlotte deemed it wise to move on. Trying to look nonchalant, she lifted the bouquet to her nose and breathed deeply.

"What do you know of a rather introspective man named Weatherby?"

Mr. Rountree shook his head. "That one is as bad as the others," he said in a tone of distaste. "Devoted to smoking his life away. I never knew him very well."

"And Uriah Lane? He rather reminded me of a bear." He was pawing his doxy at the party, she remembered in revulsion.

"Lane! Why the man thinks of naught but—" Mr. Rountree stopped again, his manner agitated. "My lady, you have me worried with all this talk. Are not the Rosebuds monitoring your circle of acquaintances?"

Charlotte paused on the pathway. "They're indisposed, as you know. But you've been a great help. I'll know whom to avoid now that I can see the true nature of those men."

But what of Mr. Rountree's true nature? The possibility that he could be fooling her was horrifying, yet Charlotte had to consider it. Was he so bent on his political career that he would murder those who might identify him as a former member of the Lucifer League?

"My dear lady, you must promise not to associate with these men," Mr. Rountree said, grasping one of her gloved hands. "I would gladly protect you with my life— ouch—dammit!"

Fancy had lunged, bitten, and retreated.

Mr. Rountree hopped on one foot and rubbed his ankle.

Charlotte gasped. "Fancy! Not again!"

Just when she thought matters could get no worse, a movement across the street caught her attention. Brand had emerged from his house and was stalking straight toward them.

• • •

There'd be hell to pay if Hannibal Jones was spying in the bushes, Brand thought grimly. Jones's chief suspect was about to commit murder in broad daylight.

He dodged a passing dray, never taking his gaze from the couple in the square. Rountree was capering around like a dance school failure while Charlotte hovered close, bending over to view his ankle. If Brand hadn't been so choked by rage, he'd have enjoyed the fact that Fancy had struck again.

And he'd certainly have savored the sight of Charlotte's trim backside, sheathed by a clingy green skirt. A bouquet of spring flowers filled her arm. A gift from her blasted suitor.

He cleared a low boxwood hedge and seized Rountree by the arm so that he tottered on one foot. "What the devil are you doing here?"

"Faversham! Kindly desist. I'm injured—"

"You'll be six feet under in a moment."

Charlotte released a huff. "Leave go of him at once, Brand."

"With pleasure." He drew back and landed a blow to Rountree's jaw. The satisfying jolt jarred his arm. It felt far better than any punch delivered in a sparring match at the gymnasium.

Rountree staggered backward and fell to the hard-packed earth. Holding his reddened jaw, he shook his head as if dazed.

Charlotte ran to him, dropping her flowers and kneeling on the path. "Mr. Rountree! Are you all right?"

"The bastard will be fine. So long as he doesn't come within a mile of here ever again." Brand picked up a barking, snarling Fancy. "Good show, furball. But you don't bite a man when he's down."

"You!" Charlotte flashed Brand a furious glare. "How dare you strike him?"

Brand ignored her, petting the dog in calming strokes. "Stand up like a man, Rountree. I want a word with you."

Rountree scrambled to his feet, his angry gaze on Brand. "This is an outrage," he snapped. "I've done nothing to deserve such rough treatment."

"Where were you last night?"

"At my hotel. Why do you ask?"

"Do you have any witnesses to that?"

Rountree's eyes shifted away for an instant. "Why, no . . . I was asleep."

Liar. The sod either had had a woman in his room or he'd been out slitting wrists.

"For heaven's sake, stop badgering him." Charlotte picked up her flowers and advanced on Brand, flourishing the bouquet like a weapon. "You're acting like a cretin. What is this all about?"

"Weatherby was murdered last night."

She halted, pressed her hand to her mouth, and made a sound of horrified distress.

"Weatherby?" Rountree said, frowning. "Do you mean James Weatherby?"

"Of course," Brand stated. "And I'm wondering what you know about the matter."

"*I?* What would I know of such a crime?"

"You'd know quite a lot if you were there."

A look that was equal parts bafflement, anger, and alarm crossed Rountree's face. He edged closer to Charlotte. In an undertone, he said, "My lady, the man's a raving lunatic. You'd best come with me."

"Charlotte stays right here," Brand said through his teeth. "It's you who'll go. Before *I* take a mind to murder."

Rountree drew himself up. "I shan't leave the lady unprotected."

"I'll be all right, Mr. Rountree," Charlotte said in a subdued tone. "I'll go inside straightaway, and the Rosebuds can chaperon me. You may leave now in good conscience."

"But your safety—"

"Brand is only distressed over losing a friend. I'm perfectly safe with him."

She gave Rountree her full attention, patting him on the arm, fussing over a few leaves that stuck to the sleeve of his coat. A low growl rumbled from Fancy, and Brand felt like joining the symphony.

"Move," he snapped.

Rountree had the sense to back away. Keeping a wary watch on Brand, he tipped his hat to Charlotte. "Should the need arise, my lady, send word to me at the Harris Hotel in Westminster. Anytime, day or night."

He had the effrontery to shoot Brand a quelling stare before he set off down the path, glancing back now and then as if he expected Brand to ravish her on the spot.

Brand turned to see Charlotte gazing at him with an odd intensity. She had never looked more beautiful, with strands of chestnut hair curled around her face and her eyes the mysterious deep green of a forest. The glow of vitality to her delicate features made his throat catch. She might be strong in spirit, but she was too damned vulnerable and far too trusting. He ached to pull her into his arms and protect her from harm.

Instead, he pulled the bouquet out of her hand and

tossed the hated thing at the bushes. Jonquils and violets rained over the barren ground.

"What do you think you're doing?" she said indignantly.

"I won't have his flowers in my house, that's what." Taking her arm, Brand forcibly drew her across the street. "That was a damned foolish thing to do, meeting him here."

"It wasn't an arranged meeting," she said in a milder tone, keeping up with his long strides. "I was watching for your curricle when he came to call."

"I entered through the back. There's no sense in calling for a groom to take the carriage round." Her pensive manner baffled him. What had happened to her anger? A thought gripped him. "Why were you watching for me? Has something happened?"

"No, certainly not!" She flashed him a small smile that somehow seemed forced. "It was just that . . . I wanted to know if you'd done any more investigating, that's all."

He had the feeling that wasn't all, but they had reached the house, and they went up the steps and into the foyer. After giving their coats to a footman, Brand hustled her into the library for a private talk.

He set Fancy on the floor, unfastened the leather lead, and looked up at Charlotte. Once again, she was regarding him with that rapt expression, and the hint of softness there made his pulse leap and his mind go blank to all but her lovely presence. Was she thinking about that kiss they'd shared in bed? Had she forgiven him for his arrogant trick?

God, he hoped so. More than he ought to hope. "Tell me what's on your mind."

"It's nothing, really." Her gaze lowered a fraction, then met his again, cooler now, the familiar Charlotte. "As I said, I was just wondering if you'd made any inquiries while you were out. I never imagined you'd bring such terrible news."

So she didn't want to talk about their kiss. It was better they didn't, anyway. And murder was a sobering diversion.

Brand gave her a brief summary of the events, glossing over his encounter with Hannibal Jones. "There was a note left, same as the others, but the bastard wouldn't let me have a close look at it."

Charlotte had gone pale. Seemingly disinclined to sit, she wandered about the room, touching a book here and there. "He's working on the investigation, Brand. You should be pleased about that. I know I am."

"He's only getting in the way. He doesn't know these men the way I do." Frustrated, Brand paced after her. "If I could compare that note to the handwriting samples I've collected, we'd be closer to a solution."

"Then give the samples to Mr. Jones," she said with infuriating logic. "I have some letters from Mr. Rountree that I'd be happy to contribute."

Welcoming the chance to vent his seething emotions, Brand stopped in front of her. "So you agree Rountree's a suspect? Yet you were out there walking with him."

"I was asking him questions, though I'm afraid I didn't learn anything new." She opened a book and paged through it as if to find an answer there.

"You should be afraid, dammit." Quailing at the thought of harm coming to her, he snatched the book out of her hand and shoved it back on the shelf. "You took a senseless risk. You should have come back into the house the instant you saw him."

"For heaven's sake, Brand. *You're* in far more danger than I am."

Her voice vibrated with feeling, and that big, green-eyed gaze stimulated his heartbeat—along with another part of him. "I can take care of myself," he said testily. "You're a woman and easily overpowered."

Charlotte pursed her lips. Lovely, kissable lips in need of softening. "If I may point out, five *men* have been murdered. And you were once a member of the league."

Would she truly care if he died? Stupid, irrelevant question.

Resisting the urge to touch her, he rubbed his skinned knuckles. "Then bring on the murderer. I'd welcome the chance to trounce him, too."

"Men." Charlotte shook her head. Rather than scold him, she merely gave him that contemplative look again. The one that made him uneasy about what she was thinking. "Brand, I'm sorry . . ."

"For disobeying me? You ought to be."

"Not that. I'm sorry . . ."—she paused again—"I'm sorry about Weatherby."

Why did he have the feeling that wasn't what she'd meant to say? The sympathy in her gaze seemed genuine, so soft and heartfelt he wanted to pour out his anger and grief over a wasted life. "We weren't close friends," he said in a gruff tone. "But . . . thank you."

Charlotte parted her lips as if to speak again. Her eyes certainly spoke volumes. Intense, mysterious, inviting. He wanted to forget about murder, forget about the world, and fathom only the depths of her kiss. A tender, seductive kiss that would stir her to mindless passion in the space of five seconds. He wanted to run his hands over her body and claim all that sweet, alluring femininity for himself. Watching her, he leaned forward by degrees, slowly closing the distance between them.

She glanced at his mouth, then said in a low husky voice, "If you'll excuse me, I need to go and dress. Michael and Vivien and Amy are coming for dinner." Leaving him stunned by the shelves, Charlotte headed toward the door.

Amy. Nothing else could have distracted him so completely. Had Charlotte said that on purpose? Because she *knew* something?

Hips swaying, she walked out of the library without looking back. Her nonchalance tempered his fears. If she knew the truth, she would have thrown it in his face. Charlotte would never miss an opportunity to roast him over the hot coals of guilt.

He blew out a long breath. So what the hell had been on her mind, then?

Ears perked, Fancy took a step as if to follow her mistress, then trotted to Brand and sat down in front of him, head tilted inquiringly.

"So, furball, you're puzzled, too," Brand said, pulling his gaze from the empty doorway. "What do you suppose that was all about?"

Fancy wagged her scruffy brown tail.

Brand hunkered down and regarded the dog. She was an ugly cur, but at least that bare patch on her back leg was growing fuzz. "Dammit, you're female. You're supposed to understand women better than I do."

Whining, Fancy rolled over, giving him an appealing look.

"Oh, is that it? You only want something." Brand

rubbed the dog's belly. "Your mistress should be so transparent about her thoughts."

His moody gaze returned to the doorway. He disliked this feeling that he'd missed something. He disliked even more his growing preoccupation with Charlotte. He ought to be focused on the investigation. But she had him tied in knots, locked in lust, panting at her feet like a hopeful pup.

And Brand suspected he wouldn't be free until they were lovers.

Chapter 16
MISS DARBY'S PLEA

The next morning, Charlotte was burrowed in bed, sipping tea and contemplating the mystery, when the message arrived.

The day had dawned cold and rainy. The patter of droplets on the window glass had a lulling effect. Though she'd awakened early, she'd been loath to leave the cozy warmth of the covers. Instead, she had indulged herself with a breakfast tray and thoughts of Brand.

As much as Charlotte craved to know his version of the story, she had decided not to broach the topic of Amy just yet. At dinner the previous evening, he had shown no particular interest in the girl. In fact, Charlotte would never have suspected any connection between them had Vivien not revealed that secret.

But it was best to set personal matters aside for the moment. Brand had enough on his mind with the murders. *She* had enough on *her* mind with worrying about him.

Weatherby's death served as a ghastly reminder of danger. The killer was out there somewhere, plotting and planning. What if Brand was his next target?

The onslaught of icy fear made her shudder. She gazed down into the dregs of her tea, wishing she could conjure the future like a gypsy fortune-teller. Dear God, if only she could assure herself of his safety. Given his reckless nature, the manly fool would walk straight into peril.

The door opened and Nan scurried into the chamber with Fancy, having let the dog outside. The maid's plump features were flushed with cold and bright with interest. "There be a lady waitin' for thee downstairs in the drawin' room."

"A visitor? At this early hour?" It was an unwritten rule in the *ton* that no one came calling before the afternoon.

"She's a wee thing, fluttery as a wren. Her name is Miss Darby."

Surprised, Charlotte threw back the coverlet and sprang out of bed, her bare toes curling against the frigid floor. For Clifford Vaughn's shy cousin to venture here at all, let alone at so unorthodox a time, could only mean urgent news. "I must get dressed at once."

With Nan's help, Charlotte managed to don a long-sleeved maroon gown and arrange her hair in under ten minutes. She hastened downstairs into the huge drawing room with its chandeliers and groupings of chaises. At first glance, she was puzzled to find the room empty. Until she turned and spied Miss Darby sitting alone on a straight-backed chair just inside the doorway.

The young woman made a forlorn figure. Rainwater saturated the hem of her drab gray cloak, and the damp hood draped her brown hair. Her face looked small and wan, and she clenched her gloved fingers together in her lap.

Although a fire burned merrily across the room, the place by the door was drafty and cold.

"Forgive me for keeping you waiting," Charlotte said, escorting her toward a stuffed green chair by the fireplace. "You must be chilled. Come closer to the hearth. Has no one brought you tea?"

Miss Darby perched on the edge of her seat. "Please, no," she murmured. "I couldn't swallow a drop."

"You're distraught. Would you care to tell me what's wrong?"

"Yes, thank you. I—I'm sorry . . . it's so early. I feared you might be abed."

"I was awake, so it's quite all right. I'm happy to help you no matter what time of day or night." Concerned, Charlotte took the chair beside her. "Let's not waste time on banalities, though. Something must be dreadfully amiss to bring you here in such a state."

Miss Darby gave a jerky nod. "I—I overheard my cousin talking last evening. You'll think ill of me for listening, but . . ."

Charlotte would have eavesdropped, too, if she'd lived with the Vaughns. If for no other reason than self-preservation. "I think you're clever and brave to come here and tell me about it. Go on."

Miss Darby bit her lip. "My cousin—Clifford—was making plans with Lydia. Horrid plans."

"Plans?"

"Yes. They're attending an awful event this afternoon." Tears swam in Miss Darby's blue eyes. "Oh, my lady, I can't bear to think of those poor little creatures being mauled. I hoped *you* might put a stop to it."

Charlotte felt a knell of alarm. "Dear God. What creatures?"

Miss Darby sniffled woefully. "Dogs, my lady. 'Tis a fight involving *dogs*. A fight to the *death*."

• • •

Hurrying along the downstairs corridor, Nan glanced over her shoulder. Only the stone statues in niches watched her. Still, she strove to look purposeful as if she were on an important errand for her mistress rather than planning a criminal act.

Lady Charlotte had rushed out with the earl half an hour ago. The mistress had been in a dither all morning, going on about the cruelty of some people toward animals. His lordship had tried to convince her to stay home, but Nan could have predicted his failure. When her ladyship was on a mission, nothing could dissuade her.

For all their quarreling, there was an attraction between those two. They were often in each other's company, and Nan had noticed her ladyship's preoccupation with him. She couldn't blame Lady Charlotte. The devil earl was so much more exciting than that namby-pamby Mr. Rountree.

What if his lordship asked Lady Charlotte to marry him?

If the mistress became countess, Nan's stature would rise, too.

For a moment, Nan let herself imagine living in this house forever, where meat was served at every meal in the servants' hall, where she had a warm bed in which to sleep at night. She liked handling Lady Charlotte's new wardrobe, the silks and linens so cool and smooth to her fingers. She didn't really mind her duties, either, except for the sewing and mending, which often ended in a tangled mess. And it made her proud to collect that quid at the end of the month, to know she'd earned every pence of it through hard work.

Yes, she'd enjoy staying here. If not for Giffles.

Nan looked over her shoulder again. The passageway was empty, praise Jesus. She'd chosen her time well, while the rest of the staff was enjoying a leisurely luncheon. And while the stuffy old valet had gone out on an errand for the master.

She'd originally intended to accomplish her purpose at night, when everyone was asleep, but Giffles always seemed to be prowling the house, peering over her shoulder, emerging out of nowhere and frightening her half to death. Ever since he'd caught her sneaking back into the kitchen, he had regarded her with suspicion. So she'd had no choice but to do this deed in the light of day when she stood a better chance of brazening her way out of any encounter.

Not that she intended to get caught.

Her cheap leather shoes squeaked on the marble floor. She passed huge rooms filled with gold furniture and rich draperies. Mayhap she wouldn't find what she was seeking on this floor. Mayhap it was in his lordship's bedchamber upstairs.

Then she spied it through a doorway. A desk. A big fancy one, just as Dick had told her to locate.

Scurrying into the room, Nan looked in amazement at the shelves and shelves of books. She'd never learned her letters, girls like her never did. What did the devil earl want with so many volumes? Then she swallowed hard to think how clever he must be.

A clever man could catch a thief.

Nan stood at the desk, her fingers tensed around the brass handle of the top drawer. She couldn't force herself to draw it open. Queasiness roiled in her stomach. How could she steal from his lordship? She'd be caught, sent to prison, perhaps to the gallows. How could she shame Lady Charlotte, who had been so good to her?

For Dick. It was for Dick, whom she loved and feared with a sick desperation. She closed her eyes, trying to bolster her courage with the memory of their last meeting.

"Money's like water to these rich toffs. The bugger won't even notice if ye nick a bag o' gold coins from 'is strongbox."

"Please, thee mustn't ask me. I promised Lady Charlotte—"

"An' what about yer promise to me?" Dick smoothed his finger down her cheek. *"Ye've turned soft, Nan Killigrew. Ye've fergotten 'ow I never told nobody about the blood on yer 'ands."*

"Nay, I haven't," she whispered. Except for the mistress, Dick was the only one who knew her secret, the only one who could turn her over to the court. He'd been loyal and true and she could do no less. *"All right, I'll do it. I'll steal the money and bring it to thee . . ."*

"You there."

Her eyes snapped open. A big bear of a man filled the doorway of the library. A burly toff in fancy garb.

Hiding her shock, Nan released the drawer handle and sidled out from behind the desk. She bobbed a curtsy and prayed he wouldn't question her presence here.

"Beg pardon, sir. I'll finish my cleanin' later." She was babbling, and servants were supposed to slip silently away whenever their betters needed use of the chamber.

When she tried to go past him, however, he took her

arm. "Here now. No need to run off. What's your name?"

Nan recognized the husky note in his voice, the way he stared straight at her bosom. *No.* A new sort of panic filled her. Her heart was pounding so fast, she could scarcely speak. "Nan."

The man gave her a little shove, pushing her back against the wall. "Well, Nan. You're a buxom handful. Faversham been riding you much?"

The shelves bit into her back, but she was more conscious of his bulk pressing into her. His breath stank of liquor, same as her father's once had. "Nay, sir, never. But he'll be angry if I don't finish my duties."

"I won't keep you long." He thrust the door shut with his foot, a leering smile on his broad face. "Go and lie on the desk, girl. We can have us a ride, you and I. You'll enjoy it. The other maids always do."

Trying to think of a way out, she backed slowly away. Like any girl, she liked a good tumble, but not now, not like this, not with a man whose massive size frightened her. He was coming toward her, his fingers fumbling with the buttons of his breeches. She bumped into the edge of the desk and couldn't move any farther.

"Don't stand there like a cow. Lift your skirts at once."

A touch of impatience had entered that cultured voice, magnifying her alarm. "Sir, please, I daren't. I'll lose my post—"

"Not if we're quick about it. Now quit whining and do as I say." His breeches half unbuttoned, he roughly pushed himself against her again, pawing her breasts, and Nan leaned backward on the desk in an effort to evade him. It was no use, he was pulling at her skirts and she was afraid to struggle, afraid that he might lash out with his fists in anger.

Someone cleared his throat. "Pardon me."

A rush of mortification and relief strangled her.

There in the doorway stood Giffles. Stuffy, priggish, wonderful Giffles with his white-gloved hands and dull brown suit. "I wish to inform you, Mr. Lane, that his lordship has gone out for the afternoon."

Clearly irritated, Mr. Lane swiveled his big head around. "Yes, well, get on with you, then."

The valet didn't move. "Perhaps you would allow me to show you to the door."

"I'll find my own way, damn you."

Giffles was silent a moment, a statue in the doorway. Without a hint of disrespect in his manner, he said, "If I may point out, sir, his lordship is rather fond of that desk."

Mr. Lane cursed roundly. He straightened, keeping his back to the valet as he fastened his buttons. All the while he muttered, "Hang it all. Can't a man have a bit of fun without being interrupted? Bloody desk, indeed."

Nan sat up shakily, fearing to stand lest her legs give out. Her teeth chattered and her bosom heaved. Tidying her skirts, she rejoiced at her escape—at least until Mr. Lane stomped out and she was left alone with her savior.

Giffles regarded her as if she were a slug he'd squashed beneath his perfectly polished shoe. His disapproving air cast a shroud over the library. "I'm waiting for your explanation, Miss Killigrew."

There was no hint of the kind man who'd held her while she'd wept. No sign of the tender man who'd calmed her fears. And no reason for her to feel such a desperate need to throw herself into the safety of his arms again.

The censure on his face made her miserable. "I—I know how it looked, sir, but thee mustn't think ill of me. He grabbed me, Mr. Lane did. He forced me down here. He told me t' lift my skirts so that he could—"

"Enough. I am well aware of Mr. Lane's culpability. You'll stay away from him in the future."

"Yes, sir."

"You will also cease wandering about at will. You are allowed only in the basement rooms, Lady Charlotte's bedchamber, and the attic. You've no business whatsoever on this floor." His gaze suspicious, he took a step toward her. "So why were you here?"

The gold coins. Her thievery gone awry. Oh, why hadn't she been more quick about it?

Too late, she realized that it would have been better to let Giffles think she'd arranged the tryst with Mr. Lane. "The mistress asked me t' fetch her a book," she improvised. "For when she returned."

"Which book?"

Nan's mouth went dry. Her gaze flitted over all the volumes with the mysterious gold-leaf lettering on the spines. There were so many it boggled the mind. She snatched one at random. "This one."

He took it from her. "Macqueer's *Elements of Chemistry*. Unless her ladyship is having trouble sleeping, I doubt she'd ask for this."

"She told me that any book would do."

Giffles raised an eyebrow as if he saw right through her transparent fib. Turning his attention to the shelves, he chose a volume and handed it to her. "Here you go. The ladies always enjoy the sonnets of Shakespeare."

Like the master, Giffles was lettered, too. He was more than quick enough to realize she'd been up to no good. He would be watching her even more closely now. Yet somehow, Nan felt worse at the knowledge of his ill opinion than at confessing her failure to Dick. "Thank you, sir. I didn't know."

Aware of his keen gaze, she mustered a show of confidence as she left the library. But inside, she was quaking at the closeness of her escape.

Chapter 17

AN UNEXPECTED VISITOR

Brand cursed himself for letting Charlotte talk him into something so damned risky.

As they emerged from the coach in a tumbledown area near the docks, he scanned the array of fine carriages parked along the narrow street. The rain had slowed to a fine mist that left the pavement slick. From inside the brick warehouse came the shouts and cheers of men.

"Oh, dear *heavens*," Charlotte said in a strained voice. "We have to hurry. They've already begun."

He clamped his hands onto her shoulders and held her immobile. She was pale, her lips compressed, her slender form taut with resolution. Beneath that sensible green bonnet, wisps of lustrous chestnut hair curled from the damp weather. She looked strong in spirit, ready to take on a throng of angry men, and it scared the devil out of him.

"You'd be better off waiting out here with the coachman," he said for the umpteenth time. "This is no place for a lady."

"I'm going with you, Brand. And that's that."

He recognized the set of that dainty jaw. "Have it your way, then, but you'll abide by our agreement," he warned. "I'll take the risks, not you. One wrong move, and this whole fool scheme could fall down around our ears. Do you understand me?"

Charlotte nodded crisply.

He had his doubts about her compliance. But short of binding and gagging her, he could only hope she'd have the sense to obey.

If indeed Charlotte Quinton had ever shown any sense.

According to plan, two of his most trusted footmen accompanied them. Raleigh was the husky son of a tenant farmer on the estate in Devon, while Hayward's family had served the Earls of Faversham for the past century. Both had been instructed in their roles. And both appeared eager to participate in an adventure. Brand acknowledged his own rush of high anticipation.

Inside the warehouse, flickering oil lamps augmented the meager daylight that trickled through the grimy windows. The air was pungent with the odor of sour wine from the huge wooden casks rolled against one wall. But today, the place had been put to use for something less innocuous than storage. The cavernous interior had the atmosphere of a carnival.

In the center of the room, a crowd of perhaps a hundred gathered around a square enclosure formed by stakes and ropes. Gentlemen stood elbow to elbow with rough characters from the neighborhood. The only other woman present was Lydia, standing at ringside with her husband, their avaricious attention on the pair of growling, snapping dogs in the arena.

Charlotte let out a moan that was almost inaudible in the clamor of voices. She stood on tiptoe, trying to see over the heads of the spectators. It was better she didn't see, Brand thought grimly. When it came to animals, she was too tenderhearted for her own good.

He stopped her in the shadows of a pillar. "Stay right here," he ordered. "If you move an inch, Hayward has my permission to take you back to the coach, willing or not." He nodded at the tall footman who took up a stance at her side.

But she paid the servant no heed. Her big-eyed attention was on Brand. "Do you have everything?"

"Yes." He patted the pocket of his greatcoat.

As he turned to go, she touched his arm. "Be careful."

A man could drown in those fathomless green eyes. That was why he'd agreed to this damned plan. Because of that blasted, heartfelt, I'm-depending-on-you look.

No, it was the fact that he relished the task to come. Dogfights were a cruel sport he'd always shunned.

He motioned to Raleigh, and they headed toward the ring. As Brand made his way through the crush of shouting men, he earned numerous angry looks and curses. Raleigh endured the same, coming up to the corner of the ring from the other side and elbowing a path to the front.

It was a brutal exhibition. Bred and trained to fight, the two bull terriers battled like gladiators, one white and one gray, wrestling and lunging and biting. At a whistle from the timekeeper, their handlers broke the dogs apart and took them back to their respective corners for a brief rest.

At the start of the next round, one dog would be held in place and the other released to rush across the ring and resume the fight. The match would continue in that manner until one of the dogs was so sorely injured he'd refuse to attack. The other dog would then be allowed to finish off his opponent.

It was the white's turn to strike. Judging by his challenging stance, snarling and straining at his trainer's grip on the collar, he was clearly the stronger, more vicious dog.

Making a slight alteration of plan, Brand came up behind the Vaughns, who stood close to the corner of the ropes. The couple didn't notice him; they were too busy exhorting the gray dog that lay there, bloodied and weak. "Get up, you little bugger," Lydia snapped. "Kick him, Cliffie."

"Don't be stupid," Vaughn said. "He still has enough in him to shred my leg."

"Better that than lose fifty guineas."

"Hah! You do it then. Your skirts will protect you. Oh, never mind, the old boy's getting to his feet."

Brand wanted to knock their fool heads together. Better yet, toss them into the ring. Now there would be a sport worth watching.

Raleigh was in place, waiting for the signal. Brand slipped the flask out of his pocket. The timekeeper announced the next round, the white dog was released and came charging across the ring, straight at the gray.

While the crowd roared, Brand held a deep breath, pulled out the cork, and splashed the entire contents of the flask onto the floor inside the ring and directly in front of the quarrelsome Vaughns.

Lydia yelped, staggering and coughing, clinging to her husband, who suffered a similar reaction. As the fumes rapidly spread, every man around them began choking and cursing, retreating from the ring in a mad rush. Even the handlers and the timekeeper fled with eyes streaming from the acrid ammonia stench.

To shield himself from the worst of it, Brand knotted a length of cloth over his nose and mouth. He took advantage of the confusion, ducked under the ropes, and made straight for the dogs. Raleigh already had a grip on the white's hind legs and was wrestling the aggressive dog backward. Brand subdued the gray in the same manner, hauling him to the opposite side of the ring.

The terrier didn't put up much of a fight. His head and body was a mass of bloody gashes, and he labored for breath, as affected by the fumes as the spectators.

Charlotte came rushing out of the crowd, a handkerchief held to her nose. When she saw the dog, she let out a small keening cry and dropped to her knees beside him.

"Dammit," Brand said, yanking off his makeshift mask. "I told you to stay put."

Ignoring him, she focused her full attention on the panting animal. "Poor little creature. We have to help him."

She reached to the dog, and Brand thrust out his arm to stop her. "For God's sake, don't touch him. He'll snap at you."

As he spoke, Brand took the muzzle from his pocket and eased it over that torn and bloodied face. Charlotte immediately bent over the dog, crooning and dabbing at the wounds with her handkerchief. Amazingly, the gray terrier wagged his tail slightly, resting his head against her knee as if he recognized a kindred spirit.

"Oh, you poor dear. You poor, poor dear. Don't worry, I'll take care of you now." She cast a distraught, teary-eyed glance at Brand. "He won't die, will he?"

"He's a tough bloke," Brand said, grimly hoping for

the best. "He's somewhat incapacitated by the fumes, that's all. None of his injuries appear to be mortal."

"We can't give him back," she said in a low, passionate tone. "They'll hurt him, Brand, make him fight again. I *must* keep him."

That look of wretched desperation wrapped around his chest like shackles. He should have anticipated such an appeal.

The fight had been routed, the crowd had dispersed, and Brand had accomplished his purpose. That was all he'd agreed to do. "You don't know what you're asking, Char. He's bred to kill. He'd eat Fancy for breakfast."

"We can keep him out in the stables," Charlotte said rapidly. "And once he's recovered, he might be taken to Devon, to live in the country. Please, Brand. If you give him back, you'll be signing his death warrant."

She was right, dammit. And he had to admit he too had a soft spot for the terrier, who managed to lick feebly at his bloodied, mangled paw despite the muzzle. He seemed to possess a somewhat gentler nature than the growling, malevolent dog that Raleigh and Hayward had subdued a short distance away.

From across the warehouse, the owner came charging forward. He was a stout, short-legged ruffian much like the bull terriers he bred. And every bit as vicious-looking. " 'Ere now, what're ye doin' there? That's me property."

Charlotte shot to her feet. "I'm Lady Charlotte Quinton, and I'm confiscating this animal on charges of flagrant cruelty."

"I don't care if ye're flamin' *Queen* Charlotte. Paddy belongs t' me."

Bloody hell. Brand stood up and gave the man his

lordliest glare. "I'm Lord Faversham. I'd like to purchase the dog."

A crafty gleam entered the man's eyes. "Purchase, ye say? This one's me best fighter. 'Ad a bit of a ill luck today, but 'e's worth 'is weight in gold."

"Forty pounds, then. Send your bill to my house in Grosvenor Square."

"Aye, m'lord." Rubbing his hands, the man trotted away with nary a glance for the esteemed and wounded Paddy.

Charlotte looked somewhat deflated to be knocked off her high pillar of righteousness. But she gave Brand only a speaking glance before returning her attention to the dog.

Raleigh carried the injured animal out to the coach. The Vaughns were nowhere to be seen. With the abrupt ending of the fight, most of the carriages had gone, taking the nobility off to some other illicit pursuit.

Gad, he was sick of them all. At least for the moment.

Charlotte wrapped Paddy in a rug and sat down on the floor of the coach with the dog, murmuring noises of sympathy and succor. While the vehicle rumbled over the cobblestoned streets, Brand reclined against the cushions and moodily watched the two.

He watched Charlotte.

Five years ago, he would never have imagined himself assisting her in such a harebrained scheme. And yet was it so unusual? An old memory surfaced of the time when she had been perhaps eight years old to his fifteen, and she had begged him to help her liberate an old monkey from a traveling fair. He'd ended up paying half a crown out of his allowance for the sorry, flea-bitten creature. She had taken it home, defied the objections of her parents, named it something silly that he couldn't recall. But he did remember how she had wept when it had died months later.

She'd weep now if Paddy died. He didn't want to contemplate *that*, so he kept his mind on the past.

Yes, Charlotte had always been like this as a child, rescuing fallen birds and stray dogs, setting out corn for the deer in the winter and greens for the rabbits. The burns had changed all that. She had turned into an embittered young woman with an acid tongue and a penchant for mischief.

A penchant for betrayal of the worst sort.

But there was more to Charlotte than the vindictive hellcat. Maybe the past five years really *had* changed her. Maybe the rancor had gone forever.

Brand shifted uneasily on the padded seat. People didn't change, not so drastically. Yet it was daunting to see that the lovable little girl still lurked inside her. What other woman of his acquaintance would have devised such a wild scheme? What other lady would have sat on the cold floor of a coach to soothe an injured beast? They were all too engrossed in the latest fashions and the choicest gossip. They weren't like Charlotte with her fascinating blend of softness and savagery.

All the hot blood engendered by the rescue now pooled in his groin. He needed a good stiff drink, not a good stiff prick.

He needed an ice-cold bath, that's what.

Rather than dropping them off at the front door, the coach went around back to the mews, in accordance with Brand's instructions. Dusk had fallen, and the misty chill of the air did little to relieve his overheated body. He picked up Paddy, rug and all, and handed him to Raleigh.

"I'll take him to the stables, then," the footman said.

"I'll go, too," Charlotte said instantly. "It's cold and damp and you'll need a fire lit. I'll see if the head groom has some bandages on hand."

Brand stopped her. "Raleigh has had experience in these matters. Let's leave it to him."

"Aye, m'lady," Raleigh said calmly. "I've cleaned up after dogfights many a time as a lad on the farm."

"Go on, then," Brand said. "You and Hayward take turns watching over him tonight."

The two footmen carried Paddy into the stables.

Brand expected an argument from Charlotte, and he didn't know quite what he'd say to her. Truth be told, he didn't want her to get any more attached to the dog than she already was. Despite what he'd said to her, he wasn't entirely certain the injured animal would survive the night.

As he put his hand at her waist and gave her a little push toward the house, Charlotte looked back over her shoulder. But she didn't start a quarrel. As she turned to regard him, a happy glow shone in her eyes.

She slipped her arm through his. "Isn't it marvelous?" she said. "We did it, Brand. *You* did it. You ended the fight and rescued Paddy."

Her admiration made him edgy. Still, he was taken by the thought that maybe she'd forgiven him for tricking her. "It was your idea to use copious amounts of smelling salts to clear the room. You were the brains, I was only the brawn."

"Oh, do stop." There was a touch of affectionate humor in her voice. "You're not really as bad as you'd like people to believe."

"I'm worse. You think I did a philanthropic act today? I like danger. I was looking for an adventure and nothing more."

"Whatever your reason, you helped Paddy. Just as you once rescued Bodwyn."

Bodwyn. That was the old monkey's name. "It was the only way to stop you from nagging me. Both times."

"Perhaps," Charlotte said softly. "But I'll never forget what you did today. Thank you."

They had reached the verandah, and as she mounted the first step, she turned around, gave him a soul-stirring look from beneath her lashes, and kissed him. A sweet, virginal brush of the lips that ended as swiftly as it had happened.

She left him standing there and vanished through the back door. It took a few seconds before he could cudgel his stunned body into moving. Then he charged after Charlotte like a lovesick mooncalf.

Lovesick, hell. It was lust. Absolute, undiluted lust, as fierce and hot as he'd ever known. She had to have done that on purpose, to torment him. And if she hadn't . . . he'd enjoy setting her straight once again on how a kiss could affect a man.

She was already halfway down the dimly lit corridor that led to the front of the house. He lengthened his strides, and Charlotte had to have heard his heavy footsteps, but she didn't acknowledge his presence. He caught up to her by the staircase, but her attention was on the library.

"Dammit, Char—" His voice died.

His grandmother stood in the doorway of the library.

She leaned on her cane and regarded him with an oddly stricken look. "For pity's sake, where have you been? You're never around when all hell breaks loose."

Hell? Grandmama had said *hell*?

And what was she doing out of bed?

He went straight to her side. "What is it? What's happened?"

"*You* tell *me*, boy. Get in here right now. You've quite a lot of explaining to do."

Then he looked past her and every fiber of his body went cold.

Standing in the library near a grim-faced Lady Stokeford and a fluttery Lady Enid was Hannibal Jones.

Chapter 18

BRAND'S CONFESSION

Charlotte had known the Rosebuds might eventually find out about the murder investigation, but not in this manner. Not from the Bow Street Runner whom she had trusted to handle the matter properly.

And not in such a way that had them all in a dither.

The moment she and Brand walked into the library, Lady Stokeford snapped, "Make haste, Brandon. This man has been searching the house from top to bottom."

Lady Enid seated herself in a leather chair by the desk and used her good arm to fan herself with her handkerchief. Despite the cheerful orange turban on her head, she looked tense and distraught. Upon getting a closer look at them, she gave a cry of distress. "You've blood on you. My stars, Charlotte, has the murderer come after you?"

Charlotte glanced down to see a few brownish smears on her gloves and pelisse. She hadn't been aware of the stains, and she hastened to the old woman's side to reassure her. "We rescued a dog from a fight, Grandmama. I'm perfectly fine. Please don't be worried."

As she spoke, Charlotte peeled off her gloves and removed her outer garment, dropping them on a stool out of her grandmother's sight. Brand did likewise with his coat.

But he paid no attention to Charlotte or the Rosebuds. He headed straight to Hannibal Jones.

"What the devil is this all about?"

The lanky officer didn't move from his stance behind the desk. He unscrewed the small gold crown on the end of his truncheon, tapped the wooden club against the edge of his palm, and removed a rolled-up piece of paper from the hollow center. A faint sneer on his cadaverous face, he passed the paper to Brand. "I've a proper search warrant, my lord. You'll see that everything is in order, signed by the magistrate."

"Devil take your trumped-up warrant." Brand crumpled the document and hurled it into the fire. "There's not a damned thing for you to find in this house."

"Isn't there?" With an air of oily triumph, the Runner drew open the top drawer of the desk. "How can you explain this, then?"

Both curious and irate, Charlotte moved closer to the desk. There could be nothing incriminating in there. She had seen the contents for herself only a few days ago— several quill pens, a spare pot of ink, writing paper embossed with the Faversham crest.

Now, however, the drawer held tidy stacks of banknotes. A single row of ten stacks, each perhaps an inch thick, each bound up with string. They appeared to be the familiar black-and-white printed notes issued by the Bank of England.

Frowning, Brand said, "That money isn't mine—"

He reached out as if to pick up a pile, but Jones stopped him by thrusting out his short wooden club. "I'm confiscating these in the name of the law," he said, collecting the stacks and efficiently stashing them in the pockets of his greatcoat. "They're forgeries. Excellent ones, I might add."

The Rosebuds gasped. Charlotte could only stare in utter confusion. Forgeries? How had those banknotes come to be there?

She turned her gaze to Brand. "Could someone have brought the money as payment for a gaming debt? Could your valet or butler have left it here for you?"

"No," he said flatly, staring at Jones. "No one touches this desk but me. And I've never seen that money before."

"There, you see?" Lady Enid cried out. "Brandon would never stoop to something so wicked."

"The notes looked perfectly legitimate to me," Lady Stokeford said from her chair by the fire. "Are you quite sure they're counterfeit?"

"The emblem of the Britannia medallion is missing a line," Jones said, holding one up to the light of a lamp. "These things often happen in forgeries. I've had quite a lot of experience in such matters."

"This is an outrage!" Lady Faversham snapped. Hobbling forward, she shook her cane at the officer. "Dare you accuse my grandson of being a common criminal?"

Jones quailed a little under her anger, hunching his shoulders, though his expression remained dogged. "I'm merely performing my assigned duty, my lady. May I remind you, I'm here to investigate a series of murders. And these banknotes provide evidence that his lordship may be involved in unlawful acts."

"Blastation! I don't know how those notes came to be in my grandson's desk"—the old woman sent Brandon a baleful stare—"but I *can* say it's a flimsy trail from forgery to murder."

"Not so flimsy as you might think, my lady." The Bow Street Runner stepped out from behind the desk, his movements quick and lithe for one so tall. "I've been investigating his lordship's background. If I may say, there are some sinister elements that caught my attention. One incident in particular." He gave Brand a hard stare. "That would be the manner in which he achieved the earldom."

There was a moment of silence, then the Rosebuds all babbled at once. Over their incoherent voices, Charlotte said sharply, "What do you mean, sir? His brother and nephew died of cholera."

"Did they?" Jones asked in an ominous tone. "Allow me to say, my lady, that some of the symptoms of that affliction can also be attributed to poison. Arsenic poisoning."

The ugly accusation paralyzed Charlotte. He was suggesting that Brand had *murdered* his brother and nephew. In all her life, she'd never heard such an outlandish, wrongful tale. The officer had offered no proof, only his own nasty speculations.

Her gaze shot to Brand, expecting him to be as enraged as herself, but he merely regarded the Runner with grim-faced intensity.

Lady Faversham reacted first. She swung her cane and smacked the Runner square on his legs. "Enough!" she cried out. "You will leave this house at once. And you may be certain I shall take this matter up with your superiors."

Jones flinched, gripping his truncheon as if to ward off another blow. Then he stiffly bowed. "As you wish, my lady. I'm sorry to have been the bearer of such bad tidings."

Charlotte doubted that. In the space of a few minutes, her opinion of him had sunk lower than the criminals he was sworn to apprehend. Poison, indeed!

Limping slightly, the Bow Street Runner gave Brand one last pointed stare, then left the library. From the foyer came the sound of the front door slamming.

No one moved for a moment. Then Brand's grandmother sank onto a chair, sagging over the ivory knob of her cane, her face haggard. "Dear God," she said brokenly. *"Dear God."*

Charlotte hastened to her side and rubbed that rigid back. Poor Lady Faversham, to be reminded in so vile a manner of losing George and her great-grandson. "Mr. Jones is a horrid, despicable man. And to think I was grateful to know that the law was assisting in the investigation."

"He deserved that blow," Lady Stokeford said, her aristocratic features drawn with anger. "How dared he make such a disgusting insinuation?"

Lady Enid dabbed at her eyes with her handkerchief. "Dear Brandon loved George and little Peter, every bit as much as the rest of us."

Brand still hadn't moved. There was a remote look on his face that Charlotte couldn't decipher. That in itself drew her to his side. It wasn't like him not to show the fury he must surely be feeling.

But he walked away before she could offer support, pacing to the other end of the library and turning to regard the Rosebuds. Without referring to that incredible accusation, he said, "You'll be wondering about this investigation. How much did Jones tell you?"

"He said it involved the Lucifer League," Lady Stokeford said. "That five men have been murdered in the past few months."

"Dear heavens," Lady Enid murmured in distress. "You could be next, Brandon!"

Her face pale and gaunt, Lady Faversham said, "This killer must be apprehended at once. Tell us all the particulars, Brandon. And don't leave anything out."

Brand summarized the facts in a clipped, emotionless tone, including the attack on the Rosebuds themselves.

"I always thought Tupper had shifty eyes for a footman," Lady Faversham said scornfully. "Have you tracked down the brigand?"

"Only that one time at Billingsgate Market," Brand said. "I've made numerous inquiries, but he seems to have vanished from the face of England."

"To think all this was going on right beneath our noses," Lady Stokeford said, shaking her head. "We deserved to know."

"We had to consider your health, my lady," Charlotte said. "All three of you are still recovering from your injuries. In truth, you took a risk maneuvering the stairs today. You might have fallen." Overcome at the thought, she knelt at her grandmother's feet, pressing her cheek to those familiar skirts.

With her uninjured hand, Lady Enid stroked Charlotte's hair comfortingly. "There, there, now. We couldn't allow a stranger to poke through the house unattended, could we? The moment North brought the news, we hurried straight downstairs."

"Were all of you with Jones the entire time, then?" Brand asked.

"Except for the first ten minutes or so," Lady Faversham said. She gave a snort of contempt. "I made the fellow turn out his pockets to prove he hadn't pinched the silver."

"So upon his arrival, he had time to slip into this room," Brand said.

"Yes, I suppose," Lady Stokeford said thoughtfully. "Yes, he might, indeed. What are you suggesting?"

"That Mr. Jones could have planted the forged notes himself," Charlotte answered in a rush of incredulous understanding. She stood up and paced toward him. "But why, Brand? Why would he do such a thing?"

Brand shrugged, and the lamplight cast harsh shadows on his face. "It's anyone's guess. He does seem to harbor a particular hatred for me, though."

Charlotte had to agree. Was it possible that Jones had a personal vendetta against Brand? Or that Jones himself was the killer? That seemed too improbable to believe. Yet if he had some undisclosed connection to the Lucifer League . . .

"Brandon, when was the last time you'd looked in that drawer?" Lady Stokeford asked.

"Perhaps a week ago." Brand cast Charlotte a pointed stare. "What about you?"

Determined not to blush, she turned away and told the Rosebuds, "Five days ago, I was looking for a . . . a pen. The banknotes weren't there at that time."

"Five days," Lady Faversham said, her eyes narrowed. "What visitors have been here in the interim? Blast, I do hate being an invalid and unaware of such matters."

"Miss Margaret Darby called on Charlotte early this morning," Brand said. "She's Clifford Vaughn's cousin."

"What sort of person is she?" Lady Stokeford asked.

"Sweet and shy and unassuming," Charlotte said. "Not at all the sort to be involved in criminal acts."

"Yet she's dependent upon Vaughn's largesse." Brand sat on the edge of the desk and folded his arms. "It's quite possible the Vaughns induced her to plant those bills on their behalf."

Charlotte's stomach twisted. *Was* it possible? "When she arrived I wasn't dressed yet, so she might have come in here while she was waiting for me. But . . . I simply can't believe it of her. That she would abet any wicked scheme of theirs."

Brand raised a skeptical eyebrow. "Then there was Harold Rountree," he stated in a hard tone. "Just yesterday, the bastard was in the park across the street. *He's* certainly devious enough to do the deed."

Was he? To alleviate her disquiet, Charlotte paced back and forth. "He went to the tradesmen's entrance and asked for me. But if he'd tried to get inside the house, surely the servants would have stopped him."

"We're dealing with an extremely crafty killer," Brand said. "I don't doubt that he could accomplish such a simple task."

"But *why*? If he's the murderer, why not simply . . . murder you?" The words stuck dryly in her throat. "Why go to all this trouble with falsified banknotes?"

"Because it's as effective as murder and far more clever," Brand said. "The crime of forgery is punishable by death."

Charlotte's legs gave way, and she sank down on a hassock. "You're a nobleman. Surely you have rights . . . immunities . . ."

"I've no license to commit such a grave crime. The

government takes a hard stand on counterfeiting. Britain's economy would fail if anyone could print money as he liked."

Lady Faversham released a long, quavering breath. "But you have no *reason*, Brandon. Why would you print your own notes? You aren't in debt. You're an immensely wealthy man."

"Greed," Brand stated. "There are many who would happily believe me capable of padding my own pockets."

"How utterly diabolical," Lady Enid whispered, shuddering.

Lady Stokeford made a sound of distress. She sat regally on her chair, her face as fine as seamed porcelain beneath her snow-white hair. "But even Jones must realize the weakness of his case," she said. "Else he surely would have arrested you today."

"He won't arrest my grandson," Lady Faversham said fiercely. "Not if we can prove that others had the opportunity to place those bills. We've already come up with three possibilities—Miss Darby, Mr. Rountree, and Jones himself."

"There may be others as well," Charlotte said, rallying to the cause. "We'll question the servants, find out who else might have been here."

In short order, North gave out the news that Uriah Lane had come by earlier in the afternoon, just after Brand and Charlotte's departure for the dogfight. But the butler had been in the servants' hall and hadn't spoken to the visitor.

Giffles had done the honors.

The valet reported to them at once. He was a sober man of medium build, about the same age as his master but far more ordinary, from his neatly combed brown hair to his plain brown garb.

"You encountered Lane here?" Brand asked. "In the library?"

"Yes, my lord."

"Well? Was he near my desk?"

"Er . . . yes, but he wasn't looking in it, I can assure you."

"What was he doing?" Lady Faversham demanded, thumping her cane. "Speak up, man."

The valet cast an oblique glance at Charlotte, a look she couldn't fathom. His cheeks took on a ruddy hue. "I'm afraid he was with one of the serving maids."

"Swiving her, no doubt," Brand said tightly. "I'll send that knave to hell."

Charlotte had to concur, though she didn't miss the irony of Brand condemning one of his friends for self-indulgence. But Brand at least had his standards. He wouldn't stoop to taking advantage of a helpless woman, a servant who would risk losing her post if she refused a nobleman.

"Who was the girl?" Lady Stokeford asked. "Perhaps she might have seen him hiding those banknotes."

Giffles hesitated. "Miss Killigrew," he said. "Lady Charlotte's maid."

"Nan?" A cold quiver of foreboding ran through Charlotte, and if she hadn't been sitting down, her legs would have wilted. "Why would she have been here with such a man?" *A member of the Lucifer League.*

"She claimed that you'd asked her to fetch a book." Giffles looked at her keenly; so did everyone else.

Charlotte's first impulse was to protect Nan, to pretend that she had sent the girl on the errand. Heartsore, she remembered the day she'd caught Nan pilfering a loaf of bread from a market in York, a thin frightened girl of thirteen, alone in the world and forced to steal to survive. Charlotte had brought Nan home, given her a place to stay, taught her to be a lady's maid. Eventually, Charlotte had learned the appalling story of Nan's past, the father who had beaten her, forced her into despicable acts, until one fateful night when Nan had defended herself with a kitchen knife . . .

Charlotte hoped that only simple curiosity had induced Nan to wander around the house, where'd she had the misfortune to encounter Uriah Lane. Nan couldn't have known him beforehand. She couldn't have let him into the house to leave those banknotes.

But if Charlotte was wrong, Brand could go to the gallows.

She met his stony stare. There was no trace of the warmth that they'd shared after rescuing Paddy. "No," she admitted with a heavy heart. "I didn't ask Nan to come here."

"Then an interview with Nan is in order," Brand said.

"I'll fetch the girl at once," Giffles said, censure radiating from him. He stood rigidly, his mouth compressed. "With your permission, my lord."

"Don't trouble yourself," Brand said. "I'd prefer to catch her off guard. If she's called down to face me, she'll have time to prepare a story."

"At this hour, she ought to be upstairs in my chamber," Charlotte said, rising to her feet. "I'll go with you."

As one, the Rosebuds also stood up. Brand shot them an irritated glare. "Don't you have something else to do? Where are Michael and Vivien, by the way?"

"Little William has a sore throat," Lady Stokeford

said, "so they've decided to stay at their town house for the evening."

"Nevertheless, it's time for you three to return to your chamber," Brand said. "The excitement is over for now."

"It most certainly is not," his grandmother said. "I won't rest until you're cleared of this crime."

"Nor shall I," Lady Stokeford averred, her finely aged face resolute.

"Nor I," added Lady Enid. "You can't expect us to twiddle our thumbs while you're thrown into prison."

Charlotte crossed the room and put her arm around her grandmother's stout waist. "Please, do let us handle this quietly. Nan will be nervous enough to face Brand and me. She'll be too frightened to speak a word if there are five of us haranguing her."

"You've overtaxed yourselves, at any rate," Brand said, eyeing Lady Faversham. "Don't deny it, Grandmama. I can see how weary you are."

"We *have* had quite a shocking day," Lady Stokeford said, glancing thoughtfully from Brand to Charlotte. "Come, Rosebuds, perhaps we should retire for the night. I myself would enjoy a glass of sherry and a supper tray. Your two grandchildren are quite capable of interviewing the maid in the privacy of Charlotte's bedchamber." She gave her friends a speaking look.

Lady Enid looked befuddled a moment, then she smiled wanly. "Now that you mention it, my arm does ache," she said, cradling the sling. "I confess it would be pleasant to lie down."

Lady Faversham pursed her lips and nodded. "Oh, as you wish, ladies. I suppose we could use the time to discuss all that's happened."

Brand stepped forward to take his grandmother's arm,

while offering his other arm to Lady Stokeford. "Come along, then. Charlotte and I'll escort you upstairs."

A short while later, Charlotte and Brand faced a wide-eyed Nan in the bedchamber. The soft crackling of the fire underscored the tension in the room, and rain hissed against the darkened windows.

"I shouldn't have gone t' that floor, m'lady, and I'm sorry." Nan held her chin up, but her voice quavered as she flicked an anxious glance at Brand. "Please, m'lord, I didn't disturb nothin'."

"If you didn't go to meet Lane, why were you there?" he asked.

"I—I was just wanderin'. 'Twas wrong of me, an' it won't never happen again. I learnt my lesson."

"There had to have been another reason," he said in a frosty tone. "You were poking around in my desk, weren't you?"

Brand was only prodding Nan, Charlotte knew. And yet Nan looked terror-stricken. Her eyes grew even bigger and she hunched her shoulders as if bracing herself for a blow. "N-nay . . ."

The maid was holding something back, Charlotte sensed with a dismal certainty. Dear God, had Nan somehow become tangled up with this mystery? Was she protecting Uriah Lane? Or perhaps some other member of the league?

She took hold of the girl's rough, workworn hands. "Nan, you *must* be honest with me. Completely honest. It's of vital importance."

"Be quick about it, too," Brand growled. "If you had anything to do with those banknotes, you'll swing from the nearest gibbet. Unless you cooperate and tell us the name of your co-conspirator."

"I didn't nick any banknotes," Nan cried out. "Nor any gold, neither."

Charlotte could feel her trembling. She shot a glare at Brand. "Hush. Can't you see she's frightened enough already?"

He glowered back, but kept silent.

She gently squeezed Nan's fingers. "All right, then. I believe you. But you must tell me the truth about why you went to the library today."

Nan's brown eyes flooded with tears. "I daren't, m'lady. Thee'll think bad of me."

"Perhaps so. But haven't I always stood by you? Whatever trouble you're in, I'll help you out. You have my word on that."

Nan's chin wobbled. Tears rolled down her rosy cheeks. In a very small, very miserable voice, she said, " 'Twas Dick, m'lady, who told me t' do it."

"Dick?" Brand asked. "Who the devil is he?"

"Her suitor," Charlotte said, her full attention on the effort not to show her shocked dismay to Nan. "But he's in York."

"He come t' London right after us, m'lady. He told me . . ." The picture of misery, the maid shifted from one foot to the other.

"He told you to steal from his lordship," Charlotte finished. Oh, how she'd like to get her hands on that ruffian! For months he'd tried to entice the girl back into a life of thievery. Although Nan could see the wrong of it, she felt an obligation toward Dick because he'd helped her escape the scene of her father's death on that horrific night.

The girl sniffled. "Dick said . . . he said his lordship wouldn't miss a few coins. But . . . I couldn't do it. I had my hand on the drawer, but I never opened it, I swear it. That's when Mr. Lane came in." Nan clutched at Charlotte's hands. "Thee must believe me. I never took nothin'. I *couldn't*."

Brand snorted, but Charlotte ignored him. She had an experienced sense of when Nan was lying and when she was being honest. "Yes, I believe you. I also trust this incident has opened your eyes to Dick's true nature. He's a trickster and a robber, and if he truly cared for you, he'd never, ever ask you to commit a crime."

"Aye, m'lady. I know that now."

Nan's eyes held a candid remorse that made Charlotte hope for the best. "You'll not see him again. I'll have your promise on that."

Nan nodded slowly. "Then . . . then thee shan't make me leave here?"

She looked so woebegone that Charlotte gave her a hug. "Of course not. Everyone makes a mistake now and then. So long as you've vowed to do better—"

"The devil you say," Brand broke in. "I won't have a thief in my house, would-be or otherwise."

Charlotte turned to confront his disgruntled countenance. "She's in my employ, not yours. I'll take complete responsibility for her actions. Besides, she has nothing whatsoever to do with our case, and that's all that should matter to you at present."

He continued to frown, then said in a grudging tone, "All right, then. But one wrong move and she's out of this house. Giffles will keep an extremely close eye on her. He'll accompany her whenever she leaves this chamber."

Nan made a strangled sound, but said nothing, only appeared more forlorn than ever. Charlotte deemed it prudent not to protest the order. Brand looked angry enough already.

She needed to talk to him. In private.

Turning to Nan, she said, "Why don't you go and have a cup of tea in the kitchen? Perhaps even take an early bedtime. I know you're distraught, but you'll feel better come the morning."

"She isn't going anywhere just yet," Brand said. He strode to the writing desk, dipped a quill in the pot of ink, and scrawled a brief message. After sanding and folding the paper, he handed it to Nan. "Take this straight to my valet in my chambers. It contains his instructions regarding you. And by God, if I find out you've done otherwise, done anything whatsoever to betray my trust, you'll be cast out on the streets without a ha'penny." He flashed Charlotte a sharp glance. "No matter what her ladyship says to the contrary."

Though teary-eyed, Nan bobbed a curtsy. "Aye, m'lord. I thank thee." The maid scurried out, clutching the note, leaving Charlotte alone with Brand.

Rain whispered against the windowpanes. A branch of lighted candles glowed on the bedside table, another on the table by the hearth. Charlotte wouldn't let herself think about the fact that they were in her bedchamber, or how much she longed to be in his arms. She would only let herself consider how cold and remote he'd looked ever since Hannibal Jones had made his wild accusations.

Brand was frowning into the fire, and she went to his side. "It's a relief to know Nan isn't involved," she said.

"But something bothers me. You never received a note saying, 'You're next.' "

"Perhaps because my death isn't imminent. If I'm arrested, there'll be a trial and a sentencing."

The prospect was too horrifying to contemplate. How could he act so indifferent?

Now more than ever, she *had* to find the killer. "We haven't absolved Uriah Lane. I wonder what reason he would have to kill the members of the league."

"Hell if I know. Madness, perhaps. The fellow's had the clap so long it's addled his brain."

"The clap?"

He gave her a keen glance. "A disease contracted from infected whores."

Repelled, she blurted out, "You don't have this . . . clap, do you?"

Brand shook his head. "I'm discerning in my choice of lovers. Very discerning." His gaze lingered on her lips. "Any particular reason you wished to know?"

Her heart beat erratically, and Charlotte knew she was blushing. "Only to reassure myself you won't suddenly turn into a raving madman."

"I'll endeavor to leash my savage impulses. Unless you beg me to do otherwise."

How had he managed to turn the conversation onto a seductive path? "I don't beg," she said indignantly. "And I'd certainly never beg *you* for anything."

He tenderly ran his finger down her cheek. "I could prove you wrong," he murmured. "Inside of two minutes."

His touch evoked a rush of liquid desire in her. Charlotte was aware of how alone they were, how much she desired his kiss. But despite his silken tone, there was a hard edge to his mood tonight. An underlying anger that made her both wary and curious.

She pushed away his hand. "We were speaking of the investigation. I shouldn't have doubted your assessment of Mr. Jones. He's a horrid man, and he won't get away with accusing you of murder."

Brand's mouth twisted derisively. "What, are you my champion now? I can fight my own battles."

"Not if you're sent to prison for crimes you didn't commit. And Mr. Jones has influence at Bow Street Station. He can feed the magistrate a pack of lies and innuendoes about you."

A wintry chill in his eyes, Brand gave her a brooding look. "Maybe they're not all lies."

That took her aback. "What a thing for you to say! You wouldn't go after the members of the league one by one. And to kill your own brother and nephew? I'd as soon believe my grandmother capable of the deed."

He prowled the room like a caged panther, and it was unnerving to see his tall, masculine form so close to her bed. "You can't possibly imagine everything I've done, Char. You don't know me at all."

The note of menace in his voice intrigued her. How she'd love to learn all of his secrets, to become one of his secrets herself. By inviting him into her bed. "I know enough," she murmured. "And while you're hardly a saint, you're not a murderer, either. Absolutely not."

But her avowal only seemed to anger him all the more. He stalked halfway to her and stopped, his face shadowed by a darkness she had never before seen.

"Absolutely?" he jeered. "Here's the truth, then. Jones was right about one point. I did kill George and his son."

Chapter 19
AN UNWELCOME PROPOSITION

Brand knew he shouldn't have spoken. Yet it was a strange relief to say those words aloud after so many years. And he felt compelled to convince Charlotte that she was wrong about him. Dead wrong.

He waited for the look of disgust to appear on her face, the scornful, I-knew-it-all-along expression so familiar to him.

Instead, her brow furrowed with concern. "I don't understand. They died of cholera. It was a tragedy, but certainly not your fault."

"It *was* my fault, dammit. As much as if I'd put a gun to their heads."

"Are you saying you *did* poison them, then?"

He ought to lie. But the truth was bad enough. Either way, George and Peter were dead. "They contracted the illness because of me, that's what. Because I was holed up in a Cheapside rooming house on a month-long drunken binge. George came after me, to bring me back home. That's where he caught the disease."

Afraid he would choke, Brand walked to the window and stared out into the darkness. Those weeks were still a blur to him. Wanting to sink into oblivion, he'd swallowed enough gin to float a navy. He'd done it to forget

Grace, to numb the rage and pain that she'd married his best friend. Grace had given herself to him the night before the wedding, whispered tenderly of love, then walked down the aisle with Michael.

Damn her. And damn himself for falling prey to a woman's soft words.

He sensed Charlotte's presence behind him, the rustle of skirts, the fragrance of flowery soap. "Why were you drinking?" she asked.

"What the hell does that matter?" he exploded. "The fact is, George wouldn't have become ill if he hadn't come to the filthiest part of London, trying to rescue me."

"How did you not become ill, too?"

"Me?" He gave a harsh laugh. "I was too damned pickled to contract any disease. Nothing in my veins but pure liquor."

"And what about Peter? If he wasn't even there—"

"That's the worst of it. I threw George out on his self-righteous bum, and the next day, he brought his son. He was hoping that Peter could convince me to come home."

He wanted to gag on that memory. Lolling in bed, totally soused and struggling to focus on his nephew standing in the doorway. Fair-haired Peter, so small and bewildered and frightened of the stranger his uncle had become. It had been the lowest point in Brand's life, to view himself through the eyes of a child.

"George had no right to do that," Charlotte said indignantly. "You don't drag a young child into a hellhole, not for any reason."

Brand hadn't thought so, either. But he wouldn't let

himself feel exonerated. "No? Well, his plan worked. I went home, and the next day they both fell ill. Within two days, I was making the funeral arrangements."

He kept his voice hard, though he was dying inside, the guilt as grinding as the moment he'd received the prognosis from the physician, and as shameful as his jolt of self-serving joy that he was now the earl and acceptable to Grace. Yes, that had been his secret, vile, disgusting thought in the days afterward, that he was no longer just the second son, that he was now worthy of her.

Fool.

Charlotte was silent. He could see her reflection in the darkened window, though not well enough to read her expression. She didn't know about Grace, how he had coveted his best friend's wife. He wouldn't ever tell her, either. Yet Charlotte knew enough to see his culpability in the death of his brother and nephew.

He waited for her condemnation, he craved it. He wanted her to see him exactly as he was so they could retreat to the familiar ground of animosity.

She moved to stand in front of him, her gaze holding his. An odd light shone in her green eyes, as if she suddenly understood him better than he understood himself. "It was Grace, wasn't it?" she said. "That's why you were drinking like a stupid sot. This all happened right after she married Michael."

Her words pierced him like a bullet. Every part of him went cold. She had to be taking a shot in the dark . . .

He looked her in the eye, glanced away, then drilled her with a stare. "I don't know what the hell you're saying."

She placed her hand on his sleeve. "Brand, don't lie to me. I know about your affair with Grace. And I know about Amy."

Shock paralyzed him. To hear his deepest, dearest secret stated in that matter-of-fact voice made him want to howl. He felt exposed, defenseless, his raw emotions on display for Charlotte to see. God help him, she *knew*. She knew about the worst mistake of his life, how he'd made an ass of himself over a woman. And how he'd had to watch another man be a father to Amy.

Charlotte had the gall to regard him with concern. As if she had every right to rip open his soul. As if she saw his torment and pitied him.

He thrust her hand away. "Damn you." He could barely speak, his voice was so hoarse. "You had no right to pry into my private life."

"Maybe not. But I couldn't help drawing conclusions after I saw that miniature—"

"In my desk. Where you shouldn't have stuck your nose in the first place."

She had the sense—or the craftiness—to look abashed. "I'm sorry, but I didn't have any other way to find out about the members of the league. You aren't exactly a fount of information. I've had to figure things out for myself."

Wanting to shake her, he ran his hands through his hair instead. "Then figure this out. I won't speak of Grace to you or to anyone else."

But he wanted to. He wanted to spill his guts, to unburden himself. To *Char,* of all women.

"Then I'll speak," Charlotte said softly. "I saw the look on your face when you hugged Amy. I know—I can *guess*—how much she means to you." She took a step toward him. "Oh, Brand. She's your daughter. It must be terrible to know you can't claim her as your own."

She'd shot him, and now she was probing the wound for the bullet. "Stay out of what you don't know."

"But I have to ask you about Grace. I only want to help—"

"Leave off, Char," he warned sharply. "I won't talk about her."

She pursed her lips. "I have a stake in this, too. All these years, you've condemned me for betrayal when you did the same thing to Michael."

"So I'm a bloody damned hypocrite on top of everything else. But don't think that gives you the upper hand." His insides in turmoil, he walked away from her.

She followed, clearly irked with him. "I don't *want* the upper hand. This isn't some sort of contest. But perhaps it does put us on even footing."

"And thus ends this discussion."

Charlotte laughed unexpectedly, shaking her head. "How like a man. You could be dying and you wouldn't ask anyone for help."

"Right, I'm not one of your stray dogs. I don't need saving. I'm bloody well able to manage my own affairs."

"I wouldn't dream of saving you. You have to do that on your own." Her gaze soft, she took another step toward him. "However, you *must* stop blaming yourself for the deaths of your brother and nephew. It wasn't your fault. You didn't plan for it to happen. *You didn't kill them.*"

The fire of her conviction threatened to engulf him. Was she right? Had he been torturing himself all these years over a sin he hadn't committed? Everything in him ached to believe her, yet he couldn't let himself off so easily.

Because she was standing so close, he gripped her shoulders. "You don't understand. I resented George. He was always so damned faultless, at the top of his form, captain of the debating team, house prefect."

"While you were sent down for sneaking girls into your chambers. Yes, I overheard the Rosebuds talking about that a long time ago. But it still doesn't mean you'd wish him dead."

"I wouldn't be so sure of that. There were times when I hated him."

"Because you wanted the praise of your parents and your grandmother. And when you couldn't get it, you sought their attention the only way you knew how—by misbehaving. I know, my two younger brothers were the same way, always jostling for notice."

She was wrong. She had to be wrong. "Don't read too much into it," he said harshly. "I like misbehaving. It's in my nature."

"I won't argue with that. In truth, you've taken mischief to new heights of artistry."

Her half-smile returned, causing a shift inside him, the awareness that they were alone in her bedchamber after dark, with the candles glowing over a scene set for seduction. Hell, why were they wasting time quarreling? Seduction was the perfect way to distract her.

He pulled her closer and nuzzled her brow, then moved his lips over the silken skin of her cheek. "Mischief requires diligent practice."

She drew in a breath, closing her eyes, but not pushing him away. "Stop. This is just a way to keep us from talking."

"Effective, isn't it?"

He brought his mouth down to hers, tempering those parted lips that were about to blister him again. God, she tasted good, as rich and mysterious as the finest wine. Need rushed through him, blotting out reality. He wanted to get her naked and into bed, to settle himself in the cradle of her legs. He wanted to forget the pain of the past and experience the pleasures of the here and now.

Yet he kept the kiss light and slow, tenderly cajoling, even when she surrendered almost immediately. It was gratifying to feel all that stiff, self-righteous pique melt into soft acquiescence. Her swift response was an erotic joy in itself, to know that Charlotte couldn't resist him. "Come misbehave with me," he muttered. "I'll give you pleasure beyond your dreams."

She sighed when he cupped her breast, stroking her through the bodice of her gown. Her hand came up to cover his, yet she made no move to stop his caress. "Brand, we can't. We mustn't . . ."

She was right; this was insanity. But the wispy tremor in her voice was an aphrodisiac. "We can," he said, kissing the smooth column of her throat. "And we must."

"Please. Anyone could walk in on us."

"I can take care of that problem." Releasing her, he went to the door and turned the key. That definitive click snapped some sense into him. A rational part of his brain reminded him Charlotte was no whore for him to use at his whim. She was a virgin, a lady, a part of his extended family.

What the hell was he doing, contemplating seduction? The Rosebuds were right down the corridor.

Damn, damn, *damn.*

He turned around and stopped dead. Charlotte had her arms behind her, busily working at the buttons on the back of her gown. She cast him a fervid, pleading look. "Do help me," she said. "I can't reach the ones in the middle."

Sweet Jesus, he'd just been dealt four aces. All the blood left his brain on a swift descent to his groin. Her gown slipped a little at the bodice, giving him a glimpse of pale, creamy skin and a fantasy of full breasts nipped by a lacy corset.

He was behind her in a moment, fumbling with her dress. Little pearl buttons that gave him more resistance than Charlotte herself. "I don't understand," he said gruffly. "What happened here?" *Stifle the talk. Just take the goods.* But his heedless tongue blathered on. "A minute ago you were refusing me."

She cast an enigmatic glance over her shoulder. "I've decided that I can't live without *knowing.*"

That look. A woman's look, ripe with carnal invitation. "Just like that? You decide to give me your virginity?"

Charlotte afforded him a quick, needy smile. "Actually, I've thought about this for quite a while. I'm twenty-nine years old, and I don't want to die a virtuous old maid."

So she regarded him as some sort of convenience? And why the hell should that irritate him, anyway? It had always been his philosophy to take his pleasure with no questions asked. He clamped his hands at her slim waist. "Dammit, Char. You're supposed to say no."

She dipped her chin and fluttered her lashes. "No, no," she said breathily. "Please don't ravish me, you wicked rake."

He chuckled in a state of dazed astonishment. "Wench. You shouldn't tease a man, either."

She turned in his arms, lifted her hand to his jaw, her mouth no longer smiling but soft with erotic promise. "I can't help myself, Brand. I've dreamed about you for so long. I'm aching for you."

At that, he lost any chance at saving them both from this insanity. Maybe this *was* inevitable, and had been ever since she'd sat on his lap as a precocious thirteen-year-old and made moon eyes at him. Ever since the night he'd tricked her into responding to him in bed. Ever since she'd given him that sweet little kiss outside a short while ago.

He kissed her again, deeper this time, letting her feel the intensity of his arousal. She returned the favor, standing on tiptoe and pressing herself to him. Moving his hands to her hair, he drew out the pins, and the heavy silken mass tumbled to her waist.

With a little tug, her gown slipped to the floor. He loosened the strings of her corset, and blast, his hands were shaking, making a tangle of an easy task, hardly a testament to his finesse at seduction. But once he'd rid her of the damned cage, it was worth the effort. Only the fine linen of her shift kept her from nakedness. The tempting globes of her breasts strained against the thin fabric, the nipples taut with desire.

Desire for him. Only him.

When he drew back to look at her, however, she made a furtive move as if to hide her arm. "Shouldn't we . . . get under the covers?" she asked.

He'd like that, too. Under the covers, on the floor, in the chair, and a myriad of other places. As slow or as fast as she wanted him to go.

Instead, he walked her to the full-length mirror and positioned her in front of him, clasping her close. God, it was torture holding her flush against him, torture not to slake his feverish impulses. Torture to gaze at that flimsy chemise, to notice the intriguing shadows in all the right places.

The glow of the candles showed the webwork of scarring that marred her right arm, ending at her smooth, bare shoulder. But it was her lush womanly form that held him enthralled.

She took a quick peek at herself, then looked away, her teeth sinking into her lower lip. It was shyness, not something he'd expected of Charlotte, and he felt the stirring of tenderness.

He gently turned her face back toward the mirror, his thumb gliding across that moist mouth, soothing the place she'd bitten. "Look at yourself," he said roughly. "You are so damned beautiful."

"I'm not," she whispered in an undertone of distress.

He wanted to scoff, but caught himself in time. This really mattered to her. Despite the proud face she showed the world, Charlotte was conscious of her one imperfection. Didn't she know there were far worse flaws? He played his fingers down the gnarled flesh of her forearm, caressing her a moment. He lifted her scarred hand and kissed her palm, then each finger in turn.

"You *are* beautiful," he repeated. "All of you."

Her wistful eyes met the reflection of his. "You needn't be charming, Brand."

"I mean it. You're not like other women. Forever admiring yourself in mirrors. Fretting over clothing and hats and jewelry. Believing your good looks can get you whatever you want." Brand saw the question in her eyes, the question he didn't want to answer, but he did anyway. "And yes," he forced out, "Grace was like that."

Charlotte's gaze held his. "Do you still love her?"

"God, no. What made you think—" He clamped his jaw, took a breath. "Rule of the bedchamber. There's no talk of anyone but us. Is that clear?"

A blushing smile flitted over her exquisite features. "Yes, my lord," she said with uncustomary meekness.

Trust shone in her eyes, a trust that made his chest clench and his loins ache. She was heaven's gift to man. To *him*.

His heart was thundering so fast, she had to feel it against her back. He glided his palms down her chemise, pressed his mouth to the fragrant place behind her ear. He wanted to be inside her *now*.

But by damn, he'd take it slow. She was a virgin, and he intended to give her an experience she'd never forget. He turned Charlotte to face him, then kissed her long and deep. He kissed her until small mewling sounds issued from her throat and she arched herself to him, a woman in full arousal.

Somehow he had the presence of mind to get her to the bed, to shed cravat and coat and shirt, to peel off her chemise. Keeping his breeches on for the moment in an effort to prolong matters, he tumbled down onto her glorious nakedness and kissed those lovely breasts, suckling her while his hand moved down to find her moist and hot, and oh God, so ready for him. Soft, perfect, untried by any other man.

Take it slowly.

He kissed her, caressed her, learned the nuances of her body. Then his much-vaunted self-control went up in smoke when she opened his breeches, sought daintily, and touched him with a maidenly reverence. Her skin flushed with desire, she murmured, "Please, Brand. *Please.*"

She was begging and he ought to feel triumphant, but he was too consumed to care. He pressed into her, meeting a slight resistance that gave way to his invasion. She caught her breath in a small gasp, and he paused, afraid of hurting her, yet glorying in his possession nonetheless. God! She was tight and velvety, utterly perfect.

His throat felt just as tight. Nothing, *nothing*, had ever felt so right. He was inside Charlotte, exactly where he'd always, always wanted to be. He eased himself deeper into her, as deep as physically possible, and yet that wasn't enough to satisfy him. She murmured his name again on a note of wonder, shifting her hips to accommodate him, and the world dissolved into a blur of kissing and touching and loving Charlotte.

Charlotte. In the dim recesses of his mind, he meant to draw out the pleasure and make this perfect for her, but already she was shuddering beneath him, crying out in the throes of completion. He came with her in a blinding burst of joy.

They lay together for what could have been a minute or ten, Brand didn't know. He couldn't have moved if his life depended upon it . . . maybe he could if *her* life depended upon it.

He was sprawled over Charlotte, his cheek resting on the pillow of her shoulder, her scent—their scent—all around him. Pulses slowed, breathing regulated, and he realized with a shock that he was still inside her, he hadn't withdrawn. He hadn't even *thought* about withdrawing.

Hell.

Charlotte moved slightly, her scarred hand resting against his back, her smooth, perfect one tracing the contours of his face. She was looking at him as if he'd brought her the moon on a silver platter. "Oh . . . my . . . stars," she whispered on a husky laugh. "Brand. I had no *idea* . . ."

Nor had he. He had never lost control so completely, had never forgotten to guard against unwanted conception—except for that one time with Grace. But somehow he couldn't summon the strength to consider the consequences when his body was lax with the finest contentment he'd ever known, when a cocky satisfaction made him want to crow from the rooftops. Charlotte was *his,* no other man could initiate her.

"You still have on your breeches," she murmured, her hands taking a delightful stroll over his backside. "Is that . . . customary?"

"Hell, no," he said with a gruff laugh, "and especially not the boots."

He ought to get up right now and leave, not take any further risk of impregnating her. But his brain refused to function. She looked so sinfully tempting lying beneath him in bare-breasted splendor, all that chestnut hair spread out in a tumble, her lips reddened and her face alight with the glow of satiation.

It was disturbing to realize how quick he'd been to claim her. He'd wanted to give Charlotte a memorable experience, not take her like a dockside whore in an alleyway.

Yet it had been far from sordid. It ranked as the best carnal encounter he'd ever had. And she certainly didn't appear to be disappointed by his slapdash performance.

But damn, he could do better. He *would* do better.

As he sat up and tugged off his boots and breeches, Charlotte eased into a half-sitting position, her head propped on her hand and her frank gaze on him. "I must say, the tall man downstairs is quite . . . impressive."

"He's a bit weary at the moment. But keep admiring him, and he'll become vainglorious again."

She reached out and touched him, her fingertips gliding in a feather-light caress that made him suck in a breath. She paused her exploration, gazing up at him. "Have I done wrong . . . ?"

Brand chuckled. "Trust me, darling, he loves it. Far too much."

He climbed back into bed, settling under the covers with her, fitting that lush body to his. One more time, he promised himself, to emblazon himself on her memory, and they'd both be sated enough to part.

Maybe.

Taking her face in his hands, he kissed her, one of those soft, tender kisses he found as amazingly enjoyable as wild, uninhibited fornication. Sipping, savoring, murmuring to each other in the candlelit darkness, they lay together with the rain tapping on the windows and the fire burning low on the hearth, transforming the night into an unparalleled eternity of pleasure. Perhaps it was the newness of lying with the one woman he'd known all his life, but he couldn't get enough of Charlotte. They made love again, far more slowly this time, yet with the same maddening passion, deep and rich and spellbinding in its intensity.

In the aftermath, buried inside her, he forgot all his reasons for leaving her bed. Nothing else seemed important. Charlotte was so damned sweet in the way she clung to him, smiling, whispering his name as if he'd invented lovemaking expressly for her enjoyment. God, if he'd known she was such a sensualist, he'd have embarked on this affair that much the sooner.

No, she couldn't become his mistress. They had only this one evening, a few hours at best.

He shifted position, afraid he was too heavy for her, and she murmured a protest that he soothed with a kiss. Closing his eyes, he told himself he'd just lie here with her for a few minutes longer. Anything more was just too risky.

"Brand, it's dawn. You have to leave."

He awakened to her urgent whisper. His sluggish eyelids cracked open. He was sprawled in the middle of the mattress, drugged with sleep, his head cradled by a feather pillow. For a moment he didn't know where he was; he seldom spent the entire night in his mistress's bed.

Then Charlotte was leaning over the bed to shake his shoulder. *Charlotte.* They'd coupled twice last night, no thrice, for there had been that time during the wee hours when he'd awakened to find her laying kisses over him . . .

Now she wore her chemise again, and in the faint grayish light from the window, he glimpsed the full curve of her breasts. Instantly erect, he reached out to fondle her.

She pushed his hand away. "Get up. And *hurry*."

"I am up. Quite definitely up."

She glanced down, her gaze slumberous. "You know what I mean. You mustn't be discovered here. The servants will be going about their duties very soon."

"Five minutes won't matter." It was stupidly insane to take the gamble, especially since he'd meant to depart hours ago, but he sat up against the pillows, caught hold of her waist, and tumbled Charlotte onto his lap, pushing up the chemise so that she could straddle him.

Her resistance was blessedly brief. Huffing out a breath, she put her mouth to his whiskered cheek. "We really shouldn't do this."

"Maybe not." He kept his hands under her chemise, moving up and down the smoothness of her back, flirting with the rounded globes of her breasts. "But here we are and it does feel good."

"Mmm," she said, shifting position slightly. "You're insatiable."

"So are you."

Then neither of them could speak. As he brought his hand down to caress her, she moaned, moving her hips to enable his slide into her moist heat. The coupling was quick, frantic, exquisite, and she came with stunning swiftness, clinging to him as he gave himself a final thrust into paradise.

He held on to her, his face buried in the fragrance of her hair. God, he still couldn't get over the wonder of Charlotte. One night wasn't enough, a dozen nights wouldn't be. Who had he been fooling? He had to take her as his mistress, buy a house where they could be together, where no one would discover them. Oh God, there'd be the devil's due to pay if they were caught. But surely they could manage to steal away now and then. The arrangement could work if they were both discreet.

Which they definitely weren't being at the moment.

She disengaged herself, giving him a wry, oddly wistful smile as she got out of bed. Very firmly, she said, "You really do have to go now."

"Yes." With more reluctance than he should have felt considering how many times they'd done the deed, he rolled out of bed and collected his scattered clothing. While he dressed, he watched Charlotte bend down to pick up her hairpins, her movements graceful. Her back was turned, and he had the oddest impression that she'd already forgotten his presence.

Or was determined to forget it.

He pulled on his shirt, stuffed it into his breeches, and followed her to the mirror, where she was repinning her hair. Clasping her slender waist, he brushed a kiss over the bare skin of her shoulder.

She deftly extricated herself. "You're leaving. Remember?"

Brand chuckled. "All right, darling. That was only a little farewell until we meet again." He paused, then added huskily, "I confess, I'm anxious to go out this morning and make all the arrangements."

She flashed a startled frown over her shoulder. "Arrangements?"

Her big green eyes reminded him of her naïveté, and he stroked the tender nape of her neck. "I'll find a place where we can meet. For obvious reasons, we'll have to conduct our amour elsewhere."

Her hands stilled on the pins. She turned slowly to face him. "There's no *amour* to conduct, Brand. It's over. I only wanted one night."

He didn't believe her. With her lack of experience, she didn't yet realize that the passions they'd aroused wouldn't so easily die. "Char," he said softly, caressing her cheek because he couldn't stop touching her. "You're new to this. Don't make any hasty decisions. You want me as much as I want you. If you need some time to think—"

"I don't need to think." Cool and collected, she stepped away from him. "I enjoyed what we did, yes, very much. But it's over."

"It isn't over." He paused, catching his thoughts. Charlotte didn't meet his eyes as she would if she were being honest. "If you're worrying about the Rosebuds, don't. They needn't find out, and it's none of their damned business anyway what we choose to do together."

"They're our grandmothers and they *will* find out if we continue this liaison. I won't do it, Brand. I can't. That's final."

Her adamant tone sank into him. She really meant it, she was ending it right here and now. He stared at her, so calm and deliberate, when he was a roiling mass of emotions that he couldn't control.

Anger. Yes, *he* was the one who ended liaisons.

And hurt. Hell, yes, he was hurt that she could spurn him so easily. Didn't she feel anything for him? Did she really believe she could turn her back on the incredible night they'd shared?

To keep from touching her again, he pressed his palm onto the cold wall even as a thought occurred to him. "This is like that night in the coach when I kissed you, isn't it? You wanted me, but you acted like a damned iceberg. That's what you're doing now."

She shook her head as if exasperated. "Brand, I can't make all my decisions based on self-indulgent desires.

What if I were to conceive? Do you really want to create another Amy?"

They might have already done so. The thought of Charlotte rounded with his child hurled him deeper into that morass of unwanted, tender emotions. "There are certain methods of prevention," he muttered. "Granted, I was too overcome to take them, but I shall in the future—"

"No," she stated sharply. "We have no future together. I'm not willing to take any further risks. We both know you wouldn't marry me."

He couldn't deny it. He had no intention of ever being tamed and domesticated, turned into a damned lapdog. Wedlock was for other men, predictable, proper men.

Men like his brother.

Charlotte had known that. So why did he have trouble meeting her eyes? "Promise you'll at least tell me if . . ." *If you're carrying my child.*

She nodded, then stooped down to gather her garments from the rug, a dismissive gesture if ever he'd seen one. And he had to force himself to turn away and walk to the door.

Chapter 20

IRREFUTABLE EVIDENCE

Charlotte was desperate for a distraction.

Unable to sit still, she paced the drawing room at the Vaughns' mansion, wending a path through the clutter of chairs and chaises. In the harsh light of morning, the tentlike décor looked more sordid than dramatic, the gold-striped fabric on the walls and ceiling a garish statement to overindulgence. The brass hookah was nowhere in sight, but a faint smoky aroma lingered in the air.

The Vaughns weren't home, thank goodness. She had come here to interview Miss Darby, to find out the truth about whether or not she'd left those banknotes on behalf of the Vaughns.

Or at least that had been Charlotte's excuse in the message she'd left for the Rosebuds. She'd been too much the coward to answer their summons this morning, afraid they might see the truth in her eyes, that they might guess the awakening of her passions.

She had been driven by the wretched need to escape Brand's house and the bedchamber where they had shared the most extraordinary night of her life.

Dear God. Never in her tame spinsterish dreams had she imagined that physical intimacy could be so wonderful. Or that Brand could join their bodies so perfectly. Her heart overflowed with the memories of his tenderness, his kisses, his possession. Now, a pleasant ache was all that remained.

Along with her battered heart.

He could have no idea of how difficult it had been to turn down his shameful offer. How, when he'd first announced his intention to make arrangements, her foolish heart had hoped he'd meant marriage.

She reached the hearth and gripped the edge of the mantelpiece. Closing her eyes, she relived that impossible surge of joy. Oh, how desperately she'd yearned to believe their lovemaking had created an enduring bond between them. That their closeness had awakened his loving devotion to her. That their night together had changed him as profoundly as it had changed her. She'd thought for one blissful moment that Brand wanted her to be his wife, to bear his children, to share the rest of his life.

His true proposal had been a bitter blow. And yet even in the midst of her pain, she'd wanted to accept him, to take whatever crumbs he offered. Only dignity and pride had saved her. He could have no idea how much she still wanted him, with a fervency born of love. Unrequited love.

She opened her eyes and gazed blindly at her gloved hand on the mantelpiece. One thing was certain, she no longer believed Brand to be a shallow rake, despite the façade he showed the world. He was a complex man, wholly capable of love, for she had seen the look on his face when he'd hugged Amy. He also was capable of grief and remorse, tormenting himself all these years over the deaths of his brother and nephew. And tenderness, for he had shown that side of himself to her all through the night. No, his were not the feelings of a frivolous man.

Yet he *was* irredeemable.

Her eyes filled with tears, but she blinked them back. She couldn't save him, nor could anyone else. Brand was the way he was, and only he could choose to turn from his chosen path of profligacy. And he had chosen to continue down that path.

Not even the prospect of a baby could sway him. He didn't want another child. She had seen the stark, hurtful truth of that in his eyes.

Nevertheless, her hand slipped down over her abdomen, and she wondered if their beautiful joining really might have started a baby inside her. It was a soft, magical thought and utterly wrong of her, but she almost hoped it was true. For herself. She could go off somewhere, pose as a widowed lady, raise his child on her own. There would be some comfort in nurturing his son or daughter . . .

The tap of footsteps intruded on her musings. Miss Darby came hurrying into the drawing room. She was the picture of agitation, from her wide eyes to her wobbling chin. A drab brown shawl drooped from the shoulders of her equally drab beige gown.

"My lady, you're *here*. I didn't expect you'd arrive so swiftly."

Charlotte's distracted mind struggled to make sense of the statement. "Pardon?"

"My letter. Did you not receive it?"

Charlotte shook her head. Her compassion engaged by the girl's obvious distress, she met Miss Darby halfway. "What's wrong? Has something happened?"

" 'Tis them," Miss Darby whispered, glancing fearfully over her shoulder. "My cousin and his wife . . . they've gone out, but they might return at any moment."

"Calm yourself," Charlotte said soothingly. "I won't let them harm you. What have they done?"

"Nothing as yet, but oh, my lady, they're *plotting*. The most awful, dreadful thing."

Charlotte's blood ran cold. Murder? Had Miss Darby overheard them planning to kill another man, someone they owed a great deal of money?

She drew Miss Darby to the side, out of sight of the corridor. Keeping her voice low, Charlotte said, "Tell me. I want to help you."

"Bless you, my lady. I—I didn't know where else to turn." Miss Darby wrung her small, gloved hands. "I overheard them last evening, talking to Mr. Lane. They were striking a bargain."

"A bargain?" Were the Vaughns in league with Uriah Lane?

"Yes. Oh, I don't know how to say this." The girl took a shuddery breath, then went on in a tortured rush, "They intend to *sell* me to Mr. Lane. For his *amusement*."

Taken aback, Charlotte went numb. Of all the despicable schemes she could have imagined of the Vaughns, this was the most unbelievable. They would give this innocent girl into the hands of such a hedonist as Uriah Lane. He would force her, make a violent mockery of the intimate act that ought to be an expression of love between man and wife.

"Are you absolutely certain you didn't misunderstand?" Charlotte asked.

"Yes," Miss Darby said on a moan. "My cousin is

desperately in debt. They set a steep price, and Mr. Lane needed time to get the funds. They were to meet him at his bank this morning."

Charlotte understood the girl's wretchedness. And yet she had to make certain of one fact. She gripped those fluttery hands, encased in fine kid gloves. "Miss Darby, I must ask you something. You must tell me the truth, no matter what."

"Y-yes, my lady. You've been so kind to me. I would do *anything* . . ."

"When you were at Lord Faversham's house yesterday morning, did you go into his library?"

Miss Darby blinked her watery blue eyes. "His library?"

"It's across the hall from the drawing room. Did you happen to look into his desk?"

"W-why would I?" The girl tilted her head to the side as if struggling to think beyond her own troubles. "Oh, dear. Has something gone missing? I vow I didn't take it. I *wouldn't.*"

To judge by her vehemence, she hadn't placed those banknotes for the Vaughns. "Never mind. I'm sure it was simply an oversight." Charlotte made a swift decision. She doubted Brand would approve, but she really didn't care. "We must make haste now to secure your safety. You'll come home with me to Faversham House."

Shortly after luncheon, Charlotte went out to the stables to visit Paddy. The air was cold and damp from the previous day's rain, and puddles dotted the graveled path through the gardens. She had briefly checked on the dog before going to the Vaughns and had found him weak but resting comfortably. Of course, the task was just another means to escape the gloomy atmosphere of the house.

Gloomy for her, at least.

The Rosebuds had taken Miss Darby to their collective bosoms. They had seen her settled into a chamber close to theirs and had exclaimed over her escape from the Vaughns' evil clutches. The girl had brought her meager belongings in a single satchel, for she'd already been packed in the desperate hope that Charlotte would help her. She had been touchingly grateful to be given a temporary home.

If only Charlotte could solve her own problems so readily.

The stableyard was empty except for two grooms who stood chatting by the large double doors. Seeing her, they quickly returned to their tasks. Brand had gone out shortly after their parting at dawn, and she could only surmise that he was investigating the murders. Yet she longed for him to ride through the gate on his big black horse, to swing down and pull her into his arms, to whisper that he'd had a change of heart, that he loved her madly and wanted them to spend the rest of their lives together.

The gate remained closed. The only madness lay in her impossible dreams.

Aware of a tightness in her throat, Charlotte trudged into the stables, turned down the corridor to the left, and went through an open doorway to find Raleigh crouched beside the dog's pallet. The saddles and tack hanging from hooks on the walls gave a pleasant, leathery aroma to the small room.

Paddy lifted his head slightly and regarded her, his

stubby tail moving back and forth. Charlotte knelt down beside the dog. With her emotions so close to the surface, she almost wept at seeing his mangled face with its array of ugly wounds. She wanted to pet the animal, but there were so many gashes on his head, she settled for laying a gentle hand on his warm back.

She looked at the footman's broad, kind features. "How is he faring?"

"He's been eatin' a bit, m'lady. Some beef from the kitchen, chopped up fine. 'Tis a good sign when they eat."

"You've done an excellent job. I must thank you."

A blush spread across his cheeks. He seemed to hesitate for a moment as if he were mulling over something puzzling. "Might ye know where his lordship has gone?"

The mere reference to Brand caused a resonant ache deep inside her. "No, I'm afraid I don't. Why do you ask?"

" 'Bout an hour ago, a chap came snoopin' around here in the stables. I thought maybe his lordship ought to know."

"Snooping? Who?"

"Went by the name of Hannibal Jones. He said he was on official business fer the crown."

The breath froze in Charlotte's lungs. "What was he looking for?"

Raleigh opened his broad palms in an expansive gesture. "Dunno, m'lady. But he peeked in all the rooms an' stalls. An' he told me an' the grooms not to go into the room down aways, that he'd be back soon with the watchman."

She stood up. "Show me this room."

Raleigh led the way to the last door at the end of the

passageway. "I hope I didn't do wrong in not reportin'
the fellow. He did show a paper to prove he weren't a
thief."

Hannibal Jones was an upstart, that's what. "You
were right to tell me. But why did you not tell Lady
Faversham?"

"He said he'd already done so."

What an accomplished liar Jones was! Brand's grandmother would never have given him permission to
search the grounds.

Seething, Charlotte unlatched the door and found herself in a small storage chamber. The single window shed
a dim light on an array of abandoned crates, a broken
stool, a pile of old horseshoes. It was clearly a junk room
containing a jumble of odds and ends. "Do you know
what Mr. Jones saw in here?"

"He was mighty interested in that contraption." Raleigh pointed at the table in the corner that held a large,
squarish machine.

Hastening toward the device, Charlotte noticed the
copper plate and metal levers, the blotters of ink and a
sheaf of clean paper. A black splotch of ink lay like
spilled blood on the wood-planked floor. A knell of
dread struck her. Though she'd never had occasion to
see one before, she recognized at once what it was.

A printing press.

"Dear God," she murmured. For one terrible moment,
it crossed her mind that this press belonged to Brand,
that it was here in his stables. Had he known about it?

Impossible. Someone had planted the press here. As
irrefutable evidence that Brand was a criminal forger.
Someone wanted him to be sent to prison. To die.

"Is aught amiss, m'lady?" Raleigh asked, looking alarmed.

"No . . . yes." She knew only one thing for certain. She couldn't let the press sit here to be used as evidence by Hannibal Jones. "Do you suppose we can lift that gadget, you and I?"

The footman went to the press and hefted one end. "Might need help. I can fetch one of the grooms."

"No." She needed men whom Brand trusted implicitly. "Get Hayward. Don't say a word of this to anyone. And be quick about it."

As Raleigh sprinted out of the room, Charlotte paced feverishly. Who had put the press here? Possibly one of the stablelads? And when? This didn't appear to be a room that was in daily use, so the machine may have been left at any time by anyone. Thank heavens Jones hadn't looked out here yesterday.

Think. Where to take the press? She'd like to dump the blasted thing into the Thames, but unfortunately such an act would attract undue notice. Perhaps Raleigh and Hayward could transport the machine out of the city, find somewhere safe to abandon it.

The middle of the English Channel would do.

She stepped out of the storeroom and saw Raleigh and Hayward hurrying toward her. Meeting them halfway, she murmured, "Is there a dray that we might use?"

"Aye, m'lady, there's a cart out back," Raleigh said. He looked rather mystified, but ready to do her bidding. "Horses will have to be hitched."

"Let's make haste, then."

While they picked up the press, one man at each end, Charlotte gathered the other accouterments, the paper and the ink jars. Her hands shook with the need to hurry.

Jones might return at any moment, and she had no intention of letting him haul Brand off to jail on false charges.

Following the men down the corridor, she bit her lip, realizing how exposed they were. She could probably be arrested herself for absconding with the proof of Brand's guilt. Jones had already seen the press, after all. But maybe, just maybe, she could talk her way out of the tangle, claim she'd never seen the press and had no idea what had become of it.

Thankfully, they passed no one on their way out to the mews. The footmen loaded the machine onto the wooden cart, and Charlotte fetched a horse blanket to cover it from view. Without asking questions, the footmen brought out two horses and proceeded to harness them to the cart. Charlotte resolved to make certain Brand rewarded the men for their discretion.

And how would Brand reward *her*? The thought of his kiss caused a resurgence of that sweet ache inside her. *Stop*. If she allowed such fantasies, she would only make herself more miserable. The moment, the very *instant*, the murderer was apprehended, she was heading straight back to York. With luck, Grandmama would understand.

Of course, Charlotte had no intention of telling her grandmother or anyone else about last night. That would always be her secret, Brand's secret. He wouldn't wish for anyone to guess, either. He knew the Rosebuds would only force them into marriage.

As if conjured by her thoughts, he rode into the mews on his black gelding. Charlotte knew the moment he saw her. He drew up the reins for the space of two heartbeats, then urged the horse into a trot, making straight for her.

She gripped the side of the cart as that weak, foolish desire softened her body. He sat tall and proud, the breeze ruffling his dark hair and giving him that rakish look she loved. Dear God. How *could* she resist him?

Reaching her, he swung down from the saddle. His hungry gaze moved over her face, yet a faintly quizzical quality tempered his eyes. Because of course he would wonder why she was standing in the mews with a cart.

Staring at him like an idiot when his life was at stake.

"You won't believe what I found—"

"What are you doing out here?"

They both spoke at the same time.

So did another voice. The familiar, caustic tone of Hannibal Jones.

"Plotting to hide the evidence?" he asked, loping out the back door of the stable. Another man stood behind him, a stout watchman in cloak and hobnailed boots who looked decidedly uncomfortable at being present.

Brand turned on his heel. Coldness descended over his face. "I told you to stay off my property."

"Henceforth, I will," Jones said, "now that I've found what I was seeking. Though oddly enough, it's vanished. I wonder where it could be?"

Charlotte shifted position in the vain hope of hiding the contents of the cart from his view. But he already knew, for his keen gaze was on her.

His greatcoat flapping around his beanpole form, he marched forward and twitched the blanket away to expose the goods. "Ah, what have we here? A printing press? And a copper plate etched with the likeness of a banknote? It seems your lady was bolting with the contraband. And that makes her an accessory to your crime."

Brand strode forward, frowned at the press, and flashed Charlotte a keen glance. Then he lounged against the cart and gave the officer his most lordly stare. "Don't be a bloody ass. *I* told the footmen to load the press. Just ask them. They obey no one's orders but mine."

He was lying. To protect *her*. "No . . ." Charlotte whispered.

But Raleigh's voice drowned her out. " 'Tis so," he said somberly. "We did as the master told us." Standing by the horses, Hayward nodded as well.

"You'll appear in court and swear to that," the Runner snapped. "And mind, if you perjure yourself, you'll end up in jail, too. Along with her ladyship."

Neither footman looked intimidated by the threat.

Nor did Brand.

All insouciant rake, he strolled toward the Runner. "I'm the one you're after, Jones. Leave them be, and I'll go to Bow Street Station with you. If you behave yourself, I'll even let you lock me behind bars and throw away the key."

Chapter 21

THE ENTRAPMENT

"You did exactly the right thing," Lady Enid told Charlotte later that day as they all sat in the Rosebuds' bedchamber. "There was nothing else you could have done."

"My grandson may have more than his share of faults," Lady Faversham added grimly, "but he would never have allowed a lady to take the blame."

"Olivia is absolutely right," Lady Stokeford concurred. "Besides, what possible good would it serve for you to be imprisoned, too?"

Charlotte knew that logically. Yet the support of the Rosebuds failed to comfort her. If only Jones had appeared five minutes later. If only she'd acted more quickly or had found the printing press sooner . . .

But *what if*s wouldn't save Brand from the gallows.

Unable to sit still, she paced to the window and gazed out into the gathering dusk. She was haunted by the memory of him being carted off to jail in the custody of that loathsome Hannibal Jones. The Runner had commandeered the dray and driven off with his prisoner, with the stout watchman perched in back to guard the evidence.

She and the Rosebuds had spent much of the afternoon at Bow Street Station. Brand had refused to see any of them, and due to the seriousness of the crime, the magistrate had deferred setting bail. Even the high-priced barrister Lady Faversham had engaged had been unable to secure Brand's release.

Charlotte feared Jones would try to pin the murders on Brand, too. Unless she and the Rosebuds found the killer first.

She could only hope that the plan they had devised would work. There was nothing to do but wait until seven o'clock when the Vaughns had been invited here, ostensibly to discuss the fate of Miss Darby. The grateful girl had been cooperative in letting the Rosebuds handle the matter. When Charlotte had looked in on her a short while ago, Miss Darby had been writing in her diary, content to remain safely in her new quarters with a few books to keep her company.

"I must say, Charlotte, it was quite dashing of Brandon to protect you," Lady Stokeford commented. "It would seem to indicate a certain . . . depth of feeling for you."

Startled, Charlotte turned from the window to see three sets of sharp eyes watching her. Brand had said the Rosebuds were angling for a match. How much had they guessed? "We're merely old friends," she said carefully, "and I'm sure he'd have done the same for any woman. Lady Faversham just said so herself."

"I will amend my statement, then," Lady Faversham said, her gnarled hands wrapped around her cane. "I agree with Lucy. There appears to be something deeper than friendship between you and my grandson."

"We've seen the way you two have looked at each other these past few days," Lady Enid said. "You've been much in each other's company. Dare we hope there is romance in the air?"

Charlotte wanted nothing more than to unburden herself of all the wretched misery that weighed down her soul. But how could she do so without revealing the intimacy she and Brand had shared? It was more than fear of censure that kept her silent. She wanted to preserve that wonderful night as a golden memory to be cherished in the privacy of her heart.

The Rosebuds were gazing at her expectantly, so she feigned a careless smile. "It's hardly a romance, Grandmama. You know that Brand and I are as different as spark and tinder."

"Nonetheless," Lady Stokeford said, "the two of you have quite a lot in common. Your families, for one."

"And passion, as well," Grandmama added with a naughty smile. She exchanged a glance with her friends. "Perhaps it's an ill-advised time to bring this up, but . . . we noticed that you and Brandon vanished all night. We wondered if the two of you were together . . . in your bedchamber."

Charlotte's mouth went dry. The fire on the hearth hissed softly into the silence. So they *did* know. She felt exposed, tormented, desperate to hide her wounded emotions.

But not ashamed. She would never feel ashamed for spending one wild night in Brand's arms.

In the dimness of twilight, misguided hope showed on the faces of the Rosebuds. Though Charlotte was loath to disappoint them, perhaps frankness was the best course of action. "Yes, it's true," she admitted. "Brand spent the night with me at my invitation. And I've no regrets whatsoever."

A collective sigh issued from the Rosebuds.

"Of course you shouldn't feel regrets, dearest," Lady Enid said. "Why, we understand exactly what it's like to desire a man with all your heart and soul. Someday, we'll tell you about the night all three of us met our future husbands."

"The night when we became known as the Rosebuds," Lady Stokeford said with a secretive smile.

"I've never looked at a pot of rouge in quite the same manner," Lady Faversham grumbled. "But never mind that. We were speaking of you, Charlotte, and my grandson."

"I must confess," Lady Stokeford broke in, "we left you two alone on purpose. We were hoping for this very thing."

"*I* had my doubts about the wisdom of such a ploy," Lady Faversham said severely. Her gaze drilled into Charlotte. "Has my grandson offered marriage? Never mind, I know the scoundrel too well to expect that. As soon as he's cleared of those ridiculous charges and released from prison, I shall make certain that he does right by you."

"*No.* You will not. You *must* not." Charlotte took a deep breath, her fingers clenched at her sides. "This is a private matter between Brand and me, and none of you will interfere. Nor will any of you censure him for ravishing me. If anything, *I* seduced *him.*"

The Rosebuds didn't appear overly shocked. They twittered amongst themselves, making little murmurings in their secret language.

"He is not to be held to blame," Charlotte went on, desperate to impress upon them the seriousness of her stand. "I chose to be with him for one night, and one night only. I've absolutely no desire to coerce him into becoming my husband." *But oh, if only he didn't require coercion.*

A clamor of protests came from the Rosebuds. "But he must marry you," Lady Enid cried out. " 'Tis the honorable thing."

"We can't let him ruin you," Lady Stokeford said in a reasonable tone. "You're distraught now, but you must face the consequences. After all, you might be with child."

Charlotte's breast squeezed. "In such an unlikely event, I'll raise the baby alone. But I will *not* be the next Lady Faversham. That is *my* choice. And I must command the three of you to abide by my wishes."

"Well!" Lady Faversham said dryly. "You certainly speak with the authority of a countess. You're capable and intelligent, and Brandon could never do better than you. He's a fool if he doesn't see it."

"He'll see it eventually," Lady Enid said, regarding Charlotte with a tender, anxious smile. "I've always thought you two were meant for each other."

Meant for each other. How dearly Charlotte wished that were true. But not even the Rosebuds could change Brand's nature. He had been too long the rogue. "We aren't," she stated emphatically. "Trust me, we'll never marry."

"This is no time to be making decisions about your future," Lady Stokeford said in a kindly tone. "We're all upset by Brandon's arrest. Better we should concentrate on identifying the murderer."

As if privy to an unspoken message from her friend, Lady Faversham relented as well. "You're absolutely right," she said. "Trust *me*, heads will roll over this false imprisonment. And Hannibal Jones will be the first to go to the guillotine."

Lady Enid reached over to pat her friend on the arm. "Do take heart, Olivia. Everything will turn out right in the end. We do have our plan for tonight."

"Bah, I'll do my part, but it won't work, you mark my words," Lady Faversham said. "It's far too wild a scheme. Your wildest yet, Lucy."

"It *will* work," Lady Stokeford said firmly. "The invitations have been sent, our roles have been determined, and now we can only hope for the best."

The Vaughns were the last to arrive. As usual, they were odious.

"Where is that naughty little cousin of mine?" Lord Clifford said the moment he'd shoved his coat and hat at the footman. "I've a good mind to turn the chit over my knee and thrash her."

"Stuff it, Cliffie." Lydia scowled at her husband, then aimed a phony smile at Charlotte. "We were extremely concerned when we discovered that Margaret had vanished from our house. It was a vast relief to receive your note and know that she is in safe hands. Where is the dear girl?"

Charlotte saw the poisonous snake behind that performance. "She's upstairs at present. If you'll come into the drawing room now."

Turning, Charlotte led the way through the huge entrance hall. Lydia caught up to her. "We're late because Sefton came by to relay the most fascinating rumor. That Faversham's been *arrested*."

"For forgery, clever fellow," Clifford said, trotting

along on the other side of Charlotte. "Do you know where he's stashed his printing press? I could use an extra fifty thousand pounds or so." He chortled as if at a great jest.

Though tempted to snap at him, Charlotte kept a calm demeanor. It wasn't the first time she'd been asked about Brand tonight by their guests. Apparently the news had spread like a nasty rash through the *ton*, which made her all the more resolved to clear his name.

"It was a terrible shock," she said. "And I assure you, Brand isn't guilty of the crime. I thought we could put our heads together and determine how to help him. That's why I asked you to come here tonight, you and a few other of his friends."

"I thought this had to do with Margaret," Lydia said indignantly. "Whatever could *we* do for Faversham?"

"Lyddie's right, we've enough troubles of our own," Clifford added. "We only came here to fetch my cousin. We'll escort the chit home straightaway."

"Yes, we must insist . . ." Lydia's strident voice trailed off as they reached the arched doorway to the drawing room. She nudged her husband. "Hsst. There's Lane. Perhaps we'll stay a bit, after all. At least until Margaret is summoned downstairs."

Charlotte compressed her lips. She had no intention of sending for Miss Darby. The Vaughns didn't know it yet, but their ward was staying right here, out of their clutches and as far away from Uriah Lane as possible.

The gold buttons of his waistcoat straining at his big belly, Lane sat on a chaise beside a stern-faced Lady Faversham. He looked uncomfortable, disgruntled, and ready to bolt. When the Vaughns walked in, he made a move to get up, but Lady Faversham stuck out her cane and blocked his progress.

"Stay, Mr. Lane. I'm enjoying our conversation. It's been a long time since I spoke with a man of so little brain."

"He thinks with another part of his anatomy, my lady," said Colonel Tom Ransom, who lounged in a chair opposite them, a coolly amused expression on his handsome face. "His balls matter more to him than his brains."

Lady Faversham leaned forward and poked Ransom with the tip of her cane. "Sit up straight, boy. And bide your tongue. There are ladies present."

Glowering, Ransom squared his shoulders with military precision.

Lane snickered. "Give it to him, my lady. Whack him a good one."

"I'll whack both of you reprobates. Believe me, I've had plenty of experience with my grandson."

Charlotte exchanged a glance with her grandmother who sat talking with a rather perplexed-looking Harold Rountree. Charlotte had written to him about Brand's arrest, and Mr. Rountree had arrived a full twenty minutes ahead of schedule. He'd used the time to plead with her to leave this house and avoid the taint of scandal. He'd seemed so sincerely anxious to protect her reputation, so tenderly devoted to safeguarding her, that she'd felt awkward and strained in his presence. If he knew that she'd given herself to Brand . . .

She mustn't think about that now. She must treat Mr. Rountree like all the other culprits and presume him guilty until proven innocent.

The chairs had been arranged in a circle beforehand

in such a way that she and the Rosebuds could watch the suspects carefully. Raleigh and Hayward stood like sentinels on either side of the doorway.

Lady Stokeford chatted with the Reverend Sir John Parkinson, who had shed his white robes in favor of an unfashionably plain black coat and breeches. Yet his luxurious fall of brown curls gave the impression that he'd spent hours grooming himself. Charlotte could only surmise he was attempting to make himself look like the Savior.

She led the Vaughns to the three remaining chairs, across from Lady Stokeford. Lydia sat down beside a gilt-framed mirror on the wall, turning to primp at her reflection and admire her elegant twist of dark hair.

"Eh, is that you, Parkinson?" Clifford Vaughn said, his swarthy face showing his relish at having a new target. He slapped the cleric on the shoulder. "Heard you found religion, by God. A pity we won't see you in hell with the rest of us someday. You're going to miss a blistering good party."

Parkinson's thin face took on an evangelical light. "I see you're still up to your old tricks, Vaughn. You would do well to attend one of my sermons at the Church of the True Believers. Besides our Sunday services, we meet every Thursday evening for a lecture—"

"Oh, fiddlesticks," Vaughn said, snapping his stubby fingers with exaggerated regret. "Thursdays there's usually a good show at the dance hall. Want to come along with me sometime? The dancers are quite fetching when they toss up their skirts."

His lips taut, Parkinson pointed his finger at Vaughn. "Sinner! The devil is at work in you, but *I* shall never succumb to the evil lure of temptation. Woe betide those like yourself who refuse redemption—"

"Enough," Lady Stokeford said firmly. "This is an inappropriate topic of conversation. Lord Clifford, you will refrain from making suggestive comments. Sir John, you will desist from reforming anyone tonight. Do I make myself clear, gentlemen?"

Parkinson stuck his self-righteous nose in the air, but said nothing more.

His hand clasped to his bright yellow waistcoat, Clifford Vaughn swept an extravagant bow. "Forgive me, my dear lady. I don't believe we've been properly introduced. Is it true you're one of the famous Rosebuds?"

Lady Stokeford inclined her head. "And you, sir, are one of the infamous rascals in this town."

Vaughn gave an indelicate chuckle. "Guilty as charged." He sat down beside his wife, who was busy making eyes at Parkinson, who in turn was busy pretending not to stare at the low-cut bodice of her gown.

Lady Faversham stood up, thumping her cane on the fine rug to get everyone's attention. "Now that we're all present," she said, "it's time we told you the purpose of tonight's meeting."

"Hear, hear," Colonel Ransom drawled. "I'm meeting friends shortly for a game at my club, and I can't be late."

"You'll stay until I give you permission to go. That applies to all of you." Imposing in gray silk, the countess swept her gaze over each of the six guests. Clifford and Lydia looked annoyed, Mr. Rountree alert, Lane fidgety, Parkinson aloof, Ransom displeased. "As you know, my grandson has been arrested for the crime of forgery. The charges are completely false. Someone placed counterfeit banknotes in his desk and a printing press in the stables."

"You're saying Faversham was framed?" Mr. Rountree asked in transparent disbelief. "Pardon me, my lady, but that seems a tad far-fetched."

"I must agree," Colonel Ransom said. "Granted, there are those who might wish revenge upon him for various misdeeds. But why would anyone go to such lengths?"

There were nods and murmurings from the other guests.

"Murder," Charlotte said tightly.

The word dropped like an explosive into the room. Everyone fell silent, staring at her. Their expressions bore variations of the same reaction: stunned, riveted, fascinated.

"Yes, this is murder in the making," Lady Faversham said, leaning on her cane and eyeing the suspects. "Someone has plotted to send my grandson to the gallows."

"This is too delicious to be believed," Lydia said with the avid air of a gossip. "Who would be so diabolical?" She elbowed her husband. "Cliffie, you know Faversham better than I. Who would resent him enough to plan such an elaborate scheme?"

Vaughn eyed the others. "How about Parkinson there? Faversham stole his mistress a few years ago."

The cleric bristled. "Slanderer! I hold no grudges in my heart, only forgiveness for those too wicked to follow the light of salvation. Your ladyship, better you should look at Vaughn himself. He's lost a fortune to your grandson at the gaming tables."

"And who hasn't?" Vaughn taunted. "Might as well

try to pin the blame on all the gamesters in London and beyond."

Lady Faversham rapped her cane on the floor again. "Gentlemen, cease this squabbling. We are not finished here. Lucy, will you tell them the rest?"

Lady Stokeford gave a queenly nod. Crowned by a mass of snow-white hair, she wore a pale blue gown that enhanced her delicate frame. "Indeed, the situation is far graver than we've yet revealed. You see, Brandon is not the only one who has been targeted. In recent months, five other gentlemen have been killed by various means."

Silence reigned for a moment. The tall casement clock bonged the hour of eight, making everyone jump. Like water from a broken dam, a gush of exclamations poured from the guests.

"Who?" Lydia demanded. "Who has been killed? Why haven't I heard any gossip?"

Uriah Lane dabbed at his flushed face with a folded handkerchief. "James Weatherby?" he asked hoarsely. "Was he one of them?"

"Yes," Lady Stokeford said. "And before him, Viscount Trowbridge was attacked and killed by ruffians. Lord Mellingham died in a duel. Mr. Simon Wallace fell down a flight of stairs and broke his neck. And Sir Raymond Aldrich suffered a heart seizure."

"Those were all tragic events, but hardly the work of a murderer," Colonel Ransom scoffed. "For one, Mellingham's pistol misfired. I should know, I was his second."

Charlotte studied those classic, aristocratic features, the strong jaw and high cheekbones, the perfectly groomed blond hair. Would Ransom admit to such a damning fact if he was guilty? "Brand said nothing of that."

"It's common knowledge," the colonel said with a wave of his hand. "Certainly it was an unfortunate accident, but nothing that could be attributed to some dark criminal deed."

"Murder can be made to look like an accident," Lady Stokeford said in a crisp tone. "Certain poisons can cause a heart seizure. A man can be pushed down a flight of stairs. Ruffians can be hired for the right price. And guns can be tampered with."

Colonel Ransom raised a disbelieving eyebrow, but said no more.

Mr. Rountree blew out a breath. "I'm astonished," he said. "Lady Charlotte, how long have you known about this?"

Charlotte didn't wish to become the focus of attention. "Only a short while," she murmured.

"But you never told me. You asked me all those questions. Great God! Is that why you haven't wanted to accept my—"

"Mr. Rountree, please! We'll discuss the matter later." Charlotte glared at him, and he clamped his mouth shut as if just realizing he'd almost spilled their personal concerns in front of a throng of eager listeners.

"Yes, do allow me to continue," Lady Stokeford said. "As some of you may have already guessed, there is a connection between all these deaths. A connection that goes back four years to the Lucifer League."

"That silly club?" Lydia said. "It disbanded ages ago."

"Yet every one of the men killed belonged to it,"

Lady Stokeford said. "As did Brandon and all of you gentlemen here tonight."

Uriah Lane uttered a strangled laugh. "Surely you can't be suggesting that someone is going after all of us. That means . . . we shall be killed, too."

"Stuff and nonsense," Clifford Vaughn said on a half-hearted laugh. "You're funning us, aren't you, ladies? Ha-ha. I'm an expert at such tricks."

"It's no jest," Charlotte stated. "I can assure you of that."

"It's God's judgment, that's what," Sir John Parkinson muttered, sinking deeper in his chair and glowering at the others. "We'll all be murdered in our beds, even those of us who have repented our sins."

"What rot," Lydia told him. "And you'll stop saying so this instant. Such talk gives me the shivers."

Charlotte deemed it time to introduce the next phase of the plan. She gave her grandmother a small, encouraging nod.

Lady Enid cleared her throat. "This has been very shocking news, I can see," she said, her plump face grave beneath her gold turban. "I'm sure all of you would like some refreshment. The footman will bring round the wine."

On cue, Raleigh left his station by the doorway and went out into the corridor. A moment later, he returned empty-handed and frowned at Charlotte in consternation.

From behind him stepped a somber-faced Miss Darby. She carried the silver tray of ten crystal glasses filled with burgundy wine.

Alarmed, Charlotte rose at once and hastened to the doorway. She had instructed the girl to wait in her chamber and not to venture downstairs for any reason. Miss

Darby knew only that the Vaughns had been invited so that Charlotte and the Rosebuds could resolve the problem of Uriah Lane.

Miss Darby clearly had no idea how her presence could wreck their ploy to trap a murderer.

"You must go back upstairs at once," Charlotte whispered urgently. "Wait until I call for you."

She tried to take the tray, but Miss Darby clung to it with uncustomary stubbornness. Her voice a mere breath of sound, she said, "Please, I—I heard everything. I want to be brave like you. I want to help catch the murderer."

Oh, dear God. "That's very admirable, but—"

"There you are, you naughty girl," Lydia called out to Miss Darby. "We've come to collect you."

" 'Deed so," Clifford added. "Don't run off again. Sit down right here where I can watch you." He sprang up to place another chair beside his.

"She can't stay," Lady Stokeford said sharply. "Let her go wait in the library."

But Miss Darby was already gliding forward, the tray in her white-gloved hands.

Ruining their carefully orchestrated plan to catch the murderer.

Charlotte knew she had to act quickly.

Miss Darby had stopped near Uriah Lane and set down the heavy tray on a table. As she took a glass and handed it to him, he leered at her. The girl froze, and Charlotte seized her chance.

She picked up the silver tray. "I'll take this now."

Her brief show of bravado thankfully in tatters, Miss Darby relinquished the task without a murmur. She scurried away to sit on the chair beside her cousin. She bowed her head and hunched her shoulders as if trying to make herself as small as possible.

Breathing a sigh of relief, Charlotte distributed the remainder of the glasses. Perhaps all was *not* lost. No one had paid much notice to the little scene. They were all too anxious for liquid sustenance.

"Ah, the night improves immensely," Clifford Vaughn said, smacking his lips as he took a sip. "Faversham always did have the best cellar."

Lady Faversham held up her glass. "I propose a toast to the imminent arrest of our murderer."

"I second the motion," Mr. Rountree said gravely. "The sooner the fellow is behind bars, the better."

The guests drank deeply. Uriah Lane slurped his wine with gusto, all the while casting covetous looks at Miss Darby. Charlotte fought back the urge to slap him. He must think the girl had come to the drawing room in search of him. Striving for calm, she took a sip from her glass without tasting it.

"*Is* an arrest imminent?" Colonel Ransom asked. "Are the officers from Bow Street Station involved?"

"Quite so," Lady Faversham said. "As it happens, we Rosebuds have found conclusive evidence pointing to the identity of the criminal. In fact, the murderer is sitting right here in our midst."

Lydia choked on a sip. Waving her manicured hand, she managed to say, "What? What was that?"

Everyone else glanced warily around at their fellow visitors.

"Never fear," Charlotte said, "we're expecting an officer to arrive momentarily. He'll find the murderer already subdued by the poison we've placed in his drink."

Gasps swept the gathering. Everyone froze and stared at his goblet.

Except for Vaughn, who spewed out a mouthful of wine all over his cousin's lap.

Miss Darby sprang up—too late. Red liquid stained the front of her brown dress and drenched her gloves like blood.

"Sorry," Clifford sputtered between coughs.

His wife cuffed him on the ear. "You're such a bufflehead, Cliffie. Those gloves are expensive. They'll have to be put to soak immediately. Give them to the footman, Margaret."

Miss Darby hesitated, then peeled off the gloves and gave them to Hayward. Distractedly, Charlotte noticed the dark, faded splotches marking those delicate fingers. The girl must have spilled ink while she was writing in her diary or penning letters. Miss Darby sat down at Lydia's urging and resumed her pose of invisibility.

Charlotte watched the Vaughns closely. Had Clifford spat out his drink because he feared it was doctored? Was he the guilty one?

There was no poison in the wine. The suspects couldn't know it was all a ruse, devised in the hope that the murderer would give himself away by being too afraid to drink more. The only trouble was, now no one seemed inclined to take another sip.

Mr. Rountree gazed askance at his goblet. "I say, how do we know the glasses didn't get mixed up?"

Apparently, that possibility was on everyone else's mind, too.

Uriah Lane's coarse features looked pasty-gray in the candlelight.

Colonel Ransom gripped his goblet with a white-knuckled hand.

Lydia stared wide-eyed into her glass, while Clifford looked as if he'd swallowed a toad.

"There was no mistake made," Lady Stokeford said. "Lady Charlotte is extremely competent."

"But Margaret took the tray," Lydia screeched. "That stupid girl could have moved the glasses around and poisoned me by mistake. Will I suffer convulsions and die?"

"Please be assured, only the murderer will be affected," Lady Faversham said. "The rest of you can safely finish your wine."

"I'm not afraid," Sir John Parkinson declared. "God will protect the righteous." He tilted back his head and took a gulp, though his hand was shaking and he sloshed a few drops on his sleeve.

"This is nonsense," Colonel Ransom said, setting down his goblet on a table with a definitive click. "I don't believe you've put anything at all in these drinks. You're trying to frighten one of us into confessing."

Charlotte hadn't given him sufficient credit for being so sharp.

"If you believe that," she said coolly, "you oughtn't be afraid of finishing your wine."

"I despise trickery," he snapped. "I won't be played for a fool. And the rest of you ought not play their game, either."

As if burned, Lydia quickly put down her glass. So did Uriah Lane, his broad features looking distinctly ill.

Mr. Rountree hesitated, gave Charlotte a wounded stare, then set his glass aside, as well. "Can you truly think *I* had any part in these horrible murders, my lady?"

That hurt look struck her, yet she had more important things on her mind. The ploy would fail completely if the innocent among the party refused to drink. Brand would be tried for forgery and sentenced to die . . .

Just then, Uriah Lane moaned. He clutched at his chest, and his eyes rolled back in his head. Like a toppling oak, he crashed to the floor and lay still.

Chapter 22
THE TELLTALE INK

An uproar of cries and gasps came from the guests.

"It's him!" Lydia shrieked. "Lane is the murderer."

"Good God!" Parkinson exclaimed. "Is he dead?"

Lady Faversham stepped to the fallen man and stared down in blatant disbelief. "He's suffered a heart seizure. Raleigh, fetch a physician. Hayward, get some smelling salts. We must try to revive him."

As the footmen sprang for the door, Charlotte rushed to kneel beside Lane. She slapped his cheek, but he didn't stir. A pink-tinged foam dribbled from one corner of his mouth. His fleshy form was unmoving.

Dear God. *Dear God.*

Harold Rountree crouched on the other side of Lane. Thrusting his fingers inside the white linen cravat, he felt Lane's beefy neck. "No detectable pulse, I fear." Mr. Rountree gave Charlotte a black, accusatory glare. "What sort of poison did you administer?"

Her mouth was bone dry. She slowly shook her head. "Nothing. There was *nothing* in the wine. It was merely a trick, as Colonel Ransom said."

Dear God, how had their plan gone so horribly awry?

She glanced up to see the Rosebuds huddled together,

their faces as horror-struck and bewildered as hers must be. Shakily, she got to her feet.

Lady Stokeford pressed her hand to her bosom. "Lane must be the one," she murmured to her friends. "He must have been in a dither and his heart gave out."

"I never imagined such dreadful results to our scheme," Lady Enid said, her face pale.

Charlotte heard them only peripherally. Unable to shake a dire sense of having missed a vital clue, she looked over the gathering. Lydia and Clifford clung to one another. Colonel Ransom sat bolt upright in his chair. Sir John Parkinson clasped his hands together while his lips moved in silent prayer. Miss Darby had risen from her seat and hovered like a wraith.

The expression on those dainty features arrested Charlotte. As if transfixed, Miss Darby stared down at Lane. But unlike the others in the group, she didn't appear shocked or distraught. Rather, there was an odd quality to her regard, almost like . . . satisfaction.

Miss Darby had handed that drink to Lane.

Charlotte rebelled against the horrible hammer of suspicion. Had Miss Darby added poison to Lane's wine? Was it merely an attempt to save herself from being bartered for his loathsome pleasures? Or was this incident linked somehow to the other murders?

Miss Darby had inkstains on her hand. From the printing press?

It made no sense. What possible connection could a shy, unassuming girl have to the Lucifer League?

Charlotte didn't know, couldn't imagine. But she had one thing to do before she confronted Miss Darby. Turning, she hurried out of the room.

• • •

Intent on her mission, Nan slipped out the back door and into the garden. For once, fussy old Giffles didn't dog her footsteps. He was distracted by all the commotion in the drawing room.

Mr. Lane had collapsed from a heart seizure. The mistress had looked distressed while giving Nan the urgent message to deliver, but Nan couldn't bring herself to feel a bit of pity. He was a nasty bloke, and if he died, well, that meant he wouldn't be forcing himself on any more serving maids. She still shuddered at the nightmarish memory of his meaty paws, the stench of liquor on his breath.

As she neared the back gate, she had only an instant's warning. A dark shape sprang from the shadows of a tree.

Squawking, she jumped. Her panic turned to dismay as she recognized the small, wiry form of a man. "Dick! Thee gave me a fright." She glanced behind her at the house where the candles glowed in the windows. "Thee shouldn't be here."

"That's no way to greet yer man." Dick pulled her close and planted a smacking kiss on her lips. His taste of sour sausages and smoke repulsed her. "Did ye get it? Did ye find the gold?"

Her heart pounding with dread, she wriggled free. Bracing herself to tell the truth, Nan took a deep breath of cold air. "I—I've changed my mind. His lordship—he's been good t' me. It isn't right t' steal from him."

Dick loosed a fearsome growl. "Ain't right? It ain't right for ye and me to scrabble fer a crust o' bread while these toffs live like kings. All I want is a bit o' gold, my fair share. Are ye forgettin' so quick all I done fer ye?"

"Nay," she whispered, not wanting to think of that awful night, when he had helped her flee, helped her wash off the blood . . .

Dick took firm hold of her shoulders, his voice cajoling. "Then do as I say, Nan, me girl. Ye don't want to stir me temper."

Fear flooded her, weakening her knees and her resolve. Yet the thought of her ladyship's trust gave her strength. "I . . . can't do it. I won't steal for thee. Please, thee mustn't ask me."

"Devil take ye." He gave her a shake, hard enough to rattle her teeth. "I ought to go to the law, report ye fer murder an' collect a reward—"

Someone yanked him away. Nan stumbled and caught her balance. Her shawl slipped, but she scarcely noticed.

Through the darkness, Giffles struck Dick in the jaw. A dull crack resounded. Dick went sprawling backward to land in a bush.

He lay there, moaning in pain.

The valet stood over him. "Get out," he said in a stern voice rather like the devil earl's. "If ever I see you again, I'll send you straight to hell."

Dick moved at once. Whimpering, he scrambled on all fours to the garden gate, glancing back as if to make sure his attacker didn't follow. The gate slammed and the sound of running footsteps vanished down the mews.

Giffles walked toward her. He picked up her shawl and draped it snugly around her shoulders. "The bastard won't bother you again."

Nan was so overwhelmed by a confusing mix of relief

and joy that she threw herself at the valet. His arms closed tightly around her. Her heart raced, but no longer out of fear.

She pressed her cheek to his, breathing in his clean scent of soap, turning her lips, seeking . . .

His kiss. He took her mouth in a brief, fervent, thrilling kiss.

Too soon, he drew back. His hand tenderly cupped her cheek, then dropped to his side. It was too dark to see more than the indistinct outline of his face, but she felt the force of his stare. "Murder, Miss Killigrew?"

That hard edge to his voice made her want to weep. He had heard Dick's threat. Shivering, Nan drew the edges of the shawl tighter around herself. Giffles would truly despise her now. But if she was going to live an honest life, he deserved the truth.

So she told him in halting words about her father, about the awful things he had done to her, and how she had finally fought back. When she was done, she waited in dread for Giffles to condemn her.

He took her hand, laced his fingers through hers, placing his other hand over the back of hers in a way that made her feel . . . *loved.* "We can talk more about this later," he said. "For now, we'd best make haste. You've an errand for your mistress."

"T' Bow Street Station t' fetch Mr. Jones." Nan scurried to keep up with Giffles as he went to open the gate. Her heart full of cautious hope, she said, "Will thee go with me, then?"

"Always." In a shaft of moonlight, his faint smile gleamed. "I'm afraid you're stuck with this old stick-in-the-mud. For as long as we both shall live."

• • •

Miss Darby sat on a straight-backed chair in the library. Her face was remorseful, her blue eyes watery, her hands clasped in her lap. She cowered before the Rosebuds, Charlotte, and Hannibal Jones, who sat in a half-circle around her.

"Y-yes, I poisoned Mr. Lane," she admitted, her lower lip wobbling. "I'd overheard my cousin talking. He wanted to give me to Mr. Lane. For his . . . his *pleasures*."

Jones scribbled something in his notebook. "And where would a young lady like you obtain poison?"

"Rat killer, sir. I—I found a box in the cupboard."

"So you acted on impulse? You saw the opportunity and seized it?"

"Yes, sir." Tears rolled down Miss Darby's pale cheeks. "I—I only meant to make him *ill*. So that he wouldn't . . . touch me. I didn't know he would *die*."

Charlotte's stomach lurched. Only a short time ago, the physician had pronounced Uriah Lane dead. The other guests had departed, including the Vaughns, who had slipped out during all the turmoil. Charlotte had a strong suspicion they already were spreading the news to the *ton*.

They had abandoned their ward to her fate.

Little did they realize, however, Miss Darby was quite capable of managing the situation. She was well on her way to convincing Hannibal Jones that Lane's death was an isolated incident, a crime born of fear and desperation. She would be magnificent on the witness stand, relating that teary-eyed tale to a judge and jury.

Charlotte had been a fool to trust her, to welcome her into this house. But no longer.

"Show Mr. Jones the inkstains on your fingers," Charlotte said.

Miss Darby thrust her fists deeper in her lap. "I—I don't see why . . ."

"Kindly obey," Lady Stokeford said in a steely tone. "If you've nothing to hide, then you've nothing to fear."

Sniffling, Miss Darby uncurled her fingers long enough to give the Bow Street Runner a look.

"Inkstains," he pronounced. "I can't see what bearing they have to Lane's death."

"I—I spilled a jar of ink," Miss Darby said. "While I was writing yesterday—"

"While she was moving the printing press into the stables sometime during the past week," Lady Faversham stated.

Lady Enid nodded vigorously. "Those splotches are too faded to have been acquired just yesterday."

"There was ink spilled by the press," Charlotte added. "You should have noticed it, Mr. Jones, when you found the machine."

He frowned. "With all due respect, the forger is already behind bars."

Lady Faversham shook her cane. "Blast you, my grandson is no criminal. He didn't forge those banknotes. This young chit did the deed."

Lady Stokeford laid a comforting hand on her friend's arm. But her hard gaze was on Hannibal Jones. "Another member of the Lucifer League has been murdered," she said. "You cannot dismiss the connection, Mr. Jones. It is far too extraordinary a coincidence."

Jones scratched his ear with his pencil stub. Yet he seemed to have a bulldog determination to lay all the blame on Brand. "She couldn't have lifted such a heavy press."

"So she hired an accomplice," Charlotte said. Her throat taut, she added, "Margaret Darby has sentenced his lordship to death for a crime he didn't commit."

Miss Darby made a moan of distress. "*No. I don't* want him to die."

Charlotte wanted to rage at her for lying. Yet something in that small, woebegone voice struck a chord in her. If Miss Darby could put on a performance, then by God, so could Charlotte.

Leaving her chair, she sank to her knees in front of Miss Darby, taking those small hands in hers. Warm hands that had committed cold-blooded murder.

But Charlotte couldn't allow herself to flinch. Holding Miss Darby's gaze, she said passionately, "I love Brand with all my heart. But he *will* die unless you speak up. For the sake of our friendship, I beg you, don't let the man I love be sent to the gallows."

Miss Darby's face crumpled. "All right, all *right*. I did it, I left the banknotes. It was just to stop him from asking questions. But I wouldn't have let him die. He wasn't one of *them*."

" 'Them'?"

"The men who did . . . *that* to me." Miss Darby shuddered. "The ones who tied me up and forced me."

Charlotte was only half-aware of the small gasps from the Rosebuds, the whisper of skirts as they leaned closer. She could hear the furious scratchings of Mr. Jones's pencil in his notebook. She kept her full attention fixed on those big blue eyes, now brimming with genuine tears of anguish.

"Do you mean . . . the Lucifer League?" Charlotte

prodded gently. "But the group disbanded four years ago. You couldn't have been more than fourteen at the time."

"It was three years ago that it happened, and I was fifteen. I was visiting my cousin, but he and Lydia were away from the house. His friends came to call and they"—Miss Darby tightened her grip on Charlotte's hands—"they trapped me in my bedchamber. They all took turns . . . doing unspeakable acts . . ."

"Did you never tell anyone?"

Miss Darby shook her head as another tremor ran through her. "They swore they'd kill me if I told. It was only later that I decided to kill *them*."

Charlotte couldn't help feeling compassion for Miss Darby and fury at the men who had abused her. And yet . . . to murder them all . . .

"Those men were Mellingham, Wallace, Aldrich, Trowbridge, Weatherby, and Lane. Who else?"

"Lane was the last one." Incredibly, Miss Darby's lips curved into a small smile. "It wasn't precisely the way I'd intended for him to die, but when the opportunity presented itself, I couldn't resist."

Sickened, Charlotte pictured the girl plotting murder in the privacy of her bedchamber when she ought to have had nothing more serious on her mind than which gown to wear to the next ball.

"And the attack on the Rosebuds?" Charlotte asked. "Was that simply an attempt to distract Brand?"

"Yes, he'd started making inquiries." As if just remembering their presence, Miss Darby looked over at the three old women. "I'm—I'm sorry. You were so kind to me. You and Lady Charlotte . . ." Faltering, she pulled her hands away. "I—I can't talk about this any longer."

Hannibal Jones took her by the arm and helped her to her feet. "Come along. I'll get the rest of the confession at Bow Street Station."

"And you'll free my grandson at once," Lady Faversham said, using her cane to lever herself out of the chair. "He is not to be incarcerated a moment longer than necessary."

He grimaced. "Yes, my lady. Though there will be some paperwork to be signed by the magistrate that might delay his release. I do beg your pardon for the mistake."

"Don't beg mine," she said frostily. "Better you should beg my grandson's pardon."

A short time later, Charlotte paced her bedchamber. The house was silent, and Fancy slumbered in her little basket near the dressing room. But Charlotte couldn't relax.

She needed time alone to think, to absorb all that had happened. To calm herself before Brand arrived back home.

Brand. Her heart rejoiced at the knowledge that he would soon be free. The charges against him had been dropped, his name cleared of all crime. If he walked through the doorway right now, she would throw herself into his arms. They would celebrate right there in her bed.

Foolish. Foolish. Foolish.

Charlotte couldn't allow herself to taste forbidden fruit again. *Never* again. One night would lead to another and another. And in the end, her heart would still be broken, perhaps worse than it hurt already. Brand was thirty-seven years old and he wasn't going to transform himself into the marrying kind.

Not even for her.

Stopping at the bedpost, Charlotte leaned her cheek against the brocade hangings. It served no purpose to wish for things that she had no power to change. She should leave on the morrow. Grandmama would understand. Charlotte was free to go now that the murderer had been apprehended.

Miss Darby.

Still shaken, Charlotte seized on the distraction. Who would have thought Miss Darby capable of murder? All this time, they had been investigating the members of the league, looking for motives, seeking clues, when the perpetrator was an innocent-looking girl of eighteen who had once been abused by a select few of those men.

Charlotte felt dispirited by the discovery. It was horrid, and she certainly condemned it, yet she could almost understand Margaret Darby's obsession.

What she couldn't fully fathom was how the girl had accomplished five of those six murders. Of course, she hadn't acted alone; she had hired Tupper to act as footman.

Could she also have hired a man to make Mellingham's pistol misfire? Someone to attack Trowbridge in an alleyway? Someone to slit Weatherby's wrists?

Charlotte shivered, rubbing her arms. Had Miss Darby hired the same man each time? Or different ones? And how on earth did a gently bred girl like her meet such ruffians?

That was the crux of the issue.

Or perhaps she *didn't* meet them. Perhaps she had a

man who acted as a go-between, someone close to her, someone she trusted. At the Vaughns' party, when Charlotte had confessed her feelings for Brand, that all other men paled in comparison, Miss Darby's answer had been puzzling.

Ah, I believe I do understand.

Charlotte straightened as cold certainty gripped her. Miss Darby *did* have an accomplice. Yet she hadn't revealed his identity, hadn't made him share the blame. For her to protect him even while she went to prison could only mean he was someone very dear to her.

Someone she might write about in her diary.

Charlotte snatched up a candle and hurried to the door. Cupping her hand around the flame to keep it from blowing out, she half ran down the shadowed passageway to the guest chamber that had been Miss Darby's.

The door was slightly ajar. Charlotte pushed it open and went into the darkened room, closing the door behind her. The last thing she wanted was to alarm the Rosebuds. They'd had enough excitement for one day.

She raised her candle and glanced around. The place was tidy, the bed covers straight and the pillows plumped. Except for the shawl draped across the back of a chair, the room looked as if it had never been occupied, albeit for only a day.

Where would Miss Darby keep her diary? In her valise?

But Charlotte couldn't see the case anywhere. Before she searched the dressing room, she stopped to look in the desk. It was a dainty table with a single, empty drawer. The surface held only a porcelain cup filled with quills and a silver inkwell.

And a candlestick . . . the wick still smoldering.

Charlotte put out her finger and touched warm wax. *Someone was here.*

Her insides clenching, she spun around, spied a movement. The dark shadow of a man. Heading straight at her.

A scream rose in her throat. Too late.

Strong arms snatched her, stuffed a cloth in her mouth. With stunning efficiency, he threw her facedown on the bed and secured her hands behind her back. Charlotte squirmed and fought to no avail.

"This will hurt a bit," he murmured, his hand caressing the back of her neck. "Do forgive me."

That voice. *She knew it.*

A sharp pain struck behind her ear, drowning recognition and plunging her into darkness.

Chapter 23
THE DIARY

As adventures went, this one stank.

Brand didn't need to survey the tiny, dark, unheated prison cell to know that. The scant illumination came from a lamp somewhere out in the corridor. After pacing the stone floor for hours, he knew every damned inch of the cubicle. Brick walls, high slit of a window, heavy oak door with a small barred opening. Except for a slops bucket in the corner of the cell, a wooden bench constituted the entire furnishings.

The loss of freedom infuriated and frightened him. He wasn't afraid for himself but for Charlotte. It would be just like her to go after the murderer.

Dammit, she'd get herself killed.

Brand drew a deep, steadying breath. He forced himself to sit down on the bench, to think of anything but Charlotte in trouble.

Well, then, he'd think about Charlotte in ecstasy.

Last night had been a hell of a lot more pleasurable than this one. Last night had been incredible from start to finish. Why not admit it? The best night of his misbegotten life.

A week ago, he'd never have believed that the most accomplished courtesan could pale beside an untried spinster. Nor would he have believed the closeness he now felt with Charlotte, a closeness of mind as well as body. She stirred him in ways no other woman had done. And he *liked* her. He genuinely liked her impudence and her enthusiasm, her vitality and her tenderness.

He especially liked the fact that she believed in him.

Today, she had been willing to risk being arrested as an accessory in order to protect him. Not many women would have gone to such lengths, having that printing press hauled out of the stables, getting it loaded up, presumably to have it dumped elsewhere. All to save his worthless ass.

And she had been so adamant about the deaths of George and Peter. *It wasn't your fault. You didn't plan for it to happen. You didn't kill them.*

God, how he wanted to accept those words. Just thinking about them somehow eased the tight band around his chest. Charlotte had heard his worst secret, and yet still she had defended him.

He'd give his entire fortune to be in her bed right now. To be inside her, one with her, hearing her cry out his name—

A muffled shout came from another cell. A drunkard called in slurred tones for the gaoler. Then silence.

His elbows on his knees, Brand glowered into the darkness. He had to stop thinking so possessively of her. Charlotte didn't belong to him. The affair was over. She was right, it was too damned risky to continue.

Because when he held her in his arms, he lost all ability to think and reason. He couldn't trust himself not to empty his seed into her again.

And again. And again.

He quailed at the notion of relinquishing another

child. With Amy it had been different; Grace had never told him the truth and he hadn't been certain until he'd met Amy five years ago and looked into his mother's eyes. By then it was too late. By then, Amy had regarded Michael as her father, and Brand had faced the impossibility of revealing her true paternity. But if Charlotte bore his baby . . .

Hell.

The thought filled him with a punishing softness. Charlotte was the marrying kind, and he had sworn never to trod that mundane path. He must never again make love to her.

Never arouse her with tender kisses. Never undress her, inch by slow inch. Never take her on the hearthrug, in the bath, or with his mouth between her parted legs. If his hand could coax so passionate a response from her, only imagine what he could do with his tongue.

Stop.

Springing to his feet, Brand paced the narrow confines of the cell again. The time had to be nearing midnight, but he was too keyed up to sleep. Dammit, he hated being locked up, helpless. He needed to be out on the streets, finding the murderer. He couldn't trust Jones to do the job right.

And who did that leave to clear his name?

Charlotte and the Rosebuds.

Brand fought back another surge of fear. If he knew Charlotte, she was endangering herself, perhaps even at this very moment. She believed she knew the nature of the men in his circle of acquaintances. But Charlotte could have no inkling of the depths of depravity to which some of those men could sink.

He clenched and unclenched his fists. The thought of

her provoking a murderer made his blood run cold. He'd kill the man who touched her. He'd kill him . . . if ever he could escape this bloody cell.

The muffled sound of voices came from down the corridor. A door slammed. Then footsteps approached. It was too late at night to hope that the magistrate on duty had relented and set bail. Too late for anything to be done to secure his release until morning.

Maybe he'd never get out. If the false charges stuck and a jury believed the evidence . . .

He pushed down incipient panic. Better he should try to sleep on that hard bench so he'd be refreshed on the morrow, able to think of a way out of this damned cage.

The footsteps stopped outside his door. A key rattled in the lock. The heavy wooden panel opened, letting in a shaft of light.

Hannibal Jones ducked his head to enter the cell. Hostility radiated from his cadaverous form. He held a lantern in his hand, and the pale illumination made his face look like a skull with shadowed eyesockets.

"You're free to go," he said.

"What?"

"Murderer's been caught. Even confessed to leaving the banknotes. The magistrate's signed your release forms."

Disbelieving, Brand walked to the Bow Street Runner. "Who did this? What's his name?"

"Not his, *her*. One Margaret Darby."

That timid, mousy girl? Impossible. "She couldn't have committed cold-blooded murder. Five times."

"Six," Jones said. "Tonight, she poisoned Uriah Lane. They were all men who'd abused her. I've a full, signed confession right here." He patted the pocket of his greatcoat. "She's being taken to Newgate Prison."

Brand still struggled with incredulity. "Miss Darby couldn't have acted alone. She must have had help. Probably from Vaughn—her cousin."

But the Runner didn't seem to be listening. His expression twisted, he snapped, "How does it feel, m'lord, to be tricked by a woman? To almost take a ride to the gallows because of her?"

His sneering manner incensed Brand. "What the devil is eating at you? I've committed no crime."

Jones looked as if he wrestled with an inner demon. Then he said in a low harsh tone, "You seduced my sister."

"Like hell." But Brand couldn't be sure.

"You did, by God. She told me so."

"What's her name?" Brand said cautiously.

Jones hesitated. "Alice. But you'd have known her as . . . Jewel."

Jewel. For a moment Brand couldn't place the name, then he remembered. A month ago. The night Trowbridge had burst in with that note. Brand had been playing cards. He'd won Jewel's services for the night. She'd been a tall brunette well-versed in the art of pleasing a man. And definitely not a virgin.

Jones's sister worked in a brothel. Didn't the poor fellow know that?

"I'd advise you to ask her what she does for a living."

"I know what she does." His nostrils flaring, Jones shook his fist. "It's men like you who put her there. You damned aristocrats with too much money and too few morals."

Brand had never given a thought to whether or not his doxies had families. He'd used women for his pleasure and given them pleasure in return. He'd never before had to face an irate family member.

It wasn't a high point in his life.

At least now he understood Jones's animosity. Brand could even commiserate to a degree. But enough was enough.

"I'm sorry," he said, meaning it. "However, I didn't put Jewel there, and I didn't force her. Is that understood?"

Jones gave him a measuring stare. Then he averted his face, not before Brand saw a deep sadness there. "I made a mistake about you," he said stiffly. "Go on, get out of here."

Brand needed no further urging. As he strode from the cell and took in a lungful of freedom, his mind was already leaping ahead to his reunion with Charlotte.

Her abductor stood across the room.

Straining against the cord that secured her wrists behind her back, Charlotte kept a close watch on him. Her head throbbed and she felt woozy. The gag made her mouth dry. A few moments ago, she had returned to consciousness to find herself lying on an unfamiliar bed.

No, a very familiar one. Several nights ago, she had lain here with Brand. In the Vaughns' bed.

Like then, neither Clifford nor Lydia were present.

The firelight shone on the fair hair and dapper form of Colonel Tom Ransom. He was bending over the hearth, methodically feeding pages of Miss Darby's diary to the fire. The sound of ripping paper chilled Charlotte. The task would only take him a scant time.

And then what would Ransom do?

It took less time than that. He carelessly dropped the empty leather cover onto the floor. He had one last page in his hand, a blank sheet.

He turned and saw Charlotte watching him. "Ah, you're awake. Do you see this, my lady?"

Ransom held up the last paper, then touched one corner to the blaze and watched it burn. When only the bottom portion was left, he carefully blew out the flames and dropped the blackened scrap onto the hearth.

"Very clever of me, isn't it?" he said. "The authorities will think old Cliffie burned the diary. No one will know that it incriminated me, not him."

Charlotte would know. And the fact that Ransom would tell her didn't bode well for her chance at escape.

She kept her gaze steady, unwilling to let him see her panic. Again, she wriggled her wrists, but the bonds were too tight. At least her ankles were free. If she could only work herself to the side of the bed when he wasn't looking . . .

But he strolled toward her. He looked like the consummate gentleman in his blue frock coat and gold-striped waistcoat, with tan breeches that hugged muscular thighs. Charlotte knew his strength and feared it. She waited rigidly, her legs tensed. There was a slim chance that she could kick him. In a man's most sensitive place.

He stopped beside the bed. "You shouldn't have coaxed that confession out of Margaret," he said. "I was listening at the door. I heard it all."

Charlotte had thought he'd left with the other guests. But he must have hidden in Brand's house, waited until everyone was asleep before going to Miss Darby's chamber to look for the diary.

"You're probably thinking she'll betray me," he went on. "But she won't. Not ever. You see, I was the one who rescued her from her attackers. She's been devoted to me ever since. In both mind and body."

The revelation shocked Charlotte. No wonder Miss Darby had protected her mysterious suitor. And was *he* devoted to *her*? Or would he leave the girl to her fate as the Vaughns had done?

"You've ruined our plans," he said, removing his white gloves one by one. "As soon as I'd married Belinda, my darling bride would have suffered a little . . . accident. Margaret and I needed the money, you see. We were finally going to be properly wed."

Ransom didn't appear angry, though. He looked . . . excited. A flush sat high on his cheekbones. His blue eyes were bright and wide. Avid anticipation lent a cruelness to his handsome face and sparked a shiver down Charlotte's spine.

He stood over her, smiling faintly. "But when you walked in, I devised a new plan," he continued. "I'll free Margaret and punish you in the process. By the time the Vaughns return from spreading their vicious gossip, it'll be dawn. And it'll look as if old Cliffie masterminded those murders."

Striding down the passageway, Brand heard Fancy's muffled yapping.

It was after midnight and the corridors were deserted. Raleigh had welcomed him at the front door, told him the ladies had all retired for the night, and Brand had sent the loyal footman off to bed, too. Brand had no intention of disturbing the Rosebuds. He could wait until morning to see them.

But not Charlotte.

Even if he couldn't make love to her, he had to hold her in his arms again. He had to kiss her, feel her warmth, and ... kiss her again. The need burned in his blood. It was a new experience, being mad for a woman's embrace with no hope of physical relief. Stunning that he'd rather endure platonic agony with Charlotte than slake his lust with any other woman.

Maybe it was more than lust.

He didn't know, didn't *want* to know. The tender feelings she stirred in him were dangerous, uncharted territory. He wanted to see her smile, to hear her voice again. Anticipation tortured him.

He reached her door. Inside, Fancy's claws scrabbled against the wood. Odd, that. If the dog needed to be let out, Charlotte would have responded instantly.

On the first pricklings of uneasiness, he opened the door. Fancy dashed out into the passageway as Brand strode inside. "Charlotte?"

A lighted candle on the bedside table showed the empty bed, the covers turned back but unwrinkled. He glanced into the dressing room, but he'd already guessed she wasn't here.

Fancy bounded back into the bedchamber, whining, her shaggy head cocked in an alert pose. The dog didn't turn over as she usually did to invite his petting. Instead, she paced to the door and looked back at him.

"Where is she, furball? Find Charlotte." As he spoke, Brand followed Fancy out into the passageway.

The dog seemed to know exactly where to go. She trotted ahead, glancing back now and then, leading him to the sector of the house where the Rosebuds had their suite. But Fancy didn't go there. She went to a room a short distance away. She poked her nose under the closed door and sniffed, whining again.

It was an unused guest chamber. Brand grabbed a candle from one of the wall sconces and opened the door.

What he saw chilled him. The bed was mussed, the coverlet hanging half onto the floor as if a struggle had taken place there. He stalked inside, Fancy running ahead of him. She put her front paws up on the side of the mattress and gave another plaintive whimper.

God. What had happened? Was Fancy trying to tell him that Charlotte had been here?

With whom? Where was she now?

Fancy nosed underneath the fallen counterpane and came out with a small piece of paper in her mouth.

Brand snatched it from her. The penmanship didn't match the other notes. This messy, blotted script could only have been written by Clifford Vaughn. As Brand absorbed the two words, dread sank its talons into him.

You're next.

Chapter 24
ONE MORE NIGHT

"You're next," Ransom murmured in her ear. "I'll wager you didn't know I wrote those notes. I'm an expert at disguising my handwriting."

He bent over her, his warm breath on her neck sending a chill throughout her body. Charlotte let herself flinch so that he would think her cowed and weak. It was hardly pretense.

Panic beat in her chest, making it difficult to think. The gag stifled her. The base of her skull ached from the blow he'd administered in Miss Darby's bedchamber.

She lay on her side, facing Ransom. She thanked God for that small advantage. When the moment was right, she was in a position to lash out with her feet. But at present, he was standing too close to the head of the bed for her to strike a good blow. Her skirts would hinder her. She had only one chance and she mustn't waste it.

His fingers drifted over her brow, toying with her hair in the parody of a caress. "I've enjoyed outwitting that Bow Street Runner," he said. "And Faversham, even more so. How I'd love to see his face when he returns home from jail to discover his mistress has vanished."

Would Brand even come to her chamber? Despair

pulled at Charlotte. She had told him in no uncertain terms that their brief affair was over. He might very well go straight to his own chambers without realizing she wasn't in her bed. And even if he did knock on her door, he wouldn't guess she'd been abducted.

Like everyone else, he'd think the killer was behind bars.

"I must say, my lady, you're quite a beauty with those big green eyes and chestnut hair. I might even feel remorse if not for this." Reaching behind her, he grazed his hand over her scars, then pulled back with a grimace. "They're quite hideous, you know. I wonder that Faversham can bear for you to touch him."

Brand. Last night, in his arms, she had touched heaven. They had both touched heaven. How fiercely she wished she'd spoken from her heart, that she'd told him how dear he'd become to her. She'd held back out of the need to protect her tender emotions.

She had never dreamed that it might be the last time she'd see him. Never imagined that this nightmare awaited her. That tonight she would plunge into hell.

It was no piece of melodrama to tremble, to watch Ransom with fearful eyes. If not for the gag, her teeth surely would chatter, as well.

In that caressing tone, Ransom went on. "I've never murdered a woman before. You'll be my first." He brought his fingers to her throat and traced a path across the smooth skin. "I've always wanted to slit my lover's throat at the very moment when she's in ecstasy."

Dear God. Dear God. Dear God.

He bent down to open the bottom drawer of the bedside table. "But first we must set the tableau to look like Vaughn's work," he said matter-of-factly. He drew forth a set of shackles, the metal clanking. "What do you think, my lady? Are these too heavy for your delicate ankles? Will you be frightened to have your feet fastened to the bedposts?"

Ransom bared his teeth in a smile. The irons dangling at his side, he strolled toward the base of the bed. The moment he turned toward her, she struck.

Using all of her strength, she landed a hard kick to his loins. His grin vanished. Groaning, he dropped the shackles and bent over, cupping himself.

Charlotte swung her legs to the floor. Her head swam, but she caught her balance. Finding her footing, she ran for the closed door.

She spun around, fumbling to turn the handle with her bound hands. The latch clicked, thank God, it wasn't locked.

Ransom spied her and lunged. She wheeled back, feverishly nudging the door open with her foot.

Too late.

Cursing viciously, Ransom clamped his hands on her waist and wrestled her down to the floor. She fought and twisted, her screams muffled by the gag. He pinned her, and it was really no contest.

The skirts wrapped her legs and her wrists were bound. Charlotte could only lie there, breathing hard, gazing up in wretched helplessness at the fury that distorted his classic features.

"Bitch," he snapped.

He drew back his hand to strike her. This time she refused to flinch. Drawing on a well of pride, she held up her chin and stared at him.

But the blow never landed. From the doorway came a fierce growl.

A moment later, Ransom loosed a yelping curse and let go of her. And Charlotte spied a brown dustmop attached to his leg.

Fancy?

Right behind the dog, Brand burst into the chamber. He took in the situation at a glance and seized Ransom.

Fancy retreated to Charlotte. Tail swishing, the dog bounded up to lick her face in warm, raspy, wonderful strokes.

Torn between joy and fear, Charlotte struggled to sit, her gaze fastened on the two men. They were pummeling each other. The dull thud of the blows resounded. Brand hit an undercut to that square jaw and Ransom went stumbling backward, knocking over the crystal decanters on a table, sending them crashing to the floor.

Ransom fell on his rump and shook his head as if stunned. When Brand went after him, yanking him back up, Charlotte saw Ransom reach down into his boot and draw a knife.

Terrified, she surged to her feet. The gag muffled her scream of warning.

But Brand had seen the blade, too. He thrust Ransom against the wall, caught his wrist and squeezed hard, applying pressure until the knife dropped to the floor. He followed up with another powerful punch to Ransom's jaw. Blood trickled from the colonel's mouth and he struck back viciously, but Brand parried the attack and launched his own. Within moments, Ransom was fighting a losing battle.

Charlotte ventured close enough to kick the knife out of his reach. When Ransom went down again, Brand didn't quit. He was a madman, trying to kill Ransom with his fists, and she could only watch in fascinated horror.

Hannibal Jones burst into the room, followed by Raleigh and Hayward. They pulled Brand off Ransom. Ransom was nearly insensible, his face a bloodied mess. Scooping up the shackles, Jones fastened them around Ransom's wrists. The two footmen roughly dragged the prisoner upright.

Charlotte ran to Brand. He had a gash on his cheek and his knuckles were raw but he met her halfway and enfolded her in a fierce embrace. He was breathing hard, his heart thudding, as he regained control of himself. Within moments, he had the gag undone and her hands freed, and he was holding her again, murmuring her name, his fingers skimming over her face and shoulders and arms.

"Did he hurt you?" he asked urgently. "Are you all right?"

"I'm fine. Oh, *Brand*."

Awash with relief, she kissed his bruised jaw, pressed her face to his chest, breathed in his scent. She could feel every marvelous beat of his heart. The aftermath of shock had left her woefully weak at the knees. Tremors racked her body, her teeth chattered, and she would have fallen if not for Brand's support.

Hannibal Jones cleared his throat. "I'll need a statement from her ladyship."

"Tomorrow." His tone masterful, Brand kept his arms protectively around her. "For now, I'm taking her home."

There was no question as to where Brand would spend the remainder of the night. Charlotte would *not* let him leave her.

A hush lay over the darkened house. As they entered her bedchamber, she leaned against him even though she had regained a measure of strength. She wanted to cleanse his wounds, but he wouldn't let her fuss over him. With firm authority, he removed her gown and corset and shoes so that she wore only her thin shift. As he helped her into bed, she held on to his wrist. "Don't leave me," she whispered.

His gaze was intense. "I won't."

Brand vanished into her dressing room to wash up. Feeling bereft without him, she shivered. The linens were icy cold, and she burrowed beneath the covers. On her bedside table, a candle flickered in a pool of wax. Incredible to think that when she had lighted that candle earlier in the evening, she'd had no inkling that Ransom was hiding in the house.

Fancy trotted to her basket, turned around three times, and went straight to sleep. Charlotte would give her an extra treat tomorrow. On the ride home, Brand had told her how the dog had led him to the scene of the abduction and the note that Ransom had left there to implicate Clifford Vaughn. Brand had dispatched the footmen to Bow Street Station to fetch Jones.

While Brand had gone straight to Vaughn's house. Just in time. Oh, dear God, Ransom had intended to rape her and cut her throat . . .

Brand emerged from the dressing room minus his coat and boots. Wearing his shirt and breeches, he slid into bed and gathered her close, fitting her into the hard cradle of his body. His fingers stroked over her back as if he too were still shaken by her ordeal.

His heat warmed all the cold places in her, inside and out, and she wanted to weep with joy. She took his hand

and kissed his raw, swollen knuckles, keenly aware that he had saved her from certain death. For the first time in hours, the horror ebbed and vanished, and she felt utterly safe.

"Char," he said, his lips against her brow. "For a time there, I was afraid I'd never hold you again like this." He laughed wryly. "Not that I'm *supposed* to hold you anymore."

She hurt from the knowledge that his arms were only a temporary haven. Yet there was nowhere else in the world that she wanted to be. "It doesn't matter," she said, "not tonight. I *want* you to hold me. I *insist* upon it."

He chuckled. "I wouldn't have let you say no, anyway."

Their mouths touched in a gentle kiss that made her wonder if he too felt a bliss that went beyond the physical. If he cared as deeply for her as she did for him. She knew it wasn't true, that Brand could never change his wicked ways, yet her foolish heart overflowed with hope.

"I couldn't stop thinking about you, either," she murmured. "About what I'd been too afraid to say. But I'll say it now. I love you, Brand."

He went still, his hands cupping her face. A troubled intensity darkened his eyes. She saw desire there as well as regret. "Charlotte, I wish—"

Aching inside, she touched his lips with her fingers. "You needn't say anything in return. I only wanted you to know."

He kissed her deeply this time, and she gave herself up to the pleasure of being with the one man who filled her soul. Brand didn't love her, at least not enough to change himself, yet a bond existed between them that he felt, too, she was certain of that much. The kiss left them both breathing hard, unfulfilled, gripped by the inevitable pull of passion.

His hands moved up and down her arms. "You do know how to torture a man," he said with a trace of strained humor. "I want to touch you so badly."

"Couldn't we? Just *touch* . . . ?"

He needed no further invitation. His palm followed the curve of her waist and hip to draw up the hem of her shift. She tugged at it, too, in a fever of impatience. Then his fingers were there, parting her folds, gliding in slow, maddening strokes that had her gasping with mindless indulgence.

He stopped, and she whimpered from deprivation. But he only pressed her back against the pillows, pushed away the covers, and moved himself down lower, putting his mouth where his hand had been.

The sight of his dark head between her legs gave her a shock. But at the first caress of his tongue, she was lost. Lost in a well of yearning so deep she couldn't catch her breath. And then she did drown in a pleasure so profound she thought she'd died and gone to heaven.

Charlotte drifted back to awareness. He was still kissing her, soft kisses that traced an upward path across her belly and to her breasts. He took the tip of one into his mouth and suckled lazily. The sensation stirred renewed warmth inside her, a banked heat that burned more slowly this time. She loved the way he made her feel, as if she were the only woman who mattered to him. She couldn't get enough of him, the raspiness of his cheeks, the smooth ripple of muscle beneath his shirt, the lean strength of his legs. And, oh, the masculine bulge beneath the placket of his breeches.

When she undid his buttons, he stayed her hand. There was a wretched fervency to his eyes. "Darling," he muttered. "That wouldn't be wise."

"But I want to give you pleasure. As you did me."

"Char . . ."

But this time he didn't stop her when she slipped her hand inside his breeches. Sweet heaven, the heat of him. He was long and thick and silky to the touch. She explored him with her fingers, but that wasn't enough to satisfy her. Desiring his complete pleasure, she slid down the length of his body and kissed him.

Brand spoke her name on a long, raspy groan. Emboldened, she took him into her mouth and swirled her tongue over him, learning what he liked, which was virtually everything. His fingers stroked her hair in wordless beseechment. Never had she known a man could be so utterly in her power. Or that such an intimate, extraordinary act could stimulate her own desires, as well.

Abruptly, he drew her up, pressed her back against the pillows, and buried his face in her throat. His powerful body convulsed and he gave a rough, keening cry of exultation. She held him tightly, frustrated that he hadn't been inside her, where she wanted him, yet knowing they did not dare take that risk. Not ever again.

When his breathing had slowed, he lifted his head and kissed her on the mouth, a kiss so gentle and loving she felt the burn of tears in her eyes. If only she could rail at him, force him to see that he needed her as much as she needed him. But she understood him too well. Brand had been the wild, reckless one for so long, he couldn't settle down to the normality of a wife and children.

If he'd wanted that, he would have spilled his seed inside of her.

After a few moments, he rolled out of bed and went into the dressing room to clean himself. Upon his return, he gathered her in his arms and held her close. Neither of them spoke other than a few murmurings. Charlotte relaxed into him, content to use his shoulder as her pillow. She intended to treasure every moment with him, but the events of the past two days caught her in a wave of irresistible weariness. She fell asleep in his arms with her face tucked into the crook of his neck.

And when she awakened in the brightness of day, he was gone.

Chapter 25

THE MISSING BRIDEGROOM

Three months later, on the morning of her wedding day, Charlotte stood in the vestibule of the church in Devon and endured the fussing of the Rosebuds. They were entirely too cheerful, she thought, considering how upset they'd been at first to hear that she was betrothed to Mr. Rountree.

Lady Faversham adjusted the aigrette of pearls that decorated Charlotte's upswept hair. Lady Stokeford smoothed the train of Charlotte's gown of pale gold silk. Grandmama handed her the bouquet of tiny white rosebuds and trailing gold ribbons, then gave Charlotte a kiss on the cheek.

"You look absolutely lovely," Lady Enid said, her brown eyes brimming with happy tears. Her arm had healed, and she no longer needed the sling. "How long I've waited for this day."

"We all have," Lady Faversham added with a fond smile, and Lady Stokeford nodded in agreement.

Like Charlotte, they had finally accepted the fact that a marriage between Brand and herself was not meant to be. A hollow anguish gripped her heart, but Charlotte firmly buried it. She had vowed not to think about him today of all days. Brand was a part of her past, and Harold Rountree was her future.

Once he'd overcome his aggravation at being considered a suspect of murder, Mr. Rountree had been extremely accommodating. A few days after the ordeal with Colonel Ransom, Charlotte had left London. Instead of returning to York, however, she'd gone to Devon for a long visit with her family. She had needed time to heal her raw emotions. Being in the presence of her loving parents and boisterous brothers and sisters had restored her flagging spirits. With the passage of days, she had come to realize that despite everything, she still yearned to be a wife, to have a family of her own.

Yet she hadn't wanted to deceive Mr. Rountree. When he had come to call, she had told him about her affair with Brand, that she loved Brand and would brook no criticism of him. Mr. Rountree had wisely held his tongue. He had courted her with flowers and small gifts. He had escorted her on quiet drives through the countryside. He had even found her a stray dog to replace Fancy, for Charlotte had given her to Grandmama.

Yes, she was making the right choice. She could find a measure of happiness with a kind, considerate man like Mr. Rountree.

The music of the pipe organ swelled. With one last smile for Charlotte, the Rosebuds hastened into the church.

Her three sisters beckoned to her from the doorway. During the past few weeks they had become reacquainted, talking long into the night. Thankfully, they and Mama had been happy to bustle around with the wedding preparations, something of little interest to Charlotte.

The seventeen-year-old twins, Jane and Jenny, were bridesmaids in pale blue silk that complemented their blond hair and cornflower eyes, while her matronly married sister Susan was standing as witness. They all looked thrilled to see their eldest sister being wed at last.

To Mr. Harold Rountree, a candidate for the House of Commons.

An unexpected lurch of panic stole Charlotte's stability. Dear God. How could she go through with this ceremony? How could she marry a man she didn't love? At least not in the wild, wonderful way she'd loved Brand.

The way she *still* loved him.

"Auntie Charlotte, hurry. Before I forget what to *do*."

Lady Amy stood in front of her, wearing a miniature version of the other attendants' gowns. She carried a basket of rose petals in her white-gloved hands.

Brand's daughter.

Charlotte's breast felt unexpectedly tight. She bent down to stroke the girl's cheek. "You won't forget, darling. Remember how we practiced? Take several petals and toss them gently, then count to three and do it again."

"All right, now *come*." Her eyes dancing with excitement, Amy slipped her hand through Charlotte's and drew her forward.

It was too late for misgivings. Jane started down the aisle with Jenny a few measured steps behind her. Dark-haired Susan flashed Charlotte a soft smile before following her younger sisters. Right on cue, Amy took a handful of petals and let them float to the marble floor. She peeked a quick, impish glance over her shoulder at Charlotte as she went after the others.

Then it was Charlotte's turn. Her portly, balding father, distinguished in a gray suit with silver buttons, stood waiting for her. He was a retired naval officer, made Earl of Mildon over a decade ago for his outstanding service to the crown. But he'd always been just Papa to her, a gruff, whiskered man who'd been away for long months at sea in her youth. She stepped into the doorway, took his arm, felt the comforting brush of his kiss on her cheek.

They started the slow walk toward the front of the church. It was the church where Charlotte had attended services as a child. Sunlight streamed through the long windows. Her two now-grown brothers, Dominic and Mark, turned to grin at her from their seats in the front. The pews were filled with guests, aunts and uncles, cousins and friends, but they were all a blur of faces to Charlotte.

Her gaze went to the altar. On the steps, the minister stood in black robes, waiting, his prayerbook in hand. Alone.

Where was Mr. Rountree?

Had he not arrived yet? She looked inquiringly at her father, and he patted her hand. Papa didn't seem to find anything odd in the situation. Had she been so preoccupied these past few months that she'd missed some planned alteration in the ceremony?

As she reached the front of the church, two men in wedding clothes emerged from an antechamber at the side of the altar. Her gaze riveted to the man in front.

Brand.

The bouquet dropped from her fingers. In the throes of giddy shock, she clung to her father's arm. Was she dreaming?

No, she couldn't be. Brand looked absolutely real, from the scar at the corner of his mouth to the warmth in his keen gray eyes.

As he walked straight toward her, his physical presence dominated the church. His heels clicked purposefully on the marble floor.

Brand halted in front of her, dropped to one knee. He gathered her limp hand in his. His gaze radiating sincerity, he looked up at her. "My dearest Charlotte, will you do me the great honor of becoming my wife?"

Sighs and ahs swept from the wedding guests.

But Charlotte could hear only the rapid beating of her heart. Brand was here. He wanted to *marry* her.

Half of her wanted to throw her arms around him, to say yes before he vanished like a fantasy born of her love-struck heart. The other half wallowed in a confusing mire of incredulity and mistrust.

She pulled back her hand. Her voice a strained whisper, she said, "I'll have a word with you."

Somehow she found the strength to step around him. Only then did she notice Michael standing nearby. As Brand stood up, Michael flashed him a faint grin and muttered, "I told you it was a shaky plan, my friend."

Brand shot him a grim look.

The organist launched into a loud hymn. The minister cleared his throat and led the congregation in a round of singing.

Charlotte marched into the antechamber and whirled to face Brand. Her hands were shaking, so she crossed her arms tightly over her bosom. She couldn't believe he was standing here, bold and unpredictable, right in the midst of her *wedding*.

He closed the door and turned to regard her. In the

sunlight from a nearby window, he looked a bit haggard, leaner in build, his cheekbones stark in his extraordinary, handsome face. His hungry gaze devoured her as if he'd been starving for this moment.

She didn't know whether to melt or weep or shout. "Where is Mr. Rountree?"

"I made a substantial contribution to his campaign fund."

"*What?* He gave me up for *money?*"

"Not . . . precisely." Brand looked uncomfortable, as if his white stock were tied too tightly. "He knew that you loved me. Because you'd told him so in no uncertain terms."

She couldn't deny it. Nor would she confirm it. Not when her throat was taut with impossible hope. "Why are you here, Brand?"

"To marry you, of course. I've a special license in my pocket, signed by the archbishop." He patted the lapel of his dark gray coat. "If we give it to the minister, we can say our vows right now."

The prospect was tempting. Far, far too tempting. "That's not what I mean. *Why* are you here, really? I found out two months ago that I wasn't carrying your child. I sent word to you."

He gave a dour nod. "I was sorry to hear the news. Truth be told, Char, I wanted you to bear my baby."

Longing thawed her insides. Did he really mean it? Had he felt the same disappointment that she'd felt?

She couldn't let herself ask. "You've ruined my wedding. I was going to be happy. I was *determined* to be happy."

"*I'll* make you happy," he said in a husky tone. "If only you'll give me a chance."

Afraid she might succumb to the urge to kiss him, Charlotte closed her eyes. "You don't understand what I need from a man."

She heard him step closer. "I'm trying," he murmured, his voice low and rough. "That's why I'm here. Maybe this was a stupid idea, but I'm hardly a prize candidate for a husband. I thought if I caught you by surprise and we were married before you knew what had happened, that it would be too late for you to say no."

She opened her eyes to find him standing right in front of her. Looking like the devil's lure to weak-willed women. "It *was* a stupid idea."

He drew a breath, gave her that rakish half-smile that always turned her inside out. As it did now. "Everyone told me so. But perhaps I've been bad so long I don't know how to do things the usual way." His smile vanishing, he touched her cheek in a feathery caress. His eyes held a suspicious moisture. "I only know that being with you made a difference in my life, Char. You made me want to reach beyond what I was."

"I never set out to change you," she whispered. "That had to come from inside *you*."

"It did, but I'm just a man. A man who wanted to die when you left London. I can't live without you." He dropped his hand to his side, gazed at her with concentrated ardor. "I love you, Charlotte Quinton. I'll always love you."

That was what she'd wanted to hear. And with it, all of her doubts vanished under a great flood of joy. She went straight into his arms. "I love you, too, Brandon Villiers. More than I ever dreamed possible."

Their lips met in a fervent kiss that held elation and desire, the attainment of heartfelt hopes. She clung to him, caressed his smooth-shaven cheek and the scar beside his mouth. He touched her in turn, his hands gliding over her face, her back, her arms, as if he couldn't quite believe she was real.

The door opened. Voices twittered. From the circle of Brand's embrace, Charlotte looked past his shoulder to see the Rosebuds standing in the open doorway.

All three of them were smiling, especially Grandmama. Beneath the white silk turban with its curving feather, her plump face beamed with happiness. "Now, children, there'll be time enough for that tonight."

Authoritative as always, Lady Faversham tapped her cane on the marble floor. Her eyes twinkled with rare pleasure. "Well, now. Are we finally ready to start the ceremony?"

Brand turned a tender, impatient, anxious look on Charlotte. "What do you say, darling? I've truly given up my wicked ways. Will you marry me?"

"Yes." Awash with love, Charlotte traced his lips with her fingertips. The adoration in his smoky gray eyes warmed her completely. "But only if you'll still be wicked at times—in the privacy of our bedchamber."

ROMANCING THE ROGUE

BARBARA DAWSON SMITH

When Michael Kenyon, the Marquess of Stokeford, finds his grandmother having her palm read by a gypsy beauty, he's convinced that Vivien Thorne is a fortune hunter. The Marquess is determined to expose her as a fraud—and Vivien is equally determined to claim her rightful heritage. Yet neither the spirited gypsy nor the notorious rogue foresee the white-hot desire that turns their battle into a daring game where to surrender is unthinkable . . . impossible . . . and altogether irresistible.

"Barbara Dawson Smith is wonderful!"
—*Affaire de Coeur*

"Barbara Dawson Smith makes magic."
—*Romantic Times*

In debt to a scoundrel . . .
Wed to a scoundrel . . .

SEDUCED BY A SCOUNDREL
Barbara Dawson Smith

Society shunned the handsome, base-born rogue, save for many women who secretly dreamed of his touch. No one expected Drake Wilder to force his way into nobility—by coercing a very proper lady to the altar. And though she despises the arrogant rakehell, Lady Alicia Pemberton agrees to wed Drake in order to save her family from ruin. But he has plans for his lovely, high-born wife. First, he will use Alicia to exact revenge on the father he never knew. Then he will work his scoundrel's charm to seduce her into his bed...

"Barbara Dawson Smith is wonderful!"
—*Affaire de Coeur*

"One of America's best-loved authors of historical romance!"
—*RomEx Reviews*

AVAILABLE WHEREVER BOOKS ARE SOLD
FROM ST. MARTIN'S PAPERBACKS

TEMPT ME TWICE

BARBARA DAWSON SMITH

New York Times Bestselling Author of
ROMANCING THE ROGUE

A rogue shrouded in mystery, Lord Gabriel Kenyon returns from abroad to find himself guardian of Kate Talisford, the girl he had betrayed four years earlier. Now sworn to protect her, he fights his attraction to the spirited young woman. Although Kate wants nothing to do with the scoundrel who had once scorned her, Gabriel is the only man who can help her recover a priceless artifact stolen from her late father. On a quest to outwit a murderous villain, she soon discovers her true adventure lies with Gabriel himself, a seducer whose tempting embrace offers an irresistible challenge—to uncover his secrets and claim his heart forever...

"Barbara Dawson Smith is wonderful!"
— *Affaire de Coeur*

"Barbara Dawson Smith makes magic."
— *Romantic Times*

*Available wherever books are sold
from St. Martin's Paperbacks*

TEMP 2/02

He was England's most notorious rogue.
Can a keen-witted spinster reach his heart?
Or is he…

TOO WICKED TO LOVE
Barbara Dawson Smith

If it weren't for the baby left on her doorstep, who
Jane Mayhew knows to belong to Ethan Sinclair, the
Earl of Chasebourne, she'd have nothing to do with
the womanizing profligate. And the last thing Ethan
wants is to become involved with the prim and proper
Jane. But sometimes, the last thing you want is the
one thing you need…

"Barbara Dawson Smith creates unusual, powerful
stories—just what readers are looking to cherish…[A]
not-to-be-missed author."   —*Romantic Times*

AVAILABLE WHEREVER BOOKS ARE SOLD
FROM ST. MARTIN'S PAPERBACKS

2W2L 6/00

©Eden Studios

BARBARA DAWSON SMITH is the bestselling author of twenty novels. Her books have received consistently high reviews and have won numerous awards including the Golden Heart and Rita Awards. You can find out more information about Barbara and her books at her Web site: http://www.barbaradawsonsmith.com

New York Times bestselling author Barbara Dawson Smith returns with another enchanting, unforgettable novel featuring the beloved Kenyon family...

One Wild Night

I have always taken pride in my bad reputation. Polite society viewed me as depraved and utterly dissolute, for I was a disciple of passion. Pleasure was my hallmark, women my pastime. That is, before the incomparable Lady Charlotte Quinton disrupted my life—again.

Due to a scandal of her own making, she had been banished from home for five years. Apparently she decided that a life of boring respectability was the key to her happiness. We might have continued down our divergent paths if not for a vicious attack on our families.

Tracking a dangerous criminal occupied my time, but the tart-tongued spinster Lady Charlotte occupied my mind—and my desires. Certainly no other woman in London was immune to my charms. Yet the more Charlotte spurned me, the more I vowed to have her. After all, I can resist anything but temptation...

—*The Memoirs of a Rake* by Brand Villiers,
 fifth Earl of Faversham

"An extraordinary author!"
—Doubleday Book Club

"Smith's writing is smooth,
and her characters lusty and likeable."
—*Publishers Weekly*

ISBN 0-312-98229-1

U.S. $6.99
CAN. $9.99